Sherryl Caulfield was born in south-east Queensland, Australia, where she currently resides with her partner. She has also spent several years living in New Zealand and Hong Kong and was inspired to write The Iceberg Trilogy following a holiday to Canada.

Seldom Come By is her first novel.

I0615843

Praise for The Iceberg Trilogy

Seldom Come By is a haunting love story set against the windswept coast of Newfoundland. The story draws you in from the opening lines and takes you on a compelling journey across time and continents, through love, loss, heartache and healing. It is a beautiful and memorable story – a great accomplishment and a wonderful read.
Julie Fison, Author

Descriptive, detailed and quite the page-turner, Seldom Come By focuses on the lives of Samuel and Rebecca (and their families), the beginnings of their romance, their separations, their ups and downs. A very good debut and one well worth reading for lovers of historical fiction and romantic historical fiction alike.
Romantic Historical Reviews

If you love deep, epic, romantic stories this is one for you.
Jeannie Zelos's Reviews

Reading Seldom Come By is like taking a long hot bath or enjoying a gourmet meal. You want to take your time and savour every single word, every single moment. Romantic and descriptive, it takes you away.
Jennifer Collin, Author

Seldom Come By is an exquisite tale of love and loss, forgiveness and healing..
The Eclectic Reader

I fell in deep with the main characters and really cared about what was happening with them, but also the people around them. It sucked me in, gave me heart palpitations and made me think about them and how to get back to them when I wasn't reading. That was what I was looking for. The last half of the book was beautiful and heartbreaking and romantic.
The Book Bosses

Seldom Come By is the beautiful story of Rebecca and Samuel. I adore historical novels and this is one of the most well written ones that I have read in a very long time. This book was just like the icebergs that the author described, beautiful, breathtaking, and the story just flowed much like I imagine the icebergs do through the water.
Goodreads Librarian

I just finished reading Sherryl Caulfield's Seldom Come By, the first novel in her new trilogy. I was transported to another life, another time. I laughed, I cried, I held my breath in anticipation, I sighed with delight and ultimately felt extremely fulfilled at the close of the novel. I liken Sherryl's first novel to Paullina Simons' The Bronze Horseman in its claim over my life and heart; its beautiful and gripping story; and its wonderful writing.
Beautiful Bizarre Magazine

Three words…startling – epic – romance! This is an epic love story that tests the wills of Samuel and Rebecca, challenges their love, duty to family and willingness to forgive.
Honey Lemon Tea Blog

Seldom Come By

SHERRYL CAULFIELD

First published in Australia in 2013 by Cedar Pocket Publishing
This edition published in 2013 by Cedar Pocket Publishing
PO Box 654 Coorparoo 4151 Australia
www.cedarpocketpublishing.com

ISBN 978-0-9923759-1-1

Cover design by Sherryl Caulfield and Mark Squires.
Cover image purchased through Depositphotos.
Photograph of Sherryl Caulfield by Lucid Photography.

Discover other titles by Sherryl Caulfield at: www.sherrylcaulfield.com

For my sister, Anita,

who makes my life possible.

And for Mark,

for the epic, adventurous love story that is our very own.

In The Beginning

1

Some days she knew they were there, just by a drop in the temperature, if they were close enough, but not today. Today she saw them first, not one but two towering spectacles. In the space of one hour they had come drifting casually into sight, carried along on unseen currents, their presence more than anything marking the shift in seasons. And had she had her head down or her back to the ocean she would have missed them. These floating, breakaway giants calved from the glacial north. Frozen formations that enthralled her with their crystal palaces, soaring peaks and mythical creatures revealed in icy magnitude. How they made the seascape come alive.

She was meant to be collecting pine cones but here she was, staring out to sea, tingling in untamed anticipation, as if something monumental was about to happen. Never before had she seen three icebergs in one day.

Two years ago one had sunk the Titanic. Even before that folks called them a curse, but never Rebecca. To her they were a promise from the veiled sea: a sign of a different life beyond the bounds of the tiny island where she had lived all her fourteen years. For they were not from here. And they were not destined for here. Yet, unless she saw them or sensed them, these silent strangers would continue slowly southwards with her being none the wiser.

It was her sense of missing things that most motivated Rebecca: her fear and awareness of missing knowledge, missing signs, missing life. Once, had she not missed signs, tragedy might have been averted. As she grew older she keenly felt the lack of some thing that she could neither define nor describe, but similarly could not deny. All she knew was she had an inexplicable fascination for icebergs, as if they in some way held the key.

One day last summer her father had yelled at her: 'If you

don't stop day-dreaming about icebergs I'm going to take you out and leave you on the next one that comes along. See what you think of icebergs after that!'

Silas Crowe wasn't one to make idle threats but on that day Rebecca almost dared him to do it. The thought of climbing on board and seeing where the iceberg might take her was magnetic. If it weren't for icebergs she didn't know what she would have to look forward to.

Rebecca lived in a faded, two-storey, saltbox house that clung to the cliffs above their cove, a good three miles from any other house on Second Chance. Once or twice a year, if she were lucky, she'd get to visit Seldom Come By on nearby Fogo Island. Seldom Come By was apt, thought Rebecca. It once had been called Seldom Go By. Boats would seldom go by without calling in, but not so much now. Still, they saw more comings and goings than Second Chance ever had or ever would.

On the westerly point of their cove was a stand of large spruce trees. To Rebecca their existence was so implausible she was convinced they had taken root long before the first wind ever blew across Newfoundland. That these monstrous uprights managed to survive while other trees succumbed was a constant source of reassurance to her; a testament that unlikely things could happen in the most unlikely places. That afternoon, after meandering through them, she walked to a vantage point where she could see their cove and the neighbouring one to her left. The water rippled below; a glaring platinum-grey, twinkling occasionally in shafts of pallid sunlight. She sighed deeply: her ocean, her coastline – as familiar as her own hands. She loved them. The vista soothed her, yet it made her yearn for more.

Staring seaward she reminisced about previous iceberg sightings. She recalled one she had seen last week ablaze in the radiant dawn, the sun's rays painting it in a rich golden halo. She remembered the one she had spotted last May, just on dusk, sliding southwards leaving a silvery trail in the starry moonlit night. She tried to decide which was her all time favourite. Oh how she loved the ones that had waterfalls cascading over the sides! And, even more, those whose melt-pool could be seen above. But whether they had come her way on a bleached summer morn, a day fractured and grey or one rare and azure, she realised she loved them all and perhaps her favourite would always be the last luring one.

Lost in her iceberg-inspired daze, it took Rebecca some minutes to realise she was looking at something unusual in the distance. Cupping her hands around her face she squinted in the direction of Coleman's Point, one of the headlands to her west. Within seconds her searching eyes found it: not an iceberg, but a small floating object, possibly a log, maybe a small dory. It was impossible to tell. She wandered along further peering down at the cliffs while she waited for the object to come closer. After a spell she scrutinised the sea again. Yes…a boat…but…no one in it. How odd, she thought.

Suddenly an arm appeared, a flash of white, barely distinct, but movement, someone waving something. Were they waving at her? Taking off her cardigan she waved it high above her head. There was a long wave back. She yelled, 'Hello'. All she heard in reply was her fading echo.

Still, something was amiss! 1914 was just four months old and already that spring Newfoundland had suffered two horrific nautical tragedies: 78 sealers from the S.S. Newfoundland had perished on the ice after being caught in a chilling blizzard far from their ship. The same unforgiving storm had claimed all 173 lives onboard the sealing vessel, S.S. Southern Cross, which had mysteriously disappeared, ship and men never to be seen again. People everywhere were holding their breath waiting for news of a third disaster.

Rebecca didn't hesitate. She raced back through the woods to the stony path that led to their beach and small wooden stage. Scurrying down the path, she leapt onto the stage, unhitched their dory, jumped in, fitted the oars and quickly put her back into rowing out to the open water, steering a course by keeping her eye fixed on a point on the cliffs in front of her. Every so often she'd steal a glance over her shoulder to see if her target had floated into view. As she rowed, she coaxed herself, 'Come on, Rebecca, come on.'

She paused momentarily to retie her blond pony tail and lock eyes on the approaching boat still several hundred yards beyond her right shoulder. Ten minutes later she halted again, peered behind her and started yelling. 'Hello! Hey over there!' trying to grab their attention. No response. No movement. Total silence. She called out again. All she heard was the wash of the sea and the occasional squawk of a kittiwake. Yet she was certain she had seen something.

With a few more strokes she manoeuvred herself towards the unknown tender. Turning to the side she was momentarily blinded by the glaring sun as she reached for the other boat, knocking it against her gunnel as she brought it close. It was then she knew she hadn't been mistaken.

Sprawled out on the bottom was a man, painfully thin, salt-crusted, bare-chested, clutching a tatty white shirt in one hand and a brown coat in the other, oblivious to the goose bumps raised all over his body, eyes shut, oblivious to her. His lips were peeling and cracked. His face, half-hidden by his beard and hair, was so blistered and mottled it looked like he could have been a leper, brown in patches, red and peeling pink in others. 'Hello,' Rebecca said in greeting and again, more loudly. She tried French, 'Bonjour!' Still no response. She picked up her oar and banged it loudly against his boat. 'Hey!'

With that he finally stirred. His head jolted, his eyelashes fluttered. He looked up as she, wide-eyed, stared down at him. He made no sound while she, in her anxiety, strangled a gasp deep inside her throat. He closed his eyes, shook his head then opened his eyes again. She was on the verge of saying, 'I am real, I'm not a ghost,' when he croaked, 'Help. Please.' Then he collapsed.

Without hesitating Rebecca pulled both oars inside her boat, grabbed her painter, climbed across into his boat and tied a clove hitch around his boat's thwart. Then she pushed her boat behind them, reached for his oars and started the strenuous task of rowing home – all the time staring in fascination at the castaway in front of her. His hair was long and sun-streaked, his eyebrows dark above brown curled eyelashes. His left shoulder had a cluster of scars, his bare chest was tanned and bruised, his nipples raw from his braces. Most alarmingly his ribs were clearly visible. He seemed tall but she couldn't tell for sure nor could she tell how old he was. She only knew with certainty that she had never laid eyes on him before.

4

2

It was her forty-six year old mother, Morna, who helped her carry the rescued boatman up to their house and lay him on the day bed in their parlour. Rachel, her older sister, immediately started sponging him down with a flannel and warm water. He didn't look any better once clean. 'Do you think I should fetch Ronnie?' Rebecca asked, unable to quell her anxiety. Ronnie Evans substituted for a doctor in their parts.

Her mother studied the stranger with her warm brown eyes. 'I doubt Ronnie could do any more than what we're doing right now.' Unlike Rebecca, her voice was steady. 'Besides, your father will be home soon. He knows more about men and the sea than any of us.'

Yes…what would her father think, wondered Rebecca? Silas Crowe was part of the local fishing cooperative that worked the outer Notre Dame Bay waters in a fleet of three 44-foot schooners moored in Deception Bay. Deception could be reached from their home by a ninety-minute walk across the barrens or by skirting the eastern side of their island in a boat, sailing or rowing, depending on the conditions. Some seasons her father worked by himself as an inshore fisherman. Rebecca knew he preferred that. Like he preferred their distance from Deception. Her father was a loner. He guarded his space. He revelled in silence. They were a perfect complement to his spirituality and his superstitions. But after a few lackluster years, he decided to sign-on to the schooners and yesterday he'd gone across to Seldom Come By to a two-day fisherman's union meeting before the season got under way.

A strange sense descended upon Rebecca as she sat beside this unknown man trying to dribble water into his mouth. It felt as if she held his fate in her hands; that, by the act of claiming him, it was now up to her to save him. For having accepted the challenge of rescuing him, she now had to face a bigger, more uncertain test of delivering him through this trial. She was still by his side, her mother and Rachel in the kitchen preparing dinner, when her father came bursting through the back door, making them all wheel around in alarm.

'What's amiss?' he blurted out.

'Nothing,' said her mother. 'Why do you ask?'

'Why?' His chest was heaving. 'I come to the top of the rise and what do I see in the distance but Lucifer in the sky looming over the house.'

'Whatever are you on about?' asked her mother.

'Come outside and see for yourself. The shape of a dragon with a raging head practically shooting flames to the sky.'

Rebecca had come to the doorway between the parlour and the kitchen. This was not the first time they had heard such pronouncements from their father and it wouldn't be the last. He was forever reading meaning into clouds, patterns in the sand, fallen branches, even vinegar in a bottle. Her mother glanced at her but without stalling said, 'We have a visitor, a shipwrecked sailor.'

'He's in here,' added Rebecca.

'God help us, he's probably brought the plague or some other terror into our home.'

This time she and her sister exchanged glances silently acknowledging their father's pessimism though eighteen-year old Rachel would never be the first to speak up. Rebecca let out a resigned sigh. 'I'm sorry you feel that way Father. I didn't think you, or God for that matter, would look too favourably on us if we left a poor stranded man to die.'

Her father glared at her with steel blue eyes, undimmed by years of squinting at the sea or snow. But Rebecca did not baulk from his glare. After a few moments he eased his shoulders. 'We must all be Good Samaritans when called, Rebecca. It still does not make me feel any better about that serpent of Satan hanging over us.'

Biting her tongue, Rebecca spun round and went back to her patient. He was looking slightly better but perhaps his improved colour was more to do with the warm glow of the lamps and the fire in the room. She moved aside for her father. Silas stared at the stranger for what seemed liked an eternity. Under his thick salty grey hair, her father had an angular head anchored by a strong nose in a face that flaunted his mixed origins. That night, his face was mask-like, only his eyes moved. After interminable minutes he uttered three words: 'What a sight.' He dragged his broad hands down his own bearded face and then placed a hand on the unknown man's forehead. Some moments later, he muttered, 'No sign of a fever. Has he said anything?'

'No, only "Help me".' Trying to keep the excitement out of her voice, Rebecca recounted how she and her mother had rescued him. While she was speaking her father peeled back the covers and gasped at the sight of the man's bony frame.

'Did you find any papers on him?'

'No.'

'Anything on the boat?'

She shook her head and felt a tinge of annoyance at her self. 'We didn't look,' she admitted. He frowned admonishingly but when he spoke he called out for Morna asking if there was any hot water.

Her mother came to the doorway. 'Yes,' she said, 'I thought you'd want to wash.'

He blinked in acknowledgement. 'I'll wash him first. Maybe a long soak will do him good. Then I'll take some clean water myself.'

The women set to, hauled the wooden tub into the living room, half filled it, brought out soap and towelling then cleared the room. Hovering in the hallway, Rebecca strained to hear her father's words as he trickled water over the man's ravaged skin. 'Where have you come from young man? What happened to you? What about the others?'

She closed her eyes and took a deep breath. It was true, there were always others.

Over dinner her father told them he couldn't find any serious injuries on the man other than chest bruises, abrasions, a lump on his head and a swollen and bruised right ankle. There didn't seem any cause for alarm. But as they theorised over the identity of the stranger her father's unease re-surfaced. 'Enough!' he yelled, slapping his hand down on the table. 'We'll find out in good time.'

'One last question,' pleaded Rebecca and before he could deny her, she asked, 'Do you think he will live?'

He stared at the table pensively before raising his eyes to her. 'That's between him and his maker. We've done what we can for now.' They bowed their heads and finished their meal in silence.

Later, when the girls were cleaning up Rebecca whispered to Rachel, 'Why does father have to be so doom and gloom about everything?'

'That's just how he is. Maybe if enough things happen to you in life that's how you become.'

'Lord spare me,' whispered Rebecca. Her brow creased faintly in concern as she reached for another plate to dry. The fact was the girls only knew some of the happenings of their father's life. Only what they could glean from their mother, which was not a lot and Silas was never forthcoming himself. For all that he was their father, he was an enigma to them in many ways. Predictable and unpredictable.

Rachel interrupted her thoughts, 'I'd say you have a fifty percent chance.'

'Of what?'

'Of becoming like our father. Shall I pray you end up more like our mother?'

She ignored Rachel's teasing, but then she felt her sister's hand on her forearm. 'Promise me you'll watch yourself and how you to talk to him?' She stared at her sister. 'I fear one of these days your tongue is going to land you in hot water. You know how he can be.'

There was no escaping her meaning. 'I don't set out to be like that,' Rebecca bemoaned in her defence. 'But all of a sudden I realise I'm at that point and all I can do to save myself is to quickly say something in jest or something prophetic, something that sounds like it might have come right out of the Bible and I hope that gets me by.'

When they finished they moved into the living room where their mother was knitting and their father was leafing through their old family Bible, looking, he said, for a scripture to help the shipwrecked sailor – help them all! – pull through.

Unlike her mother, her father only went to school till he was ten and learnt most of his important lessons in life through watching and listening to other people. Aside from the Bible, he would read the odd newspaper, thumbing regularly through a much-used dictionary. His hearing, like his eyesight, was still near perfect but his greatest asset was his keen memory, which seemed to more than compensate for his lack of education. In that respect Rebecca wanted to be like her father when she grew up.

When at last he had decided on a passage her father led them in fellowship and then they prayed for the salvation of the young man lying just a few feet away. Soon after, too soon for Rebecca, he made an announcement: 'It's time you two went to bed.'

'I can look after him,' gushed Rebecca. 'You must be tired, Father. You too, Mother. I found him, you shouldn't have to do all this extra work because of me.' She eyed her parents while silently praying for leniency.

'Rebecca!' commanded her father. 'Very soon, we will be all going to bed and there will be nobody watching over this man, understand?'

She dragged her heels upstairs where she flopped down on her bed with a huff. She desperately wanted to be below, not with her parents, but alone with the unknown.

3

Icebergs were far from Rebecca's mind the next morning as she made a beeline straight to their visitor. He'd had a restless night judging by the state of his covers but at that moment there was little sign of life.

Before long she heard the sound of her father's footsteps on the stairs, his knees creaking, then he opened the back door and went outside like he did every morning upon rising. Twenty minutes later he returned with the words, *Mme Nightingale,* which both Rebecca and her mother had overlooked yesterday in their haste to carry the man up to their house. They were painted on the stern. The name meant nothing to any of them. They would ask around after church, her father announced. Suddenly Rebecca wanted it to be Saturday all over again. She did not want to be going to church that day. She quickly offered to stay home to mind their guest, but matters had already been decided: that honour was to go to her mother.

'This morning fellow parishioners our reading is from the Letter of Jude. He warns against false teachers who claim to be believers.

'Some godless people have slipped in unnoticed among us, persons who distort the message about the grace of our God in order to excuse their immoral ways and who reject Jesus Christ, our only master and Lord.'

Rebecca tried her best to be attentive, not to slide her feet back and forth. She glanced at her father. He looked worried.

'They are like the wild waves of the sea, with their shameful deeds showing up like foam. They are like wandering stars, for whom God has reserved a place forever in the deepest darkest hour.'

'I've heard all this before,' she whispered to Rachel.

'It won't hurt you to hear it again.'

After the reading came the sermon. Could it be any longer, any slower? She didn't think so. When it was over – finally! – and they were outside, Silas approached Herbie Elliot to tell him of their news and ask if he had any reports of the missing ship, Madame Nightingale. The men asked around. Everyone drew a blank. Rebecca and Rachel stood close by, keenly following the discussion.

'Do you want me to telegraph through to St John's?' asked Herbie.

Silas twitched his face. 'Perhaps in a few days, if we have no answers.'

'What state is he in?' chipped in Ronnie Evans. He was older than most and because of his status as the community's de facto doctor, one to whom they all deferred.

'When I last saw him, a deep slumber,' her father replied. A few chuckled.

'Do you want me to come and take a look at him?' Ronnie asked.

Followed by, 'Do you want me to come round in the morn and help you move him across to Ronnie's?' from another.

There was a muffled murmur amongst the men. Rebecca's heart was racing. She had to speak up. 'Can't we leave him be? I think the poor man's been through enough without moving him any further.'

Her father turned towards her. 'Tom's suggestion is not such a bad idea. We don't know anything about that young man. He could be a thief, a murderer, or a madman for all we know.'

'Surely you don't think that, Father, or else you wouldn't have left Mother at home with him.' Rebecca twirled her head. Rachel was speaking up!

'He's not about to do any harm in the state he's in,' retorted Silas. 'But very soon I'll be out on the boat every day and you women will be the ones alone with that stranger.'

'We'll manage,' said Rebecca. 'Besides we shouldn't judge him before we know him.' She tried to suppress the fluttering in her stomach. She would be chastised when they got home for being so outspoken, but on this point she did not want to capitulate. And as always, she'd felt emboldened with Ronnie so close. He was like the grandfather she never had. But it sickened her the way she chafed her father, the way they chafed each other, neither doing it deliberately. Wishing it could be different, she braced herself for her father's displeasure.

But before her father could rail at her Ronnie spoke, "Silas, if you think that the young man needs more medical attention than you can provide then I am happy to take him, or come check on him every day. But if not then why don't you keep him at your place till he wakes up and you get some answers.'

Rebecca's eyes met Ronnie's in a silent offering of thanks.

Silas waved him off. 'We can manage. We've been trickling fluids down his throat. He doesn't have a fever or any major injuries that we can tell, aside from a swollen ankle. He wasn't any better or worse this morning. We may have missed something, who knows?' Silas shrugged.

'Well, if he shows no sign of improvement by the morn, send Rebecca to fetch me.'

Rebecca tried to silence her relieved sigh. To think if she had got her way earlier and stayed home her father would have had his way just now and the unknown man would soon be unknown and unavailable!

She left her father to talk to the men while she doubled home with Rachel on Mica, riding in and out of patchy fog. The mare was a part-time workhorse, part-time play horse, named after the pearly flakes that flecked the granite rock scattered throughout Newfoundland. Mainly she was bought for Rachel to shorten the trip between home and Deception, for Rachel had been born with one leg marginally shorter than the other. Consequently she limped, not excessively, but noticeably, and at times her awkwardness pained her but she never complained. The family made unspoken allowances for Rachel, giving her less taxing jobs, while Rebecca, Miss Hewer of Wood and Drawer of Water, carried a heavier responsibility. She never complained either.

'Any change?' asked Rebecca, coming up to her mother in the kitchen.

'Not really,' she replied, 'though he has been a bit delirious at times, mumbling words I can't even catch.'

Rebecca looked for herself. The man was practically lifeless. Privately she worried if he would ever waken. While her mother and Rachel prepared lunch she sat next to the stranger trying to dribble water into his mouth, willing her rescued boatman to waken and swallow, stir and swallow, anything and swallow.

Sunday afternoons in their home were spent resting – her father being the very definition of a God-fearing man, God-serving man. Usually the family would retire upstairs to their rooms, lie down and try to sleep – in Rebecca's case read – sleep was always a lost cause. Some Sundays her mother would sit at the kitchen table and write letters. That day both her mother and Rachel were writing letters. There was no way Rebecca was going upstairs to lie down. 'I have to finish that Les Misérablés book Miss Drysdale lent me,' she announced. 'I thought I would read to our patient.' Her mother said nothing. Her raised eyebrows said plenty. Rebecca didn't care.

Ten minutes later, she was engrossed in a passage: *'All sorts of reveries reached him from space, and mingled with his thoughts. What a spectacle is the night! One hears dull sounds, without knowing whence they proceed…'*

When Rebecca paused in her reading to drink some water, she was surprised to find the man looking up at her. Not just looking – staring – his eyes glazed and dreamlike.

'Don't stop,' he murmured.

Her eyes flew wide open. Before she could stop herself she said, 'It lives!' Her face flushed. 'I mean he lives,' she stammered. What a dimwit! She bit her lip and tried again, this time with a wide, elated smile and placid eyes. 'You're alive.'

'I am,' he swallowed, 'though God knows where I have been.' He spoke slowly, his voice deep and rough, faint from lack of use. 'Where am I?'

'You're in our home.' Rebecca smiled.

'Yes,' he drawled, 'and where might that be?'

'Second Chance Island.' His squinting eyes and furrowed brow told her he needed help with his bearings. 'Near Fogo, Seldom Come By. In Notre Dame Bay. Newfoundland.'

'Is that so?'

Rebecca nodded, wanting to look at his eyes again without him noticing.

After a pause he cleared his throat. 'How did I get here? Did your father bring me?'

'No, I did.'

'You brought me here?' His tone disbelieving.

'Uh-huh,' Rebecca nodded again. This time she risked a glance. They were unusual. A tawny gold, with flecks of brown or was it green moss, the whole iris outlined in a dark ring, the likes of which she had never seen before. She looked away but then steeled herself to meet his gaze. 'You were in your boat waving and I thought you were in distress, so I rowed out and brought you back to shore.' Then she admitted, 'My mother helped me carry you here.'

'Is that so? Well, I must thank you and your mother for rescuing me.'

She smiled shyly at him. Lowering her gaze to her lap she muttered, 'It was nothing.'

'What is your name?' he asked, peering into her face.

'Rebecca,' she whispered.

'Rebecca,' he repeated. 'Thank you, Rebecca, for coming to my aid.'

'You're welcome,' she said almost inaudibly, holding his golden stare for two seconds before looking away.

He cleared his throat. 'Do you live here with just your mother?'

'No,' she smiled, 'with my father and my sister too. Would you like to meet them?'

'Yes, but I don't think I can get up just now. Would it be possible to have a glass of water?'

'Sure,' said Rebecca, looking at her empty glass beside him. 'I'll bring you one straight away.' Walking into the kitchen, Rebecca was unable to hide her delight. 'Our guest is awake and asking for water.'

'Hallelujah,' said her mother, clasping her hands. 'What did he say?'

'Nothing much, just wanted to know where he was.'

'So he speaks English?' asked Rachel.

'Uh-huh.'

'What happened to him?' asked her mother.

'We didn't get that far.'

'Well what's his name then?'

And it was then that Rebecca realised in her pained timidity she had forgotten to ask one of the burning questions on her lips.

When they returned to the room, he had fallen back into a deep, still sleep; the satisfied sleep of a satiated man, even though he was far from it. They moved around the living room quietly, content to give their guest his peace, relieved he had at last awoken if for only a short while.

4

In the middle of the night a snowstorm arrived from the north – not that common in Newfoundland for that time of the year, but not unheard of. Outside the wind was nearly gale-force, the world a complete whiteout of wild turbulent snow. No one was going anywhere.

'Did you pray for this weather?' mused her mother when Rebecca came down the stairs the next morning.

'No' she replied, beaming with joy. There would be no going to school that day. Normally Rebecca enjoyed everything about school, even Latin! Like Rachel, she was very bright and loved reading. So much so that her teacher, Miss Drysdale, would lend her books from her personal library which her father, through her mother, would deem suitable reading for his daughter. Her father was not too fussed about schooling but when he married her mother she had extracted a promise that all of their children would go to school at least to the age of fifteen. Morna was a strong believer in education and in this Silas obliged, even though Rebecca had once overheard him mumbling that education made children more impertinent.

Rachel's school days were well over. If they had money her parents could have sent her to boarding school at Gander or St John's. If she were stronger, she could have worked in the saltworks or the cod liver oil press but they didn't want her to have a job where she was on her feet all day. So she helped her parents and did odd jobs for people, more often in exchange for something other than money.

On gloomy days, Rebecca would wonder what was going to happen to Rachel and herself. She was just a few weeks off finishing school for good. Were they going to stay on Second Chance all their lives? Marry some local fisherman or cooper and bear a tribe of children? She knew one family who had fourteen! That was not the life she wanted. She groaned at the thought. She wanted to run away and have adventures, be kidnapped even! But to where? And to do what? And who with? Once, she asked her father if she could join him on a fishing trip. His reply: 'No, Rebecca, it's no place for young girls.'

'When I'm older then?'

'No, not even then.'

Where did that leave her? She feared her life was going to be like the unchanging rocks she walked over every day, taking an eternity to vary or break away.

In the parlour, her father was stoking up the fire, coughing and spluttering along with it. Rebecca watched from the doorway.

'Hello,' ventured a strange voice. He was awake again! She wanted to move closer but held back waiting for her father.

'Good morning,' said her father as he squatted by the day bed. 'How are you today?'

'I've been better,' came a raspy reply.

'We'll get you better.' Her father held out his hand. 'Silas Crowe.'

'Samuel Dalton,' said the man offering his hand and trying to sit up.

Ah, Samuel Dalton, Rebecca's heart sighed. Lost in her thoughts, she missed hearing Samuel's quick intake of breath, but not her father.

'You got some bruises on your chest. Perhaps you cracked a rib or two. Nothing much we can do about that – they'll heal in their own time. We can strap them, but mostly you just need to take it easy.'

Samuel nodded. 'Thank you for having me in your home sir, for looking after me.'

'Och, think nothing of it. Just get well. Are you up to some breakfast, some porridge or eggs or something?'

'Yes thank you, I'll try a little bit.'

'That'll be it, little meals for you for starters. What about some tea?'

'I'll get it.' The two of them looked towards her smiling face.

She returned with her mother and sister in tow. 'I believe

you met Rebecca yesterday,' said her father. She smiled again. He nodded. 'This is my wife, Morna, and our other daughter, Rachel.' They all said hello and rearranged the pillows to help Samuel sit up. He was finding it hard to get comfortable and feed himself, but before Rebecca could offer any assistance, Rachel limped to his aid. 'Here, let me'.

Samuel slept throughout the day waking on and off to take food and drink as it was proffered. The bad weather continued its barrage on Tuesday, benefiting nobody bar Rebecca. Samuel continued his rhythm of rests and refreshments until finally he was up to having more than one line conversations.

'Do you remember what happened?' asked her father.

'To a point, though I feel I'm missing a large chunk of it.'

Rebecca was hovering in the background, keeping busy but quiet, trying to catch what was being said, snatching glimpses whenever she could. She wasn't alone: her sister and mother were doing likewise.

'Whose boat were you on?'

'My Uncle Michel's. From Montreal.'

'Where were you headed?'

'To Cartwright, then up to Goose Bay, then we were going to come back and stop off at Tilt Cove.'

'So you didn't make it to Cartwright then?'

'Not that I remember.'

'You would have been one of the first boats through.'

'That was the plan.'

'What did you hit? A berg? Some rocks?'

'No.' He shook his head. 'Maybe a whale.' Samuel's brow was furrowed. 'But I'm not certain. I was up on watch and the night was black as tar. It was a 52-foot rig and it practically crumpled in half,' his voice tapered off. 'I never saw anything like it. There were four of us on board, lots of supplies for the fur trappers and the miners. I yelled out below for all hands on deck. I knew we had to abandon ship. I rushed over to loosen the tender and lower it overboard. Something crashed on my head from behind. I don't know what– maybe the mast. I remember coming to on the deck, the dinghy's rope still in my hands. The boat was going down fast. I was thigh-deep in water yelling for the others, for Seb, for Louis and for Luc.' He licked his dry lips then sighed heavily. 'I don't know what happened. At the very last I jumped into the dinghy. I think that's when I hurt my ankle, hit my head once more, was out of it again for a while.' Only the day before had Samuel discovered his injury when he tried to go outside to the privy.

'What about the others?' asked Silas.

'When I came round there were bits and pieces of flotsam, the odd large barrel,' Samuel swallowed, struggling to find his way. 'No sign of life.' His eyes glazed over.

Silas squeezed Samuel's hand. 'You can't help that so don't go tearing yourself up over it. The sea's a hard taskmaster at times.'

Samuel was silent for such a long time Rebecca thought he had drifted off until he stirred. 'I should send word. To Michel. Let him know what happened. Is there a place around here I can do that?'

They could send word through Deception, her father said. 'It's not too far. Do you know where you were when you went down?'

'We were two days north of Belle Isle.'

'What date was that do you recall?'

Samuel stared off in the distance trying to remember, absent-mindedly rubbing his cheek. And then he stopped as if he saw something very clearly. Once more he sighed heavily.

'What?' her father asked as if reading Rebecca's own mind.

'I didn't have this beard then,' said Samuel, his voice deep and certain. 'It must have been a few weeks ago. What day is it today?'

'The thirty-first of May,' sang out Rebecca.

'Well, the middle of May,' said Samuel. 'At least.'

'Hmm,' said her father. After several moments he added, 'There's no point rushing bad news. It can wait. Your crew wouldn't have lasted long in those waters.'

The man raised his troubled eyes to her father. But before he said anything, her mother spoke. 'You've come a long way, Samuel, over two weeks at sea by yourself. Did you have any food or water on board?'

'Everything happened too fast for that. I had some water. It ran out after a week and then I only got by on what I could catch from the rain.'

'Did you catch any food?'

'I only had a small knife with me, no tackle or anything. I tried to kill a gull once, but I only managed to frighten it away.'

'Too bad it wasn't June,' noted Silas. 'The capelin would have been jumping into your boat like fleas.'

Rebecca watched her parents exchange glances, and heard her mother faintly say, 'No wonder you're wasted away,' but she couldn't hold back any longer.

'So are you from Montreal? You don't sound very French.'

Rachel shot her a look – a look that said, 'What would you know? You've never been to Montreal, never met a person from there.'

'No, I'm from Toronto,' he replied, 'but I have grandparents who are French and live in Québec. I speak French. We all do in my family.' Rebecca could hardly contain her excitement; despite his tale of devastation, she had never met someone so well-travelled!

'Is your family still in Toronto?' Silas asked.

'Yes, sir. My father, mother and sister. I have an older brother, Matthew,' Samuel swallowed, 'he's in Montreal.' After a pause he added, 'I'm the youngest.'

'How young would that be?'

'Nineteen, sir.'

'And what does your father do?'

'He's a doctor.'

Her father's eyebrows shot up at that – they weren't the only ones.

5

The gull's cawing woke Samuel. It took some effort, but he managed to prise open his weary eyes, to steer a line through his mind's haze and focus on the small black eyes of the creature in front of him. How long did he lie there gazing at the seabird gazing at him? No feathers rippling. No breeze. His bleary mind still registering. Just. Did the gull's appearance signal the proximity of land?

Struggling with untold exhaustion, he slowly raised his head to peer overboard, to stare into the face of nothingness. Nothingness masked as non-descript greyness. Lazy, forlorn, fog. Absolute silence.

Days of drifting helplessly – but not hopelessly – had robbed him of many things. But through it all he still believed. Believed he was too young to die. Too young to be lost at sea. Too young to depart this life when he felt he was only starting to live it. And so he convinced himself that his time had not yet come. And he blocked everything else out. The cold. The aches. The ceaseless hunger. The almost unbearable thirst and willed himself to live. To save himself or be saved.

Samuel lay in the dark of night trembling. He wasn't dreaming. He was remembering – recalling the random details of his misadventure as they became more and more lucid. He had spent all night and all day rowing around the area where he thought the boat had gone down, but to no avail. He'd only managed to exhaust himself and then he had spent the next day simply lying in the tender, not wanting to row away and give up on his friends but not wanting to admit they had gone. Then on the third day he decided to make a point of rowing towards the Evening Star, towards sunset every night and away from the sunrise, away from the Morning Star every morning, if he could see his bearings through the fog and the mist and the squalls. He believed his salvation lay due west. But he was like a tiny cuttlebone bobbing around in that vast endless sea, helplessly subjected to the errant waves and the currents of the ocean. Eventually it took all his energy just to keep afloat. But movement was good. He could never remember being that cold or hungry. He had a knife, a water canteen and a piece of flotsam he had scooped up which he carved into a rough pail to bail out the water from the waves. He tore part of the sleeve from his shirt, secured it to the pail and an oarlock. Likewise his canteen, afraid he might lose those two pitiful tools overboard, into oblivion, along with his remaining strands of hope.

DAD. MOM. SHRIPWRECKED BUT SAFE. WITH CROWE FAMILY, SECOND CHANCE ISLAND, OFF FOGO ISLAND, NEWFOUNDLAND. WILL WRITE SOON. WIRING MICHEL NOW. SAMUEL.

That message was relatively easy. It was the one to his uncle that he deliberated over. He had never been the bearer of such onerous news. Finally he settled on:

MICHEL. BOAT & MEN LOST. SORRY. HEADING TOWARDS CARTWRIGHT AROUND MID-MAY. SUSPECT WHALE. WITH CROWE FAMILY, SECOND CHANCE ISLAND, OFF FOGO ISLAND, NEWFOUNDLAND. WILL WRITE SOON. HOME KNOWS. AM RECOVERING. KEEN TO HELP. SAMUEL.

On her way to school Rebecca delivered the messages to their merchant, which served as their local telegraph office. She returned with a pair of crutches from Mr Evans. Samuel thanked her for carrying them all that way particularly through the fresh snow.

'It's melting quickly,' she said with a shy smile. 'You'd better hurry up and get used to those crutches else you'll miss it.'

He didn't feel like trying them out just then with an

audience but as she had gone to such an effort he felt he needed to make some attempt. His Friday morning practice around the living room and the kitchen went much better. On Saturday he ventured outside for some fresh air. The last two days had warmed up quickly. Aided by a constant southerly the snow had practically disappeared. They set him up in a chair near the step-less front door. As the day got warmer he started to walk around. He came across a large barn, the smokehouse, the outhouse, the woodhouse and their cellar. Above the barn, working a garden bed, digging in sheep droppings and kelp, he found Rebecca.

'What are you going to plant there?' he asked, coming up to her.

'Potatoes, turnips, cabbage,' she replied. She looked up at him. 'Do you have a vegetable garden in Toronto?'

He told her they did but they bought most of their food from the market in town. 'We've got a large herb garden though. My mother uses lots of rosemary, bergamot, thyme and the like in her cooking.'

'So your mother is French?'

'Oui. Yes. French Canadian. Some say Canuck.'

'What about your Dad, is he French too?'

'No,' he said shaking his head.

She paused to wipe her right palm on her skirt as she looked directly at him. 'Most French people are Catholics, are they not?'

Samuel smiled at her mild interrogation. 'Yes, but we are not strict Catholics and our parents didn't make us go to Mass that often, only on special occasions.'

'What about praying? Do you pray in your home?' she asked.

Was she merely curious or worried about his eternal life? 'We say grace, but no we don't pray – not like your family.' He threw her a sideways glance.

'Did you pray when you were lost at sea?'

So serious he thought. 'I was out for most of it and when I wasn't I was yelling and begging through the fog to whoever would hear me – does that count as praying?' He raised his eyebrows at her, a smile toyed at the corner of his mouth.

'Don't tell father that.'

'Wouldn't impress him?'

'Uh-uh,' Rebecca said shaking her head and looking back to the garden bed. She slid her hoe under a grey spider crawling over the dirt and transferred it to the grass.

'Bad luck to kill spiders, eh?'

'Yes. Though they say if you kill these rain spiders they bring rain – sometimes that might be good luck, don't you think?' She smiled and with her smile something changed.

'True. Why do they say it's bad luck to kill spiders? Do you know?'

'Of course I know. Everyone knows.'

'I don't. Tell me.'

She wiped her hand across her brow before glancing at Samuel and looking back to the soil in front of her. 'It was a spider who saved baby Jesus from Herod's wrath when he ordered all first-born male children to be killed.' She took a breath and continued almost as if she were prophesying. 'After the decree, Joseph, Mary and Jesus fled to Egypt and on the way they came to a forked road. They went down one road and when they had gone a spider spun her web across the path they had taken. When Herod's soldiers came to this fork they wondered which road they should take, and while trying to decide they discovered the spider's undisturbed web. "No one could have gone this way," they said, so they took the other road, and that's how Jesus escaped.' She pressed her lips together and looked at him.

Samuel was six two, although perhaps not today leaning on his crutches. Rebecca was the tallest of her womenfolk but even she was still a good deal shorter than him. He put her at five six. He ran his right hand through his hair. 'Thank you, for enlightening me. My father was adamant we had a well rounded education but it obviously didn't cover everything.' Keeping his voice even he asked, 'Tell me, do you believe that?'

Rebecca looked straight ahead considering his question. 'It's possible,' she murmured. She turned to him. 'What do you believe in?'

'What do I believe in? What sort of question is that?' He gave way to a laugh, not wanting her to take his response as a put down. He glanced at her and could tell she was waiting for an answer, wanting something from him, but what? He gathered himself.

'Let me see, I believe in life, that's for sure. I believe in myself. I believe in the value of education and experience. I believe in possibilities and in being rescued.' He gave her a warm smile, which she returned in kind. 'And lucky for you, I believe in questions and the right of people to ask them.'

'Do I ask a lot of questions?'

'Does the name Nellie Bly mean anything to you?'

'No.'

'Never mind.' She gazed at him, a puzzled look on her face. 'Go ahead,' he said, laughing and opening his hands to her in a welcome gesture.

She averted her eyes. 'I'm sorry if I'm being rude and impolite. It's just…well…you are so new and different.' Her eyes darted to his then peeled away. 'You are the first real visitor we have had to our home in years. And you've seen and done much more than I've ever done in my life – probably more than I'll ever do.'

'Whoa, Rebecca! You have your whole life ahead of you. Anything could happen. Don't you have dreams? Don't you believe in possibilities too?'

'Oh I have dreams.' She spoke the words with quiet certainty. Then in a resigned voice added, 'My dreams are way too fanciful that's all. I doubt anything will ever come of them. It's just that life here is so…' she hesitated, searching for the right word, '…suffocating at times.'

'So what are you going to do when you finish school?'

'Work.' She quickly added, 'I don't have a problem with hard work. I can do it.'

'I can see that.'

She sighed heavily. 'Work here though doesn't inspire me. Maybe if I could do some sort of men's work it would be different. Like go to sea.' Now she looked at him, almost in a silent plea.

'Maybe when you're older you can.'

She held his gaze for a few moments, glanced away then brought her eyes back as she asked, 'Did you always want to be a sailor?'

'No,' he said shaking his head lightly.

'What did you want to be?'

This girl, he thought, almost in exasperation. He couldn't believe that here he was fifteen hundred miles from home and he was still getting asked the same questions. She had her father's penetrating eyes, but where his were cobalt blue, hers were turquoise, striking in their rarity, but more than that she had this openness and innocence about her that was rendering him completely malleable around her. He'd never felt like this with a woman before, or anyone for that matter. Perhaps he was still suffering from his ordeal, but, he could only respond with raw, unmasked honesty himself. Her forthrightness demanded that from him, and he owed her that – hell – he owed her a lot more for saving his life.

'Rebecca, let's sit for a while. Too much standing for me right now.'

She helped him onto the grass then sat a little to the side waiting for him to speak.

'Well,' he began, 'as you know, my father is a doctor, so too is my grandfather. My elder brother Matthew is also a doctor – he graduated last year. When I was in my last year of school I felt this overwhelming pressure that I was expected to follow in the family tradition. It was crazy. Now I see the pressure came more from me than them, but I didn't realise that at the time. I just couldn't see myself stuck inside four walls dealing with sick people all day. That didn't seem like living to me. My father had said, "Well, son, the choice is yours. What would you rather do?" And I couldn't answer him.' Samuel paused remembering the exchange.

'I had a schoolfriend, Billy Sarginson, who had distant relatives living up at a place called Fort William. Have you heard of it? It's almost a thousand miles northwest of Toronto. They work as lumberjacks for most of the year up there. We hatched a plan to run away and live life in the wild and earn our keep felling timber. I was sixteen. I could hunt well enough. Our father taught both my brother and me to shoot when we were growing up. So I started stashing things away, getting ready for our escape when one night my father came into my room, quite unexpectedly and caught me with my kit lying around.'

Rebecca gasped lightly. 'Did you get into trouble?'

'No. I thought I would, but he just asked me lots of questions and then he said to me, "I'm not giving this trip my blessing just yet but I promise you, your mother and I will talk about it. Don't run off until we do." Then a few days later he said, "We think your going away for a while, having a change from here, is perhaps not a bad idea, though we'd rather you were around people who could keep an eye on you." He suggested I go and work with my Uncle Michel – he's my mother's brother. He lives in Montreal, has a merchant trading business there and in Québec. I had never thought about this option but the idea appealed. So I agreed. I had to finish secondary school first though.'

'Do you like sailing? Is that what you want to do with your life?'

Samuel brushed his hair back off his face. 'I'm not sure now's a good time to answer that.' He inhaled deeply. 'Certainly till now I've enjoyed it. It's hard work and there are many sleepless nights. But I've had some great adventures and I've met people completely different to those I grew up with. My uncle's got a few boats in his fleet and after working with him for twelve months I more or less had my pick of jobs. Last summer we sailed this tall ship all the way down to the Bahamas. What a trip that was. Water, the most beautiful teal-colour, so warm you could swim in it all day. Sand like alabaster, glittering like crystal, grove after grove of green swaying palm trees. Great clumps of rainbow coral, tropical fish and food, some of which I'd never seen or tasted before. It was summer there too and I'd never been so hot. The heat of the tropics is a completely different heat to summers in Toronto. A wet, hanging heat. You're in a sheen all day waiting for the moment when these big dark voluminous clouds burst and the heavens break loose and when it does, the downpour releases you – not just from the heat but from the build-up as well. It's kind of like a birthing every day. You really have to experience it to know what it's truly like. It's… '

He broke off, suddenly aware of his insensitivity.

What was he doing regaling her with such far-away fantasies when she had just told him of her despair with this place? It was the way she had looked at him all the while he was speaking, taking in every word, rolling them around like a ball of twine, building it all up inside her so that any moment she too was going to hurl it out, just like his story – but most likely in tears. How heartless of him. 'I'm sorry, Rebecca. I got carried away.'

'No, don't be.'

'No, I am. I wasn't thinking.'

'No, it's fine, really. I want to hear all your stories. Promise me you'll tell me all your stories, Samuel.' She looked at him in a way he found beseeching.

'Do you like to torture yourself?'

'No!' she shook her head. 'It will give me something to think about when you are gone.'

And that was the moment, the seminal moment. Years later he would look back and remember that moment, remember the two of them sitting side by side, their eyes searching, he deciding to stay, rather than rush away as soon as he was well, as a kind of a thank-you gift to her, hoping his presence would postpone her passage into a life of dreary domesticity. Exhaling, he turned to gaze at the sea. 'It's not that bad here. The air is clean and fresh. You're surrounded by nature. Trees, ocean, sky, wide-open spaces. It's got its own kind of beauty.' He thought briefly of quoting a few lines of Keats' *To Solitude* but having never lived in a city the distinction would probably be lost on her.

Rebecca sighed heavily. After a few moments she said, 'Yes, it is beautiful, particularly this time of the year. Winter sure drags on though and the fog can weigh you down, weigh everything down. But it's sometimes on the clearest, bluest days, when the whole world is fully revealed, that you most feel it calling.'

Samuel sat there pondering her words, but he was no longer looking out to sea. He was staring at Rebecca, amazed at this girl, young woman rather, who could speak of such longing and such loss for things yet to be discovered, yet still mourned for. How was it that he should find such a kindred soul here in the midst of nowhere? Or was it merely the voice of youth, echoing his own sentiments?

After a little while, he returned his gaze to the ocean and in the far distance saw a vague white spot where the sky and the water fused.

'Hey, is that fog rolling in over there do you think? Or is it a cloud? Maybe even an iceberg? Just before that headland to the right.' He raised his hand and pointed to the east.

'I see it,' she said staring hard at the skyline. 'I think it might be a berg, but it's too far away to tell right now.' She paused, her eyes far off, peering at the horizon. 'That's how I found you, you know?'

'No. How? Tell me. Was I carried here on an iceberg?' He smiled faintly.

She laughed softly. He liked her laugh. It was gentle and assured. He wanted to hear more of her laughter. He hadn't heard enough laughter lately.

'I don't know about that,' she replied. 'No, watching icebergs is my favourite past time. It's what spring and early summer are all about. I just love them. They're the slow-moving mistresses of the sea, don't you think? Ancient and wise yet graceful and unique. It's as if they each have their own story to tell about what they are, where they've come from, where they're going. It's almost like I hear them calling for me to climb on board, "Come sail the seven seas with me",' she gushed. Then she stopped. 'You probably think I'm foolish, childish,' she shrugged, looking uncomfortably at the grass.

'Not at all.' He wanted her to lift her head, to look at him, to know he did not think her callow. 'So did an iceberg tell you where to find me?'

'No.' She threw a twig at a small stone and watched it bounce away. 'I was scanning the sea for icebergs and that is when I first caught a glimpse of your boat, near Coleman's Point.'

'Where's that?'

'Over there.' She pointed her face and hand to the left. 'I'll show you one day.'

'Did you see me on board?'

'Yes, you were waving your shirt. I thought perhaps you had seen me on the headland?' She looked at him, her expression hopeful.

He almost hated to disappoint her. 'I have no recollection of that,' he said at last.

'Maybe one day you will.'

'Have you ever been up close to an iceberg?'

She shook her head. 'I heard tell how some folk on Fogo, that's an island not far from here, well they had their bay sealed in one year when a giant iceberg ran aground. They had to wait three months till it melted enough before they could get their fishing boat out into the open sea. They weren't too happy apparently.' That half-laugh again. 'What about you?' she asked turning towards him.

'No.' His gaze still levelled at the horizon. 'I've only had about eighteen months at sea and this is my first time this far north. Our major objective was to steer clear of icebergs. But you know it would be something, to be able to get up close and have a look at one, don't you think?'

'Yes,' she sighed, in a way that was more an inhalation than an exhalation.

That night at dinner after Rachel said grace and everyone said Amen, Silas looked down the table at Samuel and said, 'Rebecca tells me that you've sailed as far as the Caribbean.'

'Yes, sir. Last year. It was fascinating.'

'Was that on the Nightingale?'

'No, it was on a much bigger vessel. La Paon – The Peacock.'

'That's a masculine name for a boat!' exclaimed Silas.

Samuel faintly smiled. Michel would be enjoying himself right now. 'My uncle likes to snub convention.'

Silas huffed.

'Where did you go?' asked Rachel.

'We left Québec and headed out through the St Lawrence. When we hit the Atlantic we headed due south to Guadeloupe, Martinique, St Lucia.'

'What did you bring back?' she asked.

'Pineapples, sugar cane, cassava, sweet potatoes, plantains, rum, oranges...'

'Rum! That's the devil's drink.' Silas's disapproving eyes glared at Samuel. 'Did you have that on board the Nightingale?'

'Yes,' drawled Samuel, wondering where the conversation was heading.

'You see, maybe that was the problem with yon boat that went down. Someone up above was not too pleased with what you were carrying.' Silas pointed to the ceiling with his fork as he spoke.

Samuel halted, thinking, I hear what he's saying, but I just don't believe it. He glanced around the table. Only Rebecca's clear eyes met his. Her eyebrows were slightly raised, her eyes wide. They weren't full of warning – rather they held a look that said, 'This is what he is like sometimes.' I could let this slide thought Samuel, running his fingers through his hair, but maybe…'Well Jesus didn't seem to have a problem with alcohol. He drank it at the Last Supper.'

'A very solemn occasion,' noted Silas.

'And at other times,' continued Samuel.

'That was wine, not rum.'

'Perhaps so, but it was still alcohol. Besides, alcohol also has its medicinal purposes. It has relieved a lot of suffering in its time. My father would vouch for that and raw alcohol is one of the best sterilisers available.'

'That's different, that's for a very specific use. Tell me, is your father a drinking man?'

'My father drinks from time to time…as does my mother.' Perhaps not a good time to say everyone in my family drinks, thought Samuel.

'Well, the French are known for that.'

'Tell me, Samuel, how long did it take you to sail to the Caribbean?' inquired Morna.

'About a month ma'am. Some days we made good time if the trade winds were in our favour.'

'Did you like being out on the open water for that length of time?' Morna smiled in encouragement.

'You get used to it. I'm sure Mr Crowe would agree.' Samuel was hoping there were some things they could agree on or else he'd be out on his ear soon. 'The stars at night are wonderful. You see some different ones down there than you do up here.' He looked up from his end of the table. 'Mr Crowe,' he said, 'can you tell me about some of the voyages you've had at sea? The waters around here are still a big mystery to me.'

Everyone turned to look at Silas who eyed Samuel intently while he continued to chew, as if he were weighing up whether to indulge or deny the request. Samuel had no idea that for

Silas, being the centre of attention was like a voyage into strange and unchartered waters. After a very protracted period he swallowed and much to everyone's relief, obliged.

He started gingerly at first, it appeared he was choosing his words carefully – not wanting to cause the women too much alarm, or perhaps overly entice Rebecca. But after a while he answered their eager questions. Like any old salty dog, Silas had his share of tales and as the night wore on, Samuel was inclined to think that what Silas didn't know about seafaring didn't bear thinking about. In Samuel's estimation, he held under lock and key a trove of stories as rich and as infamous as the Grand Banks. He couldn't help wonder, not without a touch of irony, what might be revealed if Silas was well-oiled with half a bottle of good ol' Jamaican rum.

6

Next morning before breakfast, Silas said to Samuel, 'Would you like to accompany us to church? Are you up to it do you think?'

Was Silas testing his faith or inviting him into the fold? He cast around for Rebecca, like a blind man seeking guidance. 'How far to the church?'

'Oh, about ninety minutes by foot, the same in the boat on a good day.'

'He can ride Mica with me,' Rachel said, coming in on the conversation.

'That's what I had in mind,' said Silas.

Samuel looked at Rachel. 'Don't worry, she doubles Rebecca and me all the time.'

The trip to church was a welcome respite from the days he'd spent lying inside going over events in his head. Being outside, seeing the rustic, unfamiliar landscape made Samuel feel like he was starting to breathe again, see again, live again. The whole countryside was scattered with outcrops as if a meteorite had exploded.

'I see why you fish here rather than farm,' said Samuel loudly, hoping to engage Silas in a conversation. 'This is one of the rockiest places I've ever been to.'

'Oh we don't mind the rocks,' said Silas. 'God was being extra thoughtful when he made Newfoundland.'

Rebecca called out, 'Samuel, do you want to know how the rocks ended up here?'

'Yes, why?'

'Well,' she said, turning around to walk backwards as she looked up at him.

'The story goes that the rocks were the ballast that Noah used for the Ark and when he was passing over here the waters were getting lower so he started throwing out the ballast and this is where he dumped most of it.' Her cheerful upturned face was daring him to believe her.

Shaking his head Samuel smiled back at her. After about an hour they came over a rise where nestled below was the fishing village of Deception Bay. To the right were some thirty buildings straddling rocky slabs and buttresses, many single storey, a few two storeys high with steep pitched gabled roofs and dormer windows. With the exception of the red boatsheds along the waterfront they were all white, the majority with charcoal-coloured roofs, the occasional one draped in the same boatshed red of the foreshore. There were no trees in sight, only shrubs and grasses.

The largest building was at the head of the bay, obviously the salt works. At its front a large jetty jutted out into the sea. The same structure hugged the shoreline for a few hundred yards either side, covered in thin flake structures. He could see other stages, smaller ones with dories leaning up against sheds and neat stacks of wooden lobster pots. It was undeniably quaint and, on this still blue morning, undeniably serene; no motors humming, no clanging or hammering, everyone observing the Sabbath. Samuel could not help wonder if little had changed here in over a hundred years.

Half turning to Rachel he asked, 'Why Deception?'

'See how far the wharf extends?' He nodded. 'Even though it may not look it from here, the Bay is deceptively shallow and before they built that wharf any boat that was more than half laden would ground itself at low tide. Even today very few large boats come in. They go to Seldom Come By just across the way. See you can make out Fogo Island in the distance. Everything is plied back and forth.'

Samuel was wondering where they got the timber from for the upkeep of the jetty when he noticed a solitary church on a rise to the east, its tall black steeple the highest man-made mark in sight. Behind it, flanking the hillside, almost casually strewn, were tombstones and crosses, more than he expected to see, given the size of the township. After they dismounted, Silas led him towards a group of suited men and made introductions.

When he met Ronnie, Samuel said, 'I believe I have you to thank for the crutches.'

Ronnie inclined his head ever so slightly. 'How is it?'

'On the mend,' Samuel replied.

'Good to hear. I told Silas last week, I'm happy to take a look at things for you if you want. I'm no expert I might add.'

'Thank you,' said Samuel, looking him straight in the eye. 'Perhaps later.' People had started moving.

He sat between Silas and Rebecca and shared Rebecca's hymn book. Each time the organist struck up a new song, she looked at him with raised eyebrows as if to say, 'Do you know this one?' He only knew one hymn. Had he failed some test?

When they came round to reciting The Lord's Prayer Samuel realised with a jolt he was still to write to his parents and his Uncle with the full details of what had happened. On Friday afternoon, Rebecca had returned from school with two telegraphs.

After the service he ambled outside feeling overwhelmed at all that was still ahead of him and all that was behind him…all the losses from his misadventure – not just life, that was tragic enough and three weeks later time had done little to ameliorate his despair, but the boat and now being here he was conscious of people in places even more remote, who counted on supplies and news getting through. They had lost out as well. Being here with these islanders, somehow brought it home to him, in a way that drifting aimlessly in the tender never had. He knew he was unbelievably fortunate to be alive, yet he felt no sense of elation whatsoever. He was just awash with failure and powerlessness. He still seemed to be enveloped in a shroud of incredulity – at what had happened and at his own survival. The fleeting feelings of optimism he had earlier were just that – fleeting.

As he mounted the horse, Ronnie called out. 'Don't forget to come and see me, I'm the fourth house on the right past the coopers.' All Samuel could manage was a nod.

The outing and the subsequent letter writing exhausted him. He wanted to lie down, but first he needed to talk to Silas. He was outside checking some canvas bags he'd been drying. Samuel hobbled up to him. 'Excuse me, Mr Crowe.' Silas lifted his eyes and cocked one tufted eyebrow. 'Can I talk to you for a minute?'

'I'll just finish this and I'll be with you directly.'

Samuel turned towards the sea, that afternoon a gunmetal grey swelling in the shadows of darkening clouds. A little while later he heard Silas say, 'Right, what can I do for you, Samuel?'

He turned back. 'I just wanted to acknowledge everything you have done for me sir. You have been very good to me, your whole family has. I want you to know I appreciate everything you are doing for me and I will organise to repay you. Please know that.'

Silas's eyes flicked over Samuel's face. 'That's very kind of you to offer, Samuel, but it's not necessary. We may not be wealthy folk, but we can manage.'

Not wanting to insult, Samuel said, 'I know you can manage. But I am responsible for the situation I'm in and to me that implies financial responsibility as well.'

Silas sucked in his cheeks giving serious consideration to Samuel's words. 'Well, I don't know about that,' he said at last. 'Seems to me Rebecca had something to do with it too.'

Samuel couldn't help but break into a semblance of a smile at Silas's joke. Silas even smiled a little himself.

'Samuel,' he said, 'if our situations were reversed and by some stroke of foul weather or bad luck, I was homeless and penniless and stranded on your doorstep, would you not help me out in the way we have helped you? I know you and I are different, but I don't believe we are that different.'

'No, we are not that different,' agreed Samuel.

'Well then it's settled. Best get yourself well. That's all you need to worry about.'

7

Samuel had been on land for over two weeks. His ankle was going down and his appetite was increasing along with his restlessness. Ever since Sunday's outing to church, he made a point of going outside on his crutches and walking further each day to build his strength. Most days there was a steady onshore breeze from the northeast that added an extra challenge to his walks. He'd go once in the morning and again in the afternoon so he wouldn't be there when Rebecca arrived from school, wanting to give the family some time alone without him.

Yet each afternoon when he returned from his wanderings Rebecca would be outside doing something, almost as if she were waiting for him.

'Did you see any icebergs today?' was the first thing she would ask.

And after they talked about icebergs or the lack thereof, she would inquire, 'Where did you get to today?' He would tell her how far he walked, what he'd seen and then ask her, 'What did you learn at school today?' and let her carry on. But it wouldn't be long before she turned whatever she was talking about into a question about his life or his views or his plans or his likes. She had a way about her, vicariously trying to eke out her existence, through his experiences.

One day when he was feeling better Samuel decided to pay Ronnie Evans a visit. He hitched another ride with Rachel into the village. During their forced proximity on Mica, Samuel was able to ask Rachel all manner of questions about her life that he couldn't seem to broach in her home. He noticed she talked freely but not enthusiastically. She had a calmness about her that her younger sister lacked. Where Rebecca was restless, Rachel seemed resigned. Resigned to what, he wondered? While Rebecca wanted to live a lot, Rachel needed to live a little more, or so it seemed to Samuel. What sort of life did she see for herself?

In another place, perhaps another life, she would have significantly more choices than what she had here.

Rachel had inherited much from her mother. Now that he thought about it she, and for that matter Mrs Crowe, actually reminded him of portraits he'd seen of Nellie Bly, the American journalist his mother followed with keen interest, one a younger, the other an older version of the photograph in her book, *Around the World in Seventy-Two Days*.

Rachel was a more petite, darker version of her mother, with large brown eyes that seemed to glow in certain lights setting off her brown hair, fringed at the front and permanently tied in a bun at the back. She had her mother's oval face and her mother's round cheeks, gentle, even lips, in fact he would have to say perfect lips. She would not be out of place in some nineteenth century European painting.

Rebecca on the other hand had been stamped with many of Silas's features; an oblong face, a clear strong brow, a defined jaw line, a long slender neck and there was no avoiding it — his eyes. They weren't so much deep set or protruding; they simply stood out because of their striking colour and the way they were fringed in golden brown lashes. A blue forged with copper and cobalt like the teal blue waters of the Caribbean. Alluring. But she also had another intriguing feature, one his eyes were drawn to more and more. Her philtrum, the two fine lines that ran from her top lip to the bottom of her nose — in most people barely visible — was carved clearly on her face like a Rodin sculpture. Between the two lines was a pronounced indentation, which seemed to emphasise the curve of her lips even more. To top it all off she was crowned with the soft flowing hair of a young girl, a light chestnut blonde. The overall impression was one of startling originality.

Samuel suppressed a wry laugh. Thinking about these women as he had was surely a sign that he was coming back to the living. It certainly would be for his brother.

In Deception Rachel introduced him to Jonah, Toby and Michael, three lads around his age who worked in the cooperage and had gone to school with Rachel. Toby asked after Esther, Rachel's sister, who years earlier had married his cousin, David, from Salvage. They chatted amicably for a few minutes until Rachel excused herself to run some errands and Samuel excused himself to go find Ronnie.

Ronnie sat Samuel down on a chair on his porch, grabbed a footstool to rest his leg, pulled on a pair of wire-framed glasses and proceeded to peer and prod gently at Samuel's ankle while waiting for a pot of tea to arrive. He was easy to talk to, much easier than Silas. Ronnie had done several ocean voyages himself when he was a lad, working as an assistant to a medical officer on board large seafaring vessels that traversed between the eastern seaboard and Europe. That was the extent of his medical training. That and whatever books he could lay his hands on.

'Where's the nearest doctor?' asked Samuel.

'There is a doc over at Twillingate. But it's a few hours by boat and if they can last the trip maybe they should have stayed behind, you know what I mean? And more often than not you have to deal with what's immediately in front of you. Stop the bleeding, stitch a person up, bandage a break. The doc keeps me well-supplied. Sometimes you get a visiting quack working for the Grenfell Mission who will come through on a steamer and leave you some bits and pieces. Mostly they're young doctors and nurses come here from America for the summer, their 'down north' experience they call it. The very sick they take on to St Anthony's at the tip of the big island. It's easier to get there in summer. You don't want to get sick in winter I tell you. You have to deal with dogsleds and then in spring, ice floes and growlers.'

'My father's a doctor,' Samuel volunteered, 'and my brother.'

'Well I'll be. You should be treating yourself, lad. Where's that then?'

'My father is in Toronto. Matthew's in Montreal.'

'No doubt your father has seen some things in his life.'

'I imagine he has,' agreed Samuel.

'He would have seen some things if he doctored here, I'd wager you that.' Ronnie stroked his aging brown beard. 'It's not for the faint-hearted. The young ones are the worst. Silas knows plenty about that.'

'How's that?'

'Hmm, well, a couple of years back, late April if my memory serves me correctly, Silas went to check on the Wright family. They lived about four bays around from the Crowes. Bill Wright used to fish on the same boat with Silas. Anyway, a group of them had planned to go to Seldom Come By and Bill didn't turn up so they went without him. And when they got back a day later, there still hadn't been any word. That's what you go on round here, you know. You tell people what you are doing and you stick to it, then if you miss a date, people come looking. So Silas set out the next morning, pulled then rowed his boat out of his bay and headed north. The bays don't freeze up completely here, only around the edges, even so there are lots of ice pans floating around. Well anyway, Silas approaches the Wright's bay and what does he see jammed up against some rocks but an upturned boat.

'As he gets closer he sees the Wright's nine year old daughter strapped to the top. Miraculously she was still alive, but her legs were buried to the shins in the frozen ocean.' Ronnie snatched a glance at Samuel's disbelieving face. 'True.' He nodded emphatically. 'It seems Bill's wife and two sons had succumbed to a mystery illness and Bill was not about to wait round for him and Charmaine to follow. So he piled her into their dinghy. From what we can put together the boat must have hit a rogue wave or something, upturned and Bill couldn't seem to right her, so he lashed Charmaine to the top, climbed on board himself, who knows what he was thinking, maybe that the boat would drift back to shore and he could start out all over again.

'Well, he slipped away at some point, and Charmaine slipped a bit too judging by where her feet ended up. What a sorry mess it was. And Silas had to deal with it, all by himself.'

'What did he do?'

'Well, what could he do?' Ronnie replied, his palms upturned. 'He didn't have much choice did he? He had to chop her legs off. He tied tourniquets around her shins, put her stumps in a bucket of icy cold water and they landed here about three hours later.'

Samuel was speechless, his stomach turning as if he had just witnessed Silas committing the brutal act. After a spell he managed to say, 'The poor girl, she must have been in agony.'

'It wasn't too bad actually,' said Ronnie. 'Her legs were already numb and he saved her life. That one we did send through to St John's. I believe they had to take some more off her legs but she came through and was sent to live with her mother's sister down near Carbonear.'

Shaking his head in wonder, Samuel asked, 'How did Silas cope with all of that?'

Ronnie licked his thumb and with it rubbed a dry red spot on the back of his hand. 'Ah well, you know Silas, he doesn't say much. I suspect he prayed about it. But often it doesn't pay to think about these things too much.' He glanced at Samuel when he said that. 'Anyway,' he tapped Samuel on the thigh, 'he won't be chopping your legs off any day soon.'

'Thank Christ for small mercies,' mumbled Samuel.

Chuckling softly, Ronnie continued, 'Even so, I think you should stick with the crutches for another week. Most likely you've damaged your tendons. Keep your ankle strapped and start to walk on it with the aid of just one crutch and take it from there. How's everything else?'

'Alright,' said Samuel with a nod. 'I was sore here on my side for a while.' He touched his ribs. 'But that's not bothering me now.'

'You're looking a lot better, even if you are a bit scraggy. You seem to have lost that drawn look you had when I first saw you. You must be getting plenty of fluids. Is there anything else I can do for you?'

Samuel hesitated. There was something he wanted but he hated to ask. He felt like a beggar. But Ronnie had already touched on it. 'I don't suppose I could borrow a razor?'

'No problem,' said Ronnie slapping Samuel on the back as he stood up. 'Let's get you cleaned up.'

An hour later when Rachel returned, not only was Samuel clean shaven, he was clean all over, sparkling from his head to his toe and sporting a newly donated and well-fitting shirt, jacket, trousers and braces. They were a gift from Ronnie. Samuel had refused at first but Ronnie insisted saying they were passed onto him for the very purpose of giving to people in need. Little did he know they had belonged to the long departed Bill Wright.

Samuel broke into a wide grin when he saw Rachel. He couldn't help himself. She reminded him of how startled Rebecca was the day he first awoke. 'It lives,' he joked. Yes today he did feel alive, as if he was coming out of some long self-imposed exile.

'Why Samuel, I hardly recognise you.' She blushed as she tried to snatch quick glances of his clean hair, his beardless face, his generous grin. When Samuel grinned, really grinned as he was doing today for the first time, he showed all of his teeth, not his top row but his bottom row as well.

'Do you approve?' he asked, holding his hands out wide.

'Yes much better. But now you look like a stranger to me all over again.'

'Well do you fancy a ride with a tall not-so-dark stranger?' he teased.

His suggestiveness rendered her speechless, not so Ronnie. 'Get on up, Rachel, before he changes his mind.'

'Come on now, don't by shy,' teased Samuel.

They mounted Mica, Samuel at the front holding his crutches across his lap, Rachel behind, with a knapsack on her back. Tapping the crutches, Samuel said in farewell, 'I'll return these in a little while and we can talk some more.'

'I'm not going anywhere.' Ronnie waved them off. 'I'll be here or down at the forge.'

Samuel was in such good spirits he felt like cantering home – a dash bareback to totally awaken his senses. 'How does Mica handle a canter?' he asked.

'With you she'll probably buck us off and run all the way home.'

'You're just having me on. I'm sure you and Rebecca race her all the time.'

'Rebecca might, I don't. Besides,' she said, 'I have some things in my pack that I don't want to damage – including a package for you that I collected from the merchant.'

'Great, but you're changing the subject. Let's offload everything and go for a gallop.' Samuel turned his head and grinned at Rachel in invitation.

'So it's a gallop now is it?'

They decided to go home first, unload, then walk Mica back up the slope beyond their house so they could canter along the plateau. Despite the two of them, the horse had no problems breaking into a canter. Rachel and Samuel kept on bumping into each other. At one point the horse shied at a rabbit and they nearly lost their balance, but recovered in time squeezing their legs tightly around the mare. Rachel got the giggles. 'See I told you she would try and shake us off. Now do you believe me?'

When they stopped to gain their breath, they saw Rebecca off in the distance, racing along then slowing down to gather herself before breaking again into a run. She was in her own little world, blowing along like a thistle flower in the wind.

'Is she always like that?' asked Samuel. 'The only way I'd ever race home after school was if I were late for dinner.'

'Well, that's Rebecca for you,' said Rachel, her voice a quiet study of pride.

8

Rebecca had been counting down the days left before she was finished with school for the year, for life. It was a bittersweet ending. She had no illusions. The end of school would be the demarcation line between growing up and the rest of her life. And until Samuel had floated in like flotsam, she wasn't in a hurry to get on with the rest of her life.

However with Samuel's arrival she felt torn. She wanted to leave school tomorrow so she could spend every waking moment of every day with him. She was Robinson Crusoe and he was her treasure chest. And as the days passed and Samuel's body and spirit returned, she started to worry that before long he would head back out into the wild blue yonder and not only would she not have spent enough time with him, there would be absolutely nothing she could do to prevent his leaving.

Lost in her thoughts she didn't notice Samuel and Rachel until they charged past, Rachel yelling, 'Woo hoo, Rebecca.' She lifted her eyes and watched Samuel rein Mica to a halt.

'Are you two trying to kill me?' she yelled. She knew it was out of character for her but she was completely unsettled. The two of them were delirious with the speed, with the wind, with laughter. While she was at school they were gallivanting around having a good time.

And as they approached, Rebecca saw a new Samuel: a vividly alive, dazzling with the day new Samuel. His hair shone as if it had been dusted in silver and gold. His eyes sparkled, his teeth gleamed. His whole face just glowed in beautiful, captivating, cheerfulness. She had never before seen such a good-looking young man. As she stood in front of him, she was flustered in a way she had never been. Before, with his beard, he was this gentle, well-considered, older brother person whom she held in awe. A man, whom, once she got over her initial shyness, seemed to be her new best friend; her confidant; her first real life teacher. Even though he was only nineteen, with the beard he looked much older, and oddly, far less intimidating than he did right now, in front of her, astride their horse, grinning from ear to ear. Grinning with his clean-shaven face, his confident jaw, his square chin and his sensational smile. She had never seen such a transformation.

What's more, standing before him, Rebecca felt her own body opening like a sunflower facing the sun, enlarging, changing inside and out, of its own accord. She could feel her skin tingling, her legs shaking. She didn't know what to make of this new Samuel. It seemed her sister had no problems coming to terms with his latest reincarnation. Rebecca had rescued the old Samuel for her own. Now it seemed Rachel had claimed the new one.

'What's the matter?' asked Samuel.

Her breath caught in her throat. He had detected something amiss! She wanted to instantly flee but knew that would betray her unease even more.

'Nothing,' she said, dryly

'How was school today?'

'Fine.'

'Learn anything new?'

'Not much.'

'Want to go for a ride?'

'Another day maybe.'

'Rebecca, want us to carry your bag for you?' asked Rachel.

'No thanks, I can manage.'

'Anything we can do for you?' said Samuel.

'No, I'm good.' *Please leave me alone. I need to understand what I'm feeling and why. I can't do that with you standing there looking at me.*

'Alright, see you at home.' He turned the horse's head and gently kicked her on.

As Rebecca watched them take their leave she knew she didn't understand what was going on. Not so much with them, but with her. How all of sudden she felt she couldn't breathe properly when she was standing there looking up at Samuel. How for some inexplicable reason she had felt scared and exposed, as if he could look inside her and see things there that she couldn't even see.

Setting off again, this time walking slowly, she tried to relax, tried to reassure herself that while she may have not been herself just then, Samuel was hardly to know it was because of him. But how was she going to be the next time she was around him? Was she going to have more awkward moments punctuated by monosyllabic replies? Why was she so uncomfortable around him all of sudden? Why was she upset? Was she angry? Angry at whom? Somehow she needed to sift through these thoughts and make peace with herself and with them, before she walked through their back door. She prayed. She prayed hard. But even so, she didn't feel any better as she walked down the slope. Opening the door with dread, she was almost relieved to see her father at home.

'Hello Rebecca,' he said. Her father was in a good mood. When he was sullen or absorbed he never said hello first.

'Hello Father,' she said with a smile. 'How was the catch?'

'Overflowing.' A brief smile split his beard, even his eyes seemed softer. 'The most fish we've caught at the start of the season since 1908.'

'Splendid news,' enthused Rebecca. She was genuinely happy. It boded well for a good year.

Her mother was handing out mugs of root beer.

'My,' said Rebecca. Her father must be feeling extremely indulgent and jubilant.

'I suppose everyone on Second Chance is celebrating,' noted Samuel.

Swallowing a fizzy mouthful Rebecca said, 'Everyone except the women at the saltworks. They celebrate when they put their feet up. Isn't that right, Mother?'

'They're still celebrating, Rebecca.'

She looked at her mother then quietly took another sip.

'Samuel, do you like fresh cod?' asked Rachel.

'Do I have a choice?' he joked and before Rachel could reply, said, 'Actually, I'm yet to find a fish I don't enjoy.'

'Just as well,' Rachel said with laugh. 'You're going to be living on cod for weeks.'

'You know, Rachel, somehow I think I will manage.'

Rebecca watched Samuel run his fingers through his blonde gold hair from his temple to his nape, his teasing eyes twinkling at her sister and hers glowing back.

That night they had succulent fresh fish dipped in milk and flour, pan-fried and served with a sprinkling of home-made vinegar. Simple, yet delicious. Everyone enjoyed it and the dinner seemed to hold a festive air even though Rebecca was the most withdrawn she had been in weeks. She would glance at the faces around the table and back to her plate, saying little. Everyone seemed to be bubbling along with Samuel's effervescence. He was the most talkative he had been since his arrival and her father too was uncharacteristically vocal. Rebecca wondered if aside from the favourable catch, he was buoyed by the presence of another man in the house.

'When you're more hale we'll get you out on the boat with us, Samuel. Though I have to say you're looking much better than that chap who washed up here a few weeks ago.'

'Count me in,' said Samuel. 'In a week or so, I hope to be rid of the crutches altogether and back to normal. And, if you don't mind, I'd like to stay on for a few weeks and make myself useful before I head off.'

There it was! Rebecca rested her relieved eyes on Samuel. He wasn't going to desert them straight away. Maybe by the time school finished, she would have calmed down and things would be back to normal and she could once again look forward to spending time with him, just like she had up until now.

'So I was wondering,' continued Samuel, 'now that I've started shaving again, is there a mirror around here I can use?'

'That we do not have,' said her father between mouthfuls.

'No problem,' said Samuel. 'I suspect I can manage or sort something out at Deception. Ladies, would you like a mirror to adorn your wall?'

Four heads immediately turned to look at him.

'Don't you know, Samuel, that mirrors bring bad luck,' said Silas. 'Did you have them on board your boat? Break a mirror and you get seven years of bad luck,' he warned. Silas sat there staring off into space shaking his head.

'Worse though, Samuel,' said Rachel, 'if a mirror in your house falls and breaks by itself, someone in the house will die soon.'

For some unknown reason Rebecca felt compelled to add to the mounting pile of evidence. 'And they can attract lightning during a thunderstorm, so you have to run round and make sure they are all covered up.' Rebecca glanced at her mother who had not said a word and then she looked at Samuel who looked like he wanted to say a word, and did.

'That's just old superstition. Surely you don't believe it?'

'Call it what you want,' said her father. 'Ignore it at your own peril. But we don't want any mirrors in this house.'

Samuel glanced around the table till his eyes found hers. She felt him silently communicating a message to her, one she couldn't fully decipher, or was it one she didn't want to acknowledge.

That night as they lay in bed, Rachel whispered to Rebecca, 'I can't believe how different Samuel looks, can you? It's like he has been born again. When I was with him on Mica I imagined him on a great steed draped in caparisons, a knight in shining armour. He's very assured on horseback. You should go for a ride with him one day, Rebecca. We had a grand time.'

'Yes. Maybe.' Silence. 'Have you been riding with him much?'

'Only today.' Seconds of prolonged silence ticked by till Rachel wistfully added, 'I hope he doesn't leave for a while. I've decided I like having him around.'

Don't we all, thought Rebecca, staring at the ceiling. She lay there for a while then turned towards her sister. 'Rachel, do you ever wonder if we've learnt the right things growing up? Do you ever wonder that we should have learned different things?'

'Like what?'

'I don't know. I just wonder if we've learnt how to live here and only live here and how it would be if we ever lived some place else. Would we know how to get by?' She swallowed before continuing. 'It seems Samuel knows a world quite different to ours.'

'He does know a world quite different to ours. He's from Toronto. He's been all over the place!'

'No, I don't mean it like that. He thinks differently, as if he has knowledge that we haven't. It makes me wonder if the people we know have not informed us properly.'

'You're talking nonsense. Our parents, our teachers, they

have given us what we need to live in our world – here. But more than that, I'm sure they have done the best they could. And they have done right by us. What more do you want?'

'I don't know.' Each word came out slowly, separately. 'Whatever it is I feel I'm missing.' She rolled back the other way.

9

My one and only brother,

"At night, in solitude, in tears. Not a star shining, all dark and desolate."

Samuel Oh Samuel. I can't bear to think of what might have been. Of you living in the world below the brine. When I think of you, I think of us, inseparate. It will always be for me "we two boys together clinging." Thank you for writing and easing my mind that you are well on the road to recovery and still the engaging, optimistic and brave brother I love and adore. I yearn to have you with me again so I can squeeze your very flesh and blood between my fingers and see the bright light in your eyes.

I know you need some time before you are ready to come home. Do what you must to feel alive and whole again, but do come back soon as our days are long without you. Don't feel bad about Uncle Michel's boat or the supplies. "They mean <u>nothing</u> to me Matthew," he said. It is just you and the men he weeps for. He too won't let you go when next he sees you.

The folks have taken your news in their stride, thanks to Grandpa's ever calming influence. No doubt Lottie would have had palpitations had she read the letter you sent me. Leise, believe it or not, has had an epiphany. She told me, 'Matthew, I nearly lost my baby brother and I realise I don't treat him like a brother. I have been given a second chance and I'm not going to squander it.' Expect a letter any day.

And what an angel, this Rebecca Crowe. You write but little of her and her family, but in your next letter, I want to hear more about this remarkable girl and her beneficent family. My life of late has been adventureless to a fault. In a good week, Friday night El Latino, Saturday night the club, on Sunday a ride if I'm lucky. Other times it's the hospital from dawn to dusk and beyond.

Next summer <u>we</u> are going to Parry Sound together. Gliding through moonlight, pearly pink granite, shooting stars and twilight song.
Love Matthew

Samuel read Matthew's letter twice, picturing Parry Sound, recalling their canoeing trip nearly four years ago. He was right; a holiday together was overdue. Somehow, Samuel didn't think it would be that year. Strangely he was in no rush to return home. Ought he to write and tell them so? And what would he tell his brother of the remarkable Rebecca and her sweet sister. His brother who from the age of sixteen, appeared as a man of the world, a man with stature and confidence, with dark features and a carefree urbane manner. Matthew was handsome in a dangerous sort of way, aloof and charismatic. For now Samuel wouldn't be indulging him with detailed descriptions of any Newfoundland nymphs. Nor would he be retelling what had transpired that afternoon. For when he and Rachel had come across Rebecca on the barrens he didn't know what to think. Of late, Rebecca craved his company. That afternoon, she was decidedly distant.

10

The next morning as Rebecca was getting breakfast in the kitchen Samuel came up to her and casually asked, 'Are you feeling better today?'

She looked at him and once again couldn't get over how different he looked. What alchemy occurred at Deception yesterday? With his face healed and his beard gone she saw his skin for what it really was: beautiful, like a three-month old baby's, smooth and even and golden, the skin of a prince. Was her skin like that she wondered? Or was it because of his mother's French blood? Next time she saw Miss Drysdale she was going to ask her if she had a mirror! But right now the absence of a mirror didn't change the fact that in all her born days Rebecca had never encountered a man more handsome, and that disturbed her. First it was his eyes. His eyes! From the very beginning she had a bizarre weakness for them and now this. She felt the trembling start up inside her again. 'Yes, why?' She wanted to yell at herself, 'Stop being ridiculous. It is only Samuel!'

'You just didn't seem yourself yesterday, that's all.'

'Oh,' was the only reply she could manage. A feeble oh. She uttered it again, when she came home from school and found Rachel lying down on their living room floor with Samuel beside her, his hand on her leg. 'What are you doing?' she managed, once she found her powers of speech.

'I'm making myself useful. I'm measuring Rachel's legs. I'm going to make her a cleat for her shoes, so she doesn't have to limp.'

'You have to do that on the floor, lying down?' she said, taken aback.

'Yes, this way her hips are even, giving a true measure of the length of each leg,' he said, tape measure in hand. 'Then I can work out how high the attachment needs to be.'

'Have you ever made a shoe cleat before?' asked Rebecca, trying not to sound dubious.

'Well, no.'

'Rebecca,' said Rachel, pushing herself up onto her hands, 'let Samuel be. As long as I don't break my leg in the process, there's no harm in him trying, is there?' She smiled at Samuel who smiled back.

'No, it's your leg.' Rebecca tried to be conciliatory. 'Good luck.' She turned and walked towards the kitchen, any place away from them where she could deal with her latest quandary, that since yesterday had been added to her equation of angst: herself.

Rebecca's world was in a spin. She'd oscillate between wanting to gaze upon Samuel's face, but not wanting to catch his eye, as then the hollow, sickening feeling would start again and she'd barely be able to breathe. To steady herself, she plotted a raft of questions to ask him as his replies would always entrance her. How long do you think icebergs last for? Where would you like to travel to next? And whenever her interest was piqued she was able once more to gaze into his animated face, to ask every question, to tap every last ounce of information and experience he had to offer.

But every so often in their conversations, Samuel would pause and stare at Rebecca, almost as if he was wanting to ask her a question, something entirely different to the topic at hand but then he would swallow before continuing on. At times like this she couldn't handle looking into his eyes. Instead, she would lower her gaze and stare into his mouth, at his teeth and his tongue and watch the words as they came out, listening to the rich deep timbre of his voice. And that was something else about him that stirred her; how someone who was only nineteen could possess the most masculine soothing voice she had ever heard.

On Saturday her mother gave her a rare afternoon off. What to do?

Maybe she could walk out to the point and scan for icebergs. She hadn't done much of that lately, though today she would be lucky to see a thing. A large bank of fog hugged the shore. At least the wind had died down for a change. If it were a wet day, she would stay inside, read or do something with her sister. But it wasn't a wet day, grey though it was, and the last thing she wanted was to be with Rachel, hearing her whisper worship-like about Samuel.

Last night at dinner when Rachel said grace, she also said, 'Thank you Lord for sending Samuel to us.' And then when they opened their eyes she said, 'I'm sorry you had to go through what you did to get here Samuel but I'm so happy you made it.'

Rachel had good reason to be elated. Samuel's shoe cleat was a resounding success. Rachel now walked evenly, no bobbing up and down. So why didn't Rebecca feel thrilled for her sister? What was wrong with her!

If only she had a friend who lived close by, a friend she could confide in and laugh with and lose herself with. There was no one. But there was Mica, whom she loved, whom she rarely rode for pleasure, unlike Samuel and Rachel. She would ride her and when she was far away dismount her and lean into her neck and cry like she did sometimes, and be comforted by the horse's warm muzzling lips, her hot damp breath, her sympathetic eyes. That is what she would do.

When she was younger Rebecca had dreams of having her own horse, dreams of Rachel and her riding together enjoying a few hours of windblown exhilaration. And unlike her other dreams, these were well-founded. Late one spring she and Rachel watched in wonder as Mica's foal, Slate, a young colt entered the world. Rebecca instantly fell in love with the gangly creature and his huge brown eyes, spiky mane and crazy cavorting manner. As soon as Mica would let her, Rebecca started handling him. She couldn't wait to ride him, which her father said they would organise for her twelfth birthday.

The summer of 1910 however had not been a good summer for the Crowes and that year Rebecca learnt that bad summers meant bad winters and just how bad things could be. Come March all of the family's supplies were gone and they were reduced to living on cups of tea and bread smeared with the thinnest layer of butter and jam. Their diet soon took its toll. They had nasty cankers, the odd carbuncle. They were listless and constipated. Her father would rise early, sneak out in the pre-dawn light to see if he could bring down an erratic hare or a wintry fox, anything that moved. For days he returned empty handed, then one afternoon Rachel and Rebecca came home to the smell of meat roasting in the kitchen.

Rebecca remembered that. She remembered walking in and smelling the air and how the aroma had only served to intensify her hunger pains, accentuating the emptiness that within hours, perhaps minutes, would know once more what it felt to have food inside.

'Did father get lucky?' Rachel had asked.

'Yes,' said her mother, not raising her face to her daughters. 'He prayed to God and God answered.'

But in mere minutes Rebecca knew the horrifying truth. She returned from the barn with a dread so deep it almost prevented her from walking. And worse, that night, despite her protestations, her father ordered her to the dinner table.

'I'm not hungry,' she had dared to replied. It was true. Her hollowness had been filled with betrayal, and a shocking, seething, loathing for her father which she was doing her best to mask, feeling justified over it, yet also feeling terribly ashamed of it.

'You'll eat when hunger gets the better of you and then we'll see how proud you are.'

'She's not proud, Silas, stop it,' said Morna.

'Why couldn't you have killed a sheep!' Rebecca couldn't help herself, she practically yelled at her father. 'We have a dozen sheep. Why did you have to kill Slate? He was little more than a baby. He's not stock! He was my pet, more than my pet. He was my friend.'

Her father had slammed his hand down on the table. 'Those sheep are worth more to us than that young colt ever would be! We need those sheep for wool and lanolin. That horse was expendable and God told me so. I put my trust in him and he provided.'

Her father pointed his knife accusingly at her. 'You'll understand one day, Rebecca, and you'll thank me and God when you realise why you are still alive.'

She sat there stonily until her Mother told her to eat some bread and jam. Then she went upstairs and cried herself to sleep.

Rebecca's childhood ended that day. From that day onwards something was not right about the world. She couldn't fathom how her parents could do such a thing. But more than that she couldn't understand how God could let such a thing happen, particularly, after all of her prayers. Did he not care for her and Slate? And those thoughts too weighed her down. On one hand he gave her gifts and on the other he took them away. She wondered had she done something wrong to be punished in such a way. She never understood the reasons why and wondered if she ever would.

That was the year Ronnie Evans became her and Rachel's Guardian Angel. Without meaning to tell tales Rachel had told Ronnie about the woeful happenings over the hill. Within days a mysterious food hamper appeared outside their door with provisions to last them a good month. Silas could not refuse it for he did not know to whom to return it, nor was he about to ask around as to the identity of their benefactor.

For weeks afterwards every time Rebecca saw Mica's searching, sorrowful eyes she would just hang her own head and walk away, drowning in fresh misery. Had she known what her father was capable of Rebecca would have taken Slate away and saved him. How would Mica ever trust her again? It was Ronnie and Margaret Evans who helped Rebecca find a path through her troubled existence. Ronnie was the only adult who truly acknowledged her pain. He told her that the reason her heart was breaking was to make room for Slate to live on inside so she would always remember and love him. He said Mica and Slate would have forgiven her because she was so remorseful. They wouldn't want her to keep on suffering.

And once Ronnie had soothed her ailing spirit, once he had shared with her some of the sad and fathomless happenings of his own upbringing, he started telling her happier tales from his early life, from his adventures at sea, of his travels to strange lands and her injured soul found a way to breathe again as it found other things to hold onto.

Samuel came across her when she was leading Mica by the halter back to the barn.

'Can I walk with you?' he asked.

'Sure.' What could she say?

They walked along slowly in an awkward silence until Rebecca could bear it no longer. She cleared her throat. 'How's your foot?'

'It's the least of my worries.'

That made her look directly at him. 'Your worries?'

'I'm starting to think about what I do when I leave. Do I go back and work in shipping with my uncle or do I return to Toronto and do something else. As lovely as here is, I can't stay forever.'

'When are you leaving?'

'Not for a while, not till I've pulled my weight around here, but I don't want to overstay my welcome.'

'You're not overstaying your welcome.' She didn't want to think of him leaving; she'd done enough thinking of his leaving already.

'Rebecca, about Rachel…'

Oh, here it comes. 'Yes?'

'Well, about Rachel's shoe, actually. You see, I made that for her as a thank you present. While you've been at school she has done a lot for me, made me lunch every day, done my washing, lots of things.'

'It's okay, Samuel, you don't have to explain.'

'But I want to. Coming up with something for Rachel was easy, obvious. And I'm wondering now if I have gone about this the wrong way. I know that when I first came to, dazed and groggy, I thanked you for rescuing me. I meant it then and I mean it now. You saved my life. And, of all the people in your family, I am indebted to you the most. I will be forever grateful to you. You must know that.' She nodded, her eyes downcast. She could sense him waiting. She looked up into a smile that spread across his face. She breathed out. It was going to be alright.

Samuel continued, 'It's important to me to thank you in a way that is meaningful to you, but I'm struggling with what that is. I know you would like to get off this island for a while. I would love to take you on a trip somewhere but at fourteen I don't think your parents would allow that.'

'I'll be fifteen soon.'

'Even so, you know what I mean.' They were outside the barn. Rebecca looped Mica's halter over the hitching post.

'Excuse me.' She ducked inside to grab the horse's curry comb and brush. When she returned, Samuel grabbed her wrist. She glanced down at his hands and then slowly raised her eyes to his. They were incredibly earnest, that golden hazel, edged in ebony, framed in bronze lashes. They were unwavering. She felt herself unable to breathe again, unable to break away.

'Please know that if there is anything I can ever do for you, anything I can help you with, you only have to ask, even after I'm gone. Just write to me. I am in your debt. Okay?'

'Okay' she said almost inaudibly.

He released his hand and she turned to her horse. She started brushing Mica's mane and forelock, which were heavily tangled. In her exertions, her hair fell out of its loose braid and swayed gently as one of her hands brushed Mica's mane and the other stroked it. Sensing Samuel watching her, she looked up. He was staring at her, with a perplexing, narrowing gaze, looking through her, into the past. 'Samuel,' she said, stirring him out of his trance-like state. 'Samuel!'

'I remember now,' he exclaimed, coming up to her.

'Remember what?'

'I remember you and my boat and you peering into it and your hair,' he said grabbing strands of it and watching it glide through his fingers.

'You do?' she asked with delight.

'Yes, I thought I'd run aground on Sable Island, and you were this inquisitive equine creature come to explore a piece of driftwood.'

'Are you saying I look like a horse?' she asked half-indignant.

'No, it was just your hair,' he tugged it, 'I don't know, maybe your yelling sounded like neighing. My mind was quite crazed at the time. Perhaps I thought you were Pegasus come to bear me away to the heavens.' He paused. 'Am I in heaven?' He twirled, his arms outstretched, his eyes skyward, 'Are you an angel?', he grinned. There was no escaping his smile. For the first time in days, weeks, she felt her heart glow.

'Where is this Sable Island?'

'Don't you know about Sable?' His eyes twinkled. 'Well, let me tell you.' He paused, collected his thoughts then he began.

'Picture this. In the middle of the steel blue Atlantic, 200 miles due east of Halifax, Nova Scotia, not far from the main shipping route between the eastern seaboard of North America and Europe, lies a golden arc. A shimmering crescent of shifting sand dunes battered by winds stronger than you could ever imagine. From the French it has been given the name Sable, meaning sand. For that is largely what you see: sandy dunes that rise from sandy plains that vanish in a sandy mirage.

'If there's bad weather to be had in the North Atlantic, you will find it around Sable. Winter storms wreak havoc on the shifting shore, cyclones reshape it and the currents are some of the trickiest to be had in ocean sailing. What's more the island is one of the foggiest places on earth.'

'Foggier than Newfoundland?'

'As foggy,' said Samuel, smiling at her. 'With such foul weather and treacherous tides even the best captains steer off-course and run into trouble. Large barques, schooners, steamers, fishing trawlers working the Grand Banks have been shipwrecked there by the hundreds.'

'How big is this island?'

'Roughly a mile wide by twenty-five miles long, but curved like a new moon. More than a speck in the ocean but it's largely flat, a totally treeless terrain, so it's not that easy to identify even in daylight – not like the cliffs around here. Anyway, with numerous vessels getting stranded there, the British government in the 1700s established two lighthouses in the midst of that roaring remoteness, one at the western tip and one at the eastern tip, and to this day they have been manned by keepers, their families and lifesaving crews. Aren't you glad you weren't born there?' Samuel said in an aside. 'Two to three boats still go down every year. But now whole crews are saved, some, walking off their boats at low tide, crossing the sand bars and taking shelter with the local residents.'

'And eating them out of supplies,' laughed Rebecca.

'Probably,' laughed Samuel as well. 'Anyway, around the time they put up the lighthouses, a Boston clergyman sent horses to graze on the island.'

'He did what?' asked Rebecca in disbelief.

'Surprisingly, there are large parts of the island covered with grass and other low-growing, vegetation. And there are fresh watering holes, which is a good thing, for the lighthouse families as well. But sadly the first band of horses was stolen by privateers and fishermen. Then in the 1850s, a Boston merchant landed about 60 horses on Sable, animals abandoned by deported Acadians leaving Nova Scotia. These horses did survive. And over time, they lost their domesticity and became the wild Sable Island horses with long flowing manes and tails.'

Rebecca noticed his eyes taking in her hair. 'So they still live there wild and free?'

'Yes, about two hundred or so. Though every so often, some of them are rounded up and shipped off to work in the Cape Breton Coal Mines.

'Oh,' she paused, 'I don't think I wanted to hear that.'

'Well Rebecca with the amount of questions you ask, you are not always going to like the answers you hear.'

She held his eyes for a moment, wondering if he was referring to something else, then breaking eye contact she asked, 'Have you been there?'

'No, as tempting at it sounds. But you see as I was drifting for days on end, lost in the North Atlantic, I did wonder about my chances of being washed up on Sable. I knew if it were to happen, I would be saved.' He stroked Mica's forelock lost in reflection, then his eyes found hers again. 'Do you want to go for a ride and pretend you're wild and free on Sable Island?'

'Yes' she whispered. 'Would...' she trailed off, lowering her eyes.

'What? Do you want me to come riding with you, Rebecca?'

She raised her tentative eyes to his teasing ones. 'Yes,' she inhaled, 'I'd like that very much.'

'Me too,' he said softly.

When they approached the barrens Samuel asked Rebecca to pull up and to close her eyes. Her eyes immediately sprung wide open. 'Why?'

'Because I asked you to. Trust me! And don't open them.' She hesitated then obliged. 'Now, Rebecca,' he said, sweeping her hair around to one side of her neck and speaking softly into her ear. 'Imagine in front of you is not the sodden damp moor that half of Newfoundland is famous for, but rather a vast white beach full of gentle golden sand. It's a new landscape. A new seascape. Pure and pristine, unravelling like a glorious sash of silk. The sun is shining. The sky is dazzling. You can hear the hush of the tumbling surf, softly surrendering itself to the shore. The air is laced with salt, but on the edge of the breeze is the soft scent of rushes and rare pink orchids. If you look closely you can see them hidden amongst the straggly beach grass, and, oh, what delight, a dainty white tussock moth is flittering through the grass. Then a shadow floats by; a large black-backed gull, soaring skywards. All this is before us as we canter along. And when we start to tire at the end of a long sandy straight, what do we see, but the softest, greyest seal, a new born pup with moist dark eyes looking up at us, pleading to be left alone, which we do, because on Sable Island every living creature deserves to live life fully and freely.'

Rebecca was mesmerised. She was back in Samuel's world and his world was on Sable. There was no other place she wanted to be.

'We're going to start riding soon and I want you to keep your eyes closed and look for everything I've just told you. And when you see something, I want you to call it out and tell me where it is and what it looks like. Are you ready?' She solemnly nodded. 'Here we go. Don't worry, I've got you.'

Rebecca was floating, gliding on silver currents across a new crescent moon. It was so peaceful, so luxuriating. She had never had a ride like it. In her mind's eye she was on the beach, the water lapping softly at Mica's hooves, touching her lightly like feathers.

'Where are you?' whispered Samuel.

'We're on the beach. I don't want it to end. I want it to keep going forever. It's softer than snow, like what I think satin must feel like.'

'A-ha.'

And then a few moments later, 'I see the grass. It's swaying, gently lulling back and forth. And over there,' pointing to two o'clock, ' are white fluffy butterflies, perched on single blades of grass.'

'What about the gull? Do you see the gull?'

'Yes, out of the corner of my eye. He's resting on my shoulder.'

Samuel hugged her with his elbows.

'And the pink orchid?'

'He's picked one for me and brought it to me in his beak.'

'Do you see the seal?'

'No, I see more horses. They want us to play with them.'

And then they petered slowly to a stop.

'You can open your eyes now.'

'I don't want to.' She released Mica's mane and looped her arms over Samuel's and squeezed him tight. He responded in kind, hugging her from behind.

'How was that?'

'It was amazing!' She opened her eyes and twisted herself part way round to look at him. 'How do you know so much? How did you learn to take me to another world, just with your voice and your words?'

'Did I do that?' he teased.

'Yes,' she said, bumping back into him, 'I will never forget that ride.' Her face was flushed and ebullient. 'Thank you.' Shyly, she turned and pressed her face into his chest.

'Do you want to do it again?' he asked glancing down at her.

'No. I just want to remember that one.'

They walked Mica home in comforting silence. When the house was in sight, Rebecca asked if he had taken Rachel riding to Sable Island.

'No,' he said. 'I just took her racing across the moors. That was as much as she could handle.' She could hear the smile in his voice. It warmed her heart.

11

Although it was summer Samuel wondered if the mercury would ever hit 70 and the looming grey clouds, the swirling fog and the hanging damp would let up so they could shed some layers and once more enjoy the reprieve of sunshine and warmth and bright blue skies. They had marked the longest day a week back and now another milestone, for Rebecca at least – the first day of the rest of her life. School was out, for summer, for life.

The occasion coincided with Samuel's full return to health. He was ready to make the most of the warm, work season. Samuel was busy. Silas was busy. Everyone was busy. Silas would leave on Monday mornings and not return till later in the week when their catch was full, sometimes doing two trips in one week. In his absence the women turned into gardeners and harvesters and homemakers.

With Rebecca's help they hauled the Nightingale onto the dry dock. He had wanted to wait for her father, but she insisted she could manage and that was when he started to get an inkling of the strength hidden beneath layers of light summer clothes. Over the course of one week he sanded it, resealed it with tar and painted it. Often he would get so engrossed that he would look up to see Rachel in front of him with his lunch wrapped in a napkin. He would always take a break, rinse off, put his shirt back on and they would eat lunch together.

He enjoyed those restful moments with Rachel. She did not have her sister's inquiring mind. She was less interested in Samuel's travels, instead harbouring an appetite for the smaller things: the school he went to, the house he grew up in, his sister Analeise and her recent wedding to Randall, an architect. Then one day quite unexpectedly she said, 'I was meant to be married this summer.'

And all Samuel could do was pause in his chewing, stunned by her admission as he struggled for a response. Swallowing he asked, 'What happened?'

'Connor drowned. He was driving logs on Rattling Brook.'

'When?'

'Last April. Two men from the lumber company saw it happen but couldn't get to him in time,' she sighed. 'They found his body by jigging in water about 300 yards from where he fell. He could swim well enough, but he'd been crushed. They didn't know if he drowned because he couldn't force himself between the logs to get his head above water or whether he was crushed first,' she volunteered.

'I'm sorry to hear that.' Samuel glanced at her but she showed very little emotion as if the accident had happened many years ago. 'When did you become engaged?'

'He asked me and my parents at Christmas a few months before my seventeenth birthday, before he went away and they said, when I turned seventeen I could get engaged and when I turned eighteen and Connor nineteen we could be married.'

'That seems young.'

'It's not that young for women around here, Samuel. Maybe a little young for men, but Connor was a hard worker and would have been a good provider. Besides there was no one else on Deception I would have wanted to marry and probably no one else on Deception who would have married me. You may not realise but most men around here want strong and able women who can work the stage and work the house and work the plot. I can do all that but I don't have the strength or stamina of someone like Rebecca.'

'People should love you for you are, not what you can do,' noted Samuel. 'What was his rush in getting engaged?'

'He was going away and didn't want me being snapped up by someone else.' She gave him a half-laugh, similar to her sisters. 'As if that were likely.'

'Did you love him?'

'Yes.' Rachel paused. 'In a warm your heart way rather than a fluttering heart way. He was always the boy looking out for me – even from a young age.'

Samuel studied her pensive face. 'Well that must have been difficult, tragic, losing your friend and your intended.'

Rachel made no reply.

'You hide it well. How do you feel about it now?'

'It all happened so fast; we were only engaged for a couple of weeks. We didn't really have a courtship.' She sighed. 'Mother told me it wasn't God's plan for me, that my prince was still to come.' She gave him a hopeful smile.

Samuel smiled in return. 'One day. What about Rebecca, has she lost someone just as dear? She has dark days at times.'

'Rebecca…what can I say? She dreams too much. She can't help losing herself in her restless unrealistic heart.'

After the boats were completed, Samuel volunteered to check the roofs and clear the chimneys. 'Do you like heights, son?' Silas asked, handing him a stack of cedar shingles.

Samuel shrugged. 'On the boats I'm forever climbing up and down the masts. I'm used to it.'

While he worked on the roof the ever-present cloud and fog finally rolled away. The air stilled. In no time he was warm. He lowered his braces, peeled off his shirt hoping that even a slight breeze would spring up to dry the beads of perspiration dotted down his spine, all the while hammering and nailing, gluing and painting. His able body became stronger, his torso tauter, his skin bronzer and his spirit even brighter as he stepped off the ladder – the ladder that you never walked under – and smiled warmly at his waiting entourage. Samuel didn't give his shirtlessness a second thought. He and his brother had spent years running wild in the summer. That was what one did. But here, things were different or so they used to be.

After her week of delivering sandwiches to Samuel, Rachel was accustomed to the sight of seeing him without his shirt on. Samuel could tell it no longer embarrassed her. If anything, it enthralled her. That day her eyes swept slowly down his body from his exposed neck to the expanse of his shoulders, over his smooth chest with the brown button nipples all the way down to his narrowing waist where his braces hung from his trousers.

Rebecca on the other hand was studying Samuel's body like she was trying to peel off his skin to understand how this male body was manufactured, how the muscles flexed and wrapped around bones. How they gave him strength and power.

Morna saw it all: a strapping specimen of masculinity, one daughter's shameless admiration and the other's intriguing innocence. 'Come, Rachel,' she grabbed her daughter by the forearm, 'I need your help inside.' Over her shoulder she called, 'Rebecca, maybe Samuel needs a clean shirt.'

'The one I had on this morning was clean,' yelled Samuel looking for where his shirt had landed. He wasn't unaware of what was going on. He didn't mean to offend, however he did find the situation rather amusing.

Just as he was about to pull his shirt over his head Rebecca touched his left shoulder. 'Samuel, how did you get those scars?' They were clearly visible: three rough slashes on his left outer shoulder raised in a keloid ridge. 'I remember now seeing them the day I found you.'

'I got them from not being careful,' he ventured. 'For being so engrossed in nature I ignored it.' Her puzzling eyes drilled his face. 'I got swiped by a black bear,' he explained, 'and if it weren't for my brother Matthew I probably wouldn't be here today.'

'When was this?' she asked, looking at him with a mixture of alarm and awe.

'Eleven years ago. We were holidaying on Lake Nipissing. I was eight at the time, Matthew was twelve. We were lying down on a beaver wall, facing each other on opposite sides of what we thought was their entrance, waiting for a little dark snout to appear when something made Matthew look up. About six feet behind me was this black bear sniffing suspiciously. We immediately jumped up and started flapping our arms and hollering to scare it away. But then Matthew glanced behind him and what did he see but two bear cubs on the other side of the bank.'

'No!' Rebecca's eyes widened. 'What did you do?'

'Well, first we pried a branch loose and tossed it in the water upstream, hoping the bear might think it was a fish, but that didn't work. Then Matthew pulled a large stick loose and stood tall, hands and arms and stick above me and growled at the bear. She swung her front paw to knock the stick out of his hand but instead she caught me on the shoulder and knocked me into the river. I surfaced to see Matthew nearly jousting her with the stick, hissing and growling. He yelled, "The canoe, Samuel, the gun." So I dashed and grabbed the rifle but when I got back there seemed nowhere I could stand to take a clear shot at the bear without risking his life. And I'd only shot the rifle a few times before. So I scrambled along the beaver wall and said in my shaking voice, "I've got the gun."

'Matthew passed the stick he was holding to his left hand and reached behind. Then he said, "Okay, Samuel, let's go, to the canoe. Back-up."

'I started to move but he didn't. I said, "Are you coming?" I was practically crying by this stage.

'And he said, "I'll be there when it's safe. Go now." And his voice sounded calm and assured – like our father's – so I backed up. And he yelled at me to get the canoe in the water. All the while holding his ground. When the canoe was ready he fired a single shot. I thought the bear would collapse in a big heap, but she just reared up, veered to the right, and bounded up stream after her two young ones. And in a flash he was with me and we were out of there.'

Rebecca was gazing at him with a look halfway between stunned wonder and relief. 'You're like the cat with nine lives, aren't you? How many more near-death experiences have you had? What happened to the bear?'

'She didn't die by our hand.' Samuel looked deep into her eyes. 'Matthew sent the shot flying over her left shoulder to frighten her. He said he couldn't kill her and leave those two cubs without a mother. So I walked away with three gashes on my shoulder, one for each of the lives Matthew spared that day. And he risked his own life to save mine as well.' He paused for a moment. 'There you go. That is where my weakness for nature got me.'

'You must be close to your brother?'

'I am. He's the best.'

'So how can you bear to live your life so far from him?'

Samuel tried not to smile, "I'll ignore that pun, shall I?" Without pausing he said, 'We just do. He's very involved with medicine but we make the most of the times we are together. And we will spend time together in the future. Probably like you and Rachel. You two are close, but one day you will live apart.'

'You know, Samuel, all the time I've thought of getting away from here, dreamt of myself in some other place, I've never consciously thought about leaving my family. But maybe you're right, maybe there will come a day when we are apart for awhile.'

'I hope for you, there is because that is when you really can be the master of your own destiny. And nothing will be the same again.' He brushed his hair back off his forehead. 'I'm hot enough for a swim. Do you want to join me?'

'The water will be cold.'

'I'm counting on it!' He grinned at her doing his all to encourage her.

'Maybe another day.'

'Come on, it's summer. When are you going to swim, if not in summer?' And then a thought dawned on him. 'Do you know how to swim?'

'Yes, I can swim a little. My mother made sure Rachel and I learnt to swim when we were young. She didn't…' Her voice trailed off. 'Maybe I'll just come down with you and see what the water's like and swim another day.'

'What, are you telling me the water is too cold for you? You being a local and all,' Samuel teased.

'No it's not that.' She was avoiding his eyes. 'We'll see. I'll go in and get changed and grab some towels.'

Rebecca returned dressed in the same clothes, holding a single towel in her hand. 'Mother needs me. I'll come another day.'

'She can't even wait twenty minutes?'

Shaking her head, she stepped back from him and his look of pity, at a loss as to what to say to him for she wasn't that disappointed that her mother had asked her to make up some starch. As keen as she was to spend time with Samuel, she had been torn when he asked, knowing it would mean contravening her own personal breaking the ice ritual, which she didn't want to explain. She knew he thought her family had enough odd beliefs. And this one she had concocted all by herself. For the year she had learnt to swim, the first time she had donned her bathers, had been in a pond on the occasion of her fourth birthday. And she had taken to the water like a fish and everyone marveled at her natural ability to float, to hold her breath underwater, to glide through the water with calm and steady strokes. It was if she were a natural born selkie. And aside from knowing that her parents were pleased with her, Rebecca also felt that God had been pleased with her by giving her this special swimming gift for her birthday – for she had prayed the night before, 'Dear God, let me not drown, let me be a good swimmer, let me learn quickly so I can be a strong swimmer and look after Rachel so Mother and Father don't have to worry.' And God had answered. And every year since she would honour him on her birthday by remembering his kindness in taking care of her on her very first swim and she would swim anew as a mark of respect and as a kind of safeguard against the year to come.

Even though her birthday was just days away she would wait. When the blueberries were ready for picking, when the sightings of icebergs were few and far between, when the calendar marked the fourteenth of July she would brave the waters, come rain, shine or fog, and have her first swim of the year.

12

On the morning of Rebecca's fifteenth birthday Samuel rose early to prepare a treat for her and her family. His mother had sent him many things in her care package that had arrived a week ago, but it was a simple delicacy, the birthright of every Canadian – a bottle of maple syrup – that he prized the most. Yesterday they had gone to pick blueberries on the barrens. Today he was making French toast with fresh berries, cream and maple syrup as a birthday surprise. Midway through his preparations he was startled by Rebecca coming into the kitchen from the back door with a towel draped around her shoulders and wet hair. 'You're up early,' he said. 'Most people I know indulge themselves on their birthday by having a lie-in. What have you been doing, washing your hair?'

'No. Taking a swim.'

He hadn't expected her to say that. 'You're an odd one, Rebecca Crowe. The other day when we were melting with the midday heat you wouldn't go swimming but today, at the crack of dawn when there's still a chill in the air, you take a dip.' Lowering his voice he said, 'You should have woken me and taken me too.'

'Maybe next time I will. What are you cooking?' she asked coming towards him.

'A surprise. Hey,' he turned towards her, 'I almost forgot.' He bent to her, whispering, 'Happy birthday,' and in that moment he wanted to kiss her on her tender young mouth. He checked himself and kissed her on the cheek instead. 'I'm sorry I don't have a birthday present for you. Breakfast is as good as it gets.'

'That will be perfect, I'm sure,' she said, unable to look at his eyes, unable to look at his mouth even, noted Samuel. She settled on the shallow dip at the base of his throat and then turned away as she heard footsteps on the stairs.

'Samuel, this…is…delicious," enthused Rachel.

'It's heavenly,' said Rebecca, now composed and helping herself to another spoon of maple syrup. 'I'll take it over molasses any day. I think you're going to have to send me maple syrup every year for my birthday,' she laughed.

To celebrate her birthday Silas suggested Rebecca take Samuel hunting on the barrens. She looked at Samuel, her expression unreadable, before glancing at her mother and saying, 'Mother do you need me to help make jam?'

'No she doesn't,' said Silas. 'She needs you to bring her home something mouth watering for dinner.'

They set off, Rebecca wearing men's trousers for a change and carrying her father's shotgun while Samuel carried spare shells, a burlap bag, and a knapsack with water and food for their lunch. As they walked Rebecca described the birds they might come across – specifically grouse and rock ptarmigan – and how to distinguish the male and female.

'You seem to know a fair bit about them,' noted Samuel.

'Well they are my favourite bird,' she admitted with a grin, 'taste-wise that is, so that does help to hone one's skill at identifying them. Wait till you try them.'

Sometime later, a few hundred yards ahead in the sky, they saw a peregrine falcon, seemingly suspended. Rebecca nodded in its direction. 'It's onto something.'

She loaded the gun and clutching it in both hands at chest level started walking quietly but steadily forwards. The bird circled and circled and then, as it dived, Rebecca took off. It stooped low and captured its unsuspecting prey. As it did the small flock of ptarmigan startled in surprise and flew about twenty frightened feet before setting back down. In those few, perilous seconds, Rebecca whipped the gun to her shoulder, aimed and fired bringing down three of the larger birds.

Samuel was already by her side. 'You made that look easy, too easy.'

'Not always,' she replied, unable to suppress a small satisfied smile.

Finding them though was a completely different matter.

'How come you don't have hunting dogs?' asked Samuel after five frustrating minutes. 'You live in Newfoundland for crying out loud. Aren't you meant to have a Newfoundlander?

A retriever or a Labrador even?'

'No chance of that,' said Rebecca. 'When we were little Rachel and I wanted a dog but father wouldn't have a bar of it. Said he'd been bitten by a dog when he was a boy and his leg got so badly infected he nearly died. For years he was convinced dogs had venomous fangs like snakes. Even today I think he thinks they're onside with the Devil.'

'Your father,' said Samuel shaking his head. 'He's one of a kind.'

Eventually they found the three birds and walked on. Rebecca offered to carry the bag suggesting Samuel carry the shotgun but he told her to keep it for now.

They decided to spread out and do a sweep and see what might take flight when surprised. They walked about eighty yards apart keeping each other in clear view. Every so often they would run for a short burst and when Samuel flushed a bird it took off, travelling fast. Simultaneously Rebecca's gun went to her shoulder and she followed its flight waiting till it was a good distance from Samuel, clear against the stark sky before squeezing the trigger. She took three on the wing, not missing a single one.

'When did you shoot your first bird?' asked Samuel, coming up to her, delighting in her prowess.

'When I was eight.'

'Eight!' He couldn't hide his astonishment. 'I didn't start till I was twelve.'

'That's seven years too,' she said, fast with her maths, 'so we're even.'

He smiled at her, shaking his head. He didn't think he was her equal.

'I wanted to be a crack shooter after hearing all about Annie Oakley,' Rebecca confided.

'Did you? Stories open up the world and make you dream of bigger things, don't they?' He paused. 'When I was eight my grandfather showed me this painting of a bison hunt, Caitlin was the artist, and I remember thinking when I grew up I wanted to be able to ride a horse and hunt like a native, even though they hunted with spears, not rifles. Looking back I'd say it was the motivation for me wanting to learn to ride a horse and be reasonably accomplished at it.'

'That you are,' said Rebecca, beaming at him.

He smiled in return. 'I have an idea!' he exclaimed, suddenly excited. 'When I go back home I'll send you a book on the French masters. It's full of the Impressionists and all their beautiful watercolours and it's got Matisse and Gauguin and his vibrant paintings of his time in Tahiti. It's even got Rodin in it. He's an amazing French sculptor. I am in awe of his work. One day I hope to see his statues in real life.'

'Do you? What are his statues of?'

'People mostly, sometimes the odd animal. He is so talented that when he produced 'The Age of Bronze' all the critics couldn't believe he had created it by hand. It was so lifelike they were convinced he made it out of a cast mould. But he hadn't.'

'What's this Age of Bronze statue of?'

'A Belgian soldier, a naked one.'

'Naked!' She stared at Samuel, her expression dubious.

'Yes. Naked and life size.'

'Are most sculptures naked?'

'Yes, a number are. He's—'

'Does he make these up from his imagination or do people…

'Yes,' said Samuel, unable to stifle his laugh. 'People do take their clothes off and pose.'

'No!'

'Yes!' Their eyes met and held while he shook his head in wry amusement. 'Tell me Rebecca, what do we learn from the human body when we keep it hidden? It is something to marvel at, to explore, to study and admire. It is not something to be ashamed of. Like everything else in this world, it is something to appreciate and understand.'

'Maybe,' she conceded.

'Maybe? Come on! We are born naked, not wrapped in a blanket.'

'Well, yes. But mostly we need to keep covered up.'

'Granted there's a time and a place for everything and shelter, clothing and protection are basic human needs. But I'm not talking about that. I'm talking about function and form and humanity. I'm talking about skin and senses and spirit. Artists understand this as do doctors. My father has had to study human bodies in all their forms, alive and dead. And even dead, he says they're fascinating. Inside and out.'

She gazed at him and in her eyes he saw her trying to grasp something new.

'And another thing,' Samuel continued, 'Sometimes when you're clothed you don't really feel things. You don't feel the tickle of your dog's hair across your chest as he pounces on you and licks you under your chin. You don't feel the rain splashing on your back in a thunderstorm, you can't experience the floating sensation of total immersion in water, you can't feel the sensuality of another person's skin.' He paused thinking perhaps he better stop there, but then temptation got the better of him. 'Have you ever swam naked?'

'No! Of course not!' Her eyes were downcast.

They walked on in silence. After several steps Samuel felt perhaps he should apologise for making her feel uncomfortable. He was about to touch her arm when Rebecca turned to him and said, 'I guess having a bath doesn't count?'

He laughed loudly at that and she with him.

'So I gather you would you happily pose nude for a sculptor?'

'You bet!' He flashed her a grin. 'If I were lucky to model for Rodin I would gladly pose nude, be carved in marble or cast and dipped in bronze for posterity. He has this way of making anyone look beautiful, strong and self possessed – clothed or not.' He paused. 'You'd make a great model, Rebecca.'

'What, beautiful strong and self-possessed?'

'Yes. He'd capture you in your hunting garb, gun raised to your shoulder, the whole world in your sights. It would make a magnificent subject. Newfoundland's version of Annie Oakley immortalised in France. And people would look at it and go, "Who is this woman? What is her story?" '

'She doesn't have a story. You're the one with the stories, Samuel.'

'She does have a story. We all have stories. That's what I love about art. It's a glimpse of another world through someone else's eyes, someone else's interpretation of a story. I think you would find it fascinating.'

Rebecca agreed but then said, 'There's just one problem with that book as you describe it.'

'What's that?'

'If my parents got hold of it they would burn it.'

That night after they had dined on delicately roasted ptarmigan with sage and wild parsley stuffing followed by rhubarb and blueberry pie, Silas said their little band of hunters and collectors had done rather well.

Samuel looked sideways in admiration at Rebecca. 'Your daughter's a fine marksman.' Although he had ended up shooting two more birds than Rebecca, it was only because she had set it up that way.

'She doesn't do too bad,' acknowledged Silas, 'and she can land a fish or two. As can Rachel.' His eyes darted from one girl to the next.

Two days later, the three of them, again at Silas's urging, went salmon fishing at Anchor Brook, a reportedly high return spot at the base of a waterfall in a cove, four bays to the west of the Crowes. There, Samuel discovered that Rebecca did fish as well as she shot, though to his astonishment she wanted to throw the first one she caught back.

'Please tell me you are throwing this fish back because it's undersize which somehow I doubt, or loaded with eggs!' Samuel implored.

'Please tell me you are not throwing this fish back because your father once told you not to keep the first fish of the day or else you will be unlucky for the rest of the day, for time immemorial.'

He couldn't get over how two intelligent girls were so unquestioning in some matters, so falsely indoctrinated.

Rebecca and Rachel exchanged a quick glance. 'What do you say, Rache?'

'I tell you what I say,' said Samuel wresting the fish from her. 'I'm keeping this fish whether you like it or not. Whether your father likes it or not.' They stared at Samuel. He stared back. 'Really you two, that notion is just ludicrous. And Rebecca, if you believe that, then you know what? The other day when you shot down your first bird, you should have cast it skywards, to ensure you had good luck for the rest of the day. Because otherwise it's a complete double standard. Talk about superstitious nonsense.'

'Maybe,' said Rachel, springing to Rebecca's defence, 'it's more about giving thanks and honouring the fact that God has provided.'

'You do that when you say grace,' said Samuel, his voice softening, 'and you do that by not being greedy, by not taking more than you need. But here I'd say you could do with all the provisions you can get.'

They fished for another hour and were rewarded with three more fish and then not a bite for quite some time. All the while Samuel's eyes would go from staring at the water in front of him, to tracing Rachel's line up towards her hands and then up further to her placid, smiling face, then back to the water in front of him, then to his left, to Rebecca and the pendulum of emotions on her unguarded face: one moment melancholy, the next, when she caught his eye, a smile of shy joy. Something about her blazing tumescence dissolved him. Something about her quiet capabilities humbled him. Sometime later she stood up and stretched. 'Samuel,' she turned to him, 'would you like to swim now?

'Yes!' He shot up winding in his line. It was a sensational summer's day by any standard. Only the odd wisp of cloud stretched across the royal blue summer sky. He was ready for a swim at nine o'clock after he had rowed the ninety-minutes over. But they told him he'd frighten all the fish away if they went swimming first.

'I'll show you the cave as well.'

'What cave?'

'There is a cave behind the waterfall.'

Samuel went on ahead while Rebecca changed into a charcoal-coloured outfit with three quarter length pants and sleeves. Rachel decided against swimming, volunteering to prepare lunch instead. When they waded into the water even Rebecca gasped a little. The water temperature stole their breath away.

'You have to keep moving don't you, or else you feel like you will seize up,' said Samuel.

'Yes, even when it's sunny like today. At least here with the fresh water flowing it's not as cold as in our cove. Let's go.'

She took off towards the waterfall. He followed. When it was just two metres in front of them, crashing down in a sheet of white water they halted. 'We go round here to the side,' yelled Rebecca, 'it's easier. You still have to kick hard and strong but you'll get through and when you feel the pressure on your knees, swim to the surface like this,' she held her hand at a 45 degree angle, 'and then you can ride the bubbles to the top.'

'Let's go together.' He grabbed her hand, 'on the count of three.' She took a deep breath and dived down and he was right beside her. Breaking the surface on the other side, they gulped in air and smiled at each other. Rebecca went to pull away, but Samuel held on, marvelling at her. 'You're a mermaid that's what you are, a naiad. I have read about creatures like you,' he teased, 'but I thought they were only myths.' Rebecca smiled at him in delight. 'Is there anything you can't do?'

Her grin wavered. 'Yes, I can't stop you from leaving.'

Their eyes met and held. After interminable moments he reached out and touched her face. 'I know.'

She led him to the right, where they scrambled up the rocks and crawled to the small cave carved out by the forces of nature, barely three feet deep, nearly four feet high and across. 'Here,' she patted the rock as she moved to sit on the ledge and dangle her feet over the edge. She took a deep breath, turned to him and gave him a smile full of sheer delight. 'It's magic isn't it?' They gazed out at the waterfall at the sparkling curtain of light, droplets glowing in the strange soft backlight. He reached for her hand again and she let him take it, clasping his strongly in her own. They sat in the crashing silence looking from the curtain of water to each other's smiling face and as they did, a grateful look passed from one to the other as if they had just shared a special childhood celebration, like a rite of passage and both were aware of its significance.

13

They had been rowing for about twenty minutes when Samuel spotted a boat coming towards them. Both girls turned around. 'It's coming from Petrie's Bay,' Rachel said. 'Slow down, Samuel.'

'Who's rowing it?' asked Rebecca, squinting. 'It must be...William?' She exchanged looks with her sister. 'Back, Samuel, towards the boat.' As they came closer, Rebecca called out. 'Hello William, we see you, we're coming.'

The lad stopped and looked over his shoulder. When they came alongside, Samuel was surprised to discover that William could be no older than ten.

'What's up?' asked Rebecca.

'It's mother, she's had a fall. Hurt herself real bad,' the boy panted.

'Oh no,' said Rebecca.

'Come here,' said Rachel reaching out to help William across. 'We'll tie your boat to ours and go see what we can do for your mother.'

Rebecca moved across and took an oar from Samuel and the two of them rowed like they were in a rowing race. When they reached the Petrie's stage, Samuel told them to go ahead. Coming to the house barely a minute after, he found Rebecca and Rachel leaning over the silent figure of Annie Petrie at the foot of the outside stairs, a bloodied towel wrapped around her head. But Samuel didn't need to remove it to see the state of her. Her puffed face was grotesque. He was relieved to feel a pulse in her neck. 'She's alive, but she needs a doctor. Here, help me roll her onto her side.' The girls obliged while three anxious tiny faces stared at them: William, together with his younger sister, Mary holding on her hip her whimpering baby brother, Franklin. At the base of Mrs Petrie's skull, about an inch above where the spinal cord ends, where most people have a slightly raised bump was a bloodied mess of splintered bone. A pool of blood lay on the flat stone underneath.

'How did this happen?' Samuel asked.

'I didn't see it happen,' said William. 'She was carrying a basket of wood and I guess she slipped and landed on her head.'

'She landed on her head alright,' said Samuel, shaking his own with dread.

'Oh, it's all my fault,' wailed William. 'I should have been carrying the basket for her. I told her I would do it before it got dark. I just got busy with my snares.'

'Hush,' said Rachel, 'it's nobody's fault. It's just an unfortunate accident.' She put her arm around the trembling lad. 'When's your father due back from the Grand Banks?'

'Not till the end of the September.'

Rachel, Rebecca and Samuel all exchanged looks. 'We'll have to move her to Ronnie's, maybe even to Twillingate,' said Samuel. 'There's a doctor there, right? She's got pressure building up inside her head that needs to be released somehow. I've heard about this from my father. The brain swells up and because of the rigidness of the skull it's under enormous pressure – see how puffed her face is because of this?'

'You two take her,' said Rachel. 'I'll look after the children. Call in and tell mother on the way so she doesn't worry.'

'William, say goodbye to your mother,' said Rebecca. 'You too, Mary and Frank. She's got to go away for a little while.'

'You take her to doctor?' asked Mary.

'Yes, to Doctor Ron to start with,' said Rebecca.

'Will she be alright?' asked William, his voice shaking.

'We'll pray for her,' said Rachel, patting his shoulder once more.

'Here, Samuel, you take– ', but before Rebecca could say, 'her feet,' Samuel had bent down and hoisted Mrs Petrie up in both his arms.

'Rachel, grab some blankets. We need to keep her warm. She'll be in shock.'

The sisters raced ahead and climbed into their dory ready to take Mrs Petrie as Samuel lowered her across. 'Here,' said Rebecca, handing Rachel two trout. 'We'll be back tomorrow.'

They made Mrs Petrie as comfortable as possible. 'Let's take it in turns to row,' said Samuel. 'I'll row first and then you can row when I get tired.'

Samuel didn't think Mrs Petrie's prospects were all that promising, but he didn't want to voice his doubts. One thing he had learnt from his father, never talk in doomed tones in front of patients even if they were unconscious. But he was amazed at how rough life was here for these people on the edge of the earth. How a simple mishap, doing something as common and everyday as bringing in firewood could result in this precarious life and death situation Mrs Petrie now faced. That these people somehow managed to carve out a life here in asperity, in largely tenuous, subsistence circumstances was commendable. And part of him could understand its appeal. But what about it's downside? Limited educational possibilities, scarce work prospects, minimal social engagements, and now highlighted by the plight of this woman, even more so than his ordeal, the desperate lack of medical services. Rebecca definitely would be better off this island, he thought.

'Samuel, where are you? You seemed lost in your thoughts.'

'Am I?' Between exertions he said, 'You know, it's hard to believe that in a place as quiet and as remote and as peaceful as here you can still have major accidents.'

'Is this major?'

'This is major. Head wounds can be serious.'

'Do you think Ronnie will be able to fix her?'

'I think Ronnie will need help.'

After a while, Rebecca said in a hushed voice, 'You know Samuel, sometimes I think that the only way I am ever going to get off this island and see another place is if I were to have a major accident.'

He paused mid-row, alarmed by her admission. 'Don't be silly.'

She shrugged. 'I don't know…tragedy, death, touches every family around here. And occasionally I wonder that in my wanting to escape, to see beyond this island, that my dreams, my prayers will be answered in a shackled kind of way. That somehow I'll inadvertently have a major accident or perhaps I'll be granted my wish but it will be something like this: "Here you go, you can get off the island and see the world, but oh, I'm sorry, you have a mystery disease and you are going to go blind very soon."'

'That's a tortuous form of rationale Rebecca. You are feeling guilty about having dreams and desires and you are letting that guilt get the better of you. You need to banish those thoughts. You will leave this island one day and in perfect health.'

'You think so?'

'I'm certain of it.'

'How can you be so certain?'

Smiling, Samuel said, 'Because you want it so badly. You will make it happen. Even if you have to swim off this island to make it happen you will. I have seen what you do when you put your mind to it and I believe you could do anything you wanted to.'

'Really?' she asked, her voice hopeful.

'Yes. You just have to decide what it is you really want and go after it.' He paused. She was looking at him in total rapture, her eyes on fire catching the light from the slowly descending sun. 'What?' he asked. He wanted to stop rowing that instant, reach out and stroke her face like he'd done just a few hours ago. To remember this moment, not just with his eyes but with his fingers also.

'No one has ever said anything like that to me before. No one.' She shook her head. 'You are the first person who has ever said they believe in me.'

'I'm sure your parents and Rachel believe in you. Your teachers probably did as well. Your parents probably don't want to encourage you that's all.' Leaning into her, in his huskiest voice to date, with a small smile teasing his lips, Samuel said, 'What is it that you really want Rebecca?'

She averted her eyes turning her head to the side so he saw her only in profile. 'I already told you,' she whispered. She sat staring at the water, not meeting his gaze.

'What can we do about that?' he murmured as he started rowing once more.

An hour later, they pulled into their cove. 'I'll stay here,' said Samuel, reaching for the buckets of fish to transfer to the stage. 'Sort out this lot.'

'I'll do that,' said Rebecca. 'You go. If she were to wake I think it would be better for her to be with someone she knows.' Samuel was off, taking two steps at a time. When he returned five minutes later he was panting. 'Your mother's coming with me. She wants you to ride Mica to Deception. You'll get there before us and you can help Ronnie prepare. Telegraph Twillingate.'

Rebecca rode hard and fast to Deception. Samuel rowed hard and fast to Deception, only stopping to take a drink from a canteen when Morna offered. They talked little. At one point she said, 'Thank you for doing this, Samuel.'

'Mrs Crowe,' he said pausing to wipe his forehead with the back of his hand, 'after everything you have done for me, there is absolutely no need to thank me. I am only too happy to assist.'

'I know, but thank you all the same.' A little while later, she spoke again. 'This could have been me, Samuel.' She shook her head. 'Some years ago I took a nasty fall, one January on some black ice. I had a wooden pail in my hand with some dried fish I'd got out of the store and some eggs from the barn. I knew I was going down but for some stupid reason I didn't want to drop the bucket because I knew I would break the eggs. How ridiculous was that. How foolish. So what did I do? I hit the ground completely, landed on my lower back here.' She reached around behind herself. 'A dreadful blow, must have hit my kidneys or something. Of course I was still holding onto the wooden pail but my elbows were in agony. Excruciating pain. They too had somehow managed to take the full force of the blow, which was probably a good thing as my head didn't hit the ground. My neck jerked back though. I remember that. I had a terrible strain, it took weeks to get better, but that wasn't the worst of it. The worst of it was I broke my waters and less than a day later Paul was born.' She sighed, her eyes glazing over.

'He was just too young, too tiny. His little lungs weren't properly formed and he couldn't breathe. What a nightmare. It's such a terrible torture to see one so tiny, so helpless, struggle for every breath. You can't help but imagine the pain the wee one must feel. You can see it with every stolen breath they take, almost as if they are slowly drowning right in front of you. And you stand by all the time just helpless What can you do? His tiny face was so blue, like he was being strangled, dark blue beneath the translucent skin. I put my mouth over his nose and mouth and blew air into his lungs. Hour after hour I did that. I'd do it for five minutes and then I'd give it a break for five minutes as my head was totally in a spin. I was so giddy and then I'd do it again for another five minutes,' she said, shaking her head at the memory and looking away from Samuel across the sea at the sun slowly sinking to the horizon. 'Silas stopped me in the end. Said I would run out of air myself and then what good would I be to him, to Esther? Poor little Paul. He didn't even last a full day.'

Samuel thought she had finished, but after a spell she said, 'What a painful time all round,' her voice tight. 'I wouldn't wish that experience on anyone. I hope to heaven Annie is not with child.'

He heard Morna take a ragged breath and then she was quiet. 'I'm sorry,' he said into the stillness.

She waved him off. 'It was a long time ago now.'

'How long?'

'Well, Esther is twenty-six,' she sighed. 'That would make Luke twenty-four and Paul twenty-three. So twenty-three years ago.'

'And Luke?' asked Samuel, surprised at the mention of another sibling he knew nothing about. 'Where is he?'

'He was stillborn.'

Samuel softly gasped. 'I am sorry. That must have been hard…losing two sons.'

Morna looked at him and nodded, her eyes grave. Then in a barely-there voice she said, 'We lost four boys.'

Samuel halted in his rowing. 'You lost four boys,' he repeated, almost dumbstruck. 'What happened?' Then as an afterthought he said, 'I'm sorry, do you mind talking about them?'

Morna gave him a faint smile. 'It's fine to talk about them once in a while. After Paul I had two more boys in quick succession. Simon and Isaac. Had they lived they would be twenty-two and twenty-one.'

'And were they born healthy?' ventured Samuel.

'They were brimming with life and boyish curiosity,' Morna

smiled faintly at the memory. 'You couldn't hold them back. They were little rascals the pair of them. Then one year when I was working on our stage and Silas was away, I left them for about twenty minutes while I went up to prepare lunch thinking they would be right by themselves. They weren't babies; they were nearly five and four. Esther was up above doing the ironing that day. She was nine going on ten. When I came back I discovered they had tried to row off in the spare tender, trying to be big strong fishermen like their father, who knows. We allowed them to play in the boat but only when it was tied to the stage and one of us was present. The boat capsized and they drowned.'

Her sigh was unmistakeable.

'I was pregnant with Rachel, my big belly bobbing out in front of me. I couldn't swim out to them in time, though I tried, how I tried.'

Samuel shook his head in sympathy; it was all he could do. 'How wretched for you,' his voice solemn. 'I'm surprised you didn't up and leave.'

'My word, Samuel, some days we did want to but we'd only end up somewhere else by the sea. Silas was born a fisherman and he'll die a fisherman.' Morna became silent, seeming to go inside herself. Then in an unfamiliar voice she murmured, 'They, were hard times.'

Samuel looked into her eyes. In their depths he had a glimpse of her sorrow and how it must have weighed her down like an anchor dragging the seabed of her soul.

Trying to be optimistic, he said, 'Then you had Rachel...'

'Yes,' Morna quietly agreed. 'It wasn't a time of great joy though...she seemed part of a different world for a while, not our world. Rachel was a small baby and for the first time ever I hardly had any milk, she grew slowly and she was gone two before we noticed the problem with her leg. I worry that I caused that somehow. And I can't tell you how much I lived on tenterhooks when I was pregnant with Rebecca.'

'I'd say it was high time your luck changed.' His words lingered.

'So did your mother only have the three?'

'Yes, as far as I know.'

'Well lucky for her that she only had to go through three

births to get three. My odds weren't so good.' She looked away from Samuel. Softly she said, 'Then again, I should be grateful that they're all in Heaven now.'

Annie Petrie died that night at thirty-seven minutes past eleven. The telegraph from the doctor at Twillingate advised that they were to keep the patient elevated and place ice on her head to reduce the swelling. That much they could have figured out themselves, thought Samuel. He and Ronnie merely sat with the dying. After she had passed away, Samuel said, 'You know moments like these make me wonder how islands like yours are still inhabited. The odds seem so stacked against folk here.'

'Oh, I don't know, Samuel, wasn't it Daniel Boone who said: "A population of ten to the square mile was inconveniently crowded"?'

Samuel gave him a look.

Ronnie sighed in agreement. 'It's not an easy life for sure. But for most, it's the only life they know. They're not working in polluted factories; their children are not in some dingy place losing their eyesight or their lungs. They're not living in crowded hovels, which most likely would be their lot if they were to move to the city.' After a pause, he looked directly at Samuel. 'You seemed to handle this episode well. Very calm and clear-headed in the face of an emergency.'

'I must be my father's son,' Samuel said, matter-of-factly.

'Maybe you're meant to be a doctor after all.'

'Maybe,' he breathed out, keenly aware that had he been his father or brother, Mrs Petrie's outcome perhaps would have been dramatically different.

14

Samuel was out at the end of the peninsula when he first saw it. Resting his bone-weary shoulder after spending a good hour chopping a fallen spruce, he had wandered through the small forest to the end of the point where he stopped to stare at the enormous blue ocean glistening in the summer sun. And there it was. Huge, even from that distance, floating along like a gigantic nautilus shell. Near one end a cavern had been washed out by the swirling ocean currents. He was standing on the very spot where Rebecca had chanced upon him and now the iceberg was following the same trajectory he had. It was surreal and breathtaking to see such a large object simply flowing along, totally silent yet powered by invisible forces. He understood immediately how Rebecca was drawn to them. And no sooner had he thought that then the idea was upon him.

He dashed back to the house. Where was she? God she could be anywhere. He found her inside with her mother and sister and the Petrie children, helping them with the never-ending fruit bottling. It was like the tropics in there. He was mildly panting.

'There you are,' he said, smiling lightly, running his hands through his hair. 'Mrs Crowe, I need to borrow Rebecca for a while if that's alright.'

'Why, Samuel, of course. Is everything alright? Do you need two extra pairs of hands?'

'No, thanks, I'm good. Everything's fine. I just need her help for a few hours.'

No sooner, were they out the door, when Rebecca asked, 'What is it, Samuel?'

'I can't say just now but quickly, we need to put to in the Nightingale.' That was all the explanation he gave as he tore down the hill to the Crowe's stage, Rebecca in eager pursuit.

After they launched, she tried again.

'No, Miss Curious, I can't tell you, but I will tell you this much: I can take it from here. You just sit over there and close your eyes like you did that day we went riding on Mica to Sable Island.'

She smiled warmly as she moved away from him, but after a few seconds she said, 'Come on, Samuel, give it up,' her eyes practically begging.

'Haven't you ever heard, curiosity killed the cat? When have I ever denied you and not answered your questions?' She stared at him silently. 'That's right, never, so have a little trust,' he admonished her but in a playful way. 'And just to be sure you keep your eyes closed I'm going to bind them.' He cast around for something to use. There was nothing in the boat.

'With what?' said Rebecca, a smug smile on her face.

'With my shirt.' He undid the top two buttons, pulled it over his head, rolled it into a bandage and knelt down in front of her to tie it around her head. 'Like that,' he said.

Rebecca could feel the slightest breeze on her body, or was that their movement through the water creating that breeze. And she could smell Samuel on his shirt, his sweat and his Samuel smell, mixed with the sharp tang of freshly cut, evergreen pine. After a while, he told her she could sing if she wanted to. 'It might make the time go faster.'

'I'm not singing, I'm listening,' she replied.

'What do you hear then?'

'Birds, the water lapping the boat, you dipping the oars, you grunting every so often, but that's enough, I'm not falling for your questions because then I won't be able to listen and work out where we are going.'

But as Samuel pulled the oars through the water she sensed the chill in the air and gasped in realisation at what they were about to uncover.

'What's the matter?' he asked, concerned.

'Nothing,' her voice catching. Any moment she was going to cry. She took a shallow breath and smiled her biggest smile for him. She wasn't about to deny him this. She breathed hard. She almost wanted to lean over and press her face to his chest like she had done on Mica that day.

A few minutes later she asked, 'Do you see anything?'

'Yes,' he replied, 'your face. It looks most expectant.'

Rebecca laughed and the laughter eased her emotion.

She heard him say, 'Getting close.' Not long after, he slowed his rowing considerably. A few minutes later they bumped up against something.

'What was that?' asked Rebecca, steadying herself on the seat, then moving her hands to her head.

'Rebecca! Leave it on! Just a little bit longer.'

'Okay, but what was that?'

'It was nothing,' he said.

'It was something!'

'Yes a nothing something.' He stopped rowing. 'Give me your hands.' She gave him her hands. 'Now slide off the seat and sit on the bottom of the boat and slide down like you are lying in bed.' With his help she squirmed into place. 'Right, I'm going to come over and join you.' Steadily, he moved across. 'Now I'm going to take off your blindfold but keep your eyes closed till I say you can open them.' He pulled his shirt away from her head. 'Okay, open.'

And she did, almost cautiously, slowly adjusting her eyes to the blue light all around: a brilliant blue filtered light, sparkling in patches like sapphires and diamonds and aquamarines. She glanced at Samuel and found him bathed in a blue aura, a holy light, like the second coming, such an ethereal moment.

'Where are we?' she whispered.

'In an ice cave, floating along with an iceberg.'

In a million years she never would have expected this. Astonished, she sat up. To her right she could see the brighter, whiter light beyond Samuel where the opening was. 'You rowed us out to an iceberg? Not just any iceberg but one that has a cave like Aladdin's?' Now she did cry. But through her tears her face radiated absolute joy. She was mesmerised, and not just with the iceberg. 'I don't believe it.' Slowly she lowered herself back down. 'I must be dreaming.' Rebecca folded her hands across her chest and stared in awe at the crystal dome overhead. Her eyes glinted, like the shimmering blue light above, taking in the entrancing expanse of the blue cavern.

'Samuel, this, is, amazing. Thank you!' She glanced at him

and could see the abundant pleasure on his face. She touched his bare chest shyly, gently, in gratitude. She felt the exhilaration of discovery, of something new, of being fully alive. Her heart was in her throat, such a transcendental moment. She reached for his hand and squeezed it. 'Is such a thing really possible?' she whispered. She held onto his hand while they both stared in wonder and awe at nature's creation. 'Look,' she said as she released his hand and pointed to a shape within the ice like a new crescent moon, a darker blue imprint in the blue surround.

But Samuel was past looking at the crystal cove above, past looking at this stunning work of nature, for he was looking at another. He just loved watching her face come alive. It became a shining light of pure innocence, a vessel full of wonder, as the melancholy slipped away and sheer joy burst to the surface. And right now there was no melancholy; there was only discovery and delight. He could not get enough of her face, her eyes, her smile.

She was as enticing as the iceberg all around her, such a magical, mystical form. He wanted to touch her. Feel her. Breathe her. He wanted to melt through her skin and be inside her, to feel her body all around him. He wanted to warm his hands around her heart. He wanted to know the place where her laughter came from and dive into her bountiful soul. He ached to understand how such an exquisite creature could just be. God, she was beautiful. And she didn't even know it.

'I have seen a presence that disturbs me with the joy of elevated thoughts; a sense sublime of something far more deeply interfused,' he whispered as his eyes drank in her face.

'Oh, it is something, isn't it?' She sighed and turned to find him looking at her, intensely. At that point he was done for. Completely. And so was she. Their eyes locked as awareness filtered through.

Smiling softly, Samuel touched her cheek. 'You're something'. Then he kissed her. He couldn't help himself. He knew she was only fifteen, but he could not let the moment pass him by. In the icy cavern they were in, her lips were surprisingly warm, summer warm and soft. She kissed him back, tentatively, tenderly. He kissed her slowly, lovingly, exploring her lips with his. He opened his mouth. She opened hers. He moved his arm around her waist, all the while kissing her. She put her hands on his head and continued kissing him. 'Oh Rebecca,' he sighed into her mouth. And she murmured and kissed him some more, an amazing kiss for one so young, so innocent. He never wanted this kissing to stop. He wanted all of her right there and then. But she was so young. He had to stop.

He pulled himself away. Rebecca opened her eyes. She was willing him to kiss her again; he could tell. It was palpable. He smiled, touched her cheek with his right hand and gazed longingly into her eyes. 'I will remember you, I will remember this,' and then he couldn't help himself, he kissed her once again, a shorter, yet still exquisite kiss, then withdrew, not trusting himself to leave his lips on hers for any longer.

Her eyes were closed and a dreamy smile floated across her lips, her face. She did not trust herself to utter one single word or to open her eyes. The iceberg and the kiss. She must be dreaming and if she spoke, she would wake and it would vanish forever when all she wanted was for it to keep going.

'Rebecca,' he said shaking her lightly.

'What?'

'Open your eyes. Say something.'

'I can't. I'm so happy'

'Are you?' She heard the happiness in his voice too. 'Why?'

'I think you just kissed me or was that a dream? Is this whole iceberg a dream perhaps?'

He squeezed her and kissed her on the brow. 'Why did you kiss me?' she asked opening her eyes.

'I think that's obvious.'

'Have you kissed my sister?'

'You know the answer to that.' He placed his hand on her chest, below her throat, 'in here.'

Her breath caught in her throat. Moment later she ventured, 'Would you kiss my sister like that?'

'No,' said Samuel, shaking his head, his smile genuine. 'I kissed you because I wanted to kiss you. I've wanted to kiss you for a while. I like your sister but not in the same way.'

His eyes roamed all over her face. 'I don't want to kiss her.

I don't desire her.'

Ah, desire. That was the word. That was the feeling. It pulsed through her body. 'Kiss me again,' she pleaded.

'I can't,' he sighed.

'Why not?'

'Because if I start again, I might not be able to stop.'

He was looking at her lips. She was looking at his. She wanted his lips on hers again. 'Please,' she said.

'You know, it's probably a good thing I'm leaving soon.'

'Don't say that!'

'I'm sorry, but more kisses like that could lead us into trouble and I'm not ready for trouble.' He gave her a grave look. 'I have a question for you for a change.'

'What?'

'Where did you learn to kiss like that? Have you kissed a few boys before?'

'No, I've never kissed a boy before.'

He eyed her closely.

'But I have kissed a man.'

'Have you? Who was that?'

'You,' she whispered as she raised herself to plant a kiss shyly on his lips.

'Well, all I can say is you've got great intuition.' He kissed her quickly, 'But you better stop now, we'd better stop now,' he said between more kisses then he pulled back, but still held her head in his hands. 'Look, this has been a beautiful moment, but that's all it can be for now.' Rebecca thought she saw a flash of sadness in his eyes. 'Think of it as something to look forward to…when you're older.'

'Will that be with you?' she asked, placing her hand on his chest, hoping to extract a promise.

He sat up and looked away. 'Come, we best head back soon and I'd like to look around some before we do.'

15

That night Silas arrived home with a letter from Matthew.

Samuel, Samuel,

We long to see you but more than us there are others who need to see you.

I have been to see Seb and Luc and Louis' family. You would not know that Luc's wife Marissa is pregnant with their first child – she never got to tell him. A tragedy yet a silver lining on the dark clouds hanging over her.

I know you've written and said you feel indebted to these good people, the Crowes, but there are others to whom you also owe a great deal.

As a doctor I have seen death first hand and I can only share with you my experiences but what I can tell you is the family always wants to know everything they can about their dearly departed. They want to know everything they did since they last saw them, everything they said, everything they thought, everything that happened to them, when they laughed, what they ate, when they slept, and importantly, when they talked about their loved ones and what they said. And the reason they want to know this so desperately is that in the telling they feel they are walking by the side of their loved ones, this side of death. It's moments and hours they can claw back for themselves to sustain them through their uncertain future.

Samuel, you are the only person with all this information. It's inside you, waiting to come out and they are waiting and wanting to hear it.

If you need me, I can be there to support you when you tell your story and their stories. Telegram your arrival date in Québec. I beseech you not to delay this any longer.

Remember, keep your face always toward the sunshine, and shadows will fall behind you.
All my love,
Matthew

Samuel felt bad for his brother had spoken the truth. He had been dragging his heels and it had nothing to do with not wanting to face Luc's wife or see Louis' or Seb's families. It had nothing to do with being frightened of the voyage home being on open-water again out of sight of any land mass, it had nothing to do with an imminent reckoning with his uncle.

It did have something to do with his summer on Second Chance feeling like a mythical Scheria, something to do with his knowing that such a long idyl without responsibilities would never come again this lifetime, something to do with not being ready to face his future and answer the question, 'What now, Samuel?'

But in unguarded moments like the one behind a teeming, twinkling waterfall was the undeniable truth of what it most had to do with: Rebecca. He wanted her, wanted her in a way he had never wanted another, for she warmed his soul, more than that, she filled his soul. And he knew it. Deep down inside he knew it. Like the moon and the tide she pulled him to her and over the past few weeks he had started to realise he could not get enough of her. Nothing was ever enough. Her face was the one he sought out when he walked into a room. Her company was the one he relished the most. Her eyes on his face as they darted from his eyes to his mouth would put his head in a spin. Could she see that? Could others see that? Why would anyone be in a hurry to leave? And all that was before today.

So now if he was to do what his brother asked, leave immediately, which part of him knew was the right thing to do, than he'd be doing the ultimate kiss and run. Is that how he wanted to leave? On one hand he felt he should broach the subject of his departure over dinner and yet on the other, why spoil what been the most magical day?

Samuel wasn't sure if Silas had a sixth sense about what

had happened or whether it was just pure coincidence, but oddly that night, as they were enjoying a meal of fish and brewis, he said, 'We've got two empty position on the schooner going out the day after tomorrow. Phil Gresham and Robbie Coombes have to go across to Twillingate for some unexpected business. Young Toby Henderson is going to join us but we're still one man down. What do you say about lending us a hand, Samuel?'

For some time he had been expecting such a request. How could he refuse now? How could he say, "Sorry, I can't, I'm heading home next week"?

He did not look at Rebecca. He put on his happy-to-help face, his please forgive-me-Matthew face and said, 'Count me in,' looking at Silas with all the genuine interest he could muster.

The morning they set out Silas asked him, 'Do you think you'll be fine being out on the open water in the middle of the ocean, in the middle of the night?'

'Honestly, I haven't given it much thought.'

'I figured it would be good to get you out there again. You've been rowing that dory around getting the feel of water again. But some people, I'm not saying you, Samuel, when they have a fright at sea, develop a fear of it, and they have a devil's own time getting over it. Best not to leave it too late before you get out there.'

There were six other men on board the schooner that set sail just after eight a.m. on the twenty-seventh of July. They sailed northeast for five hours on the first day of their planned six-day voyage making the most of the prevailing northeasterly.

Samuel found it quite exhilarating being amongst the waves again. Most of the men on board felt the same. Coming up to him, Toby said, 'Don't you just love the ocean? So grand, so mysterious. It hooks you in it does. Has this strange way of binding you to it.'

'Yes,' agreed Samuel. 'I've had some unforgettable experiences on the water. Things I would never have thought possible if I had stayed on land.' The next day during a lull between hauling in nets Samuel found himself alongside Silas.

'It's a hard life you have here on the edge of the Atlantic,' noted Samuel, 'I suspect it takes a special type of person to live here and work these waters year in and year out.'

'I don't know if we really do endure more hardships than other folk. Whatever the case, there is no other place for me. Besides, we're small fry.' Silas's hands were busy untangling part of a net. 'We play it safe. Most of us are older and have families and responsibilities. We're not big risk takers. If we were big risk takers and after the big dollars we'd be working the Grand Banks. I did that for three seasons. One of the boats I worked on even took loads of salt fish to the markets in the West Indies, like your little trip last year. I could have sailed down there, but I decided not to. I'd just met Morna and it was not the life I wanted for us. We mightn't make as much money this way, but unlike Annie Petrie, God rest her soul, Morna knows that even in our busiest times, she will see me once a week, when we come in for the Sabbath.'

'Sounds very civilised, Mr Crowe, even though life on-shore is almost as strenuous.'

He narrowed his eyes at Samuel. 'Have those women been weaving you stories? Their lives could be a lot tougher, a lot tougher. I've chosen a much easier life for my family. Morna knows Tamar had it much harder.'

'Tamar?'

In a hushed tone, Silas muttered, 'She was my first wife, died in childbirth when we were floaters on Labrador. In those days you lived on board the boat over the entire summer, sometimes you would build rough summer huts and flakes to cure your fish. The women worked alongside their men, for some people their whole family lived on board. But I should have known it wasn't a good idea. Never a good idea to have a woman on board a boat, at least not a working one.'

'You have had your share of misfortune,' said Samuel, stirred by Silas's admission. 'Is that why you won't take Rebecca on a trip?'

'Partly. Rebecca is the closest we've got to a son. That's why I've taught her to shoot and fish. If something were to happen to me,' Silas knocked on the boat three times as he spoke, 'I know Rebecca could look after Morna and Rachel. She's not coming on board. She's where she needs to be.'

'But is she where she wants to be?' asked Samuel.

'That really has nothing to do with it,' said Silas. 'Her duty is here, to her family. She can read books and you can fill her head with stories till its full, but this is where her home is. This is where she belongs. Where can she go by herself? What can she do?'

'Well,' said Samuel, 'My father has written and he wants to repay you for all that you have done for me. He has offered– '

'Samuel, I've said before– '

'Yes, you have and just like you have your way, my father has his. I think he would feel gratified to be able to do something for your children like you have done for me. And he has sent money for this very cause. It's not an insubstantial amount. If you wanted to, if your daughters wanted to, he would be happy to fund their further education in Gander or St John's. They could continue their schooling at a boarding school. Rachel seems to have a way with children. Maybe she could train as a schoolteacher. Maybe through more education, Rebecca could discover her true calling.'

'Like you have done?' scoffed Silas.

'I'm getting closer.' That was all Samuel could say about the process he was working through.

'This is our affair. I know you mean well.'

'I respect that it's your affair. All I'm saying is that they will always have this life here. You've taught them admirably well in that regard. But this could be something they could fall back on. They could have another skill, another occupation somewhere; it may even end up being here. But they could have another type of life, which could still be of help to your family, possibly more so and put them in a better position to help their own families one day.'

'We couldn't afford to have both girls away from home. Morna needs their help. She's had many hard years, coping on shore with young ones while I've been out here trying to provide for them. It's only in the last few years things have gotten a little easier. You might think our life is hard now, Samuel, but in reality it has never been better.' With this last comment, Silas once more knocked three times on the side of the boat, 'Touch wood.'

'It's true you don't seem to want for much,' admitted Samuel. 'But this is a wonderful opportunity nonetheless.

Perhaps for Rachel initially and then Rebecca later.'

Silas smiled begrudgingly. 'I'll say one thing about you Samuel, you don't give up easily do you?'

'No. If I did I wouldn't be here to chew your ear.'

They were meant to be away for six days but on the Saturday they became becalmed, stranded in the midst of an ocean that was as flat as a millpond. Silas took to whistling for a breeze. Occasionally some of the other men would join him. But there was nothing to it. They were adrift, at the mercy of the tides. It wasn't till mid-morning on Monday that the wind picked up and they were able to set a course back to Deception.

They weren't the only ketch that came crawling into port overdue from lack of wind. One of them carried the diminished and desolate Thomas Petrie, for if ever there was a man, who looked like the bottom had fallen out of his world it was him. Thomas wanted to hear from Samuel all about his wife's last hours. Matthew's words echoed inside his head. Samuel glanced at the ocean, an oily grey in the late afternoon light to match the taupe grey skies overhead, the air heavy and damp. He did his best to lengthen the hours Annie Petrie lay dying.

Silas insisted Thomas and the children stay the night. Over breakfast, when Morna and Rachel were talking about what supplies were in the Petrie's house and what they could send across, Silas dropped his knife on the floor. As he picked it up, he muttered, 'I wonder who this will be,' and then more loudly to Thomas, 'We'll wait a while before we head across.'

Samuel, never ceasing to be amused by Silas and his superstitious convictions, said, 'Do you really believe that, Mr Crowe? That if you drop a piece of cutlery, you are going to get a visitor. I drop cutlery all the time and I'm quite sure I don't get a visitor whenever I do. Call me a sceptic but how can you put so much faith in it?'

'Ah Samuel, perhaps that is the difference between you and me. Maybe if you believe in it, it will happen and if you don't believe in it then it won't. Either way, no harm done, except my way, I'm better prepared.'

An hour later when Silas and Samuel were outside packing up the bags they had cleaned yesterday on their return, a rider came over the hill. 'Look Samuel, we have a visitor.' Samuel looked towards the rise then to Silas who was smugly nodding. He yelled, 'Ronnie Evans and on a horse no less.' As Ronnie ambled up to them, he said, 'Is that Bill Sweeney's nag?'

'It is indeed. Morning Silas, Morning Samuel.'

'Hello Ronnie,' said Samuel. 'How are you?'

'Not bad, not bad. How's everyone here?'

'So so,' said Silas, 'as you would expect.'

'I've come to pay my respects to Thomas. Is he about?'

'He's in the living room with the young ones.'

'Apparently he called in to see me yesterday when I was out. And as I was about to head off a telegraph came through for him from a Beth Dundas.'

'That would be Annie's sister, from down Trepassey way. Anything else happening?'

'Yes,' said Ronnie. He looked from one man to the other. 'Apparently, Britain is at war.'

'At war! Who with?' asked Silas.

'Germany. You probably haven't caught up. Last week Germany invaded Belgium. England gave them an ultimatum to pull out which they ignored.'

'What about France?' asked Samuel.

'Germany declared war on France on Monday. So they're in bed with the Brits for a change.' Samuel and Silas looked at each other, almost ominously.

'And Canada?' asked Samuel.

'Haven't heard anything yet, but it's probably just a matter of time. But here my lad, we are in Newfoundland, where we are a British dominion. We, therefore, are at war with Germany by default.'

16

Was there another word in the English language, so short, so simple to pronounce yet so potent with dread? War.

'What will it mean,' asked Rebecca, as soon as she had digested the news. 'Do you have to go off to war, Father? Samuel?' her voice strained.

'Usually, it's the young single men who go off to war,' said Samuel. 'So I suspect your father's safe for now.'

That was no relief for Rebecca whatsoever. 'Please tell me you won't have to go off to war?'

'I'm not going off to war, if I can help it. Canada's not at war. Though I wouldn't mind a trip to Paris,' he quipped. Rebecca turned to see a look of dismay on Rachel's face. She was sure hers mirrored it. She heard Samuel say, 'Before I was born my grandfather served in the Boer War as a medical officer and do you want to know what his verdict on war is?' Anxious faces looked in his general direction. 'Avoid at all costs.'

'Sometimes people don't have much say in the matter,' said her father.

'True, but I belong to a long line of men who believe in saving peoples lives, not destroying them. If I have to go, it will be to that end and in that much I expect I do have a choice.' Everyone was looking at Samuel. He dropped his eyes then raised them again. 'Although the timing is the same, it is for completely unrelated reasons that I need to make plans to leave you all.'

For Rebecca, it was almost a relief to hear him say that, so long had she been dreading the words. Her mother must have heard the silent screams of her heart.

'Rachel, Rebecca, go with Samuel, enjoy these last few days. I can manage. Just be back to help with dinner.'

It would take Samuel over a week to travel home given

what he had to do on his homeward journey. When to leave? After much deliberation he settled on Friday.

'No, you can't leave on Friday,' Rachel told him.

'Why not?'

'Because you never start a sailing voyage on Friday! You just don't, Samuel. Very, very bad luck.' She was adamant.

'Well then it'll have to be tomorrow, Thursday.'

'Please don't leave tomorrow,' said Rebecca.

'Saturday then.'

'Stay for the week-end,' stumbled Rachel.

'Monday.'

'Tuesday,' said Rebecca.

'Tuesday,' echoed Rachel.

'Tuesday it is then.' He would leave on the 11th August.

The three of them walked down the hillside, two sisters and one young man, strangers less than three months ago, but each knew in their hearts, they had shared moments and experiences that they would treasure all their lives. Moments filled with joy and laughter, gaiety and hope. Rebecca tried to put on her bravest face. 'Well if you're off, Samuel, you're off. There's nothing to it. We'll just have to plan for your return.'

'Yes, when do you think that might be?' Rachel laughed.

'Who knows,' said Samuel. 'Maybe you two can come holiday with my family in Toronto, or on one of the lakes even.'

The girls looked at each other, both not wanting to voice what they felt with certainty. That although their parents might let them visit their sister in Bonavista – though it was yet to happen – the likelihood of their ever going further afield was nigh on impossible.

'That would be lovely,' said Rachel.

'Yes,' said Rebecca, 'How much will it cost for you to get back home Samuel?'

'I honestly don't know. Maybe twenty dollars.'

Rebecca glanced at Rachel, her eyebrows raised just a fraction. Another impediment to any possible voyage.

Two nights later Rebecca and Samuel came racing home shortly before dusk with a brace of hares. Rushing into the house, Samuel said, 'I'm sorry we're late. They only showed their heads about an hour ago. Do we have time to skin them before dinner?'

'Of course,' said Morna. 'Let me get you a pail for the scraps and show you where to hang everything.' Morna followed Samuel outside. Rebecca went in search of her sister.

When her mother returned Rebecca was sprawled out at the kitchen table, her palms faced down, her arms outstretched, her face buried in a mass of tousled hair.

'What's, up Rebecca?' asked her mother, 'Are you tired?'

'A little,' her voice muffled.

'Are you sad?' she asked, leaning into her.

'A little.'

'Is it something else then?'

Rebecca raised her flushed face. 'Do you know what Rachel's been up to all afternoon? No wonder she didn't want to come hunting. Actually, she's been up to this for days! Weeks!'

'Stop speaking in tongues.'

'She's knitted Samuel a jumper. It will be finished by tomorrow or the next day. Definitely before he leaves.'

'Has she?' Morna met Rebecca's eyes, both fully aware of the old wives' tale about knitting a hair into a garment to bind the recipient to them.

'Yes,' said Rebecca after a prolonged pause. 'Meanwhile, I have absolutely nothing to give Samuel as a farewell present.'

'I'm sure you can come up with something. I thought we could send some jams and bottled fruit home to his family.'

'That's a good idea,' she said, standing up. 'What shall we pack it in?'

'Maybe one of those canvas packs your father takes with him on his fishing trips.'

Rebecca went to clean one. Her sister had trumped her, yet it wasn't even a competition. If anything she knew she should be grateful for stumbling across Rachel sitting upstairs on the landing, knitting away, catching the last rays of light coming through the window. Until that moment, the idea of a farewell gift for Samuel hadn't even entered her mind, yet it kept her awake half the night.

The next morning she declined Samuel's invitation to go across to Deception with him – much to his surprise. He was off to invite Ronnie and his wife Margaret over for dinner. 'I won't be gone that long,' he said.

'Then I won't miss you too much,' she replied. 'Are you going to take Mica?'

'I hadn't thought.'

'Leave her behind and I'll come looking for you when I'm done.'

Without Mica Samuel would be away longer. As soon as he was gone, Rebecca got out the drawing paper and pencils they had dragged out for the Petrie children. She wanted to draw the iceberg they had rowed out to that unforgettable day. After two hours, she was finished. How to wrap it? Racing upstairs, she grabbed her hairbrush and proceeded to brush and brush her hair then she plaited a thin section at her nape, which she tied off tightly with cotton thread. Racing downstairs she rifled through her mother's sewing box till she found her dressmaking scissors. She snipped the plait almost to the base of her skull. And then she tied more cotton around the top, rolled the drawing up and secured it with her braided hair.

Then she had another idea. She raced outside, found Mica, led her to the barn and brushed and plaited a long section of her tail before shearing it off like she had done with her own. This she brought back inside and stitched onto the strap of the canvas bag she had selected the night before.

That afternoon, she and Rachel helped Samuel cook rabbit bourguignon, his farewell treat for them. They had just finished mixing the marinade when Morna walked in from outside. 'Toby Henderson has come to visit.' Toby followed her inside, doing his best to tame his dark curly hair. 'Put the kettle on please, Rebecca,' said her mother.

Hellos were exchanged all round. After they had poured tea, softly-spoken Toby said, 'I wanted to let you know I have signed up for the Newfoundland regiment. I'm off to war.'

A piece of coal pinged in the wood oven. And another.

'Goodness,' said Rebecca, breaking the silence. 'That's very…brave of you.' Her first thought was "reckless" but she couldn't say that.

'That is big news,' said Morna. 'What do your parent's think?'

'Mom's not over the moon. Dad said, "It's your life, son." '

'What about Jonah and Michael? Are they going too?' asked Rachel.

'Nah, they think I'm mad. But,' he paused, 'it will be an adventure.' That resonated with Rebecca. Part of her would have jumped at the opportunity too.

'You could get killed!' exclaimed Rachel, the alarm evident in her voice. 'Like we need more ways for our young men to get killed.'

Everyone felt the aftershock of Rachel's comment.

In a restrained voice Toby said, 'That's not my intention.'

'But it could be your reality, Toby.'

'Well if we all sat back and left it to someone else, countries and people would be walked all over by these German aggressors. Today Belgium, next month England, next year Newfoundland.'

'Like that's likely to happen,' she mumbled.

Before Toby could reply Samuel asked if he had strong feelings about what was happening in Europe.

'Some,' he said. 'Certainly not to the degree I would feel if it were happening here in Newfoundland. It may start over there, but where does it stop?' He shrugged. 'It will make a man out of me.'

Morna hushed him. 'You're already a man.'

'When do you head off?' asked Rebecca.

'I leave on Tuesday.'

'Same as me,' said Samuel.

Toby had rested his cap on his knees, but now he was rolling it nervously in his hands, his eyes downcast. 'Umm, Rachel,' he glanced up at her, 'can I write to you?'

Rebecca felt as if everyone's head just snapped to attention while Toby's words hung in the air. After what seemed like a minute, but was probably only a few seconds, Rachel replied. 'Sure.'

'Will you write to me?' Her sister's head was bowed, her cheeks flushed. Rachel nodded, slowly raised her head to look at Toby, and nodded some more. 'Thank you.'

She gave him a faint smile.

'Will you sit by me in church on Sunday?'

Rebecca saw Rachel pale. 'Toby,' she said, 'please will you sit with us at church on Sunday? And I'll write to you occasionally too. We won't forget you over there.'

Everyone was sombre after he left. No one said a word. Rachel, Rebecca and Samuel returned to their dinner preparations.

That night around the big table in the parlour, Ronnie said to Samuel, 'Well lad, back home to Toronto to see your family and then what?'

Rebecca's eyes were on Samuel, her ears alert. They had not talked about the future. They avoided it, but now she was keenly interested in what Samuel had to say.

After a few pregnant moments Samuel sighed, deferring his head slightly towards Ronnie. 'The way I look at it, I have three options: back to sea working for my uncle. That still has appeal, though I have done that for a while and I now know it's something I can turn to at any point in my life.' Samuel glanced towards her father. 'I will visit my uncle on my way home. He is very enterprising and probably can already see plenty of business opportunities between here and France with the war. I'm not sure I want to be involved in all of that. The second option is war, and I don't really have any desire to go off and dodge bullets let alone fire bullets, so I figure the third and only viable option is to get involved in something that will keep me out of the war for as long as possible, yet still serves my country.'

'And do you know yet what that is?' inquired Margaret.

'Yes, what, Samuel?' Rebecca said under her breath.

Samuel's eyes flicked briefly to Margaret before settling on Ronnie. With a small smile he said, 'Would you believe medicine?'

'I knew it!' exclaimed Ronnie. 'You have the makings of a fine doctor, son.'

Rebecca's heart gave a little jump. Samuel was going to be a doctor! Her eyes had never left Samuel's face all evening. At that moment they glowed in admiration. Everyone around the table was excited for Samuel.

'That would be a fine thing if you were to become a doctor, Samuel. You could come and live here and all our worries would be over,' said Ronnie.

'You never know.' Samuel's eyes shone at Ronnie, then he glanced at Rachel before bringing his gaze to rest on Rebecca.

17

There was no denying what was upon them. Each day brought more news from the outside world, of events happening outside their control, like a tornado heading their way, so that before long the inevitable had happened.

'August 8: Britain accepts Canada's offer of 25,000 troops. Canada is at war', screamed the headlines of the Twillingate Sun which landed on the dock at Deception the day before Samuel departed, along with a telegram for him from Toronto.

SAMUEL. COME HOME POST-HASTE. MATTHEW IS OFF TO FRANCE TO SERVE IN A HOSPITAL. WE WANT ALL OUR FAMILY TOGETHER BEFORE HE LEAVES. TRAVEL SAFE UNTIL WE SEE YOU AGAIN. LOVE M&D.

If it hadn't been before, their fate was certainly sealed now. 'I'll telegram them tomorrow from Twillingate,' said Samuel, 'let them know I'm on my way.'

His last day with the Crowes, his last opportunity to pull Silas aside and hand over the money his father had sent through weeks earlier. As expected, Silas was as stubborn as ever. In exasperation Samuel said, 'What am I meant to do with this money? My father will consider my powers of persuasion sorely lacking if I return home with it.'

'Well that will be your problem,' said Silas, clearly enjoying Samuel's predicament. 'Samuel, it has been our pleasure to help you – really it has, despite some of my initial misgivings. And you have helped us in return. You have more than proven your gratitude. And that is all the thanks we need.'

'If you don't want to take it for yourself or Mrs Crowe what about for Rachel and Rebecca?'

'I don't want to take it for any of us.'

In his situation Samuel would probably feel the same. Silas was virtuous and certainly not materialistic in any sense of the word. But Samuel was frustrated that he wouldn't see this as a windfall to do something for his family, to consider and to provide for them in a way that he might not ordinarily be able to do so. He would broach it another way.

That afternoon Rachel, Rebecca and he went for one final walk out to the headland where Rebecca had first spotted his drifting boat. When they were gazing at the iceberg-less sea, being buffeted by the wind, he brought it up.

'How do you repay someone for saving your life? How do you repay a family for welcoming you into their home and treating you like family?'

'Samuel, what are you talking about?' said Rachel. 'You have more than done that.'

'Yes,' nodded Rebecca, 'one hundred times over.'

'Maybe I have, but my father and mother haven't. And they want to and they seem to be thwarted in their efforts. I don't mean to speak ill of your father, but he's steadfast and won't accept what my parents have extended.'

'And what is that?' asked Rachel.

'Payment for having me these past three months.'

'Money?' said Rebecca.

'Yes, money, which could go to any number of uses, to your further education even.'

'How much money?' asked Rachel.

'Two hundred dollars.'

'Two hundred dollars!' the girls exclaimed in unison. 'That's a colossal amount. No wonder he wouldn't take it,' said Rachel.

'He didn't even know the amount. Trust me.' He paused. 'I'm wondering if you can take it on his behalf.'

'We couldn't possibly do that,' said Rachel. 'Besides, what need do we have for money like that.'

'You might not have need for it now. But you never know what you might need in the future. Prices always go up in wartime. Goods become scarce. It is something for the two of you to have for a rainy day. I would have liked to see you take it and put it towards further study somewhere.'

Rebecca and Rachel looked at each other considering Samuel's words. After a few moments Rachel said, 'Your offer is very tempting. Study aside, it could pay for a holiday for us to come visit you. But Father's right, we can't take it.'

'Why don't we take the money and keep it here for safekeeping. We won't spend it and then you can come back in a little while and collect it,' said Rebecca.

'Brilliant idea!' said Samuel.

'Rebecca, how can we take his money? How can we explain it to Mother and Father if they ever were to find it?'

'How are they going to find it? We will hide it. Samuel's right. We have no idea what is in store for us.'

The girls looked at each other. Rachel's mouth was drawn in tight. Rebecca's brow was creased. 'What about if we only take half the money,' suggested Rachel. 'That way your father knows that it was accepted in the spirit it was given, but we are also able to say, it is not necessary. We do not need this money, but we will accept it because we understand it's important for you to give it.'

'Yes!' said Samuel.

'Yes,' said Rebecca, nodding her head.

'Yes,' said Rachel. 'But we will only hold onto it till you come back and claim it.'

It was their last night together, their last supper.

'Your first visit to Newfoundland is over,' said her father. 'You had the best of it my lad, the warmest summer we've had in years and the wind has behaved itself as well.'

'Maybe you brought the weather with you,' said Rebecca, thinking, you brought a lot of good things with you, Samuel.

'You couldn't have picked a better time to get shipwrecked,' noted her father. 'In winter you feel cooped up. Too much cabin fever at times, ain't that right Morna?'

'Yes, and it's all ahead of us,' said Rebecca, dryly.

'What do you do in winter in Toronto?' asked Rachel.

'Go ice-skating. Play ice hockey with my friends. Some people, like my sister for example, like to hug the hearth. I like to be outdoors doing something if I can, crunching the snow, but then I get incredibly hungry. I could eat a horse some days.'

'You wouldn't really eat a horse, would you?' exclaimed Rebecca.

Samuel looked at her for a long moment then shook his head. 'No,' he murmured. 'Not if there were other choices.' She had told him about Slate.

'Speaking of winter,' said Rachel, 'I have something for you.' She went to the wool basket, moved aside some of the dyed balls on top to pull out a naturally coloured bundle. 'Here.' She handed the item to Samuel. 'Newfoundland wool to keep you warm this winter.'

He took the bundle from Rachel and unfolded a jumper of homespun wool with a faint herringbone pattern across the chest. He stood and held the crew neck under his chin and each sleeve end by his hands. 'It's beautiful.' He smiled at her.

'Try it on,' urged Morna.

Pulling it over his head, Samuel had to also pull his hair out from the neck of the jumper, it was that overdue for a cut. But the warm natural hue of the wool made his summer skin look even more bronze. Rebecca thought he looked impossibly handsome. She imagined Rachel thought the same.

'Perfect.' Her mother admired the fit. 'Well done, Rachel.'

'This must have taken you days,' said Samuel. Rachel didn't elaborate; she just smiled at him. 'When did you manage to do this?'

'Obviously, when you weren't looking.' Her eyes shone.

'Thank you. I will treasure it always.' He rubbed his hands up and down the sleeves.

Rebecca felt her mother nudge her. She rose, went to the pantry and returned handing the canvas bag to Samuel. 'Here this took mother hours too.'

Samuel looked inside the bag and exhaled with pleasure. 'Oh my, this is wonderful. Thank you.' He looked sincerely at Morna. 'I think I am going to return home twenty pounds heavier than when I left.'

'You certainly need to be heavier than when you arrived,' said Silas. Everyone laughed.

Morna said, 'The bag is one of a kind,' drawing attention to the effort Rebecca had gone to. Samuel ran his finger along the horsehair strap. 'Where did this come from?'

'From Mica,' said Rebecca, smiling with her eyes. 'It is her little farewell gift. She wants you to come back and take her riding again one day.'

'Does she?' His eyes twinkled at her.

Rebecca continued to smile warmly at Samuel remembering their Sable Island ride. And then feeling everyone looking at her, she cleared her throat.

'I'm afraid I can't claim to have spent hours on your farewell gift. But it comes from the heart as well.' She handed over her present. Samuel looked down at the scroll in his hand and touched the finely plaited braid. He looked up at her, then he untied the bind and rolled out the picture. A smile appeared on his lips and his eyes softened, melting her heart. Across the bottom rolling like waves she had written the words: '*I will remember you. I will remember this. Rebecca Crowe. 1914.*' She heard his inhale.

He raised his head and his eyes glowed. 'Thank you,' he said, ever so softly.

'Please show us,' said Rachel, unable to contain her curiosity. Samuel turned the drawing around for all to see.

'Oh, Rebecca,' said her mother, 'how delightful,' her eyes shining at her Rebecca.

'It's great,' said Rachel. 'You should do more drawings.'

'She should, shouldn't she,' said Samuel.

'Very fitting,' said Silas. 'You know if it weren't for her fascination with icebergs, she would not have found you.'

'I know,' said Samuel. 'I am a lucky man.'

'You are. I'm amazed you didn't die out there of exposure or frostbite or something. The Lord must have decided we'd had enough sorrow for one year.'

'Yes,' drawled Samuel. 'The will to live was strong and providence was on my side.'

Everyone rose early to have breakfast with Samuel, yet no one was hungry. He needed to leave just after seven to be at Deception for the nine a.m. sailing. They were all keen to come and see him off, except Samuel. 'Please, I'd much rather say goodbye to you here. I'm not one for public farewells.' Rebecca and Rachel were petulant.

But Silas was onside. 'I think that's the right idea, Samuel. That way you can have some time to yourself before you get on board.' Samuel nodded his thanks. He was counting on that. Silas came towards him, his arm outstretched. Samuel shook his hand and patted him on his right shoulder with his left arm, 'Thank you again sir, for everything.'

To Morna he said, 'Thank you too, Mrs Crowe. I will never forget your many kindnesses.' He took both her hands and kissed her the French way; left cheek, right cheek then hugged her. Turning to Rachel he said, 'Rachel, what can I say, there are so many things I will remember you for. You've been truly wonderful. Thank you.' As with Morna, he took both her hands and kissed both her cheeks, but as he started to release their embrace, Rachel leant up and kissed him on the lips. He never thought Rachel would be so forward. He smiled warmly and did his best to put on a charmed look, at the same time hoping not to encourage her.

Lastly he turned to Rebecca, sweet, sorrowful Rebecca. He couldn't put if off any longer. She wasn't smiling. She was biting her lips, doing her utmost not to cry and failing miserably. His whole heart was giving out. All of a sudden he hated this farewell. It was way too public even. He wished he could have said his goodbyes separately and then just disappeared before they arose. Never again.

'Come on Rebecca,' he said. 'The first thing I saw when I came to on this island, was your beautiful smiling face and it's the last thing I want to see when I leave.' He opened his arms to her. She leant into his shoulder and released her tears. He gently rubbed her back. 'Without you there would be no farewell. And my heart would not feel as it does today. Be well, my little ice mermaid, my Newfoundland naiad.' He looked fondly down at her then he pulled back a little to kiss her on each check and then a gentle soft kiss on her lips, before pulling away and rubbing his thumbs across her cheeks to brush away her tears. 'Smile for me, please! Be happy for the past. Be happy for the future. I'll come again one day.'

And that is when she lifted her eyes, lifted them to cling to the promise in his. And she held on to that. Releasing him in the flesh only, stepping back with a slight nod and the tiniest tremble of a smile as if to say, 'Well, I'll see you again too. I'll be waiting.'

The Epistles

18

When Samuel returned to Canada it was as if he were returning to a different country. In the days following the declaration of war people's lives were pervaded with a sense of urgency unlike any he had ever witnessed. Everywhere they were outputting, transporting and stockpiling. It was surreal, almost as if Canada was preparing itself for an invasion. In many homes men put up their hands, then frenetically put in place arrangements for those they would leave behind. Even the discussions around the Daltons' table concerning Samuel's future were akin to military planning and strategy. Over dinner on his first night home Samuel laid his one and only card on the table. Suddenly all three generations of Dalton men were full of their own declarations.

'Fantastic news,' said Matthew, squeezing Samuel's shoulders. 'But why did you have to wait till I was leaving?'

'Good plan, eh?'

His brother elbowed him. Matthew had their mother's colouring, olive skin, dark hair with dark brown eyes almost jet black in colour, but his features, like Samuel's, defined him as his father's son. Their natures, though, were vastly different. Samuel was sensitive and quietly self-assured, Matthew, boldly confident. Yet they both gave as good as they got.

'Well there's no question about it. You simply have to go to McGill,' he said.

'I knew you were going to say that.' Samuel flashed a smile.

'He's right,' agreed Grandpa. 'It's the finest institution in Canada, if not the entire North American continent. Thanks to Osler.'

'And McCrae,' said Matthew.

'Yes, John's a fine doctor,' said Leonard, their father. He could have been Samuel's double, only thirty-years his senior. Just as tall, more heavy set, lightly bronzed skin with dark golden brown hair, greying slightly at the temples.

'It's possible,' said Matthew, 'that this year's intake has closed.'

'I'm sure between you three doctors you have enough contacts to open doors,' said Lottie, their mother, 'and I can always see who Michel knows.' Charlotte Sibonne, daughter of one of Montreal's most successful and respected merchants, was, above all things, well-connected and well-liked.

'Do you really want to do this, son?' asked his father.

'Excellent question,' exclaimed Grandpa. 'I was just about to ask, "What's brought on this change of heart?"' Grandpa Dalton was a thin man with severe, deep-set eyes almost as if he had seen too much in his life and wanted to retreat. Yet, they weren't cold eyes: they often glowed with optimism and love. He was the standard bearer for calm and patience in the Dalton family.

'Dad, I don't think I have a burning desire to be a doctor like I imagine you or Matthew or Grandpa had. But right now, of all the options in front of me, medicine is what appeals the most. I would like to be able to save people's lives and over the last few months I've come to realise how being of service in that way can be rewarding and also how little I know.'

Over the next twenty-four hours Samuel's father, brother and grandfather feverishly wrote letters of introductions and personal recommendations to any contact they had at McGill. His father phoned colleagues for character references on Samuel, and Samuel himself penned a heartfelt letter apologising for his lateness in applying, explaining his recent revelations and desire to become a doctor and, short of pleading, said he would consider it an absolute privilege to be accepted at such a prestigious academy, from which his brother had not long graduated with first class surgical honours.

When they had finished Samuel and Matthew helped Grandpa Dalton move in to the Dalton family home. The night after Samuel returned from Newfoundland Analeise and Randall joined the family for dinner with news of their own: Analeise was with child. Grandpa's second words were, 'Well it's time you moved out of that flat into something larger,' and with that he surrendered his home to the young couple.

Overnight, the extensive Dalton library doubled in size, Grandpa only wanting to bring his books and his bed with him.

It felt like the end of an era and the beginning of another. Not unlike an Indian summer and the tinge of sadness it heralds knowing the best of the season is over. But rather than be melancholic, the Daltons rose to the occasion. Pachelbel's Canon in D Major, Mozart's Eine Kleine Nachtmusik and Dvorak's Symphony No 9 filled the house. Their mother played piano. The gramophone twirled. Their father came home from his practice early. Analeise and Randall were ever present and a ceaseless flow of friends peppered their days. They ate, drank their fill, laughed loudly and smoked the odd cigar.

After one whirlwind week, Samuel and Matthew departed – Samuel's acceptance at McGill pending a series of interviews with the Medical Faculty. In Montreal the brothers had a night on the town then Matthew caught a crowded railway carriage to Québec to see their grandparents before heading to the Valcartier military training camp eighteen miles outside the city.

On the 18th September came the letter Samuel had been waiting for: his acceptance as a freshman at McGill. After two weeks in Montreal, thinking about Rebecca and the Crowes, getting flashbacks of his sea ordeal all of a sudden, doing odd jobs for his Uncle Michel's while he was in Québec, familiarising himself with the McGill campus, Samuel had had enough. He skipped orientation and headed to Québec to grab what time he could with his brother before his imminent departure.

In Québec his uncle had gone into partnership with two local photographers, set up a studio in his waterfront warehouse and a canteen at Valcartier, and somehow managed to bankroll thousands of photography plates to capture for posterity the thousands of young men going off to war in all their military finery.

'This is a veritable gold mine, Samuel,' said Michel, his brown animated eyes flashing above rotund cheeks and a neatly trimmed beard. He was in his late forties but still boasted a youthful head of hair. A tall man, tending to portliness, yet with a surprising amount of energy, he had a unique smell which Samuel sensed whenever he hugged him, a blend of cologne, mild sweat, spices and smoked wood.

'Every one of those young men is a guaranteed customer,' Michel continued in a torrent. 'Photos for their mother, their grandmother, their missus, their sweetheart – how I love women!' He kissed his fingers. 'It's a good job you showed up, my lad. We could use another pair of hands around here.'

In his uncle's midnight blue 1912 Model T Ford Samuel began courier runs between Québec and Valcartier. He heard the call of war even before he saw it: rifle ranges echoing with the sounds of firing practice and the boom of big cannons blasting across the plain. He was amazed at the size of the encampments that had sprung up in only a few weeks. Row upon row of white teepee tents graced the grounds either side of the Jacques Cartier River. Any minute he expected to see Indian braves with war paint and chiefs with their feathered headdresses riding towards him. But there were few Iroquois, Tuscarora, Mohawk or Cree here. There were some, but mostly there were British and Scottish and Irish immigrants and generations of Canadians descended from the mother country.

While the troops were being mobilised and trained, Matthew and other civilian doctors received a crash course in the operations of a hospital service in the war zone. After two weeks of drills and exams he was gazetted a Lieutenant in the Canadian Army Medical Corps, one of 1,100 medical staff off to England in military uniforms and white medical jackets. With them would be going provisions for two general hospitals, two stationary hospitals, one clearing hospital and three field ambulances, along with 7,000 horses, motor vehicles and wagons.

On Thursday 24th September 32,000 recruits began marching to the Québec wharves: their last weekend on home soil, their last Moosehead, their last Molson. Departing from one French port they would ultimately end up at another. The 80,000 strong city of Québec was like the swollen St Lawrence River after the spring melt, bulging under the military influx. The atmosphere was carnivalesque as friends, family and locals came to send off Canada's brave. Amidst the furore, Matthew yelled at Samuel, 'Do you wish you were coming with me?'

'In some respects, but if I went now it would be as cannon fodder. That's not how I want to end my life.' Samuel shook his head with quiet certainty.

'No,' agreed Matthew throwing his arm around his shoulder, 'but how do you think you are going to cope settling down to life on the land, little brother?'

'Do you have to use the word, 'settle'?'

'Settle, settle, settle,' said Matthew digging Samuel in the ribs as he tried to squirm away. 'Oh look, don't worry. Once you get into university life, you'll love McGill. I did. And the summer breaks are long. Longer than you ever had at school.'

'I'm already looking forward to it. That and whatever voyages Uncle Michel has planned.'

'Maybe next summer you can come across to the continent and we could go see 'gay Paree' together. The Eiffel Tower, the artistic centre of the world, the sin capital of Europe? What do you say?'

'Baudelaire, here I come. Le Louvre, Les Dames du Sacré Coeur, Le Moulin Rouge.'

'Boy, I've missed you, Samuel.' Matthew squeezed his shoulder. 'Shame I'm leaving. We could have had such fun in Montreal together.'

Next morning after baguettes and coffee they took a stroll around the city's most famous landmark, Le Château Frontenac. The stately hotel built thirty years previously over the cliffs of Cap Diamont combined the sturdiness of Scottish brick with the style and elegance of the French Renaissance. Both men admired it immensely. High above the St Lawrence it gave a commanding view of the fleet readying for departure and the activity of Québecois that Sunday morning. Horses and motorcars vied for space on the cobbled road. Cafes were getting ready for their Sunday trade and on the terrace an orchestra was setting up for an afternoon concert. The promenade featured large black iron cannons, a reminder of the days when the city was a fort and the scene of bitter bloodshed between the British and the French. Now they were in league with each other.

'I'm glad you're leaving from here,' said Samuel.

'Why's that?'

'This is one of my favourite places. I love this walled city. It's charming and has this wonderful sense of community. I always have such fond memories of my time here.'

'Me too. There is something comforting about the old town, something mysterious as well. I remember once when I was about ten wanting to stay here with Grandmère and Grandpère and not go back to Toronto when school started. You'd stayed home those holidays. You had come down with the measles or something just before we were due to depart. I can't remember why Analeise didn't come. Anyway, I'd had Grandmère and Grandpère all to myself and I practically had free run of the entire town as well. It was such a wonderful holiday and I badly wanted it to keep going. I was certain that if I went to school here it still would be one big holiday.'

'You must have been disappointed you didn't get your way?'

'No, not really,' he smiled looking at Samuel with his warm ebon eyes. 'Grandmère convinced me that you, Samuel, of all people, would be most upset if I didn't return.'

'She was right. Leise only ever played with me under sufferance.' Watching the river below, Samuel said, almost as an afterthought, 'I probably had more larks with the Crowe sisters this summer than I've had with Leise my whole life.'

'It was probably just an age difference back then,' assured Matthew. 'She's a changed woman since your near death experience.'

'True. I think she just found me an annoying little brother when I was young.'

'Do you think you'll ever see the Crowes again?'

'I'd like to.' Samuel's mind was drifting as was its wont lately. Coming back to the present he exhaled. 'That girl was something else.'

'Who? Rachel?'

'No. Rebecca.'

'The younger one? How old did you say she was again?'

'Fifteen.'

'Fifteen,' drawled Matthew, his voice dreamy, spellbound. 'Did you kiss her?'

Samuel could not contain his smile.

'Look at you. You kissed her!'

'Yeah, I kissed her.'

'And?' Matthew grinned encouragingly.

'There was no more "And?". There couldn't be.'

'Really?'

'Yes, really, Casanova.'

'You obviously weren't swept away. It can't have been much of a kiss.'

'Au contraire.' Still grinning, Matthew raised his palm to Samuel's forehead. 'Cut it out,' said Samuel swiping his hand away.

'Alright,' said Matthew, chortling. 'It's a good job you're off to Montreal. Plenty of fine women there to distract you.'

'Matthew, I guarantee that you would only have to be with her for five seconds and you would understand. She is Artemis the huntress, eternally young, with a beautiful face, the equal of any man.'

'Artemis, the protectress of virginity?'

Samuel ignored him. 'As we know, girls go from Artemis to Aphrodite, the woman born of the waves. And she is that too.'

'Celebrated for her perfect face, the sparkle of her eyes, her smiling mouth and the beauty of her breasts.'

'That's right.'

'She was also meant to be proud and cruel.'

'And she offered Paris the most beautiful mortal, Helen, whom he chose over kingship of the universe and invincibility in war.' Samuel sighed. 'She is the embodiment of all three.'

Matthew looked directly at Samuel. 'Unbelievable,' he said shaking his head, an expression of dazed wonder on his face, 'I finally get it: the one who seldom comes by all the way from Seldom Come By. This girl I have to meet. Promise me you are not going to race off and get married while I'm away.'

'There's no chance of that happening any time soon. But yes, I would like you to meet her. Aside from you, I've never felt closer to anyone,' he cast his brother a quick glance and caught his eye.

'I see,' said Matthew, suddenly very serious.

'Yes,' continued Samuel. 'Leaving was very hard indeed.' Samuel wondered if part of the reason he found it hard was because he knew he was coming back to a world soon to be void of Matthew. The one person he could always rely upon to brighten his days.

'Maybe you can have a short stopover in Newfoundland when you come across to visit me. Think up something that will have Michel chomping at the bit to send you off.'

'What, in one of his boats? Dodging German submarines?'

'It might be safer than how we're travelling. We aren't half advertising our presence.'

A little while later they returned to their grandparents for Samuel to collect his duffel bag and say his farewells. Saying goodbye to his grandparents was easy. He had been seeing them regularly over the past two years and with his move to Montreal he would still be close. Matthew was a different matter. As they strolled down the hill to the train station Samuel had a flash of, 'What happens if I never see him again?' He quickly shook his head dismissing the thought. But he couldn't pretend this was just an ordinary goodbye. The air was thick with emotion.

They stood on the platform waiting for Samuel to board his train. 'Write to me, please!' said Samuel. 'Let me know how you're doing, what I'm missing.'

'I will,' said Matthew looking affectionately and warmly at his brother. Coming up close Samuel embraced him in an almighty bear hug and then they kissed each other on their cheeks – the custom they always followed in this city when they said their farewells, but this time they held on for many moments, neither of them wanting to be the first to release.

'Go well, little brother. Study hard. Dream large.'

'Keep safe, big brother. I will think of you every time I play Satie.'

'You do that. Lucky for you – lucky for me I guess – that I left you my gramophone and copy of *Trois Gymnopédies*.'

19

Eight days after he left Newfoundland the Crowes received a telegram:

AM HOME. THANKS AGAIN. SAMUEL.

And then two weeks later, a letter addressed to Mr Silas Crowe from Mr Leonard Dalton and his wife Charlotte of 15 Claredon Crescent, South Hill, Toronto. And then – finally! – at the beginning of October, a letter from Samuel telling them of his life at the McGill University Medical School, his move into the Montreal house Matthew used to share, and his sister Analeise expecting a baby in February. Much to their delight he included a photograph of himself and his brother.

Rebecca knew Samuel would write. It was just a matter of time. But as the days wore on and her doubting mind got the better of her she started to think she had built up the significance of what had passed between them like some big billowy cloud that was just as likely to dissipate as bring much needed rain.

Her thoughts were not helped by the seasonal change. Samuel was blissfully ignorant of what amazing summer weather they had had. Any outsider would be. But to Rebecca it really was as if the Heavens had parted and God had shone down his favour on them and blessed them, day after day, with bright clear blue expansive skies. And when Samuel left he took away the sun.

Already they had started hunkering down. The frosts were getting heavier, the skies greyer, the days shorter. Before long their world would descend into a snowy shutdown. She didn't mind the snow. She rather liked the whiteness of it. It reminded her of icebergs. She just found its duration taxing. But it was the fall, the sense of everything dying off, of contracting, of dreading the worst that disturbed her the most. It pervaded everything and only seemed to add to her sense of loss.

When they received Samuel's letter she wanted to carry it around across her heart, every minute of every day, but she knew there was no possible way she could do that. She and Rachel decided to place it in the bottom drawer of their armoire so either of them could read it at their pleasure.

In those darkening days, the unspoken became spoken and Rebecca realised that the days weren't just dark. They were doomful. Moments earlier they had finished writing their first joint letter to Samuel when Rachel, not looking at her sister, said, 'I think I love Samuel, Rebecca. And I think I know what true love is now. What I felt for Connor, God rest his soul, pales in comparison to what I feel for Samuel. It's different and I know in my heart Samuel senses it too. I'd marry him tomorrow if he asked me.'

It was the most frighteningly awkward experience of Rebecca's life. She could look at her sister but could she say a word? No, she couldn't. Her mind raced. She couldn't express excitement or delight for Rachel. She shied away from any notion of encouragement. And she dared not mention the iceberg interlude she and Samuel had shared. She was frozen in panic and around the edges she felt overwhelming sadness. Sadness for Rachel knowing her most fervent dream was unlikely to be realised. Sadness for herself knowing for certain if the truth ever came out it would strain their relationship. And sadness for the two of them, knowing that for the first time ever they couldn't enthusiastically celebrate a development in the other sister's life. All she could manage was a dry swallow and an, 'I see what you see in him.' And, after a while, 'It's a pity he doesn't live closer.' Then finally, 'Let's hope he comes back one day.'

Who was she, a fifteen-year-old girl, to have designs on a man older than her sister? What did she know of love?

All she knew was ever since that day at the waterfall when they sat on the ledge in the soft light, their hands clasped together, with the water thundering down beside them, without any words being spoken, Rebecca saw what Samuel couldn't say. It flowed between them warming in its embrace.

The strange anxieties she had felt about Samuel had dispersed and though she could not name what she felt, she felt at peace, because she could see that Samuel felt the same way. It was a knowing and with that knowing came relief and comfort. Later came the iceberg and the kiss.

She felt one way about Samuel and her sister, no doubt, felt the same way. Only Samuel could decide their fate. That summer Rebecca felt Samuel had chosen but she only had his word to go on. He could have just as easily kissed Rachel on one of their many excursions, but Rebecca decided he hadn't. At the core of her being she knew that Samuel was unflinchingly honest. That is why she knew in her heart he would return one day. He was a person who kept his word. But where did that leave them? And would he still feel the same way about her when he returned? Would she feel the same way about him? Would Rachel?

20

1915

Toby's letters from England arrived sporadically yet were penned regularly - the best the Newfoundland and British postal and military systems could manage. Upon their arrival in England the Newfoundland Regiment had trained it with the Canadian Expeditionary Force to the Salisbury plains. They spent many muddy months doing marching exercises and drills and, unbelievably, some men were dismissed because of fallen arches: flat feet. Rachel sent up a private prayer that Toby was not one of them. In his latest letter they had re-located to Stobb in Scotland and had had a week-end off to visit Edinburgh Castle.

'Just sounds like one big holiday so far,' mumbled Rebecca.

'Don't be glib,' said Rachel frowning. She made a point of replying on the same day she received any letter from Toby as if they were a mail order she had to complete and return. When she first wrote she asked Rebecca, 'Do you want to add a few paragraphs?'

'If you like. I know I said I would write to him, but don't you think it might disappoint him not to receive a private letter from you?'

'Rebecca! I said I would write to him. I didn't say I would give him my heart.'

Rachel felt sick with dread when she thought of Toby. Dread that something might happen to him. Dread as to what his expectations would be when he returned. As much as she tried to make her correspondence platonic, each letter she sent felt like another arrow from Cupid, as if she was actively encouraging him whilst at the same time actively deceiving him. But she could see no way out of the situation.

Her only tactic was to make sure in every letter she

included some tidbit of news from Samuel and indirectly any update they received on Matthew, thereby legitimising her writing about the Dalton brothers, hoping that eventually Toby might put one and one together. Meanwhile anyone and everyone at Deception had started asking her, had she heard from her 'Blue Puttee' – the nickname given to the Newfoundland Regiment due to a fabric shortage, which saw the regiment wearing blue rather than the standard olive drab. All she could think was: if I were engaged to Samuel, none of this would be happening.

They received news from Samuel that his sister had a baby boy, Benjamin Taylor Landry, on the 28th of February and also that the Medical Faculty at McGill where he studied was to supply the entire personnel for a general hospital in the rear. It was to be known as the No III Canadian General Hospital. Matthew was stationed with the No II Canadian General Hospital. His unit had gone across to the Continent in January 1915 ahead of the Canadian Forces to help establish the hospital in a golf club at le Toquet, close to the Belgium coast.

Until the war, gangrene had been a text book topic, but as Matthew discovered the toxins spread with a speed that was hard to believe yet with a certainty that was undeniable due to the gagging, putrid odour. Limb after limb had to be sacrificed to save life. Matthew had expected to see death on a large scale, he knew there would be screams of warfare, the incessant crack, crack of rifles, the anguished struggles and laboured breathing of dying men, but the countless limbs he had to sever, the sickening smell of gangrene in war was something no one could prepare for.

Whenever he got a break, he escaped to the beach or the woods to fill his nostrils with the welcome scent of salt and pine. Clean air had never meant so much to him.

Matthew wrote to Samuel, "If ever I have a few spare hours of daylight, I go riding. For fresh air, for sanity, I just do what I can to get away for a while. Bonne chance with your exams little brother."

Samuel received Matthew's letter in the thick of his exams.

Fresh air and sanity was what he was craving. He couldn't wait to get away. He had planned two weeks with his family at the start of his break and two weeks at the end. The rest of the time he would be working for his uncle in Québec. Would there be any voyages to Labrador or Newfoundland? To Samuel the word Newfoundland had almost become a synonym for Rebecca, the mere mention of it punctuating his thoughts with nostalgia. In Montreal he'd made many friends, both male and female, some of the young ladies were delightful, one girl, part Portuguese, part French, certainly did sparkle. But she was no Rebecca.

21

In May, just as the first icebergs were starting to majestically appear on the horizon, after weeks of dank fog, the Crowes travelled to Salvage to visit Esther, whom they hadn't seen in over four years. Of all the girls, Esther was the only one who looked like a cross between both parents. Her nose and cheeks, eyebrows and hairline were her mothers. But her mouth, her jawline, her neck and her eyes – albeit a paler, peaceful blue – were her fathers. Rebecca always remembered her sister having blonde hair like hers, but now it seemed much darker.

'That's because I'm not outside as much and when I am I wear a hat – like you should. Have you started wearing hats yet, Rebecca? When I was your age it was the bane of my life trying to get you to keep your hat on.'

Rebecca laughed. 'I don't remember that at all.'

'Well you were four at the time if I recall.'

'She's still the same,' said Rachel. 'She never wears a hat.'

'Sometimes I wear a hat,' Rebecca said in her defence. But secretly they were right. She loathed wearing hats. The only time she felt like wearing a hat was in winter or on bitter cold howling days when there was no denying that a hat would keep a lid on her escaping heat. Mostly hats just made her feel more constrained.

The biggest surprise of the visit was however not Esther's hair colour or Rebecca's head coverings or lack thereof but Rebecca herself. At five foot nine, nearly sixteen years of age, the youngest daughter of Silas and Morna Crowe ended up being the tallest. 'I wish we had a camera and could get a photograph taken of us all,' said Rebecca.

'Me too,' agreed Rachel. 'We could send a copy to Samuel.'

'I want to hear all about this Samuel,' said Esther, pulling out a chair.

Rebecca had been looking forward to the trip for weeks – Bonavista Bay being the farthest she had ever ventured in her life. However to her dismay, life at Salvage was not that different to life in Deception, only different people. She and Rachel spent hours playing with Esther's three children: Ruth, five, Deborah, three, and wee Joseph who at ten months was into everything. They had picnics and went to two dances. She laughed like she had when Samuel was with them – easily. All the women cried when they left.

They returned in time for the trapping season and for Rebecca to begin her first paid job, though she would never sight any of the money – it being factored into her father's account at the merchant. She worked splitting the fish on the main wharf at Deception for the Co-operative, while her mother and Rachel managed things at home with the help of Mica. Every second night Rebecca stayed with Ronnie and Margaret Evans so she would only have to travel one way each day after such long days on her feet. Rebecca rather enjoyed staying with the Evans and she didn't particularly mind the work on the Deception stage either.

She knew this summer would be vastly different to her last which she reasoned was fine, as long as it wasn't going to be like most of her other summers before that. One night around the dinner table she said in quiet certainty, 'Summer will not be the same this year without Samuel.' She could picture him so vividly, running his fingers through his golden blonde hair.

Her father replied: 'You'll soon be that busy you'll have no time to think of him.'

In her defence her mother said, 'Rebecca is a woman, capable of thinking of umpteen things at once while still getting the job done.' She was inclined to side with her mother.

A few days after the end of his first year of study when Samuel rejoined his family in Toronto they received a long letter from Matthew detailing the latest medical emergency on the Western Front – lethal chlorine gas – launched at the Canadian troops in April during the Second Battle of Ypres. "A crippling unthinkable horror" he called it. His account was gruesome. It sounded like grown men were drowning on dry land. Samuel was relieved when discussions turned to Ernest Shackleton and the extraordinary feat of survival for the men of the Endurance in the wild Southern Ocean – even though it stirred up memories that he would like to have forgotten. It had been a year since he was lost adrift in the North Atlantic. Nothing had ever been seen or heard of from any of his companions. He still found it hard to believe that he alone had survived.

20th July 1915
Dear Samuel,

A quick note to thank you for remembering my birthday and for the wonderful presents. The blue satin sash is just beautiful. Mother says it matches my eyes perfectly. And it was such a delicious treat to enjoy maple syrup and pancakes again this year for my birthday, then I had to bolt out the door to the Bay, but as it was my birthday I was able to ride Mica over and back. She looks ever so smart in her new bridle – thank you. If I had a camera I would take a photograph to send to you. If you were here I would give you a big hug.

x Rebecca.

Dear Samuel

The boots you sent me could not have been more perfect. Thank you. Where did you get them made up? I am so impressed that you remembered my shoe size. You must come back so we can dance together again. I will wear the lace that you sent me with pride.

Fondest Regards
Rachel.

Yes Samuel, words cannot express how touched we were to receive such generous and thoughtful gifts. My velvet shawl and brooch have received numerous compliments from the ladies at church. Silas looks ten years younger in his new blazer and feels he ought to be wearing it to a wedding! I'm sure he would write and thank you himself but he has turned in, exhausted after spending the last three days making hay. Rebecca and Rachel are also working very hard of late, a credit to themselves. We don't know how we would ever manage without them.

I trust you enjoy your canoe trip with your father.
Warm Regards,
Mrs Morna Crowe

All along Rebecca had been counting on Samuel not turning up that summer. She had, however, expected him to remember her birthday, though she was stunned at the luxury of the gifts he had bestowed upon them. But if Rebecca could have had one gift for her birthday from Samuel, one wish, it would have been this: to know when he would return. He said he would come back one day and she had faith that he would. But once she had a date she would know what was halfway. She would know when the days ahead of her, the countdown to when she would see Samuel again would be greater than the days behind her. Life would be much more uplifting then.

In his next letter though he did send her a sign that he had not forgotten her. He wrote that two of his house mates – James and Anthony who were in fourth year medicine – had volunteered to join the Canadian III General Hospital in France, and that Matthew had just had ten days leave in Paris. At last, he wrote, Matthew has made me jealous of his being over there. He ended his letter with a description of the Notre Dame Cathedral in Montreal, which Matthew had recently claimed was, by and far, more impressive than the Paris one.

The ceiling of the church hovers around 150 feet high and the whole interior is of a blue material, which appears to radiate a heavenly blue light over the entire surface. It has three large rose-tinted windows set directly in the suspended ceiling. Their vermilion light mingles with the azures, purples and silver of the surrounds and the shimmering gold leaf stars dotted across the vault. Below are hundreds of intricate wooden carvings and life-size religious statues in every type of timber imaginable from light blond through to ebony black. The whole effect is breathtaking. Strangely it reminds me of my time in Newfoundland. I would love for you to see it one day.
Au revoir for now,
Samuel

22

In August, Rachel got news from Toby that the Newfoundland Regiment were in Egypt acclimatising to the warmer weather before heading to the Dardanelles in Turkey.

'Egypt!' said Rebecca when she heard. 'The pyramids! I can't believe they have been away for a whole year and seen no fighting.'

'Be thankful they've seen no fighting,' admonished Rachel, and when she read the words: 'Don't worry, when we see the action, we'll do Newfoundland proud,' she couldn't help but squirm.

They were anxious for Toby after they learnt from Samuel that the nearest hospital was on the island of Lemnos, forty miles away, whereas on the Western Front, Matthew was working at a Casualty Clearing Station (CCS) just five miles behind the trenches.

When Matthew wrote to Samuel about his experiences at the CCS, he told him out of everything he'd seen so far in the war, what he saw at the CCS was the most heartbreaking. Most of the life-saving abdominal surgery in the war took place at a CCS but while many of the victims were able to hang on till they got there, they seemed to surrender themselves the moment they arrived thinking they had made it. Distressingly, their vital signs, recorded on a cardboard sling around their neck, were often significantly lower than the earlier entry taken at the Regimental Aid Post (RAP), and when their body temperature and blood pressure were too low – many read as low as 65 over 40 – he could not operate. They were classified as being in severe shock and his hands were tied.

He felt utterly desperate not being able to give them what they needed to live. It was gut wrenching to pass over brave and helpless young men and look for patients who had stronger vital signs and a better chance of survival. He got to the point where he avoided their eyes.

At the end of his letter Matthew had written:

How is my nephew? Crawling around on all fours? We don't see any babies here, that's for sure. It would make a pleasant change to breathe the milky wholesomeness of young life and to hear their giggles untainted by anything.

'Backward, turn backward, O Time, in your flight. Make me a child again just for tonight!'

God it sounds like I'm going soft in the head. Give him a special hug from me.

All my love,
Matthew

In November 1915 the Crowes experienced day after day of silver thaw – freezing rainstorms that didn't let up, temperatures hovering just above and below 0 degrees. Their wood fires burned constantly. Rebecca had cabin fever. To relieve the boredom, she and Rachel rearranged the furniture and storage items in their spare bedroom upstairs so she and Rachel could have their own rooms – something they had talked about for years but never got round to doing. Together with their mother they spent weeks knitting garments for the war effort – socks, vests and mufflers to send to the Women's Patriotic Association in St John's for the Newfoundland soldiers overseas. They also sent two sets under separate dispatch directly to Toby. Rachel had even written to Samuel asking for Matthew's details, plus, she knitted a set for Samuel appending a note: 'I hope you feel closer to him when you wear these.'

In December they received a card and letter from Toby on the Gallipoli Peninsula.

Dear Rachel, Mr and Mrs Crowe and Rebecca,
It is hard to believe we have only been here for two months, believe me when I tell you it feels more like six. Our trials come anytime of the day or night.

The Turkish Army controls the high ground surrounding the beach and pour a constant stream of artillery and sniper fire down upon us. Re-supplying our water and food is a never-ending challenge. We pray for black nights so our boats can come in.

Early November we had some success and managed to advance our line to what we are now calling Caribou Hill. I lost some pals in that battle but don't worry about me Rachel. They say it takes three tonne of metal on average to kill a soldier and I've got some ways to go yet.

When we're not on the ridge we spend most of our days inside cubby holes – dugouts reinforced by wood – that the Australian and New Zealanders first created. The ANZACs are now called Diggers because of them and until recently these fixtures served their purpose well.

Not long ago condition here went from bad to worse. Three days of torrential rain and driving sleet washed away trenches and supplies. The temperature fell rapidly and the rain turned to snow.

We Newfoundlanders are no strangers to bad weather, as you know, but conditions here are dismal, a number of men have suffered frostbite and some even have died of exposure. The situation is desperate. Please send what warm clothing you can spare. I think of you all back in Newfoundland around your winter fires, hoping that by picturing the warm glow it might warm me a little inside.

Looking forward to your next letter to bring us some cheer.

Warm wishes,

Toby

'By jove!' exclaimed Silas, 'If the hardy men of Newfoundland are finding it desperate, that says it all.'

They prayed that Toby received his parcel and Rachel immediately started knitting him another two sets of everything.

Rebecca looked up Turkey in the atlas that Samuel had sent them not long after he had returned home. She compared Turkey's latitude to theirs. Gallipoli was at 40 degrees; they were at 49. But then she thought: what do I know? I've been one degree south at best, what do I know of their summers or their winters.

8th December 1915
Casualty Clearing Station No 44

Dear Studious Samuel,

How is life back in Montreal? I ran into James and Anthony purely by chance last week. It seems we all had three days to warm ourselves around the braziers and bars of Malo les Bains. They were well, albeit a little shell-shocked themselves. While one can read about the conditions here, reality can be far different but they have risen splendidly to the occasion.

I received a letter and parcel from your friends, the Crowe sisters, this week – you can imagine my surprise. I think you may have passed on my particulars – thank you. They said they hoped I didn't mind their writing to me. They mentioned that although they hadn't met me, they felt as if they knew me as they had a photograph of you and me on their dresser. Now I am even more eager to meet these girls! In my reply I told them naturally I was delighted to make their acquaintance even if via mail. The main purpose of their letter was to send me some homemade Newfoundland socks and vests. They thought I might appreciate such high-quality clothing from their little island, which I did.

In fact the clothing could not have come at a better time. The rain hammers down here. I fear the conditions underfoot will soon be worse than what we experienced last winter in England, as if that could be possible, but there you go. At least the fleas and rats don't like the cold either and seem to have gone quiet on us.

Mother has written to say everyone is going to Québec this Christmas and to celebrate Grandmère and Grandpère's 50th wedding anniversary on the 30th of December. I wish I could join you. I have sent them a small parcel, but in the event that it does not make it please give them my very best love and have a dance with Grandmère for me.

Merry Christmas Samuel and Bonne Année,
Matthew

23

1916

Each New Years Eve in Deception Bay a church service was held for the season of the Silent Prayer, when worshippers had to be silent during the last moments of the old year and the first moments of the new. It was a very solemn occasion; quite different to the mummering outings Rebecca and Rachel had been on over preceding nights with some of the younger folk.

The address that night was based on Deuteronomy 31 verse 8. *'The Lord himself will lead you and be with you. He will not fail you or abandon you, so do not lose courage or be afraid.'*

The sermon was dedicated to the Newfoundland soldiers. Rebecca thought briefly of Toby, but mostly the 'He' in 'He will not fail you or abandon you' was Samuel.

The path to Deception was a deep trench with snow banks up to three foot high in places. As winter deepened the cold air became crisper and dryer and the frosts more severe. Rebecca would often wake to find thick frosts on the inside of their windows. In the dwindling darkness she would place her mother's thimble on her forefinger and go around and limn pictures on them. Some days she drew icebergs.

Samuel always scanned the paper for news on the Canadian and Newfoundland Regiments. He read with interest Rachel's updates, her last one telling him the Newfoundlanders were now down to a quarter strength – 250 men. When Samuel read that he said out loud, 'Good on you, Toby.' What odds! Even though he was land-tied, Samuel would travel the world with those updates from Turkey and France and Newfoundland. The letters seemed to have a higher value than any he had ever received previously – more interesting, more woeful, more joyful.

8th February 1916
Casualty Clearing Station No 44

Hello Samuel,

I got your letter written over the Christmas holidays. What do you mean, stay away from Newfoundland? Don't you trust me? You know I would never make a play for a woman if she were yours. The question is: have you made your play yet?

We hear there are English female pilots who deliver new aircraft to the allied hangars near Furness where the French, Belgian and British planes are housed. Maybe I should go on a little sortie to Furness on my next break. I fancy having a pilot as a girlfriend. They are using those new Curtiss flying boats – the N-9 seaplanes – to patrol the channel for German submarines. I've decided I want one of those. Imagine flying one from Lake Ontario and landing in Parry Sound. Perhaps I should become a pilot when this war is over.

Right now I wish I could fly home to be with you to celebrate your 21st. Happy Birthday for the 10th of March. I enclose a small piece of artwork that I picked up from the markets around Sacré Coeur when I was in Paris last fall. I hope you like it. It's not a Gauguin I'm afraid but it is reminiscent of his work. What most appealed was its tropical richness and colour, such a vivid contrast to my present surroundings.

Think of me raising my champagne glass in your honour. I imagine you will celebrate with the family at Easter but have a few drinks with the boys in Montreal won't you? Even if you do have exams the next day, I don't care! I would be buying the rounds if I were there. I believe in living for the moment, now more than ever.

Please know that if anything should ever happen to me over here that I have especially loved having you as my brother. You have given me such wonderful memories and I look forward to many more joyful ones when I return.

Affectionately yours,
Matthew

In late March, Toby's unit was moved to France to recuperate and await for fresh recruits. Rachel was relieved to read he was away from the fighting and then her relief quickly turned to something else entirely once she read: 'When I return from the war, will you marry me?'

'Oh I knew it!' she exclaimed. She glanced at Rebecca. 'Don't you dare laugh!'

'Why would I laugh?' said Rebecca, doing a terrible job at not laughing. 'Toby's a fine chap. He's rather pleasant to look at. Granted he's not too tall' – he was around Rebecca's height – 'but you could do a lot worse than Toby.' Rebecca spoke the truth. Toby had a cheerful disposition and was bordering on handsome. Plus, his family was lovely.

'Yes he's all those things, but, I, don't, love, him. And I'm not going to marry him if I don't love him.'

'Well don't,' said Rebecca. 'No one's forcing you.'

Rachel replied:

I have enjoyed getting to know you more through our correspondence. I worry for you over there and naturally my utmost concern is for your safety. I hope and pray everyday that you will survive this war unscathed. As you know I already have had one engagement, which was torn asunder by an unspeakable tragedy. I would not like to endure another. Please let's revisit this when you return to Newfoundland.

At the end of May Samuel finished his second year and went straight to military training camp for a month – it now being compulsory for medical students during the first three years of their degree.

At the same time McGill University started running summer courses so graduating fourth year medical students could complete their fifth year and graduate at the end of 1916 rather than spring 1917, and be in France by early 1917. The Canadian Army Medical Corps could not get enough trained recruits.

Samuel said to his father, 'Those chaps will be studying for fifteen months straight.'

His father replied, 'Think of the poor lecturers, they will be working for two years straight – no rest for them at all.'

And there Samuel had to concede, though his mother did ask, 'When was the last time you studied or worked for 15 months straight, Leonard?'

20th June 1916
Casualty Clearing Station No 44

My dear family,
No doubt you've heard recently that the Canadians have been engaged in heavy fighting around Mount Sorrell in Belgium. They say it is the fiercest bombardment yet experienced by our troops – and they're not wrong. Thousands of casualties have passed through in just a few weeks, the figure approaching 8000 I believe, over 600 victims of gassing.

Today I found myself walking through the ruins of a small French town, now just crumbling facades. Here, you are reminded that war kills much more than just human lives. All the vegetation – trees, grass and plants – is completely destroyed. The roads and other infrastructure have become totally non-existent.

Mom, it reminds me of a painting you have in that book from the Hudson River School – the one of Monument Valley. I saw a solitary stairwell, still intact, leading skyward like a timeworn tower of Arizona rock. My memory of that collection is that the power and beauty of nature was manifest. Here it is the power and destruction of man and machine. Those artists with their rich pallets brought the colours of the distinctly American landscape to life. Here the colours are all muted spliced with the sanguine of blood.

How I long to see a garden bursting into bloom.
Your faraway Matthew x

24

Toby made no mention of Rachel's reply in his next letter. He told her he had fully recovered from dysentery and was fit for service and in May he'd gone into the line facing Beaumont Hamel, a particularly strong part of the German line. He did rotations of one week in and one week out.

Then, in early July, newspapers were full of a major allied offensive aimed at breaking through German lines along a 25-mile front north and south of the River Somme in northern France.

```
THE   BRITISH   ARMY   HAS   STRUCK   THE   ENEMY
ANOTHER HEAVY BLOW
```

The story quoted General Sir Douglas Haig saying:

```
'I  am  well  satisfied  with  the  results  of  the
gallant  efforts  of  the  First  through  to  the
Seventh  Armies  yesterday  and  today.  The  enemy
has  lost  heavily  and  is  severely  shaken.  We have
not  yet  completely  broken  down  his  resistance on
the   front   attacked   and   there   is   still   hard
fighting  to  be  done,  but  we  have  gone  a  long way
towards  beating  him  and  a  considerable  success
is within our reach.'
```

The report was upbeat and although the Crowes thought Toby may have been involved in the conflict, something about the optimism conveyed in the article seemed to allay any fears they had concerning his safety. It was not until two weeks later when accurate reports were released and filed that all Newfoundlanders knew the devastating truth:

```
ONLY  68  OUT  OF  801  ANSWER  ROLL  CALL  ON  DAY
2 OF SOMME
```

At 8.45 am on 1ˢᵗ July, eight hundred and one men
rose from their trenches and moved towards the
allied barbed wire cut in preparation of the
attack. The regiment had to walk across 800
metres of bullet-swept ground, with each man
carrying a 60 pound pack, a rifle, 120 rounds of
ammunition, two grenades, two sandbags, a
shrapnel helmet, a gas mask, rations, canteen,
ground sheet and field dressing. With no support
to distract enemy fire the men struggled to find
their way through small gaps in the barbed wire
while the German machine guns cut them down by
the hundreds. Only 68 men made it back to their
lines unwounded — a casualty rate of over 90
percent.

The decimation of the Newfoundland soldiers brought the
war home to every household in Newfoundland. And then,
mere days later, Toby's friend, Jonah Knowles came riding
over the hill to tell Rachel that Toby hadn't made it. Mr and
Mrs Hendersen had been sent a telegram. Rachel was almost
resigned to the fact by the time the news came. Despite their
unlikely future together, it saddened her immensely that he
died on foreign soil, fighting a war that she couldn't full
comprehend and wondered if he could either. 'You poor brave
fool,' she said under her breath as she stared out the window
and stanched her tears. The family traipsed over to Deception
to pay their respects to the Hendersens. Part way through the
visit, Mrs Hendersen said, 'We're going to have the funeral on
Sunday after the service. Will you sit with us, Rachel?' She
nodded her assent, the lump in her throat preventing her from
speaking.

They sang the hymn, 'The Old Rugged Cross.' By the end
of the service there was not a dry eye in the church. Rachel
pictured little wooden crosses, row upon row above newly dug
graves and thought how sad it was those men were buried all
the way over in Europe and not in Newfoundland, where they
were born and raised and where their loved ones could tend to
their graves.

After the service Nellie Simpson and Phyllis Mahoney
came up to offer their condolences to the Henderson's and
Rachel. Both girls were visibly upset. More upset than Rachel
could manage and she thought why couldn't Toby have
wanted to write to one of you. He deserved that. He deserved

a woman who would weep over him and mourn him as if he were irreplaceable.

They returned home to their raised garden beds that looked like long rows of graves themselves. They had taken to watering the plants by hand in the evening twilight. Newfoundland had shed all its tears on its men. There was nothing left for the soil. Everyone despaired. The dry weather did not bode well for a good potato crop or any vegetable for that matter. March was going to be a long month next year. They did not want to think about that and how they were going to survive.

After hearing about the tragedy of Beaumont Hamel Samuel wrote to Rachel expressing his sympathies. Yet it never ceased to amaze him that all over Canada; from the cities to the prairies, from the Rockies to the Yukon, men still continued to volunteer. Another two full Canadian divisions – 40,000 men – had just left for France.

Over the summer they got word that Matthew had been assigned Medical Officer (MO) to the 22nd Battalion. Everyone was anxious about the latest change to his circumstances, except Grandpa Dalton, who declared they all had to have faith that Matthew would be safely delivered. Samuel tried to take comfort in that, given his mishap at sea in 1914.

When Matthew became a Medical Officer he could have declined the posting but for many of his medical colleagues the front line had been the entire sum of their war experience. I have been fortunate, he thought, I should not shirk.

Before his changeover of duties he spent a few days at the Canadian III General Hospital catching up with several friends but largely to see a man who was not just a close friend but also his mentor, Lieutenant Colonel John McCrae, who just so happened to be in charge of the medical side of the McGill Hospital.

Matthew had worked under Jack, as he was known by his friends, when he was an intern at Victoria Hospital. Jack was a brilliant man, a wonderful teacher and surgeon and, like Matthew's Grandpa, had been a Medical Officer in the Boer

War, albeit much younger.

In this war he had been the Medical Officer to the 1st Brigade of Field Artillery and seen fighting in April 1915 in the second battle of Ypres. Matthew wanted to know first-hand how best to be of service as an MO.

Never give way to your fear, he told him. 'You are the greatest asset to your men and yourself. Put on a brave face and you will instantly feel better and so will the men around you. Go into the trenches regularly and hang out with your men – it makes them feel that you will be there when they need you. Nothing nerves a soldier more for conflict than the knowledge that everything is being done to take care of him in the event he is wounded. This is why we spend so much effort perfecting our medical operations in the war zone; it is such a great morale booster to the troops.'

Matthew thanked him and asked, 'Anything else?'

'Yes. Find something to laugh about with your men. Nothing breaks up the tension like laughter. The worst part of war is all the anxious waiting soldiers are forced to endure in anticipation of the next battle. Do what you can to distract them. Then in the midst of battle, remember the first thing: be brave and be there for your men. If you can be fearless under fire you set a fine example for your men and that is one of the most important ways of helping them. If you can do all that then your medical training will instinctively kick in and you will do your best by your men.'

Matthew wrote to Samuel and relayed everything the good Lieutenant Colonel had shared with him. Now that I'm here, I try and follow his advice. You too, little brother. Put on a brave face come what may, he'd penned.

25

In late August Rebecca was released from her duties at the saltworks and joined Rachel and a group of women on the barrens, berry picking in the dying days of summer. Mostly Rebecca enjoyed their company, their boil-ups and sing-a-longs. Although she never said, her favourite song was the *'There's a Long, Long Trail'*. She loved the line about nightingales. She wrote to Samuel asking him if he knew it.

As the seasons came and went Rebecca realised with increasing certainty and undiminished longing and a deepening sense of loss that only around Samuel had she felt truly alive. Each letter they received was like a sampler of Samuel, each one a highly prized treasure box. Reading his letters transported her back to the days when Samuel would tell her his stories, running his fingers through his golden hair, and she would listen to his mellow voice, and picture places and people in the most refined and exquisite detail, that she couldn't seem to imagine solely by herself. She feared her letters were so dreary and dull he'd eventually become bored and have no desire to ever come again.

Part of her wanted to turn up on Samuel's doorstep unannounced. Wouldn't that surprise him? When she finished at the saltworks, she deliberated over going up to the manager and asking him for her wages directly, in cash. What a stir that would cause – with the merchant and her father!

22nd August 1916
22nd Battalion

Dear family,
I have heard that this war is like no other. Now, I have seen it with my own eyes.

This is the worst. I honestly don't think it could get any more terrible than this: for there is absolutely no hope for these men whose bodies have been torn apart and randomly scattered near and wide. I wonder if they have hope in death even. When you see this carnage, you can't help but wonder if their souls survived or if indeed they were vanquished. How Dante would recognise this place. Some days, there is no aiding the wounded, it is a matter of collecting your dead – picking up body parts you have no idea to whom they belong. I wish some days to be amongst complete strangers, so I don't jerk with recognition and anguish at the faces of men I help pile onto stretchers. Faces of men I have only known for a short time, yet feels like a lifetime. One of them, a young bank clerk from Toronto, I'm sure served me in another life.

The letter stopped there. Matthew could not finish it. He re-read it once and threw it away. What was the point of writing about such unimaginable horror? How would his family react? And to all the other things he dared not commit to paper. For what Matthew could not write home about was that he lived and ate and slept in constant danger. How the trenches he walked, like the wards of a hospital, rocked with the constant concussion of cannons. How the ground would shake, and the din would echo and the whiz-bangs would terrorise, giving no warning or time to find cover before they exploded. How he had crouched behind two sandbags for protection and seen men of his regiment being blasted skywards, their bodies seemingly ripped apart at the seams, a top half cartwheeling thirty feet in the air, arms spread wide before it plummeted to earth with a thud. One life, twenty-two years in the making, dead in one second; blood and entrails flying in every bleeding direction.

Now he understood how it was for the acute insanity cases he'd seen in the early days of the war. The young men incredibly drawn who sat up staring into the distance with absolute terror written all over their faces, biting the ends of their fingers, covering their eyes and peeking through the gaps. He remembered how they would follow the flight of an imaginary shell as it gradually came towards them, looking into the distance and then overhead. All of a sudden they would get up on their knees and stare at the roof right above them and then bury their heads under the pillow or jump off the bed and dive under it, crying out in fear and panic.

No, he was not going to give voice to his fears nor to theirs. All his family really wanted to know was that he was alive. And that he was. So he took to sending them a short postcard whenever he was out on rotation.

Salutation

Having a short break here at Poperinghe / Boschepe / Saint Omer. Am exhausted but well. Thank you for your letter.
Love Matthew.

Once, for his parents, he added a postscript:

Sorry my updates are lacking in any type of news. What I have seen, I cannot write to you about.

The exhaustion part was the truth. His number one enemy – the rat – was back in huge numbers and unbelievable sizes – some as large as cats – fearlessly snapping at his boot when he tried to kick them away. They were relentless in their roaming of the dugouts and their prowling for rations. They chewed clothes, equipment, food, anything and everything even bandages and medicines. Matthew had to zealously guard them or ask a soldier to watch over them while he slept for an hour or two.

He'd seen them at night walking stealthily in murine swarms over the men as they tried to sleep, like an image out of the Black Plague. He couldn't comprehend how the men put up with it. He'd felt a rat's whiskers tickling his ears just once – that was enough. They sorely tried everyone's patience and Matthew was beginning to think that it was these hideous creatures and not the trauma and the terror of the battlefield that contributed most to the cases of insanity. Then there was the inescapable stench of open latrines and rotting bodies that a shovel of quick lime could ameliorate for an hour at best. He felt as if he were a prisoner of war himself. His only salvation was the sky, the birds that flew overhead, the occasional menacing zephyr, and the welcome stars at night.

And then he got some tragic news. Twenty-four year old

James Maplethorpe, his friend and housemate from Montreal, the same James Samuel had lived with in his early McGill days, was killed in action on 26th September, just fourteen miles north of where he was stationed. While Matthew was tending to his wounded, James took a shrapnel hit that tore away half his chest. For the first time since leaving Canada Matthew saw his whole life flash before him. The news was sobering and terrifying and he felt a part of him died with James' death. He'd had enough. It had been a year since he'd had more than a three-day break. He put in another request for a seven-day pass, ten days of leave, whatever they would allow. This time he was going to England at least, Scotland if possible, as far away as he could manage.

Samuel read the posting about James on the board at McGill University and the enormity of that news almost broke him apart. That could have been Matthew. He worried for Matthew and then for himself and what his brother-less life might be like. He berated himself for thinking such thoughts. He had never felt worried for Matthew till now. In their next letters to Matthew all the Daltons wrote about James, they all worried about how Matthew was taking his loss.

Samuel missed James; he missed his sharp mind and his thick mop of hair. He missed the men he had sailed with, now lost to the silence of the sea. He missed Rebecca. He missed the striking, hopeful young woman who reminded him of a parr, a young salmon, ready to leave the fresh waters of its home in favour of the salty sea. But some days he missed Matthew the most, particularly the gay, vibrant Matthew who seemed to be declining with each melancholic letter he sent home. Despite their four and a half year age difference they had always been close, always connected, and Samuel felt the longer Matthew was embroiled in the conflict on the Western Front, the harder, the more debilitating he found it. Every new posting seemed to reveal a deeper layer of misery and heartache and despair. And in some oblique fashion, Samuel's happiness, his emotions started to mirror those of his brother's.

26

The train trip to Cambridge took nearly two hours from St Pancras station, the cab ride to his lodgings ten minutes. Matthew was standing at the reception desk filling in the register and the date, 10th Oct. 1916, when a woman came up and asked if there were any messages for a Lenore Anderson. Before she said her name he recognised her as a Canadian, but then, in wonder he turned and said, 'Lenore? Lenore Anderson from Toronto?'

'Why, Matthew Dalton!' her face equally stunned, 'what a surprise' She hugged him. 'What are you doing here?'

'I'm on furlough. A short one.'

'I heard you were in France looking after our fallen.' She gave him a warm smile. 'I get them when you are finished with them – well, the ones who are in no state to return to the front.'

'Are you in medicine too?' he asked, the surprise evident in his voice.

'Yes,' she said, 'I'm a nurse with the Toronto hospital unit in Richmond.'

'Really? A bluebird. Are you here with company?'

'No, just by myself.' She glanced at the folded note in her hands just given to her by the concierge. 'A friend was hoping to make it.'

'Would you like to join me for dinner?'

'I'd love to.'

Half an hour later Matthew was waiting in the hotel restaurant when Lenore made her entrance. In the space of thirty minutes she had shaken off her drab grey overcoat and her damp hat and now stood before him like the relaxed and confident girl he once knew. However, gone was the Victorian-era school uniform: in its place a beautiful, long, emerald-green velvet dress that set off her clear green eyes, and draped around her elbows was a scarf the colour of peacock feathers. Her hair was glowing, part of it pinned at her crown with a rose gold clasp, the rest falling down past her shoulders in rich copper tresses. He remembered Lenore had been self-assured, spirited. Tonight she looked the part.

'What's the matter,' she said with a soft smile, 'haven't you seen a girl in a dress before?'

'It's been a very long time,' he said as he helped her into her chair, 'and that's a knock-out dress.'

'I figure we have something to celebrate.'

'What's that?'

'Meeting up after all these years. It must be– '

'Serendipity,' he said in unison with her. 'Not fate?' he continued. 'Or destiny?' he teased.

'Hmm, difficult to say at this point,' she countered. 'Certainly not design.'

'No, this one would have been a hard one to pull off. Mind you, you are a woman capable of engineering such a feat. And I would not have minded in the slightest had you orchestrated such a rendezvous.'

'Matthew,' she laughed. 'You always were a charmer. Shall we order?'

'Yes. Some champagne to begin with?'

They talked about the war and where they had served. They talked about the people they had worked with, trying to see if they had colleagues in common. They talked about England and what they had seen till finally Matthew said, 'Enough of the war, I want to know what happened to you. One minute you were studying law at McGill and the next you disappeared. What happened to you?'

She turned her deep-set gaze on him. 'You know I always used to admire your powers of investigation.'

'They're still there.'

She arched one eyebrow.

'I admit a bit dormant at times.'

'Really, I thought being a doctor and all you would have a constant call for them. Never mind, Matthew you had your hands full at the time. With a brunette if I remember correctly.'

'All right now, I'm sorry I didn't follow up on you. But you didn't follow up on me either. Please, do tell what happened.'

'My father died.'

'Oh Len, I'm sorry.'

'He had a heart attack. I managed to get home while he was still living but he died a day later. And then when we read his will and went through his estate, we found that his financial affairs were not so rosy. The doctor thought perhaps that may have contributed to his medical condition. Anyway, my days at McGill were over, I transferred to Toronto. But after six months even that was too much of a strain. We could only afford to have one of us at law school and of course that was Alistair. I didn't begrudge him that. He was in his fourth year and deserved to keep going. So he transferred to Osgoode Hall and finished his training there.'

'That's such a shame. You would have made a great lawyer with your perceptiveness and aptitude for persuasion. And one of the first female lawyers to boot!'

'Thanks, Matthew.' She smiled sincerely. 'That means a lot coming from you.'

Matthew tilted his head in acknowledgement. 'So, then what happened?'

'Oh well, I went to work as a clerk for a law firm in Dundas Street, thinking I could at least learn more about the profession that way then return to study when my brother finished his degree. But after a while that became a daily reminder of everything I had lost. At least that is what it felt like. So I left and signed on to be a nurse at St Michael's Hospital.' She raised her eyebrows, 'and the rest so they say is history. I saw your father from time to time. That's how I knew you had graduated and signed on.'

'Maybe after the war, you can go back to law school.'

'Maybe.'

Throughout the meal during small lulls in conversation, Matthew found himself looking at Lenore for longer and longer spells till finally, she said, 'Matthew, stop staring, what are you thinking?'

'I'm thinking not only have I had the good fortune to meet up with an old friend, but I also have the pleasure of sharing my table with the most beautiful woman in the room. If there were a band playing when you walked in, it would have lost its place.'

'That's very sweet of you Matthew. You haven't changed, have you? Are you going to do anything about it?'

'Yes, I'm going to take you dancing for a start. Are you up to it?'

'Too right.'

Later that night as they were walking quietly up the stairs Matthew said, 'You never told me, how long you are here for?'

'Till Monday afternoon. And you?'

'The same. Do you want to be my Cambridge tour guide?'

'Only if you promise to take me out for dinner again tomorrow night. No scooting off with the boys or girls for that matter.'

'I don't know any boys or girls here except you.'

'Just as well.' She left him with a barely-there kiss on the lips. Part of him been hoping for more.

The next morning they went to church in the historic Kings College chapel. As they listened to the heraldic voices of the all male choir the sun pierced the stained glassed windows lighting the inside in shades of crimson and amber and midnight blue. They felt they were caught in a rainbow. The light made Rubens' 'The Adoration of the Magi' almost come alive.

Afterwards, they strolled around Cambridge University, along The Backs, past the delightful River Cam, onto the weir at Jesus Green and the boathouses alongside Midsummer Common. They ambled under the beautiful vaulted archways made of ancient oak from the Sherwood forests. They sauntered across the stunning Bridge of Sighs built in salutation of its Venice namesake, over Mathematician Bridge and the graceful curve of the Clare. It was one of the most relaxing, entrancing days Matthew had spent in years.

'The world feels at peace here,' he said.

'It is calm, isn't it?' Lenore turned towards him. 'What brought you here? I thought the Moulin Rouge in Paris would have been more your scene?'

'I've already been there.'

Chuckling, Lenore shook her head. 'Why am I not surprised at that?'

'I don't know. I make no apologies for my life and the way I've lived it. I have seen more than enough death for one lifetime. I do what I can to keep sane, to know I'm still alive.'

'I don't mean to come across as judging you.'

'Don't you? You certainly enjoy giving me a hard time.'

'I'm sorry,' she gave him an apologetic smile. 'Satisfy my curiosity as to how you ended up here?'

'I needed a break.' His eyes were downcast as he strolled along. Then he halted and let out a ragged sigh. 'I wanted to put the sea between the war and me. Lately it has worn me down. I was feeling I had lost the young man I knew from my Montreal McGill days, so I came here to clear my head and to remember him, I don't know, maybe try and find him again. But perhaps that is too much to hope from one weekend.'

'Oh, I don't know. You found me and I'm part of your McGill days,' she teased. After a pause she added, 'I think your instincts were right in leading you here.'

'Maybe. You tell me something, because my instincts haven't quite worked this one out. You're what now, twenty-six, my age and here you are still single, not married to some high-flyer back home. I understand you're an independent young woman and all but I had you pegged as one who would make an advantageous match and go on to raise an elite band of academics so your influence could stretch far and wide.'

'Well you know that still could happen. I don't really want to die a spinster.'

'I don't think there's any chance of that. So why haven't you married? Don't tell me you've been lacking proposals.'

She laughed softly and shook her head. 'Maybe I haven't married for the same reason you haven't married.'

'Really?' He looked at her critically. 'Aside from the war making such things nigh on impossible, are you having too good a time living the high life, enjoying singledom and romances along the way? I know I don't know you as well as I once did, but something tells me that is not you.'

'No, but you can't tell me you're ready for the responsibilities of family life?'

'You're right about that, though one day I will need to be as I would like to have a family. With the right woman of course.' He glanced sideways at her. 'I look forward to the day when I can teach my own son to paddle a canoe like our father taught us. Teach him how to hunt and light a fire.'

'And if you had a girl?'

'I'd teach her too.'

'You would, wouldn't you? That is one of the things I always liked about you. Your belief in equality.'

'Liberté, égalité, fraternité.' After a while Matthew asked, 'Is there an answer to my question or are you still working on your rebuttal?'

'Is that what you want, Matthew, the declaration of every logical and justifiable reason why I'm not married, how beyond work and my mother, I refuse to be subordinated to anyone, or maybe the arguments as to why would women want to get married in the first place, what they forgo and is it worth the sacrifice?' She laughed shallowly and looked aside.

'So you have thought about this,' he said dryly.

Lenore held her tongue, not giving an inch.

'How about the truth, the plain and simple truth.'

'The truth?' Her laugh had a hint of nervousness about it. 'Well let's see, you're right, I have had proposals, some of them needed their heads read. I mean really! But, the truth is there has only been one man in my life that I have ever been interested in marrying. And a proposal from him has never been forthcoming.' She glanced at Matthew and pressed her unsteady lips together. 'It's not his fault really, he barely knows I exist.'

'What is this fellow, ascetic?'

'Ascetic? Aesthetic more like it. He is definitely not blind to the charms of women – nor them to him I might add. The problem is, as you know, I don't play that game.'

'Come now, Lenore, you're very vivacious.'

'I might be vivacious but I'm not flirty and really Matthew, in some matters I can be quite shy.'

'Well how is he ever going to find out? How long has this unrequited, undeclared love been going on?'

'Oh, you know, a while,' she said with a flutter of her hand. 'I have contemplated writing to him, but…after all this time, what would I say?'

'Hello? Remember me?' He stopped walking. 'So why have you waited all this time anyway? What happened to the confident girl who was a master at persuading?'

'Tell me Matthew, how would you feel, if you got a letter

out of nowhere from someone from your distant past?'

'Well it depends what was in the letter and how I felt about that person. Anything from, "oh dear" to being flattered, touched maybe, possibly even excited.'

'Yes, well.' Lenore halted. 'I waited all this time because I knew he could not give me what I wanted back then. I wasn't even ready for what I wanted back then. I don't even know if he can give me what I want now. He's just as likely to move onto another woman and break my heart.'

'What a scoundrel!' He gave her a cheeky grin.

'Oh, I don't think it was really in his nature to be hurtful. It's just the way he is, was, oh I don't know,' she said with another wave of her hand. 'But besides that, he had, has, a lot of fine qualities.'

'So, are you going to tell me this chap's name, or do I have to guess? It's someone I know isn't it, from school or university, that's why you haven't told me who he is? A bit wary that I might track him down and say something to him.'

'Oh I have no fear of that.'

'Well, hit me then.' Lenore was silent, struggling to hide her unease. Matthew thought she reminded him of a deer trapped by a band of hunters. Why wouldn't she raise her eyes to look at him? After interminable moments he knew. 'It's me,' he whispered, almost incredulously.

All Lenore could do was keep her head down and nod as the blood reddened her face and ears. He stepped up to her and embraced her, kissed her hair and with his lips at her temple, whispered, 'That was a brave thing you just did, Lenore. You deserve the Military Cross for that.'

'Too right! And for what?' She placed her hands over her face.

Matthew pulled them away but held on to them. 'Lenore. I'm flattered. Touched, excited even. I never knew you felt that way about me.'

'Well now you do, Matthew, but don't worry. I don't expect it to make any difference.' She was looking at his chest unable to raise her forest green eyes. 'I know this has always been a one-sided thing.' She pulled her hands away from his. 'I know you have never had feelings for me in that regard.' She turned away.

'That's not true.' He placed his hand on her forearm. 'You never gave me an ounce of encouragement. You were always friendly and chatty and good for a laugh and a yarn, but you always kept me at a distance. I figured that's how you wanted to keep it.'

'Matthew!' Her voice slightly raised, her eyes definitely raised. 'I had no interest in being part of your harem, another one of your sexual conquests. You seemed to go through girls as quickly as notepads when you were at university.'

'Just for the record, they weren't all sexual conquests.'

After a long pause she sighed and raised a palm in peace. 'It's your business.'

'Thank you,' he replied with a slight tilt of his head. 'So despite my sinful past and even though you haven't seen me for what – six years – you consider me a suitable candidate for a husband? I mean I could be a terrible husband, a selfish lousy lover, an irresponsible father, a reckless bastard. What gives?'

'Haven't I given enough?' Matthew waited. Swallowing, Lenore said, 'Granted, you could be all of those things, but somehow I don't think so, Mr Equality. And here's the one thing about you Matthew. You, more than practically anyone I know, know what I am capable of, my potential. You have always respected me and I know we would always be able to talk things through, be open-minded and that would be a great foundation for a relationship. And we would have someone to argue with in our old age,' she said, with a hiccupped laugh.

'What about love?'

'Ah,' she sighed. 'There is that.'

'Come on, I think we both need a drink.'

'Yes, and can we not talk about this anymore please – I know that is contrary to what I've just said, but I think enough has been said for one day.'

The next morning he woke Lenore at eight a.m. with a rap on her door.

'Who is it?'

'It's me,' said Matthew. He heard the rasp of the bolt and then she opened the door and stood in front of him in a cream dressing gown, her hair dishevelled.

'What's up?' she asked.

'Breakfast and punting, in fact, breakfast while we're punting. Get dressed. It's a beautiful morning and the kitchen is whipping us up a hamper.'

An hour later, munching on a bacon and egg roll in their own flat-bottomed punt, they glided along the Cam River past some of the sights they had marvelled at the day before, only this time, in the still early morning light, they saw enchanting mirrored reflections of bridge after picturesque bridge. 'This was a great idea. Thank you for dragging me out of bed even though it was my last sleep-in for God knows how long.'

'Yes, well, I thought that in the cold light of day, you might be lying there, moping, and mortified about what happened yesterday.'

'I thought we weren't going to talk about it anymore.'

'We're not,' he said with a grin.

The next afternoon they caught the train back to London and while saying their goodbyes and exchanging addresses, Lenore asked, 'Are you sure you want me to write to you, Matthew?'

'Of course, please stay in touch,' he said as they kissed each other on the cheek.

27

In October 2016 everywhere Samuel looked he saw the '**5 Questions to Men who have NOT enlisted**' flyers taunting him. The Medical School was like a ghost town. Half his year had taken abeyance and gone to work at overseas war hospitals joining most of the fourth year plus a large number of fifth year students who would return for their graduation in late spring. As the days wore on he kept asking himself was he in the right place? Should he be over there? Samuel was relieved he was mostly studying and working in Montreal's hospitals – he would notice the empty halls and posters less.

In November Rebecca happened to be alone early one evening trudging home through the snow. It was a clear dormant night, the sky blue black, the landscape blue white. In the northwest there was a glow, then arches and small waves and flowing curls and then all of a sudden rays of light shone straight down – violet and red at each end. They started to sway like soft ribbons rippling across the cosmos. The ribbons would disappear and then the bright lights would shine down again and go through the same kaleidoscopic effect, diffusing light all over the sky in greens and yellows and oranges and reds, almost a full spectrum of hues. She stared skywards entranced, wishing Samuel could be by her side to see the celestial wonder. And in that moment her longing for him was so immediate, so intense yet so impossible, she burst into tears.

When Matthew returned to the Front he was back in a quagmire. It had rained constantly in his absence, as if the Heavens were mourning the dead. He wondered what the Germans thought about that and if they believed Nietzsche and his 'God is dead' proclamation. The rains simply did not let up and the most appalling muddy conditions ensued. Walking out with his men, weary, sodden and submerged, he turned to a soldier and said, 'Hey Peter, weigh that coat of yours before it gets laundered. I want to know how much you are humping around on your back.' It weighed 80 pounds – nearly six stone – and then he had all of his gear on top of that. Matthew could only shake his head. He thought often of his mentor, John McCrae, and did his best to put on a brave face, for himself and the men around him. And he was brave. On the outside he was cool and suave like he always had been. Perhaps he joked a little less than he used to, but he was still well-nerved, even if other parts of his body were becoming strangers to him.

Finally some relief came with the frost and the ground froze to a depth of 18 inches, making it much easier to get about, but making shelling more fearsome and deadly. Shells detonated the moment they landed on the iron-hard ground, scattering fragments far and wide. Another Christmas and New Year came and went; his third since leaving Canada.

During that time he received many cards and letters but to his surprise none from Lenore. He noticed when one month had gone by and he hadn't heard from her. Then a second month came and went and while he held out hopes for a festive greeting he realised two things. One: she had gone out on a limb far enough. Two: any other woman he would have given up on way before then.

After their short Cambridge interlude, even though one heart may have spoken, there were no passionate goodbyes, no promises, no pledges. Matthew had got on his train and Lenore on hers, both wondering what, if anything, was to come of her admission. But over the days and weeks that followed, Matthew, for once in his life, could not get this one girl out of his mind. The French women in the street, the jovial Red Cross girls in their canteen, the international nurses casually relaxing on their days off, all only warranted a cursory glance from him. And Matthew asked himself, is the reason I can't get her out of my head because she is a lost opportunity from my misspent youth? Or is she a new challenge for me all of a sudden? A new, available, promising woman for me to have my wanton way with – as if she would let me! Or is this the key to the door that I, unknowingly, have been waiting for all these years? For in opening up to him as she had done, Lenore had clearly said she was interested but on her terms. He had to ask himself, was he interested on those terms? The terms that, although not foreign to him – he'd heard them enough over the years – were largely incomprehensible. They spelled s.e.t.t.l.e.d. They spelled the end of his carefree ways and his wandering heart. A long monogamous life with just one woman. How did that sit with him?

The unsettling truth was that Lenore Anderson was exactly the type of woman he could see himself married to one day. She was attractive, intelligent and with worldly sensibilities. She had an iron core and was high-spirited. He liked that about her. Was he going to forego this opportunity in the hope that it might come along again in a few years? Was that a fair thing to do to her? Put her off by thinking in the back of his mind that if she had waited six years, she would wait some more. All the while, he kept his options open in the event he might meet someone else who was all those things and more. And what if she were to meet someone else? In the past he would have said, 'Que sera, sera'. But, for the first time in his life he wasn't certain. For the first time in his life he had never thought about a woman so much. And he couldn't even call that farewell peck a kiss – dammit!

Clearly he had to make the first move. Clearly he had to cross that bridge and see where it took him. So in the end he sent her a two-line letter that simply read:

Happy New Year Lenore. Yes, I really do want you to write to me.

And then two days later, he followed it up with a much longer letter, a more open letter about how he felt being back in the war zone, how he filled his days, how he spent his evenings, how he could not stop thinking about her, how the thoughts and possibilities whirled around in his head and would not settle in any clear order, and how in the end he didn't want to think about them anymore, but yes he did want to talk to her, with her, to correspond.

It was a long missive; full of his mind's ramblings, quite out of character to the Matthew she first met many years ago.

In reply, he got a short letter back that read:

I'm glad we are talking. P.S. I can tell I have stirred up a hornet's nest. That pleases me immensely. More anon.

And then the letters flowed and the conversations poured and the minds met and his head really did spin, till he couldn't take it any longer. He wrote:

I've got four days leave at the end of this month. Want to go for another mini-break? Oxford? Bath? Stratford-upon-Avon? You name the place. I'll take care of the bookings.

They met at Paddington, embracing each other like old friends. But in the train carriage to Bath, his eyes kept circling her face and hers his, the air hummed with pent-up tension, their fingers itched with the wanting, the need to lay their hands on each other.

They signed the register for two rooms, Mr Matthew Dalton, Miss Lenore Anderson, and declined the offer of help with their bags. Matthew carried them up the stairs, nearly taking two at a time, following Lenore with the keys. He said, he didn't mind where he slept, she could choose. She walked into the first room, walked over to the window, glanced outside and said, 'This will do just fine,' and as she turned around he was right behind her, his luggage-free hands pulling her to him and kissing her, a commanding kiss, one that deepened and sweetened and took her breath away. Gasping, she broke off and then Matthew felt her place her own hands on his head and then she kissed him back with equal determination, opening her lips to his, the first hint of her surrender as she moaned deliciously in his mouth. His arms tightened around her as he pressed her body firmly into his own.

She broke off again and grinned at him, her smile as wide as the St Lawrence, looking deliriously happy, deliriously pleased.

'I can breathe easier too,' said Matthew, smiling and pulling her to him again and kissing her on the temple and the cheek then returning to her lips, while his hands roamed over her body, feeling her soft curves through her warm winter dress.

Finally they separated. 'Two rooms, Matthew. I didn't think you would go for that.'

'Well you have this idea that I've always respected you, Lenore. I thought it best not to disappoint you on that score. Besides, I'm prepared to take things slowly.'

'You call that kiss slow?'

'No I call it way overdue. I need to know what I am letting myself in for.'

'I hope you haven't been disappointed thus far,' she replied, arching an eyebrow.

'No I can't say I have, but I have been suffering from short-term memory loss, something to do with war trauma or denial. I'm not sure which.'

'Well we better work on that,' said Lenore planting kisses up his neck with every whispered word, caressing his jawbone, brushing his chin till she reached his lips, where she paused and nibbled them, first gently, then more firmly until Matthew took control. Breathless kisses, sensual stroking, undeniable desire. He was nearly bursting with restraint. Finally, he pushed her away. 'Come, we've got to get out of these rooms or it will be the end of me.'

This time after their farewells, as Matthew sat on the train to Folkestone, on the ferry to Calais, he felt uplifted and in a strange way relieved. It was a marvel that in the inferno that was his life, he had been given this opportunity to rediscover Lenore and to be reborn himself. Unbelievably, the thought of stepping off the plank and choosing a woman to be by his side, no longer utterly terrified him. It still terrified him, but not completely. Some of the fear had left him and in its place was…solace.

28

In March 1917, Rebecca finally got the answer to her most anguished question. Samuel was coming! That summer! Less than four months away! He had written telling them how moss was now being used for dressings in the war as it could absorb twenty times its weight in fluids. And that the best type of sphagnum moss to be found on their side of the world was in Newfoundland and Canada. McGill University was involved in sourcing supplies – could they send samples? In his letter he said the best time of the year to pick the moss was in spring, if it were summer he would come himself and then he had written:

Still, I'm hoping that I can manage a trip out to you this summer. I probably will only be able to stay for a month at most. I'll keep you posted.

When the ice had barely thawed on the peaty bogs, Rebecca waded into the dark chilly water and reached for the moss like she was reaching for her lifeline. She and Rachel dried it on the flake racks they used for drying the fish. Inside and outside she worked like she had never worked before. She barely had time for icebergs. With the spring melt her energy levels multiplied, gushing forth like a raun spawning. She worried about having to work over at Deception when Samuel came to visit. Her mother assured her they would work something out. Rebecca worked and lived with renewed hope and renewed vigour and renewed joy. And when she slept she allowed herself to dream.

29

In late March, another rendezvous for Matthew and Lenore, two more rooms, the same drill, the heat of heavenly kisses, the lust of temptation, till Matthew could no longer deny the pyre of his frustration, 'This is too much, don't you just want to do it. Let's do it. I swear this is not good for my health.'

'Oh Matthew,' said Lenore, gasping for breath, 'yes, yes I so want to do it. I'm tingling all over.'

He couldn't help himself, he groaned, the groan of a man brought to his knees. 'Yes, this is crazy. Come on then.'

'It is crazy but no.'

'What do you mean, no?'

'I mean no.'

He was incredulous. How could she kiss like that and moan like that and still hold out for him? She was some woman.

Lenore stood to put some distance between them and smooth her hair. 'Matthew, this is how you have always been, practically since the day I first met you. I know you have feelings for me. I have feelings for you. I know that now more than ever. But in the back of my mind is this little voice that says, Matthew Dalton is Matthew Dalton. I have no doubt you will love me and love me well but I'm sorry, please forgive me, there is still this little voice that says to me, careful, because chances are he will leave you. He will treat you just like he has treated all his other women.'

He stood and moved towards her. 'Lenore, listen to me before you get too wound up. One, people can change and two, believe me when I say, you have interested and engaged me on levels other women never have.'

'Hmm, engaged, now there's an interesting word.'

'Oh God help me,' he glanced away then steeled his eyes back to hers. After a lengthy pause he said, 'Okay, I give up, you win.' He gave her a faint smile. 'You just have to know what a huge step this is for me. I can't believe I am saying this, but here we go. Let's get engaged? What do you say?'

'Are you asking me to marry you, Matthew?' said Lenore, both eyebrows raised.

He looked at her and he knew his normally straight, nonchalant face was at that second betraying him. And Lenore could no longer keep a straight one. 'You should see yourself,' she laughed. 'Mm, mm, marriage. Darling, can you even say the word?'

'You are so testing my tolerance.' He came towards her wanting to unleash something – everything – pushing her along with his body till she backed up against the bed and fell on top of it. He leant over her, his hands either side of her shoulders, and stared into her teasing emerald eyes. He loved being with her; he loved playing with her. She made him feel so alive! Alive again! Only the lack of consummation in this relationship was nearly killing him. He'd left the war zone to enter a battlefield of wills like he'd never encountered before. A shadow of their interactions from yesteryear, except this was real and booby-trapped with temptation. She was achingly beautiful and he just wanted to see and touch all of her aching beauty. She inflamed him and the depth of his response to her amazed him. Every cell in his body was crying out, 'I've got to have you'. Followed by a whisper, 'You will make the war go away'. It was on his tongue, but he already knew her response. He exhaled deeply. 'You are not being fair. I have come a long way in six months.'

'Yes Matthew, you have indeed,' she said in husky solemnity. 'Now come a bit closer.' She pulled his head down to hers. Much later, Lenore sat up. 'You know, I have no interest in getting engaged.'

'You what?' He sat up himself, astonished. 'Is this a different tune to the one I heard six months ago?'

'No, my gorgeous doctor.' She laughed, covering his face with a barrage of kisses. 'Take it as a compliment. With other men, I might agree to an engagement, just as you might agree to an engagement. After all, engagements can be broken. Engagements can lead to a girl's downfall. It's marriage or nothing. It's that simple.'

'Christ woman! You call that simple.'

'Yes, no fanfare, no build-up.'

'I've been building up for months. Any minute I'm going to explode.'

She raised a single eyebrow, her lips quivering, trying not to laugh. 'Half an hour in a church, a registry office. What more do you want? A parade for acquaintances. And you wouldn't even have to buy me an engagement ring.'

'It takes a lot more than a wedding contract to bind two people together for life, Lenore, to ensure loyalty and fidelity. It takes a lifetime of honour and words and deeds to seal the deal, not a piece of paper.'

'I know that, Matthew. The question is do you think we are capable of that?'

He stood up and walked a few steps away from her, feeling he was at an absolute crossroad. He turned around. Her eyes were imploring. 'Matthew, I love you! I want to spend my life with you! There it is,' she said with a sweep of her hand, 'my innards laid bare on the table like some gaping war wound. The question is do you love me? Do you want to spend the rest of your life with me?'

'You see, it's at this point that relationships normally get too hard for me.' She looked at him in exasperation but before she could say another word, he held up his hands. 'I'm not saying that is the case here, but that is how things have generally been.'

He studied Lenore closely, weighing up his response. 'In answer to your questions…Do I love you? Yes I think the answer to that is yes. Do I want to spend the rest of my life with you? That I haven't figured out yet. Can I see myself with you in my thirties and forties say, with children, enjoying life together? Yes I can see that as a possibility and that is quite a pleasant thought. Would I like you by my side? I think the answer to that is yes. Am I ready to take that plunge right now? That, I'm not sure of. Do I want to make love to you right now? That I'm 100 percent sure of.'

'Just think, if we got married, one of us could apply for reassignment, so we could start living together as husband and wife. How sweet would that be? We could make love 100 percent of the time when we are off duty. You might think your whole life is ahead of you, but we are not getting any younger.'

He gave her a grave look as he ran his tongue across his teeth, then, relaxing, he said, 'All right, you old maid, grab your coat, let's see what this town has to offer. I don't want to spoil our time together immersed in turmoil.' After, as they were walking along the street, he took her gloved hand and kissed it. 'I'm sorry I'm being difficult. I don't mean to be. My life is not that easy right now. I'm doing my best.'

'I know.' She squeezed his arm and rested her head against his shoulder as they strolled along.

Mere days later Matthew was back in the trenches, in the wet icy cold, in the gluggy mud, in the oppressive nervous tension that enveloped every Canadian waiting for the attack on Vimy Ridge to begin. Lenore had become his oxygen mask, the promise of clean fresh Canadian air. He lived for her letters. He lived for the days when he would see her again.

Throughout the battle he would work in stretches of 36 hours, 44 hours, 52 hours without relief and then when he could, he would sleep, utterly exhausted, and when he awoke, he would think about her, wanting to wake up next to her, to reach across and make love to her in the early morning light.

And then a letter came that changed everything.

Darling Matthew

My mother has been diagnosed with an inoperable tumour. I have resigned my position and will leave in three weeks to go and care for her. I don't know if I will see you before I go. Naturally I would love to. More than ever I want this war to be over. Be well, my love. Stay safe. Enclosed herewith my mother's address in Toronto.

Yours, Lenore. xo.

In the Richmond hospital, on her last day at work, he found her. She was so surprised, so overcome, that she immediately burst into tears. He pulled her outside into the stairwell to calm her down, to hug her, to wipe her tears, to kiss her puffy eyes and her trembling lips.

'Oh Matthew,' she said, 'Thank you, thank you. You have

no idea what this means to me. What a relief it is to see you.'

She held his face and plastered kisses all over his lips and face. 'Was it hard to get away?'

'It was, shall we say, a bit irregular. I had to bring out the big guns.'

'In what way?'

'In this way.' He kissed her in fierce determination, crushing her to him with his arms and his body, until they broke off, the two of them breathless, but far from gratified. 'Nothing was going to stop me.'

'Tell me!' she implored, pulling hard on his collar.

'I showed them your letter and explained that as my fiancé's mother was dying, we wanted to go back to Canada, get married and have her blessing tout de suite.'

She looked at him in disbelief, her eyes flickering. 'Please don't kid with me at a time like this. Are you serious?'

'Well yes and no.' He paused. 'I'm not going to go back to Canada to get married.'

'Oh Matthew! Please! I– '

'Lenore, we are doing this my way from here on in. Do you want to know how long they have given me off?'

'How long?'

'Four months.'

'Four months!'

'Yes, and I am not going to waste a single day of them. We are getting married tomorrow or the next day,' he whispered, 'your choice. But there's no way you, my blushing bride, will be a virgin on your wedding day. I intend to make you blush. Come on! Let's get the hell out of here.'

The Garden of Eden

30

In a small, scattered fishing community on an outlying island off the north eastern coast of Newfoundland, in the middle of a mild summer, Samuel found her, almost as he had left her: in tears, in her mother's kitchen.

He had arrived on the four o'clock boat from Seldom Come By and gone looking for her amidst the harried women working outside on the production line at the saltworks. They all had their eyes downcast, their nimble fingers working the cod, splitting, de-heading, salting. He couldn't see her anywhere. Eventually he asked someone if they knew where Rebecca Crowe was.

'Her father was here a little while ago,' said the woman. 'She went home in the boat with him. We let her off early.'

He turned and started walking. As he approached the cooperage he caught sight of Ronnie Evans. He hadn't aged one iota in three years. 'Samuel, my lad!' Ronnie gave him a hearty handshake and a friendly hug. 'What a surprise! I heard you were hoping to visit this summer and then I heard you had to put everything on hold, something to do with your brother coming back from the war.' Ronnie kept his hand on his shoulder as he looked at Samuel, then he squeezed his shoulder and said, 'It is so good to see you again, Samuel. Fresh off the boat and all. Did you see Rebecca?'

'No, she shot through with her father.'

'Oh well, never mind. Can I offer you a drink?'

Samuel hesitated. 'How about I come by tomorrow sometime and we catch-up then.'

'That will be splendid. In the meantime let me organise you a horse so you don't have to hump that bag all the way across the barrens. You might even beat them home.'

Not long after, Samuel stood outside the Crowe's house

listening to the sounds of movement inside the kitchen. The back door was wide open. He knocked nonetheless and waited patiently. Morna came to the entrance wiping her hands on her apron. She blinked in surprise then put her hand across her heart.

'Hello, Mrs Crowe,' his facing breaking into a broad grin.

'Samuel Dalton.' She hugged him as he bent and kissed her on both cheeks. 'My, oh my. My girls will be over the moon! They were so disappointed when you wrote and said you didn't know if you could make it. Have you seen them already?'

Still smiling, he shook his head.

'Well they'll be here any minute. They might even be down in the cove already. Do you want to go and see or do you want to come inside?'

He looked towards the path that led towards the cleft in the rocks then back to Morna. He did want to see Rebecca but…he shrugged. 'I'm here now.'

'Well come in. Let me fix you something. It will be the only chance we get to have any time alone for the next few weeks, I guarantee it.'

They were sitting at the kitchen table, drinking tea, and eating lassy bread when Rebecca walked through the door. He heard her gasp before he saw her. 'It's you!' she cried as she launched herself at Samuel. There was no time for him to stand. She hugged him and cried and laughed and stood up and clapped her hands together and said his name over and over, 'Samuel, Samuel, Samuel,' and hugged him some more as she wiped tears from her cheeks. All he could do was laugh and hug her back and squeeze her tightly whenever she squeezed him tightly. She was like a ten-year old child with no inhibitions: open and innocent. And he was like a ten-year old child soaking it all up.

'What are you doing here?' she finally managed to say, her face exultant.

'I'm on special orders to make an important delivery.'

'What sort of delivery?'

Her delight was infectious. 'Maple syrup for one Rebecca Crowe for her eighteenth birthday!' he announced with joy.

'I can't believe you've come back at last.' She hugged him

again. This time he was ready and standing. He clasped her to his chest and held her as tightly as he dared, breathing in the smell of her, his fingers entwined in her long blonde hair.

'He missed you at Deception,' said Mrs Crowe, pouring Rebecca a cup of tea. 'You had just left apparently. What are your father and Rachel doing?'

'Checking lobster pots. They won't be long. They sent me up so I could have a bath. Sorry Samuel, I probably stink of fish guts.' Rebecca glanced down at her smeared front. 'We thought you would send us a telegram to let us know if you were coming.'

'I decided this way is much more fun.' He couldn't drag his eyes away from her excited eyes and her ecstatic face.

'How is your brother? And how have you managed to get away? I thought you would be spending the summer with him.'

'Listen to you. Nothing has changed. My brother is very well, thank you for asking. In fact he couldn't be better. He's happily married –'

'Married!' Morna and Rebecca exclaimed in unison. They looked at each other; their eyes wide then back to Samuel.

'We didn't even know he was engaged,' said Morna.

'Neither did we,' said Samuel, laughing. 'In fact they never got engaged.'

'This I have to hear,' said Rebecca, her hand raised to halt Samuel. 'And Rachel will want to hear it as well. Save it till she gets here. I'm going to race off and have a wash.'

Around the table that night four pairs of ears and eyes were turned to Samuel as he recounted the extraordinary tale of how Matthew had arrived home married.

'Were you surprised?' asked Rebecca.

'You can say that again. In the telegram he sent my parents he said he was coming home to recover and remember his old life. We were holding our breaths fearing he hadn't told us everything. '

'Clearly he hadn't,' said Morna, clearly amused.

Samuel, equally amused, said. 'It's much more than that. You don't know my brother, but…well, he doesn't strike you as the marrying kind that's all.'

'Is he quite solitary?' asked Rachel.

'No, I wouldn't say that,' said Samuel, choosing his words carefully. 'No, we probably thought he would get married one day, but when he was a lot older.'

'At twenty-six he's old enough,' said Silas brusquely.

'Yes he is,' agreed Samuel.

'And do your parents like his wife, what's her name, Lenore?' asked Morna.

'Yes. They were surprised for a second but then they were rapt. They couldn't be happier with his choice. They have known her for years.'

'I thought you said he met her nine months ago in England,' Rebecca noted.

'He did. He met up with her again. But he first met her at high school when they debated against each other. The two of them were very good. The first thing our Grandpa said when he met the newlyweds, was: "This is going to be fun. I want to see this." He was thrilled.'

'And so they had their honeymoon sailing across the Atlantic?' mused Rebecca.

'I think they were recovering from exhaustion mainly. No, they are having their honeymoon now. Two weeks on Prince Edward Island –'

'Prince Edward Island!' shrieked Rebecca and Rachel.

Samuel looked at them, perplexed.

'Anne of Green Gables,' said Rebecca, by way of explanation.

'I would like to honeymoon…holiday there.' Rachel blushed in embarrassment.

'Would you now?'

Rachel smiled demurely in reply. Samuel continued. 'Yes, they are spending two weeks at Prince Edward Island for Lenore – so maybe Rachel, you are not alone with your sentiments – and two weeks at a lodge in Parry Sound, Matthew's choice. And as they are not going to be at home and as they obviously didn't want any company, I was free to come away here for a month,' said Samuel with unrestrained delight.

'It has worked out swimmingly, hasn't it?' said Rebecca. 'Will Matthew be going back to the Front?'

Samuel nodded. 'He sails on the 1st of September from Québec City.'

Next, Rachel asked if they had had a ceremony in Toronto for their family and friends. And when Samuel told her they'd had a lunch with just the immediate families at the Queens Hotel, all Rachel wanted to know was what Lenore wore.

'A dress,' said Samuel, thinking what else? All the women practically glared at him. He broke into cheerful laughter as he tried to scramble together some details. 'Um, if I remember correctly, a full-length dress with short sleeves. It was a russet colour. It really suited her.'

'She got married in red!' exclaimed Silas.

'No, she wore red to a celebration that we had. I don't know what colour she got married in. What's wrong with red anyway?'

'Married in red, you will wish yourself dead,' said Silas. 'It's her life,' he frowned in concern and shook his head as if it were a lost cause.

In the brief lull Rebecca said, 'I don't want to go to work tomorrow.'

I don't want you to go to work tomorrow, echoed Samuel in his head.

'I know,' said Morna, 'but go, tell them you have a friend visiting and ask if we can take it in turns working. One of us will be there every day. They won't mind. I'll go Saturday so you can have your birthday off.'

'Thank you, Mother. Rachel, are you okay with that?'

'I guess.'

'Of course she's alright with it,' said Morna. 'And if you work hard when you're at home you should be able to grab a few hours here and there to go riding or berry picking or what have you.'

Rebecca leant across the table and squeezed her mother's hand before turning to Samuel with a relieved smile.

The next morning he doubled Rebecca over to Deception to return the horse Ronnie had lent him. After three years of separation Samuel didn't want to surrender her so quickly. He wanted her eyes on his face and never wanted them to leave, he wanted to touch her, deliberately and in small ways, he wanted her arms around him, and when they cantered they were.

Samuel spent the morning with Ronnie. In the afternoon he helped Rachel put away a boatload of fish. The season before Silas had returned from the lumber camps so flush he had finally bought a powerboat and gone back to working by himself as an inshore fisherman over the summer. As a result one of the Crowe women was always busy on the stage salting and drying fishing.

As they worked Samuel and Rachel talked about her sister, Esther, and their family trip to Bonavista two years earlier. They talked about his sister, Analeise, and her daughter, Catherine, born in April. And then when they talked about Matthew Rachel asked, 'Has your brother's wedding put you in the marrying frame of mind, Samuel?'

'All good things come to those that wait.'

'What is it that you're waiting for?'

'Rachel, have you been taking lessons from Rebecca?' he asked with a half-smile.

'Well one thing's for sure, we're glad it wasn't you who married your Toronto sweetheart. For one it would make it harder for you to visit us.'

'I'm glad I'm not married either,' he agreed.

'Do you have a Toronto sweetheart or a Montreal one?'

'No,' he said shaking his head with an easy laugh. 'Do you have one in Deception or Bonavista Bay perhaps?'

She shook her head. Then softly she said, 'You know Toby was never my sweetheart.'

'I know,' he spoke quietly his eyes meeting hers.

She held his gaze and with a slight slant of her head and a wistful sigh said, 'I think it's my destiny to marry someone not from here.'

Samuel deliberated over his reply. He wanted to encourage her without encouraging her. 'I think it would be good for you to venture further afield. As they say plenty of fish in the sea, but here it's a small pond.'

She held his eyes for a few moments more. 'Why did you come here, Samuel?'

'Isn't it obvious?' he teased. 'I came so we could have maple syrup for breakfast tomorrow morning!' She threw some salt at his hand. She didn't buy that. He didn't think she would. After a pause he said, 'I came because I wanted to see you all again. I wanted you to know that the summer I spent here was one of the most important in my life. I wanted you to know that I had not forgotten your family and all you had done for me.'

'You certainly have shown us over the years that you value our friendship and what we did for you back in 1914. We feel very close to you.'

'Same here.'

'Is that all?'

'Should there be more?' he asked looking at her.

There was more, so much more. As each mile on his voyage brought him closer and closer to Deception, Samuel could feel his excitement building. It was bursting through his veins like the boat's bow ploughing through the water. Who was it that he was really coming here to see? He knew the answer to that right enough. And for what? So he could go away and spend another two or three years thinking about her, dreaming about her. So he could know for sure that what he felt for this girl was real. To know for certain that she still held his heart captive with her longing and her melancholy, with her beauty and her joyful, youthful delight. He knew it would only take a moment, a breathless fatal moment, and yesterday it had. In three years he had not been able to get this girl out of his head and now he was overjoyed that he had failed.

He knew he wanted to be with her. On one level he always had; he had just never connected the dots. But his brother's marriage had made him think of marriage as a possibility in a way he had never done before. No, not his brother's marriage; his brother's complete and utterly delirious endorsement of his changed circumstances, which Samuel had found highly amusing at first, saying, 'Are you sure you didn't pick up trench fever over there? I heard that's going around. You seem to have got it real bad.'

And Matthew, true to his affable good nature, had said, 'Go ahead, I am quite prepared to be the brunt of all your jokes. But I will pass on this one piece of marital advice to my worthy brother, the only surviving Dalton bachelor. You don't have to marry, Samuel, hell, take your time, like I did, take longer if you want, but you do have to listen to your heart and know that the one in front of you is the one. And if you do know that then what's the point in denying the inevitable? It is a beautiful moment to get to that point of knowing and understanding about yourself and another person. That is to be celebrated and sanctified.'

And here he was in Newfoundland, dodging questions on the topic with one woman, thinking how he might raise them with another. Lost in his thoughts, Rachel came at him from a different tack.

'Samuel, please do tell me, because I am curious about how it is a fine looking man like yourself, from a good family has not met one fine young woman in all of Canada to call his own?'

'Well I haven't met all the fine young women in Canada, have I?' he replied.

31

Early Saturday morning as the sun was still climbing out of its bed Rebecca woke Samuel with a light touch on his shoulder, gently calling him out of his slumber. 'Samuel,' she whispered, 'do you want to come swimming with me?'

'Yes, little naiad,' he mumbled, 'I would love to go swimming with you. 'Tis your birthday after all.'

A half orange circle sat on the horizon as they made their way down the stony steps to the Crowe's stage. The sky was mostly grey a few shades lighter than the sleepy ocean. Off in the distance rays of pinks and ambers were just starting to light up the dawn.

Rebecca had been carrying her towel around her shoulders and dropped it on the stage. She was wearing a dark purple costume made of heavy cotton. The pants came three quarters of the way down her legs with a ruffle around the bottom. The top was a pull over design with a slit at the back with a single button making it easy to pull on and off. It was drawn in around the hips and had a small ruffle below matching the ones on the three quarter length sleeves.

'Where did you get your outfit from?' asked Samuel.

'I made it,' said Rebecca. 'Do women wear costumes like this back in Toronto?'

'Something similar,' he muttered.

'What are you going to swim in?'

'The latest sensation from Europe,' he said flashing his unmistakeable smile. He started unbuttoning his trousers.

'What's that?' she asked, smiling back, half-intrigued, half-wary.

'Shorts.' He explained that button front shorts had become standard issue for the soldiers in the war and their introduction had been met with resounding popularity. 'It's the latest in underwear, don't you know?'

'Oh…' To hide her flushing face Rebecca walked away.

As expected the water was bone achingly cold, stealing her breath away. This birthday ritual almost seemed like some bizarre form of torture. She wondered at what age she would stop doing it. But she loved the satisfaction she got from doing it and the sense of assurance she got from renewing this strange covenant. They swam to the little buoy about sixty yards from the stage, held onto it while they caught their breath then swam back. Rebecca got out first, grabbed her towel and wrapped it around her shoulders. She reached for the second towel to hand to Samuel. 'How was that?'

'Invigorating.'

She laughed. 'Are you awake yet?'

'Oh, I'm awake.' His goose bumps testified to the fact. She watched him walk across the stage to the barrel of water they used for their mug-ups and ladle some out into a bucket. He turned and called her over. She went to him and let him pour water over her head. She did the same for him. And then came her favourite part: the little routine that Samuel did as he dried himself. All the memories of three years past came flooding back. She watched him slick his hair back squeezing the water at the nape of his neck. Next, he ran his hands over his shoulders, down his arms, his chest and his legs, palming the water away. Her eyes followed his every movement. Despite the cold he never seemed to be in a hurry to dry himself, rubbing his hair and shaking it like a shaggy dog, before wrapping the towel around his waist.

Rebecca stood there, like an Indian squaw with a blanket across her shoulders, gazing at her brave, admiring his beautiful form, larger, more developed than she remembered; every fibre of his being proclaiming 'I am a man.' His shoulders broad; the muscles pronounced from months of rowing regattas; his body brown, tanned from helping his mother in their summer garden; his chest smooth and flexed with the faintest sprinklings of hair across the sternum; his nipples raised, the colour of milk chocolate.

Her fingers twitched with wanting to touch him, with the urge to lay her hands on his arms and squeeze his flesh and know he was solid and real and responsive. She wanted him to reach out and hold her and kiss her like he had that day when they rowed out to the iceberg. Was she game to search his molten eyes to see if he felt the same way? She shivered, trying to shake off the want. She could feel a pull deep inside almost like a chant calling out to her, calling out his name. On this calm morning a struggle raged inside Rebecca like she had never known before.

She became aware of Samuel looking at her intently. 'What are you thinking, Rebecca?' He took a step closer to her. Just at that moment they heard footsteps. They stepped back and turned around to see her father coming down the stony stairwell.

'You two are up early,' said Silas. 'Did you go swimming as well, Samuel?'

'Yes,' he replied. 'Do you want a hand, Mr Crowe?'

'If you're offering, I won't say no.'

Rebecca was almost relieved she never had to give Samuel an answer and they never had another moment to themselves that day or the next. Two days after her birthday, she finally got to have Samuel all to herself as they worked the stage together. Rebecca thought it was the happiest day of her life. Her grin was a permanent resplendent feature on her face. Samuel too was happy with the day, ceaselessly flashing his sensational smile. He was such a sight, more handsome than ever, his sun-streaked hair still long on top but short at the back. She was feeling light-headed as if she were suffering sun-stroke, suffering Samuel-stroke. She wanted to hug him again like the day he arrived. She longed to kiss him. Her youthful longing of a summer past had been replaced with a tangible ache.

He asked if she wanted to row over to Anchor Brook later to catch some salmon.

'Yes! Let's!' Her eyes wide with excitement. She hadn't had any fresh salmon all year, but that was hardly the point. 'I'll talk to Mother. See if she can manage this afternoon by herself. Maybe we could get father to drop us off in his boat. It will be much quicker than rowing.'

'But where would the fun be in that?' Samuel asked. 'Besides, if I remember correctly last time you were constantly worried about the fish being frightened away. Wouldn't the motorboat frighten them more?'

'You're right. Let's row.' She traded grins again.

A little while later, her eyes downcast as she salted, she said, 'Samuel, do you remember that one hundred dollars you left us for safe keeping? We haven't spent any of it. It's yours to take back now.'

His hand on her arm made her stop and look at him. 'I had completely forgotten about it till now. Keep it. Better still, spend the money on a holiday to Canada. Sail to Québec and I will show you around then we can go onto Montreal and Toronto. We can even go to see Niagara Falls. That's an exciting place to visit. I would love for you to meet my parents and grandparents and they would love to meet you too after all these years.'

She told him she'd come tomorrow if she could, but with a hint of exasperation, said, 'How do you think we could ever manage that?'

'We just need to choose a quiet time of year for you to get away. Winter's the quietest but it doesn't really work for me with my studies and all. Maybe next May or August, after the fishing season. Think about it.'

'The only thing to think about Samuel is how to convince our parents to let us go. I don't have any money to pay for anything. Only the hundred dollars we just talked about. We don't deal in cash around here. We just keep an account at the Merchant.'

'Don't worry about money. I'll pay.'

'Then you should take the money back for that purpose as Rachel and I will have a hard time explaining it.'

He agreed at last. 'I wonder if you can catch a boat from St Anthony's that goes round the northern tip of Newfoundland and through the Strait of Bell Isle. That would be an interesting way to come. The year I got shipwrecked we were going to go home through the Strait of Bell Isle. We figured the ice would have fully melted by then.' After a pause he said, 'Do you know the story of the Ile de la Demoiselle? Of the French girl and her lover?'

'Yes,' she said. 'Ronnie told me about poor Marguerite. Hard to believe a man could do such a thing to his own niece, abandon her on an island like that.'

'I'll say. But I think the greater tragedy was her nurse, her lover and her newborn baby all dying on her. To have lost everyone, knowing you are completely alone with no means of sailing away,' Samuel shuddered almost. 'I don't know if I could cope with such loneliness.'

'It doesn't bear thinking about,' whispered Rebecca. Moments later she murmured, 'I always wanted to know what happened to her.'

'Some French fisherman found her and took her back to France.'

'I know, but did she ever meet someone else? Marry?'

'I suspect a woman like her would have had another suitor. I, for one, would have found her interesting,' Samuel gave Rebecca a reassuring smile.

After a long pause, one in which she felt the longer she left it the harder it would be to say anything, Rebecca eventually said, 'Samuel?' then she coughed and cleared her throat and tried to find her bravest voice. She was unable to look at him but she continued just the same. 'Tell me, have you had many paramours?'

'Now Rebecca, gentlemen do not kiss and tell.' He threw her a very assured grin.

'Why not? You tell everything else,' she said trying to make light of the situation, but wanting an answer.

'Ho, ho, ho. Tell me this then. Have you got any better at kissing in the time I've been gone?'

In less than a heartbeat he had totally managed to unravel her. 'What sort of question is that?' she stammered. She was flustered like nothing else. Her insides were trembling. She wildly cast her mind around, attempting to come up with an answer, any answer. 'You know Samuel, I'm told practice makes perfect.'

'Is that so?'

Rebecca didn't reply, she just turned and looked at him and tried to be brave. They gazed at each other and she watched as he lowered his eyes to her mouth.

'Hard to perfect something that was perfect to begin with.'

In that moment, with those few words, he took her breath away. Her insides melted, trickling warmth throughout her body. She peered into his eyes and saw it all: the wanting, the longing, the need for each other, more intense than ever – a life force that flowed between them, their shared destiny, their shared salvation. She held his gaze, but she couldn't move, couldn't breathe, couldn't utter the smallest response. Only her trembling lips belied her emotion.

'Come here, you ice mermaid,' said Samuel, drawing her into his open arms, lowering his head and kissing her. A long, sweet, homecoming kiss, loaded with remembrance and a promise of things to come.

'My God, I've missed you, Rebecca. I've missed everything about you,' he whispered when he at last broke off. 'Now that I'm here with you again, I wonder how I've gone so long without you.'

'Samuel, I've missed you so much. I nearly gave up hope that you would ever come back.' Her eyes poured into his.

'Never give up hope, Rebecca. Sometimes it's all we've got.'

They kissed again, a long never-ending kiss full of relief and release and hunger and the faint taste of blueberries, parting their lips to touch each other with the tips of their tongues. Rebecca broke off. Leaning her head into Samuel's chest she shyly said, 'I could go on kissing you all day, Samuel.'

'I could go on kissing you all day and all night Rebecca. *We must sleep a never-ending night. Give me a thousand kisses, then another hundred'.*

'Oh, yes,' she whispered, 'but I'm frightened any minute mother will walk down the steps and discover us or father will turn up and we won't have finished putting this load away and I'll be in trouble.'

'Later then.' He kissed her on the temple then released her.

Around two o'clock they set off in the Nightingale tender. When they were underway Rebecca said, 'You know, this is the third time I've been alone with you in this boat.'

'Is it now? Do you like being alone with me in this boat?'

'Yes,' she said with a satisfied smile. 'I'm liking it more and more. Do you know when the first time was?'

'When we went out to the iceberg together?'

'I'm so pleased you remember our iceberg trip.' She looked at Samuel, her heart overflowing with tenderness.

'I have remembered that trip every day since. I have replayed the whole episode a thousand times over in my head.'

'You have!' She was nearly beside herself with joy. 'Me too. And I knew you hadn't forgotten it. I got the veiled references to it in your letters.'

'How I wish I could have written to you in private.'

'How I wished you could have written to me in private! I thought about writing to you but then I didn't know if I could manage posting letters to you without someone finding out and how were you going to send a letter addressed only to me that no one else could read. How would that look?'

'That's why I never wrote to you. But going forward we need to work out how we can.' His eyes were warm. They were like the sun orbiting her face.

'So the iceberg trip was our first?'

'No!' Rebecca laughed. 'The first was the day I found you. I rowed out in our tender and you had collapsed in this boat and I didn't have a hope of moving you, so I climbed into this boat and rowed you home, tying ours to the thwart.'

'Now how does that count! I wasn't even conscious. I had my eyes closed and all. How could I possibly remember that?'

'Yes and I had my eyes closed when we went out to the iceberg Remember? You tied your shirt across my eyes so I wouldn't peek.'

'And did you peek?'

'No,' said Rebecca. 'No peeking. Come to think of it,' she gushed, 'you weren't wearing a shirt the first time I met you either.'

'Wasn't I?'

'No, it was scrunched up in your hand. You'd been waving it about.'

'So did you enjoy staring at my naked chest?' His eyes were twinkling.

'I was in too much of a hurry and too worried to enjoy it.' Today she was in no hurry to drag her eyes away from the sight of his muscled forearms. They were bronze and smooth with the faintest showing of hair. Her breath caught in her throat.

'You see, that's why you need to take advantage of opportunities when they come your way. You never know when they may come again.'

Rebecca looked into his face.

'I try and make the most of life's opportunities, Samuel. I wish I had more.' She exhaled deeply.

'I know. What are we going to do about that?' Their eyes scanned each other's faces then hers rested on Samuel's lips like they had so often three summers ago, then their eyes held onto each other, drawing each other in, drawing each other out. Almost imperceptibly Samuel released the oars, placed his hands around her face, leant forward and kissed her. And kissed her and kissed her.

A whimpering moan escaped her mouth. Oh what comfort, oh what need. She felt herself melting again. Could she dissolve in Samuel's arms? They were breathing hard. Finally they pulled themselves apart. Samuel pressed his fingers to her lips and sat back on the seat.

After a while he said, 'Let's talk about opportunities.' He stopped rowing and looked aside as he ran his right hand through his hair, then he turned to look at her once more. 'I'm this person who's come into your life and to you and most people locally I imagine I'm somewhat different. But in my world, the people I mix with, at university in Montreal, and my Toronto family and friends, I'm not that unusual. I'm just a regular guy.'

'I don't think so.'

'I love your faith.' He touched her nose and ran his fingers down to her lips and let them linger there, but his eyes were full of concern. 'Now don't take offence at this. I know that you are not the type of person to ever take advantage of someone. I know how I feel about you and I think I know how you feel about me, but do you know why you feel that way about me and could you possibly feel that way about someone else like me.' He paused. 'What is it that draws you to me? Is it me? Is it what I represent? My background? My future? Is it because I could be your ticket out of here? You see, in your innocence and naivety of the wider world, I could be the one taking advantage of you and I don't want to be in that position. It's possible you could come back to Canada and make a life with me and find out you'd prefer to be with my pal Joel or my friend Alex.'

'Samuel Dalton, are you doubting me, doubting yourself? You, the most handsome of men. Riding the waves on a great white stallion you came to me, you the rider they call Faithful and True. You are my one true love.'

'Am I?' said Samuel huskily.

Rebecca could only nod and gaze into Samuel's earnest eyes. Any moment she felt she might cry. Untempered emotions were pressing against the walls of her heart.

Samuel reached out and stroked her face. 'But you can only speak from the position that you know about. There's a whole realm out there, another world that you don't know anything about yet.'

When she thought of the wider world Rebecca mostly thought of Samuel. That was what mattered most to her. 'Perhaps there are possibilities that I can't see or don't know about. But I know I want to be with you and maybe it's some of the things you have mentioned but they are not the essence. I feel I belong with you. I know I do.' Her eyes searched Samuel's face for confirmation.

'I was meant to find you. I feel our destiny is to be together. I may not know much but I know that much. I think you know it too. What I understand the least, aside from divine intervention or even with it, is why it is this way and also, given who you are, with your background and your future as you say, what exactly do you see in me?'

'You don't know that?' He shook his head and smiled at her as if in a daze. 'Incroyable!'

'Tell me,' she whispered.

'Not even in here?' he asked as he placed his hand across her heart.

She placed her hand on his hand and moved it to his heart. 'Samuel, I want to know. I want to hear what's in your heart. From your lips.' She ran her fingers across them allowing him to kiss their tips. 'Spoken from your lips,' she smiled.

'Alright.'

She waited. 'So tell me.'

'I will.'

'Tell me now.' She smiled eagerly. Samuel smiled eagerly but he wasn't forthcoming.

'I'll tell you later.'

'Samuel!'

'When have I ever denied you?' he asked playfully.

'Right now!'

'I'll tell you before the sun goes down. How's that?'

'Promise?'

'I promise. Come here.' She leant towards him. He leant towards her. Placing his hands on her shoulders he said, 'I'll even seal it with a kiss.'

For three hours while they fished, Samuel couldn't keep his eyes off Rebecca. She was more beautiful than he remembered, more beautiful than he imagined. His head was swirling with images of Greek and Roman goddesses, of Helen of Troy whose face could launch a thousand ships. He loved her long neck, he thought it was so sensual, he loved her profile, her crystal clear cerulean eyes that seemed to sparkle whenever they met his, her honey blonde wispy hair, loose around her face and trailing long down her back. But mostly he loved that she was a woman now, with a woman's body and a woman's desires. He knew it. She knew it. Both conscious of her breasts pressing into him when he hugged her and kissed her, kissed those lips that in a few years had become a tantalizing few inches closer to his own.

His head was spinning. To be in her shining presence after all this time, to share her comforting embrace, to kiss her once more and know what they felt for each other was real, to blot out the lonely expanse of the last three years. To be talking with her again. How he had missed their discussions. But to be having an adult conversation about them, as an entity, not a mythical dream bound entity but a real entity, discussing their future, was something else. Samuel felt himself floating in a sea of possibilities just thinking of their life together.

That afternoon, in his solitude, two thoughts kept rolling relentlessly around his head: you need to take advantage of opportunities when they come your way. You never know when they may come again; and, if you know that she is the one, what's the point in denying the inevitable. He would tell her.

They had been rowing for over an hour. The sun was below the horizon. Twilight was serenading them home.

'It's getting dark,' said Rebecca.

'So it is.' He stopped rowing. 'See that star over there?' He nodded with his head.

She turned around. After a few moments she said, 'The Evening Star?'

'Yes the Evening Star, the brightest celestial object in the sky after the sun and moon. Only visible for a few hours after sunset and a few hours before sunrise.'

'The Morning Star.'

'Yes, also the Morning Star. The heavenly body that has been guiding seafarers for centuries, helping them sail by the stars, divine a path through the oceans by celestial navigation. Such has been her brilliance and her importance. Many would be lost without her. Do you know what her other name is?'

'Venus.' She turned to face Samuel.

'Yes, Venus, one of the eight planets of our solar system. Venus, the jewel of the sky, named after the Roman goddess of love and beauty. And here in my boat, on this still summer night, under a vault of blue indigo, surrounded by twinkling water is one who is as auspicious as the Evening Star. As rare as a blue moon.'

He paused, utterly captivated by the look on her face, by the way her eyes shone, solely for him.

'Yes, my beautiful girl, you are my Evening Star, my Venus. You saved me and gave me the gift of a kindred spirit. How I love you. I love your sense of adventure. I love your hard working ways. I love you when you are exuberantly happy and I love you when you are hollow and sad. I love everything about you.' He ran his hands over her hair and smiled his brightest smile.

'From your strong body, to your beautiful, expressive eyes, to your glowing golden hair. Everything! All and in between.' He clasped her hands and looked straight into her attentive eyes.

'My brother thinks he is the luckiest man alive but he is not. I am. For I was carried through the shades of the sea, and when I was delivered from my ordeal, I woke to find that I had been placed on the chaste lap of Venus, and there is no other place I would rather be. There is your answer, Miss Rebecca Crowe. Will you marry me?'

Rebecca fell to her knees and kissed him through her tears, pressing herself into him, pulling him into her. He kissed her back with complete abandon, relishing her salt-laden breath, revelling being adrift at last in the arms of the one he loved.

32

Samuel rose early to help Silas haul in his trapping lines. In the shifting light, when the cod were feeding, the first catch was the biggest of the day. The girls were back on the stage, cutting throats, heading, splitting, laying away and salting. He joined them after they returned the second time and then with a sigh, Rebecca said, 'See you two later. I'll be back at lunch time.'

'Where are you going?' he asked.

'Ironing, baking, getting lunch ready. We drew straws and I got the short one, though Rachel, I thought you might have wanted a day inside after yesterday.'

'Maybe tomorrow I will.'

They were working side by side, idly chatting when Rachel said, 'Samuel, sometimes I feel there is something on your mind, something you are holding back, but want to talk to me about, but are unsure how to proceed. Maybe my instincts are wrong. But if not, please know that you can talk to me about anything, it will be alright.'

Not this, thought Samuel. After a few moments he said, 'You know there is something I want to talk to you about. I want you two to come and holiday in Canada with me – next May or August or September after the trapping season. I know we've talked about it in the past but I want to make it happen. Would you like that?'

'Yes, we always said we'd love to visit. Making it happen is another thing.'

'I know, but your parents seem to be getting more amenable to some things. Your father bought that boat for one and you all had that holiday.'

'Canada is a lot further away than Bonavista Bay though.'

'I know.'

'It will cost a lot more money as well.'

'Yes, but it's a cost you won't have to bear. Rebecca has suggested I take back the money I left here and next year I write to your parents enclosing it for your tickets. It will be harder for them to refuse that way. I'll get things rolling while I'm here and you two can follow through after I've gone.'

She gave Samuel a hopeful smile. A little while later she asked, 'Do you like it here on the island where we live?'

'I do. Yes.' He glanced at her then at the cliffs around their cove. 'There's something about Newfoundland that's so elemental, a certain rawness about the place that is rare. I must admit though at times I find it…– ' he struggled for the word, 'daunting, perhaps. There's beauty and sadness here.'

'Sadness? In what way?'

What to tell her? How to tell her that as beautiful as it was, it was too empty for him and at times he was hauntingly reminded of those desolate days lost at sea. For him there was a sense of loneliness that permeated the place and in some mysterious way it would sneak up on him when he was unaware. Was it the melancholic light or the fog loitering along the coast? He wasn't sure. He thought it had its tentacles wrapped around Rebecca as well, but Rachel seemed immune to it.

'I don't know. It's hard for me to put my finger on it. Your place is quite exceptional with the stand of pines. But the rest of the coastline is quite barren. I like trees around me. There's something about them that nurtures my soul on a deep level. Maybe because it's the landscape I grew up with. Some days I feel lonely here because of the lack of trees as if they have lost out to some other order. Having seen more of the world, I couldn't live all my life here.'

'I think trees like the tuckamore are amazing,' said Rachel. 'They fight hard for their survival. That's why Father only lets us chop windfalls.'

'That's very wise,' said Samuel. 'I think everything and everyone fights hard for their survival here. That wind can be fierce, howling over the rocks at times.'

'You should try February and March. You practically spend every moment cringing against the incessant wind.'

'I'd believe it,' said Samuel. 'I've only had limited exposure to life in a Newfoundland outport as you know.'

'Maybe you should live here for longer. Would you like that? Three years between visits is just too long. You sure you can't study for your medical degree in Deception?'

Laughing, Samuel said, 'It would be interesting to live here for a whole year; see the four seasons,' he paused, 'which kind of brings us full circle, about you two coming to Canada, for the experience.'

'For the experience, Samuel, nothing else?'

He looked at her then, all jokes aside. 'I think we both know it's the people who share those experiences with us that make all the difference.'

Late that afternoon, Rebecca ventured onto the stage. 'I'm done.' She sighed. 'By Jove, I needed to get out of that kitchen. I was burning up.' She called out to her father. 'What still needs doing?'

'Only lobster pots to go. I'll be up directly.'

'Why don't you let Samuel and I check them for you? I can show him how well you taught me to drive the powerboat.'

When they got to the first pot and started hauling in, Samuel said to Rebecca, 'Your sister is trying to work out if my return here has been driven by friendship and gratitude or something else.' Their eyes met. 'She's hoping that she is the something else.'

Rebecca let out a heavy sigh. 'She can't help that. You're the most amazing man we've ever come across.'

'Say that again.' Samuel broke into his best smile. Rebecca refused to be drawn in. Instead she put her hand in the water and splashed her wet fingers in his direction.

'Have you two ever said anything to each other?'

She gave Samuel a troubled look. 'I have never said a word about anything. I wanted to keep what we shared just for me and I didn't want to be presumptuous. Rachel on the other hand told me she would marry you tomorrow if you asked.'

'When did she say that?'

'Just after you left last time.' They held each other's eyes as the seconds ticked by. 'Then about six months ago she said, "Sometimes I wonder if I'm a jinx and anyone who takes a fancy to me will end up dead. Why would someone like Samuel want me with that hanging over his head? I'm a widow before my time. Who's going to want to marry a widow?"'

'Well, I'd marry a widow. If you were a widow, I'd marry

191

you. If you were like Marguerite and once had a lover and a child, I'd still marry you. A person's past is immaterial. What's important is you love the person you want to marry.'

'I agree,' said Rebecca. 'And she loves you or thinks she does.' Rebecca's face became awash with worry. 'Why did your brother have to race off and marry Lenore? You should have sent him our way.' She looked despondently at the ocean. 'What are we going to do? How can I face her?'

'I'll face her or we'll face her together. But more than telling Rachel about us I worry about what will come of her when you leave, how bereft she will be. I hated it when Matthew went to Montreal. I think that was one of the reasons that made me want to run away.'

'Maybe that's how it will be for Rachel then.'

'You think?'

'Could she not come and have a life with us?'

'Do you think she would want to be reminded everyday that she lost out? No, she needs to have something else to look forward to. That's why I want you both to come to Canada for a holiday. I'm hoping it might be an epiphany of sorts for her so that she will not just dream of a bigger life for herself but go out and make it happen.'

'What sort of life?' After a few moments of unanswered silence Rebecca shoved her windswept hair behind her ears. 'I don't want to think about this anymore today.'

'I know. It's not your fault or mine. It's just the way it is. Come, we'd better get on to these pots.'

Samuel lived for the moments when he was alone with Rebecca. Sometimes the silvery dawn was the only time he had alone with her all day. He didn't care how windy or grey the days were, he would brave any element to have such precious privacy with her, as they checked the lobster pots, as they tended the animals, as they snuck off for a quick ride on Mica.

Yesterday morning they rode Mica to the westerly point of the headland overlooking their cove and when they got to the tall stand of pines they dismounted and walked hand in hand, slowing down to kiss in celebration of a new day, in celebration of their newly declared love while the wind whistled through the trees.

And later when they mounted, Rebecca planted kisses on Samuel's neck, whispering. 'I love the back of your neck. I always have. I have wanted to do this for a long time.'

'You can do it every day,' he said, turning to her, 'as long as I can do this,' and he kissed her ardently and ran his hands down the side of her body feeling the shape of her under his hands, wishing he could feel and see her skin beneath, wanting to see and taste it all. Come lunchtime he was wishing it were early morning all over again.

Another morning and another evening, this outing handed to them on a golden platter by Silas, when Rebecca had asked if there was anything else they could do to help. 'You could jig for squid,' he said. 'Lenny Wilson hooked a good few the other night. The light's about right.'

The long hours of twilight shone tallow all around, mellow and serene in duskiness. As Samuel rowed, the pearly grey water seemed to caress the boat in an oily embrace. It would be dark by the time they got back to the cove. He should maintain his pace but the truth was he was in no hurry. He wanted to spend the whole evening in this boat, alone with Rebecca, talking with her, touching her, tasting her. He wished he could be lost at sea with her for his entire holiday. Once they got back to shore the walls around their secret love would go up so no one could peer inside.

Part of Samuel wanted the secrecy of their summer idyll to continue forever or for at least till the end of his holidays. He didn't want to invite suspicion, or scrutiny or chaperones or risk any conditions being imposed on their days of delight and discovery, on their sublime sanctuary where they were both enchanted and enthralled with each other. But his hope was like an incantation of Icarus.

Already he felt as if he were walking a tightrope in front of Rachel such was the balancing act required. The longer he stayed silent, the more time he spent alone with Rachel, the more he felt he was deceiving her and the more uneasy he was becoming.

He had already been there for ten days; another fortnight would sail past even faster. It was time to bring matters to the surface, put everyone in the picture and make plans. He stopped rowing.

'Are you tired? Do you want me to row for a while?' Rebecca asked.

'No,' he said quietly, 'I have never been more awake in my whole life.'

She smiled at him, all her teeth gleaming in lucent light. It was so easy to lose himself in her face. He drew her to him and kissed her, for many long minutes he kissed her. When he broke off they were lying across the bottom of the boat, strands of her tousled hair across his face. 'Have I told you how much I love the smell of salt water in your hair?' Samuel whispered.

'No,' Rebecca inhaled, then kissed him again, her hair pressed between their lips.

'I wish I could smell your hair every day.'

'Soon,' she sighed.

'We need to talk about our future,' he said, brushing her hair back from her face.

'We do, Samuel Rousseau Dalton,' her voice dreamy. Then she propped herself up on an elbow, her face animated. 'When and how can I come away with you?'

'That is definitely what we need to talk about, Rebecca Olsen Crowe.'

He sat up and gazed into her eyes. 'I don't want to leave without you. I want to take you home to Montreal.'

'You do?' Her eyes were shining like precious stones.

'I absolutely do. That is what I want in my heart.'

'Me too!' Her eyes mined his face then faltered as understanding filtered through. 'But there's a but?'

'Yes,' he exhaled. 'In a perfect world we would marry in the next two weeks and I would take you away with me. But I don't want to take you back to live in a house with me and three other men.'

'I wouldn't mind, I would cook and clean for you all.'

'I know you would but I don't want you to.'

'Could we not get a little place of our own?'

'Yes, that is what I would like for us,' He exhaled deeply, 'but I'm not in a position to do that right now. In two years time when I finish my studies I will be in a much better position financially.'

'I wish we didn't have to wait that long. Could I not get

work in Montreal to help us out while you finished your studies?'

'You could, but there's a third but.'

'What's that?'

'I get distracted enough just thinking of you. I wouldn't stand a chance having you within arm's reach.' He kissed her then like there was no tomorrow.

When they broke off, a breathless Rebecca whispered, 'Can you do two years study in one?'

'I can do it in eighteen months but it would mean no summer holiday.'

She pressed her forehead against his chin and let out a resigned sigh. 'Two years it is.'

'It will go quickly, much quicker than the past three years I promise you. If you come for a holiday next summer you will have that to look forward to, and then the next summer I will come here and we will marry.' He squeezed her tight as he said it. 'Right now I need to ask your parents for their permission to marry you then take it from there. It could mean our nights like this might be over for a while once they learn of my motives for their youngest daughter.'

'What motives?' Her eyes once more alive and sparkling.

He laughed, trailing his lips across her jaw. 'You're too much.'

'They trust you, Samuel.'

'I know, but I wouldn't be surprised if they place restrictions on our being together. You need to be prepared for that and not let it upset you. It is something we just have to go through. We have each other and we will be together one day in wedded bliss. We just have to hold onto that.' He kissed her and with his lips on her mouth whispered, 'When is Rachel next working at Deception?

'Not till Monday,' Rebecca whispered in reply. 'Mother is on tomorrow and I'm on Saturday.'

'I wish Rachel was on every day,' he murmured, his lips roaming all over Rebecca's face.

33

On Saturday morning, as Silas and Samuel were motoring back with their third haul of the day, Samuel asked if he could talk to him and Mrs Crowe that afternoon in private.

The four of them, Silas, Morna, Samuel and Rachel, had lunch on the stage. As they were packing up, Silas said, 'Can you wait up a bit, Morna? There's something we need to talk about. Rachel,' he continued 'you head up. Your mother will be there soon.' Rachel immediately looked at Samuel and raised her eyebrows in a small sign of acknowledgement. He gave her a small smile and nod in return. Had it been Rebecca he would have winked.

'Samuel,' Morna said, 'would you mind filling up the water barrel with fresh water so Silas and I can talk?'

He looked at her but before he could say anything Silas intervened, 'No Morna, Samuel is the one who wants to have a private talk with us.'

'Oh,' she said. 'Why didn't you say?'

'He's getting to it. Speak up now lad.'

'Shall we sit?' Samuel, pointed to the rough outdoor table and benches where they had just eaten. When they settled, he began. 'Thank you for welcoming me into your home a second time and for your family's friendship over the years.' He paused. 'You have raised two beautiful and outstanding daughters, two unique women. This has been made abundantly clear upon my return. That is why I would like to ask for your daughter's hand in marriage. I –'

'Praise the Lord,' enthused Morna, clasping her hands together. 'Rachel will think she has died and gone to heaven.'

'Morna, let Samuel speak.'

'Thank you,' said Samuel, trying to muster a smile. All of a sudden he had no idea how this was going to be received. He spoke slowly, pausing after every few words so they could take in clearly what he was saying. 'I ask for your permission to marry Rebecca,' he paused, 'and your blessing.'

Morna sat there wide-eyed, her eyebrows raised in surprise, then she lowered her gaze as her eyes scanned back and forth as if she were trying to make sense of it all. She moistened her lips and looked up at him. 'Samuel, we thought you had feelings for Rachel. You sent her that lace two years back. Men only ever do that for their intended.'

That was news to Samuel. 'I had no idea lace carried such meaning, I'm sorry. I merely wanted to send her something different to Rebecca and I chose lace because she is more traditional. I could have just as easily sent you the lace and Rachel the velvet.'

'Nevertheless, Rachel has feelings for you. She has burnt a torch for you these last three years.'

He ran both his hands through his hair as he exhaled. This was going to be harder than he thought. 'I'm sorry, really I am. But I never did anything to encourage her. You've seen all my letters. I do have feelings for Rachel, feelings of friendship and affection, but not feelings of love. It is Rebecca I love. It is Rebecca who I want to spend my life with. She is my eau-de-vie, my water of life, the one I lie in bed and think about, have thought about practically every day for the last three years.'

'But Rebecca was only a girl when you met her. Are you sure she returns your feelings? She's always held you in such high esteem, Samuel, in awe practically, but love?'

'There's no doubt in my mind whatsoever. Ask her yourself.'

Morna and Silas exchanged glances. They had managed to hide this well then, thought Samuel. He didn't know if he should be relieved about that or not.

'Did you and Rebecca talk about this when you were here three years ago?' Morna asked.

'No, Mrs Crowe, we only talked about it three days ago.' He gave her an honest smile. 'But I think in an unspoken way, we have felt it for a long time.'

'And what about Rachel, do you think she suspects anything between you two?'

'I don't honestly know.'

'She is going to be heartbroken,' said Morna.

Samuel agreed, but didn't say anything.

'Tell me,' said Silas, 'if we were to give you our permission to marry Rebecca, when would you want to marry? And where do you propose to live when you are married?'

'What I was thinking was next summer, before or after the trapping season, I'd like to bring Rebecca and Rachel to Canada for a visit and to meet my family, and then the following summer I would return here with my family for the wedding. I'm hoping you would be agreeable to such an arrangement. Rebecca will be twenty. I will be twenty-four and by mid 1919 will have finished my medical degree. In terms of where we would live that would depend where I gained a posting.'

'First things first,' said Silas. 'Do you ever see yourself living here, near our family, amongst folk like us?'

'Not in the foreseeable future. But you must know, surely, that my experiences here three years ago were what convinced me to be a doctor as I recognised that there would always be a shortage of doctors in the world. So living here or a place like here is not out of the question. That said, I would need to be able to make a living to support Rebecca and any family we might have and I would want Rebecca to be happy, so she would also have a say in where we were to live.'

'You could end up anywhere with Rebecca the way her mind works,' Morna mumbled.

Samuel's face broke into a wide grin. 'That is one of the things I love about her. You know she yearns to see more of the world and I want to give her that opportunity, be by her side as she does.' Another flicker of eyes between Silas and Morna. 'My grandpère has this saying. *The longer the cord the higher the kite flies.*' It's an old French proverb, but it describes Rebecca to the core don't you think? She was born to soar.'

Silas cleared his throat. 'What about the draft? We hear talk that any day it's going to be compulsory for all Canadian men over the age of eighteen? You could be sent to the front.'

Ready for this answer, Samuel replied, 'There is a small chance I could be conscripted, but it's unlikely I would see any action. I would be like my brother and do medical duty either here or over there.'

Silas and Morna looked at each other, their eyes still full of questions. After nearly a minute, Silas spoke, 'Well Samuel, we thank you for the honour you pay us, and our daughter, our youngest daughter no less. Morna and I need to talk things through before we can give you our answer. You have had much longer to think about this. We won't take long, just a few days.'

'By all means,' said Samuel. 'You probably want to talk to Rebecca as well,' he added, trying to be as helpful as possible.

That night Samuel could feel Mr and Mrs Crowe, watching him and Rebecca like hawks. He wondered if she could sense it too. He tried to be his normal self.

'Oh,' gasped Rebecca. 'I just remembered there is a dance on Friday night in the schoolhouse. They were talking about it today. They are looking for helpers to clean on Friday morning.'

'I can clean,' said Rachel. 'Can we go, Mother, Father? Samuel, remember I promised I would dance with you if you came back to visit and I would wear the lace you sent me.'

'I do remember,' he said with a nod, inwardly grimacing. 'Let's go dancing.'

On Monday morning, when the air was warm and still, before breakfast even, Silas and Samuel started making grass, as they called cutting hay in Newfoundland, severing the tall strands with long-handed scythes. After letting it dry for a day they raked it into rolls using wooden rakes, with Rebecca lending a hand as the final sweeper. On Tuesday afternoon when Rachel was at Deception Samuel and Rebecca were expecting to have a conversation with Silas and Morna in Rachel's absence but they gave no indication that they were ready to talk, nor did they arrange a time. By the end of the day Samuel and Rebecca were eager to dive into the ocean to rinse the clinging strands of grass from their body. Just as they were preparing to go Morna called to Rebecca: they wanted to talk to her inside.

Talk, thought Rebecca, you mean question.

'How long have you and Samuel been talking about marriage?'

She was relieved that it wasn't something she had been hiding from her parents for months or years.

'Do you love Samuel? Do you want to marry him? Do you not think it prudent to meet his family to make sure you would fit in and get on with them?'

'Yes, that's why I'd like to go to Canada and meet them.'

Had she thought about the fact that she might move to Montreal or Toronto and not like it and want to be back in Newfoundland and the complications that could entail, they asked. She was born by the sea – Toronto and Montreal were a long way from Newfoundland, they warned.

'Once you make your bed you have to lie in it Rebecca,' added her mother.

For a while Rebecca started to wonder if her parents thought she was making the wrong decision. She couldn't work out the subtext. 'Don't you like Samuel? Don't you think he will make a suitable husband?' She looked from one to the other, anxious for a reply.

Finally her mother said, 'Yes of course we like Samuel. We like him very much. We are just wanting to make sure you are not rushing into anything blindly, and trying to find the best way forward that doesn't upset Rachel too much.' Her mother gave her a pointed look.

Rebecca knew Rachel was going to be hurt and upset and she had no idea how to avoid that. While Rachel had confided in her years ago, to this day Rebecca had never openly and honestly shared with Rachel her feelings for Samuel. She stared at her mother, unsure what to say. Any comment almost seemed like an admission of guilt or deception. An uneasy frown crept over her face.

'Don't fret,' said her mother.

It wasn't until four o'clock on Thursday, after Silas, Samuel and Rebecca had transferred umpteen hay piles to the barn did Silas say, 'That was a job well done. Thank you, Samuel. Have a rinse off and come and see Morna and I in the kitchen.'

'Me too?' asked Rebecca.

'Yes, Rebecca,' said her father, 'we want to talk to you too, but first we want to have a word with Samuel. We will call for you soon.'

Silas got straight down to business. 'Samuel, our decision is yes – in the long term.'

'Pardon?'

'Our preference would be for you to marry Rachel. But as you don't wish to do that, we cannot make you. However we cannot let you marry Rebecca – please let me finish – we will not let you marry Rebecca until Rachel has met and married someone else.'

'It would just break her heart too much,' interjected Morna. 'You are the third potential suitor who has not worked out for her.'

Samuel felt like voicing that Toby and he were hardly suitors, but he held his tongue.

Glancing at his wife, Silas continued, 'She has had enough disappointments and setbacks in her life and we are not going to let this situation be another for her. So fine, if you want to marry Rebecca, then you must wait and wait for however long it takes and once Rachel is married, perhaps once she's betrothed even, then you and Rebecca may also get engaged. There will be no engagement between you and Rebecca until there is an engagement between Rachel and a suitable match. Do I make myself clear?'

Abundantly, insanely clear thought Samuel, but what he said was, 'Thank you for your permission for Rebecca and I to marry. And thank you for being happy to welcome me into your family.' He gave them his best smile. 'I am not so thrilled with the condition concerning Rachel, though. How is she going to meet someone living here? How many suitors are there in Deception Bay? How many visiting eligible bachelors come into port when she is there? Your daughter is a very attractive and intelligent young woman. She won't settle for just anyone. Send her to St John's, let her train to be a teacher, a nurse, a bookkeeper, whatever her choosing. We can pay for her tuition. Don't let pride or some other reason stand in your way. If you want to see her happy, then help her so everyone can get on with their lives. She could live with my family in Toronto for a while even. My mother would be happy to introduce her to some suitable young men.'

'Samuel, with all due respect Rachel would be a fish out of water in Toronto,' said Morna. 'Unlike Rebecca, she is very content here, and we'd rather she not move to Toronto or anywhere for that matter.'

'There is another important point you need to be aware of with regards to this whole affair,' added Silas, 'Out of respect for our wishes and consideration to Rachel, you and Rebecca will continue to be just friends around her. That is not a request. That is a condition. We will make sure Rebecca is clear on that as well. We do not want Rachel to think there is anything serious going on between the two of you. And we expect you to go on treating Rachel like you always have.'

Without hesitating, Samuel said, 'I will continue to treat Rachel as I always have. That you can be assured of, but how can we, Rebecca and I, carry out our courtship with such limitations?'

'Exactly, that is the point, there will be no courtship carried out in public,' said Silas.

'You would rather we carry out our courtship in private? Tell me this,' said Samuel, before they could reply, 'don't you think if Rachel knew the truth about Rebecca and me, then maybe she would forget about me and start to look anew at other men, other possibilities and think more widely about her future. The truth would liberate her. She deserves that! Do you want her to burn a candle for me for another three years?'

Silas and Morna sat there stonily, unwavering. Samuel was doing his level best to stay calm whilst convincing them. 'I am going to tell Rachel that I don't have feelings for her, without mentioning that I have feelings for Rebecca. I really do believe being honest with her is the kindest thing we can do.'

'And what are you going to tell her when she asks you if you have feelings for someone else?' asked Morna. 'Are you going to lie to her? Are you going to pretend you have a sweetheart in Toronto, or some place else, then some time later come back and marry her sister?'

'Morna's right,' said Silas, 'you can't do that. There's nothing you can do but bide your time, I'm afraid.'

Samuel exhaled in frustration. 'What do you think is a reasonable amount of time?'

'You and Rebecca will wait for however long it takes,' said Silas, giving the question no consideration whatsoever. He stared pointedly at Samuel.

'Oh come now! It might take years. She might never get married.'

'Why shouldn't she?' asked Silas. 'She's a fine looking young woman and her limp is not a major impediment. She is on the cusp of womanhood. And maybe when she sees that you've come here and not asked her hand in marriage, she'll be open to other proposals that come her way.'

'If they come her way.'

'Why wouldn't they?' said Morna, defending her husband.

'You misunderstand me. I merely was wondering where these proposals might come from. But more importantly, you can't seriously expect Rebecca and me to have this undefined term hanging over us. It is not fair that our lives should be put on hold indefinitely while we wait for Rachel to marry. And by your unwillingness to send her to a place where she might meet someone suitable you are not helping our quest nor hers.'

'Have a little faith, Samuel,' said Morna, smiling her encouraging best.

'Oh, I've got that. I just don't have timing.' Samuel paused to collect his thoughts. 'Look, I appreciate you have had only a short while to come to terms with my proposal and we, have all come a long way in the past five days. Thank you. I'm just not over the moon about the terms. Put yourself in our position, as to what is a reasonable length of time. I don't live here. I can't see Rebecca weekly or once a month even. So the only way we will be able to carry on our friendship will be when I can manage to visit here, probably only during summer and through letters.' Yes, they nodded. 'Private letters,' said Samuel, nothing indefinite about his tone.

Samuel and Morna exchanged another look. 'We will have to find a way to manage that,' Morna said at last.

'Thank you,' said Samuel, 'perhaps Ronnie will oblige, and also if you could reconsider our getting married at the end of my medical degree in two years time, I would appreciate that. It is a reasonable length of time. I would like my parents to be here and they would want to come. We just need to make suitable arrangements. It can be a small family affair, whatever works for you and Rebecca.'

34

Rebecca didn't welcome the news any more than Samuel. She couldn't feel the "yes" in there so wrapped up as it was in a thick web of eventualities and uncertainties. In frustration and in tears she said, 'Don't you understand? I love Samuel. I want to be with him!'

'We understand,' said her father. 'But if you truly love him and your love is blessed in Heaven then you will know most of all that love is patient and love is kind. So you will be patient in your love for Samuel and you will be kind in your love for your sister.'

'I can be both those things,' said Rebecca trying to keep the petulance out of her voice, 'but I don't think you're being very reasonable.'

Her father flinched when she said that. Rebecca held her breath and lowered her eyes, part of her expecting his outburst, part of her dreading it, knowing the shame and embarrassment she would feel, but part of her wanting Samuel to see what her father could be like at times.

His posture was erect and stiff as if he were holding himself in check, trying not to give way to anger. Rebecca knew if the next thing she said was the wrong thing, her father was liable to explode with an even more absurd and unfair pronouncement. For her sake and for Samuel's it was best to avoid such an inimical situation. But what could she say or do to make any difference.

She looked at Samuel, her eyes conveying her distress.

He reached across and grabbed her hand. 'Rebecca, it will work out. As your mother told me earlier, have faith.' He smiled and nodded his head in encouragement. Then he got up, squeezed her shoulders and left to go outside. 'I'll be with Mica when you're done.'

Outside, Samuel tried to rid himself of his own tension by brushing Mica's coat. It was fortunate Mica was a steady mare but at one point she did flick her tail at Samuel as if to say, 'Go easy. It's not my fault.' He was angry and irritated. Mostly he was upset with himself. He knew the predicament he was in could have been avoided if on his second day at the Crowes he had levelled with Rachel. If he had said, 'Actually Rachel, don't be shocked by this, but I'm intending to ask for Rebecca's hand in marriage if she'll have me.' Why couldn't Rebecca have worked at home that day instead of Rachel?

He didn't level with her then because, why? – He felt under pressure and wasn't going to comply – or he was like his brother, too secretive, too cocksure, – or because he wanted to talk to Rebecca first, understandably! to be sure they both wanted a future together – or because deep down he knew Rachel would be hurt and he wanted to avoid hurting her. For all those reasons and, if he was truthful, because he wanted to have that never to be repeated first week of love and longing they had shared in secret and rapture.

So in the end he had unwittingly played right into Silas and Morna's hand. Had he been able to say to them, 'No, Rachel doesn't suspect anything because she knows everything! I told her. Yes she was upset, but she's coping fine, don't you think?' then the whole scenario would be different. There would be nothing to hide from anyone and he would have been able to achieve his other objective of having Rachel start to think of a life for herself that didn't hinge upon him.

In trying to do the right thing, in trying to map out a future for himself and Rebecca he had backed them both into a corner. The distasteful truth of the matter was while he wanted to be with Rebecca, he knew in his heart that it was best to wait till he had finished his medical degree. So there was nothing to be gained by antagonising the Crowes when Rebecca would be left to deal with everything by herself.

Rebecca came to him still seething and told him that her father had given them his permission, yes his permission she repeated for emphasis, for them to go and check the lobster pots. Did he want to come with her?

They walked down the stony steps to the stage in silence, started up the boat and took off, not having spoken a single word to each other. When they reached the first buoy Rebecca put the motor into neutral letting it idle, but before they hauled the pot up Samuel said to her. 'Rebecca. Stop. Look at me.' She lifted her upset eyes to his. 'Is there anything I can do or say to give you comfort?'

'I'm so angry, Samuel. I don't think I have ever been this angry in my whole life.'

'I can see,' he said. 'Be angry. But is anger going to get you what you want? Remember what we talked about the other night. I said things might be different, they might be difficult but in the end we will still be together and you have to hold onto that.'

'Different, yes, difficult yes, together in the end, when? I was thinking two years but they won't accede to that in the slightest. What happens if Rachel never gets married? What happens if you get sick and tired of waiting for me, for her, and meet someone else? What happens if you get dragged into this war and end up like Toby? This is my life, Samuel! This is your life! This is our life we are talking about!'

'I know. And we will live it together – we just have to wait a bit, that's all, like the song, remember?' Their eyes were full of meaning.

Rebecca cut the motor. 'I feel I have spent my whole life waiting for my dreams to come true and just when I thought they had they are still not within reach. Waiting erodes the soul! What do you think of that ridiculous decree they have just laid down?'

'It is rather extreme, I grant you. Maybe they are counting on Rachel meeting someone in the next two years and in the end we will get married in the same time frame we have set ourselves. My hope is that will happen but my gut tells me it won't.'

'Samuel, you know my whole life I have never asked for anything. I may have dropped hints and said wishes out loud. But I never directly asked them to give me anything, buy me anything, do anything for me. I have just accepted whatever I was given gladly. Did whatever they asked of me, always deferred to my mother. I feel like I can't breathe standing here talking to you. As if the air is being forced out of me in anger. And I don't know what more can I say, or do, or give, to get the one thing I utterly want more than anything else in the world? Why won't they let me have it? Have I not been a good daughter? Is this the reward I get? Oh, I am so wild I could scream.'

'Scream, but while you're doing it, know that in my opinion you could not have been a better daughter.'

'Then why do I feel the way I do? They make me feel as if I'm so undeserving.'

Rebecca searched Samuel's face, the sky, the sea, her chest rising and falling, trying to calm her unquiet heart.

'I just feel so trapped here,' she cried. 'It's like this corset I'm wearing is a metaphor for my whole life. Oh my God,' she said gulping for air, 'I have to get out of this thing. I can't breathe!' She started frantically undoing buttons. 'Samuel, can you help me?' she asked as she peeled off her top and turned her back to Samuel so he could unclasp the corset. He gave it to her. With relief, she sat down in front of him with layers of skirts on her bottom half and just a plain sleeveless cotton slip on her top half. Her arms pale till they reached the part of her forearm exposed to the fickle sun. 'Thanks,' she said. 'I almost feel like throwing this thing away. How I hate it.'

He gave her a warm smile. 'Rebecca, it's not the end of the world. We can elope. You are already of an age where you are legally allowed to wed. While it would be desirable to have your parents' permission and blessing, it is not necessary. Granted, they hold the purse strings but they don't control your life. I suspect that come two years time, your heart and conscience will have made clear to you the choices you need to make to live the life you want to live.'

'Samuel, you make it all sound so easy.' Her voice was flat.

'Well, maybe because we still have so much to look forward to. We can write to each other – in private – and if you and Rachel can't come and visit me next summer then I will come here and then the next year we are free to be together if we decide to elope.'

He had managed to put Rebecca more at ease and himself – outwardly. Yet, amidst the disappointment, there was a gnawing, unsettling feeling about the Crowes' adamant stance. He couldn't quite put his finger on it, but he sensed it even so.

He wanted to talk to someone about it and that someone was Ronnie. While Rebecca worked the stage and Rachel scrubbed the school, Ronnie listened to every word Samuel had to say.

'One thing I've learned about Silas over the years is often the reason he gives for something – while being the truth – is not the most important reason. He's very private like that; he keeps his inner workings to himself. He knew you two could elope so by saying 'yes', he has stalled that option. He has got you right where he wants the two of you. But my question is…what is he stalling for? Because I would wager that if Rebecca were the only one at home, he would still be stalling and I think that is what you need to understand the heart of.

'Rebecca is the man about the house and she can also be the woman about the house. Rachel, has only ever been interested in being the woman and only been groomed for that role. I am constantly amazed at what that family manages to produce, given that Silas spends half his time at sea. And it's largely because Rebecca is a Trojan. And with her physical labours, Rebecca has worked harder than any man or woman I know to gain her father's approval and love. And she should never have had to. I wonder sometimes that losing his four sons took so much out of Silas that he vowed never to love his children to that degree again, never to expose himself to so much grief and heartache. Most people I know become easier on their children with age, but not Silas.'

'So your sense is that the real reason he is stalling is to keep Rebecca here?' said Samuel.

'Yes.'

'That figures. I remember him saying to me once that Rebecca's duty is here, to her family. But does that mean she has to spend the next twenty years of her life paying back for her first twenty. She's being used like a form of ransom or an insurance bond.'

'They wouldn't be the first people to have such views, Samuel, and they won't be the last. For centuries, a large family has been the best guarantee for people in their old age. And the Crowes don't have a large family. There is one solution that you may not have considered. If you were to make your home here it might clinch the deal. He would get to keep Rebecca within reach and gain a son-in-law as well.'

'Well, that might happen at some point but not in the foreseeable future and not immediately thereafter. I have to finish my degree and Rebecca is keen to see more of the world, and I'm keen to show her.'

'I know,' said Ronnie, 'that's the way with the young and how it should be. I think you have to find your heart's home and settle down.'

'Thanks,' After a pause, Samuel said, 'I wish some days you were Rebecca's father.'

'I would proudly be her father, but alas I'm not. However, I will help the two of you where I can. It will be my pleasure and don't worry, your secret's safe with me and Meg. She's as tight as a tick. If the opportunity ever arises I'll talk to Silas about your and Rebecca's situation. I'll definitely talk to him about the trip to Canada; see if I can have some influence there. And how about we have you and Rebecca over one night for a little celebration? See if you can organise that.'

The dance came. Silas and Morna stayed home while Samuel danced fairly and squarely with both sisters and every other woman in the progressive dances. Saturday, the three of them picked berries on the barrens. Already Samuel was into his last week and despite having spent the entire day with him, Rebecca was downhearted. 'Rebecca,' he said when they had a moment alone, 'Perk up. Let's live for the day and enjoy out time together. You will be seeing me again in twelve months, not three years. What's more Ronnie and Margaret want to have us over for dinner to celebrate our engagement.'

'But we're not engaged yet,' she whispered.

'Yes we are,' he said. 'Just not publicly. They are excited about our betrothal and we can bask in their blessing at least.' Samuel paused, considering the possibilities. 'Rachel and your mother will be bottling all day Monday, right?'

'They will be bottling fruit all day Monday and Tuesday by the looks of things.'

'Fine. Why don't you stay at Deception on Monday and Tuesday and I'll come across on Monday afternoon and we'll have dinner with the Evans.'

They set it up that night, Rebecca saying that she would be happy to work both Monday and Tuesday on the stage rather than being stuck in the kitchen bottling fruit. She got no objections from anyone. And the next morning at church Samuel accepted Ronnie's very public invitation to come for dinner. 'How about Monday night?'

'Monday night would be fine,' said Ronnie.

'I'll be working here tomorrow,' piped up Rebecca. 'And Tuesday as well.'

'Well you should stay over, Rebecca, like you did before Samuel turned up, and join us for dinner as well. We've missed your company.' He placed his hand on her shoulder and gave her a gentle squeeze.

35

Even before she finished work on Monday, Rebecca looked up and saw Samuel at the end of the stage, leaning against a railing waiting for her. It made her heart rejoice to look up and see him there so clean and fresh, glowing with a huge smile solely for her. 'Hi,' she said coming up to him. 'Did you bring my bag? I can't wait to have a wash.'

'I bought your bag and a berry pie from your mother.'

Rebecca's raised her eyebrows. 'A peace offering? A blessing?'

'Perhaps.'

As always, the Evans had a half-barrel of warm water ready for Rebecca to bathe in. Some minutes later she walked into their kitchen in a pale blue dress with her hair brushed and down expecting to find them drinking tea and eating cake around the table. Samuel, however, came through the other kitchen door. 'We're out here, come and join us.' But rather than wait for her to walk towards him, he walked towards her, reached for her left hand, and pressed it to his lips. 'You have never looked more beautiful,' he whispered, bending to give her a soft kiss on the mouth.

The tension she had felt over the last few days slowly started to release its hold on her. Samuel too was so at ease with the Evans.

'Come, let's celebrate our engagement.' On the closed-in veranda, Samuel handed her a glass of wine.

'What's this?' she asked.

'It's elderberry wine. Ronnie tells me it's his best brew ever. Will you try some? Had I known I was going to propose I would have bought French champagne, but this, I swear, is a close second.'

'That's it,' said Ronnie. 'Next time you come, you bring that champagne so we can compare. In the meantime, raise your glasses. I want to make a toast. To the two people I know most deserving of each other, may you have a long and loving life together. Meg and I wish you every happiness.' He exchanged a quick look and a smile with his wife.

In the dining room, not only had Margaret brought out her best silver and her best linen she had also brought out her best candles in honour of the occasion, banishing the kerosene lamps from distant sight. The room glowed with warm amber light; the conversation flowed. Samuel and Rebecca were free to be their complete unencumbered selves. To talk openly about the future and the plans they had. To touch each other lightly on the shoulder, on the forearm, even hold hands in front of company.

Why can't my life be like this all the time thought Rebecca? When it came time for Samuel to leave, Rebecca wasn't sad at all. She was warmed by the wonderful night they had shared and the prospect of a life filled with many more. She had no problems drifting off into dreamy white sleep. In the morning she awoke with resolve and a renewed sense of hope for her future.

That afternoon, Samuel rowed round to pick her up in the Nightingale.

'You're keen.' Her smile lit up her face.

'I am keen,' he whispered. 'And I need to keep rowing fit as we have regattas in the fall when I go back to University. I can't afford to slacken off. Besides, this way we get to have ninety minutes to ourselves without anyone eavesdropping or spying on us.'

'I made a decision this morning.'

'Did you? What's that?' He leant closer towards her. 'Are you going to run away with me on Saturday?'

'Have you changed your mind?' she asked, all wide-eyed.

Samuel couldn't help but laugh. 'Don't tempt me. So tell me, what was your decision?'

'Well you weren't far off. I decided that if father and mother won't let us marry come the summer of 1919 then I'll elope. I want to have that life we had last night, to be free to enjoy ourselves in front of other people. What can they do? I will be with you. That's all that matters. And it's not like they don't want you for a son-in-law. They will get over it.'

'I'm sure they will.'

They smiled warmly at each other and then Rebecca leant forward and they kissed, a comeback kiss, full of her love and commitment to him. She returned to her seat at the back of the boat and gazed in adoration at Samuel rowing her home. After a few minutes she said, 'It occurs to me that we are here in the Nightingale and you are wearing your shirt. Somehow, that doesn't sit right with me.'

Samuel removed his shirt. Her eyes soaked up the sight of his glistening body.

'Like what you see?'

'I'd like it more if I were clean and could touch you.'

'Come touch me anyway.'

She shook her head. 'You don't want my fishy fingers all over you.'

'Well then we better get you cleaned up.'

Two bays later he rowed into a deserted cove and when they were close to shore, he stopped rowing, rolled his trousers up and climbed overboard dragging the boat up onto the pebbly beach. 'Come on you scaly thing,' he said, holding his hand up to her. 'It's time you scrubbed up. Off with that fish-gut smeared dress, off with those stockings. Off with that cramped corset that you can't stand. It's time for another dip in the Atlantic Ocean.'

'Did you bring my costume?' she asked.

'No,' And with his teasing, unmistakeable smile, he said, 'You'll just have to swim in your slip or nothing at all.'

She was speechless. Coming up close to her, he reached for her hand. In tender solemnness, he said, 'When we are lovers Rebecca, you are going to be naked as the day you were born and so will I. When we are married that's how you will be. And I don't want you to be uncomfortable or shy or prudish about that.'

She was trembling and she hadn't even shed one item of clothing or put one toe into the chilly water. She couldn't look at Samuel; she could only look at her hand in his.

'What do you say, Rebecca?' he asked, squeezing her fingers lightly.

She nodded softly and lent her head into his chest. He released her hand and lifted her face to look into her eyes. She could see everything that he felt for her. O perfect love.

'Say yes,' he whispered.

'Yes,' she whispered.

And then he kissed her, a kiss that seemed to awaken parts of her body dormant all her life. She felt unknown parts of her being calling out to her saying, yes, yes we are here, we have been here all along to take you to this new place, so you are not alone. And with Samuel she never felt alone. For him she could do this. He would be gone in a few days. Her pained heart shuddered at the thought. With her nerve endings tingling she said, 'You go into the water first and I will follow. Look the other way. But wait, help me with my corset first please.'

When she turned towards the ocean she saw Samuel's broad shoulders rising out of the water, looking out to sea, his hair wet and darkened. She inhaled sharply then relaxed into it, coming up to him silently, placing her hands on his shoulders and pressing her body up next to his, the thin weight of her slip a sheer veil between them. She wrapped her arms around his shoulders and kissed his neck. He reached round behind her and pulled her closer, so her body was pressed completely against his back. Slowly she ran her hands over his collarbone and his chest, then gingerly across his nipples.

'They've gone hard,' she whispered.

'Yes because of you,' he said. 'Like yours have gone hard.'

'That's because of the water.'

'The water may have something to do with it but I guarantee you I can also make them go hard.'

She felt them tighten even more as he said that. Samuel turned to her and kissed her, a deep kiss full of longing and desire. He pulled his mouth away and kissed her neck below her ear, down to her collarbone and then he pulled her slip strap aside so he could kiss her shoulder. He ran his hands down her side, tracing her outline, in at the waist, out at the hips.

'What a beautiful body you have,' he murmured, 'and I only ever get to see a fraction. It is always covered up. I only get to see this much,' he said, grabbing her arm three inches below her elbow.

'Yes,' she said softly, 'but one day you will get to see it all and touch it all and no one else ever will.'

'That day can't come soon enough,' he whispered hotly against her lips. He kissed her with urgency, folding her in a liquid embrace, their bodies entwined like seaweed. She felt him harden and her body tingle in response not just in her breasts but also down below, a surge, a kind of urgency she couldn't name or describe, just an intemperate ache for Samuel to keep on keeping on. But then he broke off, turned and dived and when he surfaced he sang out to her, 'Come, come swimming with me.'

'You come here,' she called, but he ignored her. When she caught up with him she pushed him under. Then as he surfaced, she demanded, 'Why did you stop?'

Samuel's eyes, sad and expressive, looked deep into her own. With a heavy sigh he said, 'Rebecca, my body has been on fire for days, bristling with the desire to make love to you. But I have to restrain myself, overcome this desperate need I have to ravish you, because if I do give into the cries of my body then the future we so desperately want will never eventuate if we are found out. Has your body been teetering on a similar brink?'

'It is now.' Her breath ragged.

'So now we both know what we stand to gain and lose. Is that not fair?'

'No! Because you have just shown me yet another thing I am missing out on. Another part of Samuel's world that I am still to explore. Is that fair?'

Samuel sighed deeply and pulled her into his arms. 'I'm sorry. This has been very selfish of me, pure gratification on my part. I wanted something more than just our kisses to remember you by when I'm gone. How I wish it were 1919 already.' He kissed her again until they both were tingling and breathless.

36

On Wednesday, with Rachel working over in the Bay, Rebecca tried to speak to her mother once more about Samuel and her getting married in the summer of 1919.

'What's the rush in talking about this now? Nineteen nineteen is a long way off.'

'Yes,' said Rebecca. 'It is a long time to wait, which we are happy to do if we know in the end we can get married.'

'A lot can happen in two years,' said her mother.

'I'm hoping for Rachel's sake, a lot does,' said Rebecca. 'More to the point, Samuel has come all this way, asked for my hand in marriage and has only been given a tentative yes. What sort of blessing is that?'

'We have not said no.'

'But neither have you said when. How long did you have to wait after father proposed to you before you got married?'

'That was different. There weren't other people involved.'

'Rachel is not involved! How long, Mother?'

'Three months.'

'Three months! And you won't even specify three years for us. Do you want us to elope?'

'No, that is not what I want! Besides it wouldn't be easy for you to elope with Samuel at medical school. Do you think it right for his father to support both of you?'

'I could work just as easily there as I could here. I could support us.'

'You have no idea what would be required to finance a life in Montreal, to put Samuel through medical school. I'm sorry, but you are delusional if you think you do.'

'Well, that brings me to my second point. Maybe if I were able to go to Montreal then I would have some idea. What about Samuel's invitation for Rachel and me to visit for a month next year, to meet his family? Can't you say yes to that at least? It would give Samuel and me something to look forward to. And, be something for Rachel as well.'

'If we could afford to do that we would. We'd be hard pressed to afford to send even one of you.'

'But if Samuel will pay for us to come and visit him, then it's no cost to us, only effort. We can work extra hard before and after our trip to get all the work done around here.'

'It's unlikely that he will be paying for any such trip. It will be his parents and once again your father and I don't think that is right. We don't want to be beholden to anyone in that way.'

'But years ago Mr Dalton wrote to us and offered to help us financially if ever we needed assistance.'

'This is not a need, this is a want, a fancy. We would never ask for help in that situation.'

'I'm sure he would be happy to give it.' Rebecca took a deep breath, trying to stay calm. 'Mother, I don't ask for much.'

'No, you don't. You and Rachel are incredibly selfless. We have been blessed to have such children.'

'Then why, when I'm asking for these two things, can I not have at least one of them?'

'I'm sorry, it's not in my power to give this to you.'

Rebecca let out an exasperated sigh. She knew whose power it was. 'What did father say about the trip to Canada?'

Morna looked out the kitchen window. 'He thinks the idea of you going to Canada is just a whimsical fantasy, a fairytale. I don't think he'll ever agree to that.'

'Well, that's just great, isn't it? How would it be if I never agreed to any of the things he asked of me?'

Rebecca was despondent and downhearted. And then she thought: if she and Samuel were having this much trouble getting her parents' approval on such important matters, how would it be for Rachel when her time came? Her parents had known Samuel for three years and known him quite well and still everything was tied up in conditions. How long would Rachel have to know a beau, her parents know the man, before they gave their blessing. Oh poor Rachel! And where did that leave Rebecca and Samuel?

She had never felt more torn, wanting to honour her

parents and wanting to strike out for herself. She felt full of despair, because she knew in her heart that she would have to elope with Samuel in two years time if she wanted to be his wife, as it was unlikely to happen any other way. They could get married in the church here on the island. Ronnie and Margaret would be their witnesses. They could invite her parents and Rachel and tell them of their plans. But not to have such a momentous occasion celebrated joyously saddened her beyond words.

Samuel came into the kitchen as she was swirling in her melancholy. 'There you are,' he said. 'Do you think we might be able to manage one more bout of fishing before I go? If we head off this afternoon, then we could have salmon for dinner tomorrow night. What do you think?'

Turning to her mother, she said, 'Mother, you heard Samuel, can I have the afternoon off please to go salmon fishing with him before he disappears for a year or two?'

They were in the Nightingale, this boat that felt like their very own Noah's Ark – a tiny bob in the ocean, yet expansive in its refuge, a holy vessel as far as she was concerned. Rebecca was lost in thoughts that flowed deep inside her. When they rounded the headland Samuel said, 'Not the best morning?'

'They won't even commit to us holidaying with you next year.'

'Don't give up. I'll write to them once I've gone and you two just keep on at them. Ronnie is going to find a way of talking to them too remember. They'll yield eventually.'

She told him about her thoughts and fears for Rachel.

'Yes,' agreed Samuel, 'I think there will be conditions placed on Rachel's union as well.'

'What sort of conditions?' her interest aroused.

'Let's start with you. This is about you and keeping you here. You are more valuable to them than Rachel. I'm not saying they love you more or you mean more to them but the plain economic truth of it is you're more useful to them than Rachel. And that's why they don't want to let you go. Ronnie made the point that if I was to come out and say, "Yes I'd marry you and live here with you from this day forth for the next ten, twenty years," then they would give us their blessing instantly. I think he's right but I'm not about to put his theory to the test. They don't want to lose you most of all. I think they can see that we do love each other and I think they are happy for us to be together, but what they're holding out for is for Rachel to meet someone and marry someone and that someone will live with them. Or maybe they'd build a house and live right next door or in Deception, but they're not prepared to let you go till they have someone else to take your place.'

'But Rachel could be like my sister Esther and meet someone from Bonavista Bay or some other place and make her home there.'

'She could, but perhaps a condition of that marriage would be that her suitor would have to move here. Alternatively, Rachel and your parents could move to where her prospective husband resides, provided they could continue to lead the life they currently do. Ronnie thinks they have lost so many children over the years that they don't want to lose you all. I suspect it's a mixture of economic and emotional necessity, but they would struggle to put that into words.'

'So they are using both of us – Rachel and me – to bargain for what they want.'

'That's a cold way of looking at it, but yes, there is a price on the two of you. They see this as your duty.'

'We have been dutiful! And we'll continue to help whatever our circumstances.'

'Exactly! That's why I'm keen for you and Rachel to have other vocations and for your parents to consider such undertakings as a means of still ensuring a livelihood for them in their old age.'

Rebecca's mind was racing back and forth as her eyes zigzagged across the water.

'It's not right that they use our lives for their own personal gain. It's not right that they can say no to our marriage plans or no to the date we want to get married. No to them!'

'That's the spirit. But saying no may not get you what you want. Talk to Rachel about how you both can be in a better position to determine your own future. Consider all the possibilities and maybe together you can come up with a plan that will work for everyone. So you can say "yes," this is what we will do. Use all those feminine wiles.'

'Like the ones I tried to use on you yesterday, Samuel, but failed,' her voice deflated.

'You didn't fail. I stopped when I still could, otherwise I would have failed.'

She felt Samuel's hand under her chin, turning her face to his. 'Let me assure you, once we are married you won't have any problem seducing me.'

'Really,' she said, a smile bubbling to the surface, her self-esteem at last boosted by something that day.

37

When they asked Samuel how he wanted to spend his last day, he surprised everyone when he said: 'Working on the boat that had brought him so far.' He rowed the Nightingale tender to the mouth of the cove and with Silas' and Rebecca's help they hauled it along the stage to rest on some old wooden hoists. Silas went off and Rachel joined them. Together they cleaned the molluscs off the bottom, scraped away the seaweed, broke for morning tea of blueberry scones that Rachel had baked especially, and then they waited a few hours for it to dry out before they sanded the bottom of the boat. 'I probably should have started this a few days ago,' said Samuel watching Rachel carry the lunch basket away. 'I don't think I'll get it finished.'

'Doesn't matter,' Rebecca said, 'I'll finish it for you, after all, it's our boat, isn't it?'

'Yes. You found it and you claimed it – just like you claimed me,' he whispered, winking at her. Straightening up he called out. 'Hey Rachel?' She stopped halfway up the stony path. 'What shall we do for my last afternoon here? I'm going to leave this boat. It needs to dry out some more.' To Rebecca he said softly, 'Do you mind?'

She shook her head and smiled for him.

'Why don't we take Mica and go looking for wild irises?' Rachel called back.

'Sounds like a fine idea.' He really didn't care how they spent the rest of the day, except he did want to find a quiet moment to talk to Rachel. And he told Rebecca as much, asking her to make herself scarce at some point. Despite the Crowe's conditions his conscience wouldn't let him leave without Rachel knowing clearly where she stood and somehow he wanted to get that across to her, if she hadn't yet perceived it for herself.

They took turns riding in pairs with Samuel. Then when

Rebecca had ridden off by herself, Rachel said to Samuel, 'I hope it's not three years till we see you again.'

'I promise you it won't be. I want to see you two next summer, remember.'

'How did you get on in that discussion with my parents?'

'They didn't say no. You and Rebecca need to work on them, chip away at the iceberg. Get them into the habit of saying yes to more things.'

'It's not them, Samuel.'

'Don't you want to come to Canada next year?'

'Yes, don't get me wrong. But that's not what my heart desires most.'

'Are they stopping you from attaining your heart's desire?' asked Samuel.

'No.' She turned away from him and looked into the distance. After a few seconds she exhaled. 'You seem more at ease with Rebecca. I worry that I scared you away from me, made you uncomfortable with all my questioning.'

He laughed lightly, then put his arm around her and pulled her to him, kissing her on the top of her head. 'You didn't scare me. You just didn't get the answer you wanted, but you got your answer right?' She nodded, unable to look at him.

Samuel dropped his arm and reached for her hand. 'Rachel,' he said softly, 'some things don't always work out the way we want them to. It's good to have dreams but sometimes you just need to move the dream along a little, take a diversion and you might end up with something far better than you actually ever dreamed. Don't settle for anything less than your heart's desire but don't stand still waiting for it. Move forward.'

'Thanks,' she said, biting her lip.

He wanted to hug her again and tell her it would be alright but he didn't know for her when it would be. Instead, he squeezed her hand and said, 'I see you happy one day, your prince is still to come along.'

'Yes,' she said, squeezing his hand back, 'Or maybe I have to go and find him.'

'Maybe you do. Where are you going to start? Is there a way you can go into service with someone so you can finish school part-time. Why don't you come and live with my parents, they have enough rooms in their house, particularly with none of us children at home, they would enjoy your company and you two could finish your schooling there and get part time jobs to send money home to your parents. And remember, your parents wouldn't need to produce as much with two less mouths to feed.'

'Thanks for the offer, Samuel, and the encouragement. I think if there were more of us, it would be easier for some of us to get away, but as you know there is only Rebecca and me and our parents don't seem keen, nor are they able to manage without us.'

'They would manage if they had to. And I'd gladly give you the money back to help you on your way. Think of what you want. What can you do to make that happen?'

'I could happily live here my whole life, marry and have children. But there is no one around here I want to marry.'

'So move away and find the one you want to marry.'

'I couldn't leave Rebecca. She wouldn't cope with me going away somewhere and not her. And our parents wouldn't let us both go.'

'But they might let you go. You're the eldest, maybe if you talked to Rebecca she could see her way clear to support you going for two years and then maybe she could go away somewhere for a while after that. She might be more amenable than you think. But nothing will come of silence.'

38

That night they all turned in sometime after ten. In her room Rebecca changed into her nightgown and got into bed and lay there, not sleepy in the slightest, and lay there, wide awake, her heart beating out the seconds, and lay there, counting down to Samuel's departure. Her bed was practically above the day bed Samuel slept on in the parlour below. Could he sense her lying restlessly above him, desperate to be with him? Was he lying there looking up at her willing her to come to him?

Only a few hours earlier he had whispered to her, 'Your kiss was the one thing that stayed on my lips all the way home last time and it will be the same this time. Have faith.'

Beyond that they hadn't spoken or arranged anything, yet she was longing to go to him, to nestle up against his chest, to have his arms around her and his hands and his lips all over her. She waited an hour and then another, as the beam from the crescent moon painted its arc across her bedroom wall. Then as quiet as a ladybird she got up, pulled on her clothes, took a step and waited, then another and another, in some places taking two steps at a time to miss the boards that creaked. It took her over two minutes to descend. She made it to the doorway of the dining room where she heard Samuel whisper, 'Wait for me outside.'

He joined her ten seconds later. He had pulled two blankets from his bed and brought with him two candles. 'To our boat.' They took off, she in the lead, down the well-trodden dirt path, down the stony steps, on to the stage, across to the Nightingale up on the hoists. He crouched and tossed one blanket under the boat, and then another. 'After you.' She kicked off her boots and crawled under. He returned from their store with the two lit candles and placed them on the underside of the back seat of the boat. The light washed them in pearly ivory. Then he draped two old sails over the boat, to keep the insects out and to stop any wind from guttering the candles, though that night the air was still.

'It's like an igloo,' she said when he crawled inside.

Samuel folded his arms around her, pressing her into his chest, and whispered, 'Wouldn't this be a dream come true to go to sleep every night in each other's arms?'

'Yes,' she said, 'and to wake up in them as well.'

'One day.'

They kissed, the softest, slowest kisses, warm and wet and mellow, as if they had all the time in the world. They smiled, their faces full of each other and pressed their noses together so happy were they to be having this wonderful last night together. They stroked each other, fingers traipsing up arms, down hips, over backs, across chests, pacing themselves with sweet never-ending kisses, whispering their love and desire into each other's mouths.

'So my husband to be, do you want to be my lover?' she asked with kisses along his jaw, up behind his ear.

'As you know, I want to be that and much, much more.' Shivers down her side, down her back.

'Will you be my lover tonight?' Sliding her tongue in and out of his mouth.

'I will be your lover tonight and every night,' teasing her tongue, 'if you will have me.'

'I will have you like I had you yesterday and more,' she said.

'More,' he said, brushing her hair back from her face and looking earnestly into her eyes.

'Yes I want you to be my lover in every sense of the word. I want your hands all over me,' weaving her fingers with his, 'I want for us to be joined as one,' she said.

'I want to be inside you too.' His lips against hers. 'To have you melt and burn and swallow me completely,' taking all of her mouth in his own, 'but we play with fire, it's risky,' he breathed into her.

'Then let's risk it,' she breathed back. 'The gods have been on our side have they not? My God, your Gods, your ancient Greeks and Romans. How many God's do you have, Samuel?' she asked, rolling over and sitting on top of him, bending down so her hair created another cave around their faces.

'None, they're just fascinations, like you,' his hands stroked her thighs. 'There's a small chance, you could get pregnant.' He looked directly into her eyes.

'If I did, Father would have to let me marry you then,' she whispered as she rubbed her chest against his.

'Once he gets over you surrendering your virginity out of wedlock.' He stroked her breasts, through her blouse.

'It wouldn't be out of wedlock if he had been reasonable to begin with.' She caressed his nipples through his shirt. 'But it's mine to surrender Samuel,' she said. 'Mine. Not theirs. I am mine to give and I decide the giving. Tonight I give myself wholeheartedly to you.' She ground her way back towards his pelvis. 'So let's have this night together under the wings of our nightingale.' Her hands trailed down his chest in waves. 'Let's live in Paradise for one night and be like the nightingale and not despair at the coming of dawn.'

There was nothing hurried about that night. They drew it out, pleading for it to last, wanting its memory to sustain and nourish them in the months ahead, to bind them indelibly when they were worlds and oceans apart.

She undressed him one item of clothing at a time, completely covering every new ocean of skin with sensuous kisses. And when she was done she lay down in half recline looked up and said, 'I am yours now, Samuel, do what you want with me.'

Slowly, he peeled away the layers till there was nothing left but her slip and then he loosened the straps on either side and pulled it off one shoulder and then the other rolling it down over her breasts to her waist as he stared at her nipples like apricots in the midnight sun, neat and round, urging him to taste their delights. And taste them he did, lowering his head and taking one breast in his mouth he delicately sucked it, kissed it, trailed his tongue around the sensitive areole, as it twinged and tightened in his mouth, then the other.

And then he moved her slip down inch by inch, his mouth on a path to her naval, to her pubis where her light brown hair nested subdued in the softest light. But not her, there was nothing subdued about her. He told her she tasted of summer fruits, from the delights of the Garden of Gethsemane, sapid, pungent, his tongue roved over and round, in and out as he sampled her nectar and drank her in, 'Oh, Samuel,' she gasped and moaned, trembling then shuddering as the sensation of his lips possessed her and she came in a cascading rush.

And afterwards in the afterglow as he held her in his arms Samuel told her he had never felt anything so lush, so warm, so all-embracing as he had when he was inside her, that he had dived into oblivion when he entered her. He had slowly pushed his way in ever so carefully and she wondered if it would feel like he was tearing her apart, but no, she was anointed and embalmed and she had opened to him, completely opened, called him in, called him home and home he came, again and again as his momentum grew and he too rode the crest of the longest wave before he crashed to the shore and collapsed into her caressing calm.

He said he wished he could be like Zeus and make the night of love last three times as long. And she said let's make love three times and pretend that you are.

'You are so beautiful,' she told him, over and over.

'Rebecca,' he whispered. 'Beautiful? You don't know the meaning of the word.' Rubbing his head against hers, his voice husky, 'You so need a mirror.'

'You smell so beautiful,' she whispered.

'I smell of you,' he said.

'Ah, then I smell us,' she said. 'I want to smell us forever.'

Before the first tinge of blue in the sky they were up and gone. Walking up to the house, Samuel called after her softly, beckoning her to him, 'Rebecca look.' He pulled her into his arms, and turned her to face the east and there was Venus, their morning star, shining down on them, winking at them, blessing them with her brilliance, watching over them.

Four hours later Samuel was gone.

Revelations

39

Samuel looked at Matthew's drawn face and wondered if his looked the same. He knew he had flashes of down-heartedness, but mostly he was infused with excitement. And restlessness.

'Cheer up, Matthew,' he said, 'you're making me feel depressed. What a pair we must be. I thought we were meant to buck each other up. You're grinding yourself down as if you were back in the war zone. But you are not there yet.'

Matthew lifted his head and gave a small sigh of resignation. 'I'm sorry, Samuel. I haven't thought about it for months but I figured I ought to start preparing myself.'

'Why don't you do that once you get to England? Enjoy your last few days here.'

'I wish I could. War takes so much out of you. I'm just trying to build up my reserves and get my head in the right place.'

Samuel wanted to empathise with his brother, but at the same time he had no real idea of what he had experienced. 'If you had to name it, what is the worst part?'

Matthew sucked in his cheeks, reflecting. After a good minute he said, 'I think it's when you are in the trenches, when you witness the awakening of new recruits. Everyone goes through their own baptism of fire, and if they come out the other side a survivor they're forever a changed man. And rather than be a moment of relief and jubilation it's a moment of infinite sadness, of infinite loss. It's like their innocence, their very heart, the essence of who they were before, has been torn from them. They surrender to the destiny of front-line life, to the fighting brotherhood. And while they go on killing, it's like they don't care if they live or die any more, because they feel they've already crossed some invisible moral divide. They believe they're already damned and headed for the grave.'

Samuel considered all Matthew had said. After some time he asked, 'How do you think this has affected you?'

'Oh, I'm not sure,' said Matthew shaking his head with uncertainty. 'I think the survivors of this war are going to be a generation of emotionally impotent, morally numb men.'

'I don't think that's you,' said Samuel. 'You just told me of your compassion for your fellow man.'

'Maybe' said Matthew, his tone edged with doubt, 'but I'm worried that eventually, I, like them, will become inured to all the agony and suffering and atrocities I see around me. I'll become so hardened that I won't be able to attend to a little girl's broken wrist. It will be meaningless. And then my medical career will be over. What then?'

'You become a pilot, a cartographer. You'll find something else. But I'm sure you're a long way from such apathy. And if it worries you that much, resign your commission or ask for re-assignment.'

'I can't do that.' Matthew shook his head. 'In the grand scheme, I have nothing to bemoan. I made the most of these four months, but in a few days I'm leaving and I can't help be conscious of what I'm leaving behind and what I'm getting myself into again. It's actually easier for a new recruit. Since September last year it was hell. Meeting Lenore after all those years was my salvation. She was sent to be my lifeline, to keep me sane, to keep me going. I'm not sure how I'm going to manage with her and everyone else I love halfway across the world, that's all,' he said, dismissively.

Two days later when all the Daltons were gathered at Toronto Union Station to say their farewells, Samuel was notably absent. 'Where is he?' his father asked. Before long Samuel appeared trotting down the ramp to the platform wearing his knapsack and holding a black duffle bag in his hand.

'Don't tell me you're going back to McGill already,' said his mother. 'Please stay a bit longer.'

'Let him go with his brother as far as he can,' said Grandpa. 'He's only a few hours up the line.'

'What if I were to go all the way to Europe with Matthew?' said Samuel.

'What!' exclaimed Matthew looking sharply at Samuel.

'I'm coming with you.'

'You're not.'

'I am and there's no point arguing. Like nearly every other McGill intern I can continue my studies just as well over there as here.'

'How dare you spring this on us!' said his mother.

'Would the alternative have gone over any better?' After a pause, he said, 'Come on, I don't need your permission any more, please just give me your blessing.'

The lengthy discussion his parents could have had was reduced to one long heartfelt look between his father and mother. Samuel saw his father give his mother the barest nod. She took his cue. Caving in, her voice catching, she said, 'I'll only give you my blessing if you promise to come back to me whole and alive and soon. If not, I'll come and drag you home myself.'

'I promise, Lottie,' said Samuel, embracing his mother, kissing her on both cheeks.

She hugged him with all her being.

'I'll watch out for him,' said Matthew, hugging his father.

'You watch out for each other,' said Grandpa.

But oddly, as Samuel had surmised, everyone was relieved with his decision and Matthew was so overwhelmed with love and gratitude he nearly shed tears.

'This is a pleasant surprise,' he said when they were underway. 'When did you decide you were coming with me?'

'Yesterday. I couldn't go back to studying at McGill and spend the next twelve months thinking about Rebecca. I've done that routine for three years. I need a change of scenery. I'm so wound up. I figured this was the best thing for me, for you, for us.'

'It will be very good for us, little brother. Thank you.'

Samuel was euphoric and after the holiday he had just had with Rebecca he felt invincible. He believed in fate more than ever and that soon they would be together forever. The next two years were to him just a small speck on the landscape of their lives. And he had faith, that despite volunteering to go to the maw of death, he would remain unscathed, unlike two of his classmates who were wounded in the battle of Vimy Ridge, one fatally. But these were things Samuel did not dwell on, and certainly did not divulge to his parents.

The other matter he did not divulge was his and Rebecca's engagement. Not wanting to overshadow his brother's recent nuptials and not wanting to denigrate his future in-laws and their absurd conditions, he kept the matter of his betrothal to himself.

But what he did talk to them about with great fervour was his desire for Rachel and Rebecca to holiday with them in Canada next year and how he'd like to make that happen. His parents were completely supportive. He could see his mother mentally planning an itinerary. And then in her bewitching way she said, 'There's more than friendship at stake here. You're keen on one of these girls aren't you, Samuel?'

'That's putting it lightly,' interjected Matthew. He and Lenore had joined them for dinner.

'Which one?' asked Lenore.

'You'll see,' Samuel teased. 'Let's bring them to Toronto and see who you think.'

His mother looked at Matthew. 'Don't ask me.' He raised his eyebrows in warning.

'Come on, Samuel, spill the beans!'

'Mom, if you can't guess within five minutes, I'll take you aside and put you out of your misery.'

'Well, Samuel,' she said in feign indignation, 'How inconsiderate of you not to bring me a photograph at least. But don't you worry, I'll have it out of you before they get here.'

'Do your best,' joked Samuel, then more seriously he added, 'Would you mind writing to the Crowes again, formally inviting Rachel and Rebecca to come for a holiday?'

'Consider it done,' said his father, wiping his mouth with a napkin.

Samuel had written as well, both to the Crowes and secretly to Rebecca, but in neither letter did he mention his thoughts about going to war with Matthew. He hoped they would not think he had deceived them with his intentions. It certainly wasn't the case – merely how events had transpired. He was trusting the letter he was in the process of penning would ease their minds. After all, just two days ago, conscription had become law in Canada and would be in force by January 1918.

Three weeks after he left Newfoundland Samuel was again sailing past his homeward angel, this time with his brother. He wanted to reach out and hold her. He wanted to be in a smaller boat so he could run his fingers through the water, water that eventually might fold itself around Rebecca in a liquid embrace. He projected his thoughts to the heavens, hoping she would feel emboldened and comforted by his presence 400 passing miles away rather than 2000 distant miles on terra firma.

On boats and trains, automobiles and trucks, on foot even, Matthew led Samuel all the way to the McGill Hospital in Belgium. They arrived on the 18th September. Samuel was drafted immediately as a second lieutenant and at work the next day, assisting a doctor from Halifax in his post-operative rounds. For the first time in his war career, Matthew was also assigned to McGill. He had expected to be taken on strength as an MO to a battalion, given his experience in the field.

Not only was Matthew delighted with his assignment; he was humbled by his welcome. One of his colleagues lifted him off his feet and swung him around full circle. 'Come back to dance with the enemy, hey Matthew?'

'I didn't know if you would return,' said another, Dr Peters, slapping him incessantly on the back.

There were smiles, and handshakes and hugs all round and then they discovered he'd got married and so another round of embraces ensued. And inexplicably the nursing staff seemed to admire him even more for leaving his newly married wife to come unbidden once more to the war zone.

With Matthew's return being so heralded, Samuel was, as ever, in awe of his older brother. He was also instantly welcomed into the establishment, automatically able to mix comfortably with those well above his rank. The commitment those doctors and nurses lavished on his brother they also lavished on him: teaching him, helping him, to be the best he was capable of being. Many of the cases he encountered as an intern at McGill were continentally new. His learning and contribution, like the Lee Enfield that had replaced the ill-fated Ross rifles, had to be reliable and rapid fire. Before long, any doubts or regrets he had about leaving Canada vanished. He began to get a sense of the unique camaraderie, the never-ending challenges and the unspoken achievements his brother had alluded to in letters and conversations.

When Matthew and Samuel arrived in France the battle for Passchendaele Ridge was in its third bloody month. The British, Australian and New Zealand troops had been leading the fight and despite their best efforts had been largely unsuccessful: 100,000 casualties for little ground won. On October 26th, much to the reluctance of their Commander, Sir Arthur Currie, the Canadians entered the battle in what would become known as the third battle of Ypres. Currie warned it would cost 16,000 of his 20,000 men to take the ridge and for the medical division to be prepared. He was not wrong.

Miles in the rear, Matthew and Samuel were spared the hard-earned, paltry yet poignant progress that was Passchendaele, but they suffered in their own way. Thousands teemed through the McGill Hospital. Both men worked long hours, for days sometimes only seeing the sleeping form of the other. Samuel had never experienced a more intense, sobering few weeks in his entire life.

He'd see captains come into wards, searching for their men, gazing without speaking at unshaven faces and in their eyes he would see things that no man would speak of. And that unnerved him.

When he could summon the energy, he wrote notes in his journal and did revision. But first he'd write a quick note to Rebecca so he could send her weekly updates, hoping that something in the excitement of receiving a letter with a European postmark would offset the disappointment of him being so far away.

He was housed with Matthew and once or twice a week, they would get to enjoy a few hours together and a meal. Whenever Matthew finished at a decent hour, he would always come looking for Samuel and patiently wait while he attended to a soldier, helping him with his treatment. Samuel felt privileged to have such a brother. One night, when he came in late, he told Matthew his feet felt like lead. 'Wait till you've spent time in the trenches and have to walk out with ten pounds of mud on each foot,' said Matthew, 'then your feet will feel like lead.'

Samuel wrote home to his parents, saying everyone was calling the Canadian troops the leading storm troops of the British Army and so they were. Nine Canadians won the Victoria Cross for their valour and efforts at Passchendaele. Yet, whatever the Allies' successes, it was making little difference. That was the cold, cruel truth of the matter. Too many men were being sacrificed, too many men slaughtered, too many squandered.

40

Rebecca and Rachel were picking and carding wool in the living room. They had started two days ago and when they finished they would start on the spinning, which they both preferred. Their parents had braved stinging icicles of windblown rain to go to Deception, settle up with the merchant and order supplies for the winter. It was November. The temperature had dropped suddenly and viciously. Both fires were lit and would stay that way till April. The two of them talked little. Both were lost in their thoughts, unaware of the long skeins of silence draped between them.

Two months after Samuel's visit Rebecca realised she was carrying a moonlight child. She was like Tess of the d'Urbervilles...a fallen woman. She knew she should be ashamed, but she couldn't find it in her. She was with Samuel in body as well as mind and spirit. It was the wake from his leaving that washed over her and filled the depressions left by his absence. Now, there would be no stopping their union. Her father would have to give his blessing. She would write to Samuel and he could come back and marry her, like he had planned, but at Christmas – only a few months away! The whole charade would soon be over. And then she got his letter; the first one from Belgium, and that changed her mind completely.

The morning he left Samuel had pressed the hundred dollars on her, insisting she take it back in case of any emergency. O prescient Samuel. Was this what you had in mind? Rebecca wondered. At Reception she had refused and refused till she finally relented, placing the money under her insole and there it remained. She had never even bothered to explain it to Rachel.

In those surreal days she oscillated between secret joy and

238

sinking dread. Once her father found out, all hell would break loose. But then she asked herself, does he need to find out. She thought about taking Samuel's money and running…to where… the Daltons in Toronto, Esther in Bonavista, the Ile aux Demons? And then she realised the only person she would be running from was her father, but if she could find a way to tell her mother and enlist her help, maybe she could go away without running.

A week later Rebecca found herself baking in the kitchen with her mother. Rachel was in Deception visiting some of the women folk to talk about what Christmas supplies they could send to the WPA for the Newfoundland soldiers abroad.

'Perhaps Rachel will return with some letters,' said Morna. 'I'd like one from Esther. I'd like to know how she's getting on.' Esther was pregnant with her fourth child, due in March.

'Do you think she will be over her morning sickness by now?'

'I hope so, poor thing, having it morning noon and night. I was never that bad. It's meant to be a sign of a healthy baby getting on with its growing, you know. So in your misery you are meant to take comfort from that. It's the ones that don't make their presence known you're meant to worry about.'

Rebecca didn't know whether she should be happy or sad about that. She only had one morning when she felt squeamish, the day they made lassy soap and that could make the strongest stomach queasy.

'Like poor Iona Barnes,' continued her mother. 'That woman could never carry a baby full term. It was heart breaking for her and her husband. How I used to feel for her, despite my own losses. I got to the point that I felt so guilty telling her each time I was pregnant.'

'Guilty?' said Rebecca, trying not to shy away from the word.

'Yes, guilty,' said her mother. 'It's strange how guilt can plague a woman at various times. Like when an older woman's pregnancy is proof of her still having intimate relations with her husband, she can feel guilty, conscious that everyone is talking about her, or when a young bride feels uncomfortable, guilty almost, announcing she is in the family way, when everyone expects her to do her motherhood duty. And then there are misguided girls who get in trouble. They are garrotted in guilt.'

Rebecca felt the words pinning her down. Doing her best to appear normal, she asked, 'Do you think all women in such circumstances feel guilty?'

'Of course they do,' her mother said, her voice full of certainty, 'and so they should, for thinking so little of their virtue, for the shame and embarrassment and upset they cause their families.'

Trying to keep the tremor out of her voice, Rebecca said, 'Would you be upset if Rachel or I ever found ourselves in such circumstances?'

'Of course I would be! Upset and disappointed beyond belief!'

Rebecca stayed silent. Silence was her only safety-net as she skated dangerously on thin ice. This conversation was so close its claustrophobia was giving her morning sickness. Part of her felt like fleeing from the kitchen, so she could stumble outside headfirst into the cold cool air, but then some other day she would have to have this unwanted conversation. She closed her eyes, cleared her throat in readiness to speak but then with a heavy sigh, her mother came to her rescue. 'It would upset me more if you weren't honest with me.'

Salvation, however, was not in sight.

It was not the same night, nor the next one, nor the one after that. In fact it was many nights later, after the first snow of winter had fallen when Morna decided to raise the unpleasant matter of her youngest daughter's condition with her husband. Rebecca had retired early to her room, exhausted. Rachel was in the kitchen making bread for the morning. Morna and Silas were alone in the living room, knitting and reading. Even Morna wanted to prolong the inevitable. She got up and closed the door.

The explosion didn't come at once. Silas stopped what he was doing, fixed his penetrating eyes on Morna and said, 'Say that again.' Morna watched cautiously, as he took it all in. His anger simmered under the surface and then he launched it, jumping up from his chair, smashing both his hands down at the table and staring accusingly at Morna as if it were all her fault.

'What is it about women? From the time of Adam they can't be trusted. And he!' said Silas, slapping the table once more in fury, 'he is the son of the Devil. His arrival was ominous – I knew it in my heart!'

'You don't think that. You were quite happy for him to marry into this family.'

'Woman, whose side are you on? He deceived us, can't you see that.'

'Yes, I see that.'

'He has brought shame upon our home. And she has too.' Silas was pacing two steps in one direction, then two steps in the other.

'The shame will fade away.'

'No it's a stain. It will always be there.'

'I disagree. They will get married and move away and then it will slowly die away.'

'Yes and we will be the ones left to live with the shame. I won't have it,' he said, shaking his head, 'not for us.'

'Silas, she is not the first and she won't be the last.'

'She will be in this family, that's for sure. How could she?'

'These things happen sometimes. Maybe if we had done things differently they may have done things differently. Perhaps, like Samuel asked, we should have given them a timeframe for when they could marry and then this situation may have been avoided. I think half the reason Samuel and Rebecca went down this path was because they felt thwarted and couldn't see an end to the waiting. That, and this war hanging over everyone's heads.'

'How do you know that?' demanded Silas.

'It's more or less what Rebecca implied.'

Silas lowered his voice, almost in warning, 'If it was good enough for Jacob to wait seven years for Leah, then it should have been good enough for Samuel.'

'Yes, Silas, though I'm sure seven years was a long time for Jacob as well, but at least he knew the term, didn't he? And even then he was deceived, wasn't he? Besides they lived longer back then, maybe that's why they could wait longer.'

'It was highly unlikely they were going to have to wait seven years,' said Silas raising his voice again.

'We got engaged and married in a matter of months.'

'That was different. I was twenty-seven!'

'It's not that different.'

'Well they didn't even wait a month, Morna. Not one, single, month.' He slapped his hands down with every single word, stamping out his displeasure. 'I trusted him. I trusted her and this is how they treat my trust!' Silas strode to the bottom of the stairwell and yelled, 'Rebecca! Rebecca! I want you down here. Down here now, in the living room!'

Rebecca knew what was coming and she didn't relish it. But she knew it would be better once it was over with. After all, children were a blessing from God. And besides she had a little bit of Samuel with her now to add to her courage. Trying to keep the quiver out of her voice, she stepped into the living room. 'Yes, Father.'

'Your mother tells me you are with child. Is that so?'

Swallowing, 'I believe so, Father. I'm sorry to—'

Before she could apologise her father cut her off. 'And the father?'

'Samuel.'

His name was barely out before he walloped her across the head, knocking her to the floor. She was stunned. And then he started kicking her. She curled around herself, instinctively protecting her belly, yelling, 'Stop it, Father! Please, stop hitting me.'

'You harlot. You fornicator. You whore,' he yelled.

Her mother ran to her father's side, 'Stop it, Silas.' Both women were screaming. Rebecca tried to defend herself, while her mother tried to haul her father away but he was wild with fury and too strong for his wife. He kept at Rebecca, as if he could kick the problem away, doing his utmost to punish her to eternity or damnation for her immoral ways. It was the shot that blasted over their heads and lodged itself in the wall above the fireplace that halted her father's savage onslaught. Rachel stared down her father.

'Leave my sister alone,' she said through clenched teeth.

Barely controlling his anger, her father strode out of the

room, slapping at the rifle in Rachel's hand on the way past. Her mother was on edge, not knowing who to turn to. She ran to the kitchen and returned with a cold damp cloth, thrusting it into Rachel's hand with a 'Here, look after your sister,' as she fled the house in search of her husband.

Rebecca was a ball on the floor, still curled around herself, shuddering in shock and in pain at the brutal way her father had attacked her. She had endured his vehemence before but nothing compared to this. She expected his disappointment and judgment, even his anger but not this degree of violence. Somewhere deep inside, Rebecca felt that if Rachel hadn't fired the gun her father would have killed her in his rage.

'Let me help you up,' said Rachel, soothingly. 'Let me have a look at you.'

Rebecca's beaten back was throbbing so much she thought she could still feel his boot ricocheting off her body. Her left ear was ringing echoes, sending out aching spirals to the entire left side of her face. The only thing that had managed to escape his aggression was the little kernel growing inside her. At least she hoped it had. But she couldn't move, she just couldn't move.

Rachel knelt beside her, rubbing her shoulder, stroking her hair, whispering, 'Come on, Rebecca, it will be all right. You'll be all right. You're safe now. Come on, sit up and show me you are all right. I'm going to get you a glass of water.'

When she returned she helped Rebecca sit up. Rebecca had two mouthfuls and then groaned, 'I'm sorry,' as she turned her head and threw up and threw up and threw up and the tears started all over again.

'It's alright Rebecca, it's alright,' said Rachel as she cleaned up after her and brought more cold water.

She made her way to the day bed and perched herself unsteadily on its edge. 'Rachel,' she croaked. 'Thank you, you're a good sister. I think you saved my life tonight. How could our father be such an animal?'

'Ssh, come on now. Enough of that talk.' The two sat there staring at each other, blinking occasionally. Finally Rachel said, 'So, you and Samuel...?'

Rebecca stared at Rachel unsure of the right thing to say.

'I was standing outside the door. I heard everything.'

'There wasn't much to hear.'

'How could you not have told me? How could you have done such a thing?'

Rebecca continued to stare at her sister, her answer a long time in coming. 'Rachel, how could I not have told you? How could I tell you when it was clear that for the last three years you and I have both wanted the same thing? How could I tell you when I knew that Samuel wanted me and not you? You, the older sister who by some strange right, some divine order of the universe, should be the one going off and getting married first. It was up to him to tell you he had chosen me, and they,' pointing at the door, 'Mother and Father, forbade him to do so. Making him, us, wait until someone else came to woo you and ask for your hand in marriage. And as for the other...' Her voice trailed off.

After a moment, Rachel said, 'I would have figured a way to tell you eventually.'

'Well so did I. Though probably not the best way,' she said, wincing as she tried to get comfortable. Her eyes came to rest on Rachel. 'I'm sorry, Rachel. I'm so sorry. I never wanted to hurt you. I never wanted this to mar your happiness and I've worried for months, that this will be a scar on our relationship. I never meant to take something away from you that was yours. I wouldn't do that. But, as God is my witness, he wasn't yours to begin with.'

Rachel sighed deeply. 'I know that. I just hoped he could have been, that's all.'

'I know. We just have to figure out a way for you to find your own Samuel. Come here, please, I desperately need a hug.'

After her father's anger had cooled a few degrees, insanity set in. He wanted Morna to pretend she was pregnant so in six months time they would have a way of explaining a newborn baby in the house. It took two days to talk him out of that. He seriously contemplated sending her to Esther's, for he wanted Rebecca out of his sight, yet he asked 'Why should David and Esther have to suffer because of you?'

And in this her mother agreed, 'Esther has enough on her plate.'

'We'll send her to the Wright's house. It has all the Petrie's furniture still in it.'

'We are not banishing our daughter in the middle of winter to a house by herself that has a death curse hanging over it. You'll be doing that over my dead body, Silas.'

He turned on Rebecca, his eyes pinning her in place. 'Are you satisfied with the mess you've created? I've a good mind to make an example of you. Let everyone in the Bay treat you like the scarlet woman that you are. But for your mother's sake and for Rachel's I can't. All this time you haven't given a wit as to how this might affect the lives of your sister or your mother or me for that matter? Your immorality will wash over all of us. And see what we have to do because of your sin. Lie. You have brought everybody down. Are you happy about that?'

'No,' she said, almost inaudibly, but she couldn't understand the need for lies. When she and Rachel were young they were made to learn this scripture by heart: *Whoever wants to enjoy life and wishes to see good times, must keep from speaking evil and stop telling lies.* They could almost say it backwards.

'No wonder Samuel absconded to Europe,' continued her father in his seething. 'Nothing brave about that. He's a coward if you ask me. A prevaricator! Running as far away as possible to evade retribution. I'm sorely tempted to write to him and tell him because he defiled my daughter he is not welcome here ever again. I don't want you to ever mention his name again in my house, in my presence, you hear me?'

And on it went.

The Ten Commandments according to Silas

1. You will go to church up until New Years Eve then you will be housebound. Every time you are in public you will suck your stomach in, hold something in front of you so no one can tell you are pregnant.
2. You will tell people you are going away to be with Esther, to help her out with her young family.
3. You will stay around the house. If anyone comes to this house you will disappear to your room and never come out.
4. You will pray for forgiveness every minute of every day.

5. You will search your heart to understand why the Lord has punished you so.

Rebecca read the Bible and she prayed for forgiveness but repeatedly she kept coming back to two scriptures. One from James: *Every good and perfect gift is from above, coming down from the Father of the Heavenly lights.* And one from Hebrews: *To have faith is to be sure of the things we hope for, to be certain of the things we cannot see.*

And then five other commandments which came from her mother, who said it would be remiss of her not to tell her such things. But secretly Rebecca knew they came from her father way before Esther was born.

6. Thou shalt not raise thy arms above thy head or else you might cord the baby.
7. Thou shalt not do anything to frighten yourself. (Too late!)
8. Thou shalt not put anything to thy nose to smell.
9. Thou shalt not mock anyone.
10. Thou shalt never ever look at a dead body.

In the midst of all these sanctions, Rebecca was able to claim one small concession for herself. No one was to write to Samuel about her situation. 'I don't want him to worry about me and the baby. I don't want him to be distracted over there. He is the one whose life is in danger. I don't want to endanger it more with unnecessary worry. I will tell him once the baby is born. I will write and ask him to come via Newfoundland on his way home, so we can be married.'

41

One evening in mid-November after Samuel and Matthew had finished their rounds Samuel got to meet Matthew's hero and friend, John McCrae. The two brothers were walking along through the Medical Camps, when a man with a large English setter came walking up beside them.

'Evening, Jack.'

'Hello Matthew.' The man stopped as did his dog. 'Long day?'

'Yes, but it's over, thankfully. Hello Bonneau,' said Matthew patting the dog who had moseyed forward for a sniff. 'What about you?'

'No, not too bad actually. I managed to finish my paper work and get away for a ride on Bonfire.'

'Where'd you go?'

'Along the waterfront to the pier where we went that day. When was that again?'

'July before last.'

'That long ago! Life is a blur here. Well now that you're around we must go again.'

'I'd like that.' Turning to Samuel, Matthew placed his hand on his right shoulder. 'Please let me introduce Samuel, my younger brother. Samuel, this is Lieutenant Colonel McCrae, Dr McCrae.'

'The lost-at-sea brother? Hello Samuel,' said the Colonel, extending his hand. 'I've heard about you. Matthew told me you returned with him. Welcome here. I hope you are settling well into life at a military hospital. A bit of a change from Victoria hospital?'

Samuel shook his hand. 'Yes, rather. Pleased to meet you, Dr McCrae. I've heard about you too.' Samuel smiled. He knew about him alright. He was the McCrae from his first year Adami & McCrae pathology textbook, but more than that, was there an English speaking person anywhere in the world who did not know of him and his famous 'In Flanders Fields'? Deferentially, Samuel said, 'I was very moved by your poem, sir.'

'Thank you,' said Dr McCrae, 'it was a moving time.' He squinted his eyes a fraction. 'In some respects, it still is.'

'Have you written any more poems?' asked Samuel.

'Oh, I've got one I'm playing around with. Something similar.'

'Samuel is a keen reader of poetry,' said Matthew.

'Is that so?' asked Dr McCrae. 'Would you two care for some tea? My sister Geillis has managed to send me some excellent supplies – not unappreciated may I add.'

Outside Dr McCrae's modest quarters, they sat in canvas chairs around a brazier, drinking smoky Russian Caravan in metal mugs. 'Tell me, Samuel,' said Dr McCrae, 'Byron or Coleridge?'

'The Ancient Mariner is a great poem,' Samuel replied.

Without hesitation Matthew said: *'Water, water, every where, And all the boards did shrink; Water, water, every where, Nor any drop to drink.'* After a short pause he added, *'You'd know something about that, Samuel.'*

'How long did you go without water when you were adrift?' asked the Doctor.

'I stretched what I had over a week and then for the rest, another week, eight days, I didn't have any.'

'A week without water! Great Scott! I went two days without water once and I thought I'd fallen through the cracks into Hades.'

'Where was that?' asked Matthew.

'In Africa, the Boer War – 478 miles of horse-riding through such dry, desolate country, you couldn't even imagine it. At one point we had two days in a row of nine hours in the saddle without food and just a trickle of water in our cans. All we could do was gargle – my throat has never been so sore or swollen.'

'Well lucky for me it wasn't hot. But it was a torment to be surrounded by water and not able to drink any. Have you spent some time at sea, Dr McCrae?'

'I've worked as a ship's surgeon on a few passages between

Europe and Canada. Didn't see any albatross though. What about you, any albatross in sight when you were lost?'

'None whatsoever,' said Samuel with a single shake of his head.

'You will have to tell the tale sometime, better still, write a poem. The process of writing distils your emotions and thoughts like nothing else. I would encourage you to turn your hand to it. I would be most keen to read your reflections.' He took a sip of his tea, savouring it. 'Yes, I would say The Rime is Coleridge's masterpiece.' He took another mouthful. 'Does Coleridge get your vote then?'

'No.' Smiling, Samuel turned to the doctor and said, 'Byron. He was by far the more colourful character and a traveller after my own heart. And,' casting a sheepish glance at Matthew, 'maybe I have a soft spot for him because he reminds me of my brother and his hitherto dissolute lifestyle.'

'Oh come now, Byron was rumoured to have had over 250 lovers in one year!' Matthew exclaimed. 'I could never claim that – not even in my lifetime! Those days are well and truly over.'

'They are indeed. Tell me Samuel, are you as taken with your new sister-in-law?'

'We are delighted,' said Samuel. 'We have always thought she was quite the package.'

The Colonel looked at Matthew, his eyebrows raised, his eyes alight.

'Dr McCrae,' Samuel ventured, 'you haven't said, who is your favourite?'

'You're right I haven't. I tell you what; I'll give you a clue. With a name like McCrae, there's no guessing my origins and one of these esteemed romanticists was also half Scottish by birth and he liked to claim he was bred a whole one.'

'Byron,' said Samuel with a grin.

'Yes, and despite all his controversy, there is another reason why he is a man of my heart.'

'What's that?'

'His inordinate love for animals. Did you know he kept a bear with him when he was a student at Trinity College in Cambridge? Imagine that? Nothing like a touch of eccentricity. And he had a whole menagerie of pets over his life: monkeys, foxes, a parrot, an eagle, peacocks, herons – you name it. But his greatest joy and fondness was reserved for his best friend.'

'His dog,' said Samuel, wistfully. 'What type of dog did he have?'

'A Newfoundlander,' said Dr McCrae.

'Really!' said Matthew primed with excitement, 'just like Samuel here!' casting Samuel a quick glance and dodging a thump in return.

'Will that be in your poem too?' asked Dr McCrae.

Samuel struggled to reply. As always, Matthew enjoyed every moment of his discomposure.

'Never mind,' said Dr McCrae, unable to suppress a small smile. Samuel noticed that about him. His smile was always close to the surface.

'Back to Byron,' he continued, 'His 'Epitaph to a Dog', is one of his best-known works and possibly my all time favourite poem. Do you know it by chance?

Near this spot are deposited the remains of one who possessed beauty without vanity
Strength without insolence, courage without ferocity,
And all the virtues of man without his vices.'

'Beauty without vanity, that's so perfect,' murmured Samuel, his heart at that very moment going out to Rebecca.

28th November 1917
McGill Hospital

Dear Rebecca,
I miss you my beautiful, strong, self-possessed girl. Remember our conversation on your fifteenth birthday? Well, Auguste Rodin, the greatest sculptor of his time, of our time, has died, on the 17th of November at 77 years of age. France is in mourning and so am I.
For over 60 years he created the most inspired statues and has left an amazing legacy. I wish I had my own bronze statue of you with me. I lie awake at night and dream of your body, wanting to run my hands over every inch of it so I can forge it into my memory. We never had enough time together, you and I, but after this war we will make up for it. We will make love to wake the gods. I so

want you beside me. You are my muse and I am not the same without you.

Ever Samuel X

The men received regular letters from their family, from their friends but most especially, from their women. Rebecca's were always a few weeks older than Lenore's, mail services not being as frequent to and from Second Chance as they were from Toronto. When Samuel got a letter from Rebecca, he would go and lie on his camp bed, imagining the two of them lying together in the boat looking up at the stars, into their dreams. He would read them over and over committing them to memory but for the first reading he sought solitude so he could be completely undisturbed.

Samuel received a letter from Rebecca only a week after he had arrived. His mother forwarding it onto him with a note that said, 'This arrived a week after you left,' and a, 'P.S. now I know!' But it was the first letter he got, twelve days after he arrived back in Toronto that he carried around with him at all times, in his pocket over his heart, even though he knew every word, by heart:

I thought I missed you an unbearable amount last time you left. But nothing compares to this. I miss you so badly I can barely breathe. And when I do, my chest hurts.

When I awake in the morning for an instant I feel normal as if the world is right but then reality comes rushing in and I realise that I am here and you are there. And I have to somehow get through several more anguished months apart. My sister is stoic. She says nothing and nor do I, harbouring my emptiness, my sadness. Trying to keep the faith, that we are meant to be together, that one day you will return for me and that God will answer my prayers and deliver a suitor for my sister.

I long to wake up in your arms,
your Angel, your Venus, your Rebecca x

It was a week before Christmas and the newly arrived dispatch was likely to be their last mail till the New Year. After Samuel read Rebecca's latest letter, twice, he walked outside and sat next to Matthew, flicking through the pile, deciding which letter to open next, leaving Matthew in peace with his wife's outpourings.

'Lenore has written with the most incredible news.'

He glanced at a startled Matthew. 'Has her mother made a full recovery?'

'No, in fact there were only a few lines about her mother. You'll never guess.'

'You're right. I'm too tired to guess today.'

'I'm going to be a father. You,' he said grabbing Samuel around the shoulders, 'are going to be an uncle again.'

'You are!' said Samuel, equally astonished. And then, 'Wait a minute, why should I be surprised about that. It's a miracle you are not a father already.'

'Samuel, I have always been careful.'

'Even with Lenore?'

'Initially. We didn't want morning sickness to mar our extended honeymoon.'

'Do you mean to say you planned this baby with the precision of a military manoeuvre?'

'I'd prefer to say we used science to our advantage.'

'Then why are you so surprised?'

'I don't know. Perhaps it's still a marvel that you can create life through the simple act of lovemaking. Maybe, because it happened some time ago now it doesn't seem real.'

'When is she due?'

'Late May.'

'Late May,' Samuel repeated, his mind registering.

Matthew burst out laughing. 'I can see your brain working, little brother. We made a baby just before I left. Lenore writes, "I had a spot of bleeding at two months and was worried I might lose the baby, so your father ordered absolute rest and a month later, all is well. I'm sorry I didn't write of this before now, but I didn't want to get your hopes up if nature decided to intervene. But we are clear. We are going to have a baby! Can you believe it?"'

'What's the date on that letter?'

'The first of December. What was the date of your letter?'

'The twentieth of November.'

'You're looking worried. Are you expecting similar news?'

'No, I hope not to receive such news. Not that I don't

want to be a father to Rebecca's children you understand, but I wouldn't wish that upon her under the present circumstances.'

'Could it be a possibility?'

Samuel threw him an anxious look. 'I never planned on going there and having relations with her,' he said in exasperation. 'But some of your prophylactic packages would have come in handy.'

'Playing with fire. Did you take any precautions?'

'Yes willpower, self-control, I resisted, she resisted, right up until my last night.'

'And?'

'Coitus interruptus.'

'Onanism is not a fail-safe method,' said Matthew, shaking his head.

'I know,' said Samuel dryly. 'She seemed to think God would protect her. I know there's no science or proof in that, and no reason for me to trust her instincts. Anyway, by that stage, we half thought her getting pregnant could be a solution to our problems.' And that is when Samuel finally told Matthew everything: his feelings for Rebecca, the predicament with Rachel, his proposal, her parent's dictatorial decree.

In the end Matthew said, 'Well, if you both felt so sure of yourselves, why didn't ou just take yourselves off to the local minister, hang the parents and get married. That way if she did get into strife she'd have some comeback and so would you and they couldn't forbid any union once you were legally wed.'

'That didn't occur to me at the time' said Samuel, anxiety traipsing through his body.

'Oh, Samuel.' Matthew laid an arm around his shoulder and gave him a squeeze. 'Don't kill yourself worrying over it. If she's pregnant, you'll marry her and we'll all stand by you and that is ultimately what you want. But look, it's been over three months, she would be further along than Lenore and I'd dare say you'd know about it by now.'

It had been the one black cloud on his happy horizon. He had worried about it on and off for weeks, heavy thudding moments of guilt and angst, wondering how he had let it happen. He debated writing to Rebecca about it, but decided against it, feeling it was dangerous to commit such a question to paper. He wasn't sure how well their privacy was being respected. And, as Matthew had declared, he would have heard about it by now. He let it go and started to breathe easier. Turning to his brother he said, 'I'm looking forward to being an uncle to your child, Matthew. Congratulations.'

42

A week or two after the discovery of Rebecca's pregnancy, a day or two after the bruises inflicted by her father had finally faded, Rebecca's life nearly returned to normal. Her mother was back to treating her like she always had and Rachel, surprisingly, had made the quickest recovery of all. She had started to knit and sew a whole baby's wardrobe, which at the rate she was going would be finished by New Year, if not Christmas.

Her father on the other hand had placed Rebecca in a prison of silence. The only problem was, he was there too. One day Rachel, in front of them all, made a vague illusory comment to the fact. His reply: *'God had made all people prisoners of their own disobedience so that he might show mercy to them all.'* And then: 'Particularly those who disobey their parents. You know, honour your mother and father is one of the most important commandments.'

The only way he would communicate with Rebecca was to leave pieces of paper on the table with scripture readings for her to read. She felt like burning them in the fire. But she read them, in case he ever drilled her about them.

Lamentations 3: Punishment, Repentance, and Hope. After she read that, all she could think was, who was the enemy? Her father would not have been pleased with her answer.

A dark mood would descend over the house whenever he was around, hanging like an oppressive fog. Which, being winter, was quite a lot, too much in fact.

Eventually Morna had enough and spoke her mind. Standing silently on the stairs, out of sight but not out of earshot, Rebecca heard every word.

'This has got to stop, Silas. Come Christmas I want peace in our home. How long are you going to punish her and make everyone in this house miserable?'

'I'm not punishing her. I'm helping her see the error of her ways.'

'You are not helping!' exclaimed Morna. 'Be reasonable. Stop treating her like she's the worst person on this earth, as if she is scum. She made a mistake. We all make mistakes at times. But she is not a murderer, a thief, a cold-hearted person of mean spirit and spite. She has been and continues to be a wonderful daughter in many ways. You have forgotten that. You keep putting her down, like you are pushing her head under water. Let her come up to breathe and maybe she'll be able to find her own way again, the right way again. And enough with the Scriptures! You're the one who needs to search the Scriptures and find answers in prayer so you can find a way in your heart to forgive her, a way for you to stop punishing her and let it go. Think about yourself and not her. Think about how you can find some small offering in yourself, some token, some gesture of peace.'

'Me?' said Silas, almost incredulously.

'Yes. You. And stop glaring at her belly as if it's growing in front of your very eyes. It doesn't happen that quickly!'

It wasn't until Christmas morn that her father spoke the kindest words he had said to her in over a month: 'Merry Christmas, Rebecca. Shall we go and give thanks to the Lord for all he has given us and remember our loved ones?'

Over the following days, Rebecca came to realise that although her father had made a move towards peace she was not forgiven. The Ten Commandments were still in place. And Rebecca wondered, what's going to happen when Samuel does come back and marry me and all of a sudden a baby magically appears? What are people going to think then? Or is he going to make Samuel and me disappear in the middle of the night…and what's going to happen when we return one day with a child and people find out how old the baby is? What then?

She didn't think her father's irrational mind had ventured that far…or had it? He or God, as Silas would often credit, always seemed to have an answer for everything. She was tempted to ask him. But she knew it would only serve to inflame what was already a highly incendiary situation. More than anything, Rebecca lived her days doing her utmost to steer clear of any confrontation with her father.

News Year's Eve on the Continent was spent huddled round two crackling braziers. Anthony Clarkson, one of Samuel and Matthew's former Montreal roommates, joined them. It had been two and a half years since Samuel had last seen Anthony. He never returned to graduate. They were joined by four other doctors whom Matthew had worked with and Samuel had come to know in recent months: Doctor Martin Cameron, Marty; Doctor Bartholomew Peters, Bart; Doctor Edward Hansen, Ted or Teddy; and Wyatt Kingston. He was simply Wyatt. Samuel liked that about him.

One of them had managed to source two bottles of French champagne for the occasion. They toasted in the New Year, all wishing for an end to hostilities so they could return home to their families. Marty, five years older than Matthew, had a three year old and another one on the way. Bart was engaged to a shop assistant back home in Ontario. Ted was engaged to no one but was busy writing letters left, right and centre and Wyatt never gave an inch – he was the one big mystery in the western military zone.

When Marty refilled everyone's glasses, he said, 'Let's drink to Canada.'

'To Canada,' said Samuel and quietly, 'to Newfoundland.'

43

The long dark month of January: daylight from eight in the morning to four in the afternoon. Samuel wore his Newfoundland gloves while he wrote notes and letters by kerosene lamp. Every night at nine he would head to the mess tent for some hot water and some powdered milk to go with the powdered hot chocolate his mother had sent. That would tide him over for another few hours of textbooks and discussions. The men in his tent quarters were mindful of his studies, having been there before and were generally quiet and circumspect around him. If they wanted to talk, they would go outside, light up a brazier and chat and drink or head off to the mess if it were drizzling.

The Germans were re-organising and re-planning. The Allies were re-strategising and re-planning. The British and the French had suffered a huge public backlash at the inordinate loss of lives in 1917. No one wanted 1918 to be a repeat of 1917, of 1916, of 1915. They all waited, holding their expectant breath. It was deathly still, deathly dark and into that bleary blackness, into that bizarre tranquility came the angel of death and in the space of one week McGill Hospital would lose one of its most respected and loved men, setting Samuel's life on an unforeseen path.

On 23rd of January forty-five year old John McCrae was appointed consulting physician to the First British Army – a great honour and the first Canadian to have been appointed. When he heard the news Jack wasn't up to celebrating. He had long suffered from asthma and bronchial infections and throughout 1917 had had recurring bouts. On Friday 25th he was transferred to No. 14 General Hospital at Wimereux where high-ranking military officers were treated. Three days later he was dead, far from the battle lines, but not that far from his famous Flanders fields. The cause of death: double pneumonia, extremely virulent, with massive cerebral infection.

Matthew was devastated. He felt like he had lost an uncle, a man, whom next to his father and grandfather, he respected and admired above all others. He had only seen him last Tuesday when Jack told him he wasn't feeling a hundred percent; he'd had that old tightness in the chest again. They had planned to go riding when he was well. Matthew was so distraught he couldn't bear to face anyone. He hastily made bland excuses and disappeared.

Samuel heard the news around lunch and went looking for his brother but couldn't find him anywhere. No one seemed to know to where he had disappeared. But, late that afternoon, Samuel found him walking towards him up the main thoroughfare. He hardly recognised him. He had never seen his brother so downtrodden, his head so low.

'You've heard,' he said, coming up to Matthew embracing him, trying to take on a little of his sadness. 'I'm sorry for your loss, Matthew. He was one in a million.'

'Yes,' breathed out Matthew, a tremor in his voice. 'He was the most brilliant of men. I've never met anyone quite like him and I doubt I ever will again.'

'Where have you been all afternoon?'

'With Bonfire.'

Ah. 'Did you go riding?'

'No. I just groomed him,' Matthew admitted, his voice trembling. 'Talked to him. Told him all the things I loved about Jack that I never said to his face, that I wished now I had.' Matthew lost his composure and cried and his tears brought tears to Samuel's eyes. 'I told him,' he said, his voice catching 'how sorry we all were that Jack had passed away.'

Samuel hugged his brother, struggling for words that might comfort him. 'If his spirit is floating around here anywhere, Matthew, it would be with Bonfire and Bonneau and I'm sure he was greatly comforted by your words, not only by your words but by your deeds. If I didn't know before, I know now how much he meant to you.'

Matthew wrote to Lenore trying to describe what Jack had meant to him. He was the most talented man in the medical profession in Canada, a world-class poet, a walking encyclopaedia. But all these words sounded trite in his ears and he threw his attempts away. When he thought of John McCrae he thought of two things. He was noble in the truest sense of the word. And he had a smile of empyreal radiance, of sheer fun, uplifting, touching anyone who caught it. Matthew finally wrote to Lenore saying January has been the saddest month in his life, without fail.

I have lost a man who was both a dear friend and mentor, Lieutenant Colonel John McCrae. You may recall I have spoken about him in the past. Grandpa and Father can tell you what a marvellous man he was. In honour of him, I ask that you name our firstborn Jonathan if it is a boy, Jacqueline if it is a girl. I trust this will work with any other names you may have had in mind for our child.

My truest love, Matthew.

He always signed his letters to her, 'My truest love'. She had asked, had he ever signed his letters that way before and he said, 'No, just for you, because that is who you are.'

Even before McCrae's death there had been a reshuffle of the Canadian medical men working at Hospital City in Boulogne and Etaples. People were moved across to fill vacancies and Matthew found himself assigned to No 1 Hospital. Samuel stayed on at McGill.

44

Throughout that dark protracted winter, Samuel's letters from the front came in steady regularity. As Rebecca was grounded, Morna had taken to collecting them from Ronnie under the pretence of sending them on with her own mail to Esther. Rebecca would read the letters up in her cold room, basking in their warming effect. At times she would read them out loud, not too loud, but loud enough to share her news with her unborn child.

'Oh little one,' she gasped. 'You are going to have a cousin nearly the same age as you to play with. How wonderful will that be? How exciting!'

And then she would whisper to her baby, tell stories of Samuel and sing soft lullabies. And it would kick, and swirl and swim strokes in the sumptuous sea sloshing inside her, blowing out little bubbles of air, little hiccups of hello, letting her know it was there.

Every morning the first thing Rachel would say to her when she came to the kitchen table was, 'How is our baby this morning?'

Our baby. She liked that. Rachel and her mother delighted in placing their hands on her belly and feeling the signs of life knocking from the other side. And then Rachel, taking her role of assistant midwife very seriously, asked Ronnie if he had any books on birthing that she could borrow. So she could read up on what her sister, ahem, her sister, Esther, would be going through. Ronnie borrowed one from the midwife, Mrs Hooper, for her and said, 'You know, I would have thought your parents would have sent you off to be with Esther, not Rebecca. I would like to see you have time away from here, Rachel.'

'Thanks,' she said, giving him an appreciative smile.

Rachel relayed everything to her grounded sister. Two

nights later as she was reading, she said, 'I don't think you want to read this, Rebecca.'

'Why not?'

Her mother snatched the book from Rachel and gave her an admonishing look. 'It will spoil the surprise,' she murmured. As much as they could they relieved her of heavy duties, made her put her feet up and made her special brews of tea. In some respects it was the easiest few months Rebecca had had in years. She told her mother one night that she was feeling guilty about not doing more to help. Her mother replied: 'Make the most of this time Rebecca, because after your first, it is never the same again. Trust me. Being pregnant and having a young family is the hardest job of the lot.'

She continued to write to Samuel every week. Sometimes she would hold her letters over for a second week and send him summaries of local newspaper reports, any other news that her sister or mother brought into the home, sometimes she would do drawings for him, of Mica, of their house, their cove from the top of the stony steps, sometimes she would send him just a few lines, a few adulterated passages of the Bible, from Song of Songs, that would let him know just how much she thought of him, that might remind him of her in Newfoundland waiting patiently for him to come back and claim her:

Samuel, how I love it when we get your letters, any and all of your letters. How I love listening to Mother and Rachel talking about you and your news. I'm in Heaven when I hear your name. My whole body leaps for joy. Every part of me embraces you.

Your angel, Rebecca

Her letters would simultaneously make his heart warm and his heart ache. If she were in front of him she would immediately know the effect she was having on him as he struggled to control his throbbing heart, his throbbing everything. In return he would send her corrupted lines from Catullus, from Hugo and from himself.

The velvet night, the slinking moon, my shining, dazzling Venus. I see you twinkling down at me, casting your eyes across the

sky, sending your love across the waves. I can almost feel you beside
me, around me, inside me, your hair brushing my face, your lips
brushing my lips, your breasts brushing my chest. I so want it to be
real. My only comfort is that every night is yet another night closer
to you. Come forth the Evening Star.
Ever Samuel x

In February after the ending of hostilities with Russia one million German soldiers, relocated to the Western front where Allied forces were stretched from the top of France to the bottom of Italy waiting for more American forces to arrive for what they hoped would be a final offensive. On 21st March 1918, while they still had an advantage, Germany attacked along 40 miles of the British front near Amiens, hell-bent on one mission: to capture the rail line and starve Paris.

In a matter of days, they had advanced an unprecedented 40 miles. For the first time since 1914, manoeuvring was achieved on the battlefield. The Canadian Corps based in the Lens-Vimy sector was immediately stripped away to reinforce threatened points along the line. Sensing a shortage of medical personnel near the front, the Commanders transferred staff from their General Hospitals to their Field Ambulances and Clearing Hospitals.

Without hesitating, Samuel said, 'I'll go.' Had Matthew been there, he would have stomped on his foot and belted him around the ear. He was not happy when Samuel told him the news yet Samuel couldn't quite understand Matthew's displeasure.

'You worked at a dressing station. You were safe.'

'Only by sheer good fortune,' said Matthew. 'This is not an adventure in the wilds of Canada, Samuel!'

'I know that. You're sounding like our father. Do you think I don't have what it takes to work out there?'

'No,' sighed Matthew. 'That's not it at all.'

'Well, the way I look at it, I would rather it be me than you. If they have to pull people from the rear and send to the front, I would rather you stay here where you are undisputedly safe. You have a family now to consider.'

'Fine Samuel, but I'd rather it wasn't you either. You haven't finished your studies. You are still a medical student and you just don't know what situation you might end up in out there. You get pulled in all directions.'

'I'll be careful.'

'You need to be more than careful. You need to trust your gut instincts. And another thing, there is no way I am telling Mother and Father about this. You can be the one to deliver that news.'

Matthew was right. Their parents would not be pleased.

'Oh. Damn it all to hell and back,' said Matthew, fiercely kicking a stone at his feet. 'I don't want anything to happen to you Samuel, you hear?' Anxiety was clearly etched on his face.

'I hear.'

'Right! Listen up and listen hard as what I'm going to tell you could save your life.' Matthew came up close, his dark eyes boring into Samuel's. 'You are going out there and you will work as a dresser, you hear me, making men passable enough to return to service or to be shunted down the line if they are serious. Under no circumstances will you volunteer to be an orderly or a stretcher bearer or a medical officer. A dresser is where you should be. Working under someone more senior, under some Major or Captain, taking their orders, learning as you go. But at times pandemonium happens and all hell breaks loose. An MO goes down here, another one takes a hit there and before you can say, "I'm not trained for that, or I didn't sign on for that," you're ten yards from the front line as you're the most suitably trained there and then. So if that happens remember this:

'Your job is to stay alive at all costs. Dodge those bullets. Take shelter from those shrapnel shells. Wear that helmet at all times even when you are inside a building. And never, ever, take that white band off your left arm. It marks you as a medical man and at times of absolute danger that brassard might be the one thing that saves your life. Do what you can for your men, but do it judiciously. You're no help to them if you are dead. And I won't even begin to tell you what you are to me if you are dead. So wait for those lulls. Use your intuition.

'And you have to protect yourself from the gas at all times, especially now that the bastards have started launching mustard at us. You're no good to anyone if you're gagging with the stuff. And chances are you won't be alive for long if you do.

'There should be gas guards at the ADS but if you are out in the trenches or on the battlefield you have to listen to the soft plop and wear that mask. If you can't see, drop to the ground and wait till it passes. In fact you should be at ground level whenever you can. It's too easy to become a victim of a random act of chaos. And that's what it's like out there: meaningless indiscriminate chaos. And then you're dead by accident or design. And that is what we don't want. Getting captured by the enemy is not the worst that can happen. All that will happen to you is you will end up in one of their camps, looking after their prisoners, our men, or you'll end up attending to their wounded it's all the same. And eventually they'll exchange you for one of their prisoners. That's what they did with Dr Hart from Regina. So remember that. Keep calm and keep a clear head. I know you are capable of that. It's a Dalton family trait. So when you've got some down time, do what you can to make peace with yourself and with your head. Got that?'

'Loud and clear, big brother.' Samuel smiled in gratitude. 'I'll be careful. Ich bin ein Doktor. Bitte schießen Sie nicht auf mich.'

'Ja genau,' replied Matthew. 'Good job you learnt German at school.'

'Just as well,' said Samuel. 'I wouldn't have got into McGill without it.'

45

Samuel wondered if he had half-volunteered as a way of permanently engineering himself out of returning with the McGill students at the end of April. Matthew was still so disconsolate and downcast after the harrowing month of January that Samuel felt there was no earthly way he could return to Canada and see Matthew's offspring, ahead of Matthew. There was something innately unfair about that. He would return with Matthew whenever that would be – possibly at Christmas, failing that in April or May 1919, when they could both expect to gain leave for Samuel's graduation. He knew Rebecca would be sorely disappointed. He would write soon and break the news that they wouldn't be seeing each other that summer. He hoped she would understand.

Samuel was assigned to an Advanced Dressing Station (ADS) in the Passchendaele sector. Their station was a modified pillbox with whitewashed internal walls to improve luminescence and visibility. A large Red Cross flag flew overhead. He would be there for seven weeks then given a two-week break followed by another seven-week rotation. Samuel thought he was never going to hear the end of his brother's tirade until he mentioned he was going in with Captain Kingston.

'Why didn't you say?' said Matthew shoving him roughly.

'I was getting to it,' said Samuel. 'See, it will be almost like having you with me.'

'You are so wrong there. He won't exactly keep you company, but he will look out for you,' he said grudgingly.

The station was well equipped with enough medical and surgical supplies for treating two to three hundred men: dressings, wool, bandages, splints, scissors, soap, collapsible candle lanterns, iodine and 500cc ampoules of preserved blood. The use of preserved blood on the battlefield was a relatively recent medical advance and only since the beginning of 1918 had transfusions been carried out at advanced dressing stations and regimental aid posts (RAPs) using a syringe technique. Only group O, also termed group IV, blood was used.

One of Samuel's tasks each day was to do a stock take of all their supplies of medicines, food, water, morphine and blood and send an order through for replenishment. When they first took over responsibility of the station there was not much shelling or activity. It wasn't quiet, but Wyatt told Samuel this was as quiet as it got. They would take turnabout each morning to visit the battalion headquarters to learn about any planned action. They'd stop by the RAPs, and the Bearer Relay Posts, the Main Dressing Station (MDS), and the Field Ambulance Officers and stretcher bearers.

Samuel was always gregarious and friendly. He tried to be extra cheerful to make up for Wyatt's sombreness. In his spare time he sought to engage Wyatt in conversation. Occasionally Wyatt would throw in an anecdote, a reflection, a little bit of his youth growing up in Saskatchewan. Samuel had seen pictures of Saskatchewan. And he'd heard the line: "It's so flat in Saskatchewan, you can watch your dog run away from home for a week." Both images disturbed him. He couldn't imagine living in the midst of such a huge endless steppe without any hills or trees to break up the monotony of the horizon. He would lose himself there. Perhaps Wyatt had come to terms with emptiness and isolation. Perhaps that was why he was always so standoffish, thought Samuel. He needed his space, his nothingness around him.

Samuel would also spend his days writing to his parents, to Rebecca and the Crowes in diary-type formats. His private notes to Rebecca were shorter, but heartfelt and much, much more intimate. In writing to Rebecca as part of the Crowe family he tried not to spare any details of his surroundings and his company. He had just written telling how every soldier in the field carried a field dressing, sewn into a small pocket on the inside of their coat. The dressing consisted of an ampoule of iodine and two roller bandages, which were each attached to a pad of absorbent material – yes, Newfoundland moss! This was the first treatment an injured soldier received before any medic saw them.

On the Monday of his second week at the ADS the sleeping giant of the Hun awoke and unleashed its vengeance on the Canadians holding the line from their lofty heights on the Passchendaele Spur. In that short week, which felt more like one long never-ending day, Samuel learnt about the wastage of war and how in the crowded trenches priority of movement was given to ammunition, then reinforcements and finally to the wounded. It went against Samuel's grain. He wanted to run in, hold his hands up and say: 'Hold fire. Just let us get these men out and then you can resume your war.'

They worked steadily throughout the first day and incessantly during the night under dull kerosene light. Under the protection of darkness stretcher-bearers retrieved countless wounded off the battlefields. Samuel would go for hours without looking outside his work pit. He would finish with one casualty, say, 'next', wipe his hands, take a swig of water, then turn back to another stretcher case lying in front of him.

Dawn on the second day: the sun's rays drenched No man's land and glazed every face that had bivouacked out under the barest shelter. Samuel stepped outside to catch some air and light. It took a few moments for his eyes to adjust and he nearly had to rub them in disbelief at the sight of the wounded piled up on stretchers in long lines down the communication trenches: a sea of stretchers in front of him, a tidal wave of wounded men, many of them with blankets covering the whole body. Ones he and Wyatt didn't get to in time. He took a deep breath and with grit went back inside.

On the morning of the second day Samuel had to perform his first amputation. A sergeant's arm hung loosely and heavily by his side, wrapped in the bloodiest of bandages. Samuel unwrapped it to find a large divot and the bone missing from his forearm and a similar section missing from his bicep. Loose flaps of skin and flesh were all that was holding the arm together. It hung like the Raggedy Anne doll description he had read recently in one of Analeise's letters. Bizarrely the explosion had not managed to burst major arteries but even so the arm was lost.

He called Wyatt over for a quick look. 'Right you know what you have to do.' Samuel was hoping Wyatt would say,

'Let's swap.'

Pulling him aside, Samuel whispered, 'I haven't done an amputation before.'

'No?' said Wyatt. He glanced at the man lying on the table then back at Samuel. 'He's a good one to start with. Leave the top third of his upper arm on.'

That was all the instruction Wyatt offered. Samuel put the man under with an extra large dose of morphine, applied a tourniquet, asked for an orderly to hold his arm out, took a small saw, held his breath and cut through the bone, then with a scalpel he sliced carefully at an angle, trying to leave a large section of skin as a flap to fold over the stump. He doused it with iodine, knowing it would be excruciating if the guy were conscious. Then he tightly bandaged the stump. 'He's one for the ambulance train.' Samuel looked at the remains of the arm on the table beside him. It had to go into the bin along with the used medical supplies. It would be burned in an incinerator. He felt sick throwing it away.

After their second day he put in a request for a complete daily replenishment of all their supplies until otherwise advised. The 'walking wounded' were making it to the Walking Wounded Stations but the Field Ambulance had been collecting from ten or more RAPs and the 'liers', as men on stretchers were called, were still piling up outside. When he took another short spell Samuel noted how what Matthew once told him was true. The guns of war boomed all around, the angry growls of armoury, but Samuel seemed almost oblivious to it, intent on the men that kept appearing in front of him.

Compound fractures, broken tibias, a bullet through the lung, another with a large shrapnel wound to the thigh. 'You are fortunate,' said Samuel. 'It just missed your femoral artery.'

'Would I know it if it hit that?' asked the soldier.

'Not for long,' said Samuel.

Was it just Samuel's imagination or were the squeals of warfare getting closer? He and Wyatt were both outside on the fourth day of battle having a quick cup of tea when someone yelled, 'Incoming.'

They dropped to their haunches. Samuel automatically checked that his helmet was on. In no time they were showered in dirt and dust. They sat, waiting for more, and more did come. They could see the entry point of a shell about two yards outside the entrance to their ADS, but where did it come out? They followed the gas guard as he walked slowly around the outside of the station. Noticing the half crumbled wall on the left side he said with barely a note of surprise in his voice, 'You've got light and ventilation. Was that what you wanted?'

Samuel looked at the hole, the size of another doorway. 'It didn't come out there, surely?'

'No,' said the sergeant. 'That's from that stump that used to be over there,' casually pointing to a hole about three metres to his right. The sergeant continued to walk around the back of the building. 'Well I'll be,' Samuel heard him say.

There in front of them was the nose of an 8-inch shell, poking up out of the ground at the back of the ADS. It had landed at the front, travelled the whole length of the pillbox underneath to come out on the other side.

'Well I guess you can say it's safe to go back in,' quipped the sergeant.

'You're kidding me,' said Samuel, 'If it had exploded where it was meant to there would be no ADS standing. Maybe it's time we dropped back to another pillbox.'

At that moment they heard another coming their way. Samuel fell flat on the ground. This time the shell went over their heads towards a group of soldiers who had their backs to them, thinking they too were out of danger. The last man was hit, the shell slicing his legs off just below the knees. Samuel would never have believed it had he not seen it with his own eyes. The soldier still in motion walked forward and somehow managed to take two more steps before collapsing. Five seconds later Samuel was inside their hut grabbing tourniquets, bandages and morphine. Thirty seconds later he was with a kneeling Wyatt who uncharacteristically was doing plenty of talking, 'Listen, we've got you. And those cuts are clean. They'll heal nicely,' as both men proceeded to tie tourniquets on each thigh, and inject him with a large dose of morphia. They drenched his stumps with saline, then iodine and dressed them and handed him over to two of his comrades, who had re-appeared, stretcher at the ready to take him to the ambulance truck. He had lost both his legs in a split second but he also lost very little blood, and the morphia would minimise shock. Oddly, his chances of survival were good.

Captain Kingston ordered Sergeant Trelome to speak to Battalion Headquarters immediately to find out exactly how far away the enemy was and what in damnation was going on. Amen, thought Samuel. Along with the Hun, Wyatt had awoken.

Twenty minutes later an excited Sergeant Trelome came in puffing heavily. 'It's a goner. We've been given the order to drop back. They want this area completely cleared within four hours. Everyone who can carry stretchers with a live one is to get them up to the ambulance carts and trucks so we can move them out. They want you at the MDS by 1700 hours. The Fritzers are going ballistic. Nearly every one of them has that new sub-machine gun weapon, what are they calling it, the MP-18? And they're just cutting our men down.'

Four frantic hours followed. Samuel and Wyatt, along with every available orderly, ferried wounded men one mile westward to where they were handed over to others who had come forward to assist the Field Ambulances. All the horses and carts were out in force. From time to time shells would burst around them and Samuel found himself instinctively pulling his collar up around his neck, as if it would keep out the dirt and metal fragments like a raincoat kept out the rain.

Around 1600 hours they returned for the last ten injured. Just as they were about to head off a Medical Officer, Patterson, arrived with four stretcher-bearers carrying two fresh casualties. Patterson had shrapnel wounds to his right side, his arm and his leg. He was rather breathless but he was holding on. He could walk out he said but one of his men needed urgent medical attention, which he could no longer render. They were both captains. Wyatt and Samuel exchanged a quick glance.

'This one, I think will hold on,' said the MO, nodding to his right. 'He's been hit in the chest, could be his heart, I'm not sure. But it's quite small and he is holding up. But Captain Gaines's stomach is sliced open. Not sure if it's cut his spleen. He's lost a lot of blood. He's a good solider, was awarded the VC last year.'

'Take your heart man and go with our men,' said Wyatt. 'We'll look after the captain and bring him straight down after you. Leave two of your bearers with us.'

Patterson left, reluctantly, not wanting to surrender his man. They were close, thought Samuel, and his patient was grave. He was pale, almost white. Samuel and Wyatt caught each other's eyes.

'It's a good job they told us to abandon all our medical supplies,' Samuel muttered.

Wyatt was making a quick assessment of the man. He had a long deep slash across his upper abdomen. 'What do you think?' he asked Samuel.

'Pack with one large bandage and then stitch it up to hold it in place to seal his stomach as much as possible.'

'Yes,' said Wyatt, 'and,' he lifted his arm to rub the side of his face with his shoulder, 'I can't believe I'm saying this but I think we need to try and top him up.'

'A transfusion?' queried Samuel, trying to hide his surprise. He wasn't surprised in so far that the captain could clearly do with some blood, but he was surprised that Wyatt was suggesting it here and now when they were meant to be evacuated.

'I think best,' said Wyatt. 'He's lost a lot of blood. It will buck him up for a while longer.' He stared at the pale face of the soldier in front of him then looked up at Samuel's uncertain face. 'We must have some supplies left surely?'

Samuel walked over to retrieve a supply of blood from their diminishing stores. Over the last two days a number of bearers had been helping themselves to supplies trying to keep alive some of the men lying outside on stretchers.

'There's four lots,' called Samuel, 'One O, one AB– ' He broke off. 'I thought we were meant to get all O's out here. I should have checked this dispatch when it came in.'

'Doesn't matter,' said Wyatt. 'Just give us the O.'

Samuel wiped the Captain's arm with the iodine as Wyatt attached a glass tube and syringe to the blood receptacle.

A shadow fell across the doorway, the orderlies coming back inside. Without even glancing around Wyatt said, 'Gentlemen, either come inside or go outside, but don't stand there in my doorway when we're low on lighting as it is.'

The doorway continued to be mired in darkness. Samuel lifted his head. There standing in front of him were three German soldiers. The ones on either side were heavily armed supporting a soldier whose tunic was covered in dark wet blood.

'Ah, Wyatt,' said Samuel in a low voice, 'stay calm, but you should know our company is foreign.' Wyatt looked up.

Captain Gaines' stirred, fumbling for his revolver. Samuel placed his hand firmly on his arm and gave the slightest shake of his head. He wondered where the orderlies were. From a defence point of view it didn't matter, because none of the Field Ambulance staff carried any ammunition, but he was concerned by what might happen if they startled the Germans standing in the doorway. Samuel couldn't get over what was hanging off their bodies. Along with their pack and the machine gun, they had a standard bolt-action rifle with a bayonet and knives, wire cutters, a grenade thrower and a flame-thrower. They must have been some elite advance force to be carrying all that equipment and to be here in their midst when the Canadians hadn't fully evacuated their frontline forces.

'Doktor?' said the one on the right, pointing with his gun.

'Ja,' said Samuel looking at him steadily. 'Beide.'

'Sprichst du Deutsch?'

'Ein bisschen,' replied Samuel.

'Our friend needs help. You will look at him. You will fix him,' he said in German.

'Bitte,' said Wyatt, letting them know he knew the difference between a request and a command.

The two able-bodied men looked at each other. 'Ja, bitte,' said one.

'We will look at him,' said Samuel in German, 'provided you let all five of us go when we are done.'

'Fünf?' queried the solider.

'Yes, there are two others who will be joining us any minute.'

The soldier on the left pulled away from the man he was supporting and turned around.

Samuel yelled at the man in German, 'Don't shoot them. We won't help you if you do.'

The two able-bodied Germans looked at each other then they looked at Samuel and nodded.

'Put him on the table over there,' Samuel pointed. 'We will be with him in a minute.'

'No, you will be with him now,' said the German with the machine gun.

'Go look at him,' said Wyatt. 'I'll manage.'

The man also had a large gaping wound to his stomach. No wonder he too was nearly bled out. 'He needs surgery,' said Samuel. 'We cannot operate here. How far back to your doctors, your hospital?'

The men looked at each other and then the one on the left said to Samuel. 'How far back to your hospital?'

'Six, eight miles,' said Samuel. He thought about lying and saying twenty miles. Twenty miles and the Germans would be likely to grab him off the table and run with him back to their own medical men. But they were in a bind. Advancing soldiers did not return with wounded men. They left them for medical units and stretcher-bearers to collect as they caught up.

'You take him,' said the soldier who had hardly spoken a word. 'He is with doctors now. On our side, it will be hours before he is with doctors and it will be too late.'

'It will be too late,' Samuel agreed.

At that moment the two orderlies came walking in through the door. One said, 'Is he–' but broke off and exclaimed, 'what the hell has happened here?'

'Just keep calm, gentlemen,' said Wyatt, 'and we'll come to no harm. Two more minutes and our Captain Gaines will be right to go. We will have to strap the bottle to his chest as I don't think he will be able to hold it steady and you two will have your hands full.'

Samuel had given the injured German soldier a jab of morphia and called out for one of the orderlies to bring him Type O blood from the icebox in the corner.

'There's no O. There's only AB, A or B.'

'Bloody hell,' said Samuel, shaking his head.

'Bring them all over,' said Wyatt. 'We're covered at least.' He threw Samuel a quick look.

'Do you know what blood type he is?' asked Samuel to the German soldiers.

They looked at Samuel and just shook their heads. Their friend was drifting in and out. 'Can you ask him?' They tried but got the same response.

'You're going to have to do tests,' said Wyatt.

'Right, orderlies,' said Wyatt, 'let's get Captain Gaines on his way.' They picked up either end of the stretcher but the machine gun wielding German held up his gun in front of them, refusing to let them pass.

'Let them go,' said Wyatt.

'Nein,' said the machine gun man, pointing to his German friend on the table.

Samuel tried to explain to the Germans that they needed to give their colleague some blood to replace the blood he had lost. Samuel didn't know the word for transfusion. He said it in English. 'We need to keep him alive, till we can reach our hospital so they can operate on him. Blood is what will keep him alive. We will take your friend,' said Samuel, pointing to Wyatt and himself. 'Let these men go and they can get the ambulance to wait.'

Wyatt turned to the orderlies and told them under no circumstances were they to tell anyone they had been over-run by Germans and were treating a German. 'Just tell them, we have one last patient that we are working on and we will bring him ourselves.' They translated for the Germans and they seemed satisfied.

Samuel reached for the A Blood container; A being the most common blood type after O. They had to do a test first. Wyatt prepared the man's arm and injected 15 cc of A and then they waited.

'Have you ever had a patient react to the wrong blood type before?' asked Samuel in a low voice.

'No, I've only given about twenty – all of them Os. Do you remember what warning signs we look for?'

'Fever, which could be from another infection in his case. Chills, which could be from shock, from loss of blood. Pain along the infusion line to the chest or back.'

'Probably our best bet to go on'.

'Acute respiratory distress.'

'That too.'

'Dark urine.'

'Pass.'

'Hives, and other forms of allergic reaction. I wish I hadn't been in such a hurry to give him morphia,' said Samuel.

They waited another minute. And then their patient's breathing started to change; he was short of breath, breathing tighter. He rubbed his left arm as if it irritated him. 'Dammit all to hell and back,' said Samuel. He wiped his face with his hands and pushed his hair back.

'What now?' he said to Wyatt. 'What are we meant to do if he has a reaction?'

'We don't have time to think about that. We just have to try the next one. B, higher odds than AB.'

They connected an ampoule with Type B blood. One of the German soldiers asked him if he had any food. Samuel went and grabbed him some rations. There should be biscuits, cheese and other food in there, he told them.

'Käse,' said one of the men.

'Ja, Käse,' said Samuel. 'There's more if you want.' He waved behind him. 'When was the last time you ate?'

One of the men just shook his head and said, 'Not enough food lately. We are all starving.'

'How's he looking, Wyatt?'

'Difficult to tell if he's having any reaction or if it's the effect of the B blood.'

While they waited they bandaged the man's stomach. They waited three minutes this time. He didn't seem to be any more stressed than he had been after the last jab. 'I say we take our chances,' said Wyatt. 'Get him down there. Then we can grab some O blood once we are there. We need to get going.'

Samuel nodded. He turned to one of the Germans and said, 'Come, help me find a stretcher.' They went outside to one of the Canadian dead, lifted him off a stretcher, placed him on the ground and brought the stretcher inside.

'Are we going to be attacked by German soldiers when we try to leave here?' asked Samuel.

The machine-gun wielding soldier shook his head. 'Not if you hurry.'

'Your friend will become a prisoner of war.'

'Yes, but he will live.'

'Yes, hopefully. What's his name?'

'Thomas.'

'Thomas,' repeated Samuel. He looked at the two healthy soldiers 'Do you want to say your goodbyes?'

'No, just go. Go now. Auf Wiedersehen, Thomas. Write to us.'

Samuel had six hours sleep in four days. He couldn't remember when he had last slept, eaten, gone to the toilet and now he was running, running for his dear life, down a communications trench, down the evacuation route, hunched over like a pauper with an IV drip attached to Thomas' arm and a glass bottle, secured with strapping, his senses unbelievably charged. Something grey whizzed by, six inches in front of him. He startled for a micro second then kept going.

They ran and ran and Samuel thought, if I'd played ice hockey this year, this would be much easier. The trench was uneven underneath. He was at the rear of the stretcher and couldn't see where he was placing his feet. He kept his knees bent and tried to only run on the balls of his feet to avoid spraining an ankle.

The ambulance driver was waiting at the MDS with Captain Gaines, Patterson and his other men. 'We're it,' said Wyatt, climbing on board. 'Let's go.'

'I can't believe we waited for you to bring us a dying German soldier,' Patterson said.

'How long did you wait, Captain?' said Wyatt 'Fifteen minutes. It's neither here nor there. We can only give your man 500 cc's every four hours so what are you complaining about. We'll be there in time for his next round and they won't operate on him till he's perked up.'

Remarkably both patients held on. They were given two more blood transfusions and operated on the next morning. Samuel crawled into his sleeping bag at eight o'clock and slept soundly until midday.

After their interlude with the Germans, Wyatt said, 'I can see whose brother you are, fraternising with the enemy–'

'Finding out military secrets like they are low on food?'

'Not that, being sangfroid and all.'

'Those were my brother's orders.'

'Not just your brother's orders. You have the same survival instincts. You use your head.'

Samuel tilted the head in question. 'Those men weren't the enemy. I doubt they enjoy killing any more than our men. The men in power are the enemy.'

To his surprise, Samuel hadn't felt rattled by the Germans at all. Maybe he had been too tired to be rattled and now after rest and fresh food, the feeling of invulnerability was with him again, stronger than ever.

'My brother has always been cool in tight situations,' said Samuel, 'even as a young boy.'

'I would believe that,' said Wyatt. 'His commendation made note of that: "By his coolness and devotion to duty, many lives were saved".'

'What commendation?'

'His commendation for his Military Cross for what he did at Vimy Ridge last year. Didn't he tell you?'

'No,' said Samuel shaking his head in resignation. 'Wyatt, you should know by now that my brother is like you and keeps things very close to his chest. What else did the citation say?'

'I can't remember. Ask him to dig it out for you. If he still has it with him. That's how he was made a captain, didn't you know?'

'No I thought it was because he had served a certain term, not specifically for a single act of bravery. How did you become a captain?'

'I would have thought for three years uninterrupted duty but I was promoted for services at Mount Sorrel, though I have to say I thought the Somme was a harder, hairier experience, but there you go.'

Samuel and Wyatt had no more close encounters with the Germans but they did have to pull back twice more over the following days. By mid-April, in the space of a week, much of the ground gained at Passchendaele at great cost the year before was taken back by the Germans.

In a last ditch effort to overpower the Allied forces the Germans made another 40 mile advance towards Paris in late May before being stopped on the Marne River. Samuel and the Canadian Corps were far from the action. They had come out of the line in early May, replaced by fresh French and English troops. The Canadians were given two and a half months to prepare for a new offensive.

Samuel and Wyatt stayed on with the Field Ambulance service for the first few weeks of May, helping to do full medicals on over 5,000 men. After seven long weeks, they were given a ten-day break and told to sign back on at McGill for their next lot of orders. They headed west towards the French coast for respite and reunion with friends and in Samuel's case, family.

46

Rebecca had been having false contractions for nearly a week, like flashes of period cramps every so often, but her mother had told her not to worry. They were not the real thing. She had tried putting them out of her mind. She had been in and out of the house all morning doing the laundry, hanging clothes on the line but gradually they had become increasingly persistent. After her mother had managed to ascertain the one and only time she and Samuel had slept together, she had informed her not to expect a baby until May. 'I was never early Rebecca,' she had said, and here it was the 22nd of April.

Her father was down on the stage. He had been there for the last week, sanding and restoring the boats and all the woodwork. Since he returned from the lumber camp he practically lived down there, almost as if he were avoiding her, except things seemed slightly less strained between them. If she were to venture even halfway down the stony path she would smell the strong odour of new fishing gear and tar. It was one of those smells that immediately anchored her to spring. But going up and down her stairs each night was enough for Rebecca.

Morna and Rachel had chosen that day after the long closed in winter to go clean the church. She didn't expect them back till mid-afternoon, so there was not much she could do in their absence. By the time her mother and sister returned, they were more regular, more intense and longer lasting, nearly up to sixty seconds. Her mother eyed her closely and asked when was the last time she'd been to the toilet.

'About two hours ago,' she replied.

'Well start using the potty chair inside from now on and let me know each time you go. Keep your fluids up.'

She didn't feel like dinner. She barely managed to eat half of it. As she went to clear up her mother stopped her.

'I think you should have a warm bath and head to your room. I'll help you.'

Upstairs, dressed in a fresh nightie, her mother inspected her. 'Well, well.'

'Well, well what?' said Rebecca.

She patted her nightie back down. 'Your baby is coming.'

'When, now?' she asked in stunned disbelief.

Her mother laughed. 'Tonight, tomorrow sometime.'

'Not May?' said Rebecca.

'Not May. I certainly hope for you it won't be May else you will be in labour for a very long time.'

She was told to try get some rest and to call out if she wanted anything. Rest? thought Rebecca. The space between the contractions was getting shorter and shorter. She decided she would distract herself by reading Samuel's letters all over again. By the fifth letter she'd had enough of lying in bed and so she started pacing the room. Every time she had a contraction, she would reach for the bureau and hold it tightly, as if it were the one holding her up. Her thoughts were with Samuel, wondering what he would be doing and saying to her if he were with her right now.

And then the dull ache in her back became far from dull. She called out for her mother and put the letters away. Rachel came too. Her mother carried her sewing basket and a small bottle of olive oil. Rachel carried a warm woollen throw, which had been wrapped around a bed warmer. Rebecca took it from her, wrapped it around her lower back and leant into the rocking chair that they had moved up there only a few weeks ago in preparation for when she would be breastfeeding in the middle of the night.

'Maybe some mint tea might help,' suggested her mother.

'What can I do for you?' asked Rachel, seeing her sister silently enduring.

'You can hold my hand,' she breathed out.

'What do those pains feel like?' she asked.

'Your whole stomach goes rock hard,' she breathed out. 'It's uncontrollable,' she clenched her teeth together and gritted, her face reddening. 'Overriding,' she exhaled. 'Like the worst monthly pain you have ever experienced in your life.'

'Why do women have it so hard?' said Rachel.

Rebecca continued to squeeze Rachel's hand each time a contraction came over her. By ten o'clock the contractions were getting stronger and stronger. Rebecca barely spoke. She shuffled around the room, rubbing her own back. She'd hold onto the end of her wrought iron bed, and would stare down at the floor while her mother and sister would rub her lower back and coax her through another wave. 'Is this the real thing yet?' she cried out to her mother.

'Yes. Now you know the difference. Blow the air away.'

She moved to the bed, and lay on her back, bent her legs at the knees and placed her hands under her knees and pulled them up towards her underarms so she could round out her back and roll around side to side on her bed, moaning softly. Minutes later she asked them to help her up so she could continue the shuffling. Her mother saying, every minute, Rebecca, is a minute closer to the end.

'The baby is moving, moving slowly and it's a big job for your body to make room for it so it can come out, but you're getting there.'

Rachel kept two cold washers on hand, constantly wiping Rebecca's forehead, pressing the coolness around her face. Next time she was on the bed, her mother said, 'Let me have another look,' pushing her nightgown onto her tummy. 'You're not there yet.' She rubbed her with some oil. 'But you are getting closer.'

Her contractions were strong, coming every two to three minutes and lasting a minute or more. After another swell of pain, Rebecca said in jest, 'Maybe I should go riding on Mica, maybe that will bounce it out of me.'

'Sometimes, movement can help,' said her mother. 'If you are up to it, we can walk you up and down the stairs.'

With her mother in front of her and her sister on her side, she gingerly walked down the stairs, one hand on the banister; one hand around her lower belly, groaning every few steps, not silent and serene how she had been the night she snuck out with Samuel. Fancy thinking of that at a time like this, but she found it comforting to think of Samuel. She was having his baby. She couldn't wait to hold it in her arms. Would it look like him she wondered? She could do this, she told herself. For him. He always said she was a strong girl and she was.

Her father appeared at the bottom of the stairs. 'Here.' He handed Morna a large kitchen knife. Rebecca eyed it alarmingly.

'Not for you, love,' said her mother, as she turned her around and helped her up the stairs. 'It's to put under your mattress. It's supposed to cut away the pain.'

'Yes,' she swallowed dryly, 'cut out the pain. I'm up for any old wives' tale.' Four steps from the top, she heard a faint popping sound. Two steps more she felt moisture running, down her legs. 'Oh, I think I just wet the floor,' she said, feeling a flush of embarrassment.

'It's alright.' Her mother bent down, placed her finger in the small puddle and brought it to her nose to smell. 'It's just your water's breaking.'

Her mother placed the knife under the bed while Rachel continued to rub Rebecca's back. 'Do you want to try the stairs again?' Rebecca nodded. Holding onto each other, they slowly retraced their steps.

'How's that?' said her mother, when she came up a second time.

'I don't know,' said Rebecca, starting to cry. Her emotions were running wild; the contraction pain was intense. She was teary and exhausted. 'How much longer do you think?'

Her mother patted her on the shoulder. 'Let's get you up on the bed and have another look.' There was a lot of bloody discharge on her legs. Her mother wiped it away.

'You're getting closer. Normally, you will feel, you will know when it's time to bear down. Often when you think you want to pass a motion it is actually that you want to start to squeeze the baby out, bearing down, pushing with your stomach muscles, not just the ones here,' she said patting her upper stomach, 'but also inside. Think and feel about how you can use those muscles to help push the baby out. But, Rebecca, only push when you have a contraction, not between times. The contraction is your body's way of helping the baby move along. You need to use your muscles to make the contraction work for you.'

Her mother made it sound easy. Well, she had loads of experience, after all. Rebecca realised how desperate a situation she would be in, if she were by herself. She turned to her mother in tears. 'Thank you, Mother, for being here with me. For helping me. For not sending me away. I would be totally lost without you. You too, Rachel.'

'That's what mothers are for.' Morna embraced her. 'Now just trust your instincts.'

Rebecca faintly nodded. She didn't have the energy to talk anymore, focusing completely on what was moving through her body, working through the contractions and then recovering. After about thirty minutes she didn't want to breathe through them, she wanted to bear down.

She tried leaning over the bedrail first and then she assumed the foetal rolling position, squeezing and groaning with all her might. She made strange noises that seemed to come from a mysterious cave deep inside her, echoes of her agony and determination. She seemed to be able to breathe a little easier. But she was thirsty, incredibly thirsty. They helped her up. They gave her water. And then glancing around the room, she rasped, 'The stool. Help me to the stool.'

They placed a towel under the stool and helped lower her down. She sat on the edge and supported herself with her hands, her legs bent and spread either side of her boulder of a belly. From this position she grunted with each contraction, her face straining with the effort she was putting into each exertion as her body tensed and then relaxed.

Her mother took her hand and said, 'Feel this, you are bulging here, that's the baby's head. It's not far off now. We will catch it. But take it easy now. Nice and steady. Let it rest there for a spell, let your body expand gradually, you don't want to tear if you can help it.'

The pain was immense, like nothing she had ever felt before. She closed her eyes and thought, where are you Samuel? Where are you? And from the depths of her soul she felt him calling to her. Dive into it, Rebecca. Dive into the pain, he was saying. She let out her breath and let go and she felt like a hundred tiny little hands were swimming all around her, inside, rippling over her taut stomach, in gentle waves, holding her up, grabbing hold of her child and pulling it to the surface. Another contraction, another push, she felt an intense burning sensation. She distantly heard her mother say, your baby is crowning.

And then she heard Samuel's immortal words, the words he had spoken to her the first time he made her body come alive. 'Breathe with it, feel it completely, open every pore to the sensation, to the blood rushing through your body to whatever else is rushing through your body and ride it, ride it like a chariot bursting out of the ocean, coming up out of the sea.'

And she did. Her baby's head pierced her vulva. She was shaking and quivering, sweating and throbbing. Out came the forehead, the nose, the mouth, and…finally…the chin. Her mother reached across and wiped its face and ran her finger around the baby's neck checking for any signs of the cord, 'Rebecca,' she said, 'On the next contraction, the shoulders will come out and then the rest of the body.'

One final, painful push. Her mother caught her infant child as he slipped into the world. A boy. A baby boy. She held him while Rachel and her mother threaded knots around the cord and cut it and then she had to birth the placenta, a mere song compared to what she had just been through.

Later when she and the baby and the bedroom were totally cleaned, she lay in bed cradling her newborn to her chest and whispered to the night sky, 'A son. A son. You are a father, Samuel Rousseau Dalton. You have a son that you don't know about yet,' her lips brushing her young son's snowy hair. 'Perhaps it's time you did.'

Her son, their son, was long, twenty-two inches, with long limbs and long fingers and long nails even. Rebecca put them in her mouth and gently bit them off so he wouldn't scratch himself. He was the most beautiful thing Rebecca had ever seen and while every mother thinks that about their child, in Rebecca's case she had reason to believe it was true. He had her clear blue-green eyes, and long brown eyelashes and dustings of eyebrows. His hair was faint and blond, a perfect head, a petite turned up nose and the sweetest little ears. There was not a mark on his body. He was blissfully untouched and blissfully asleep when he wasn't blissfully feeding, his tiny fists flailing at her breast.

She couldn't wait to remove his whittles in the morning and wipe him over with a warm damp cloth and blurt raspberries on his belly. Then she'd reluctantly wrap him up again and sit on her bed and lay him in front of her. She wanted to spend the whole day and night just looking at him. But she didn't. In her supreme joy, Rebecca remembered her sister Rachel, remembered how generous and understanding she had been throughout her pregnancy, and so she let her hold the babe almost as often as she did. In fact it was Rachel who first took the boy down to show their father, saying, 'Look at your grandson, what a brawny boy he is.'

Her father looked closely stripping the boy off completely, checking him all over, counting his fingers and his toes, and measuring the length of each leg. 'Well it looks like you are all together, young, man,' he said as he pulled the clothes back on, gazed at his face and handed him back to Rachel.

She called him Samson. She couldn't christen him, but that didn't bother her. It worried her father, though: her mother telling Rebecca she had found him downstairs two mornings in a row praying for guidance on the matter. Most children were christened in the church about a month after they were born. But because of their 'lies' and concealment, they weren't going to be forthcoming in that. If a child were weak or sickly, however, a minister or a lay preacher, possibly a schoolteacher even, could administer a baptism at home. But once again that wasn't an option and besides Samson was a picture of health.

When Silas first broached the subject, Morna was dumbstruck. 'I thought your whole aim was not to reveal the pregnancy?'

'It still is! I just have this voice telling me he needs to be baptised.'

A day later, he announced. 'I will do it. I will baptise the baby. As a captain I can do that. I'll row the tender out and baptise the little merry-begot myself.'

Morna laughed when he said that. 'Silas, the cove's still half full of ice.'

But he had said, 'I am serious Morna, we'll manage. Go up and tell Rebecca that tomorrow we will baptise the boy and for her to rest up today as she'll need her energy in the morn to go down below and out in the boat a little ways with me.'

When Rachel heard, she said he was mad.

But Rebecca liked the idea. 'Tell him to ready the Nightingale so we can take Samson out in his father's boat.'

47

It is a still grey fog that greets them when they open the door the next day, as four dark figures, almost wrapped in their own swaddling clothes, make their way down to the stage. Rebecca is cocooned between her mother and sister; protected in case she should slip. When they get to the water the fog is even thicker if that could be possible. They can barely see five yards in front of them.

'Can we not just sit here in the boat and do it?' asks Rebecca.

'No,' says her father, 'I don't think that will do.'

Her mother helps her on board and she sits holding her baby, her back to the shore, staring keenly into the gloomy fog. Though she has paddled out of their cove more times than she cares to remember, for the first time in her life, she is worried that her father might hit something lurking just out of sight. In the limited visibility that she has she can see small blocks of ice everywhere, menacing and prowling. All of sudden she doesn't think this is such a good idea and wishes for her sister to keep watch with her as well.

Her father sits there morosely, silently, rowing steadily for about ten minutes till they're nearly at the end of the peninsula. 'I think this will do,' he says. Pulling the oars firmly in, he unscrews his flagon of water and pours a little into a glass bowl that her mother has given them especially for this sacred purpose.

He opens his Bible and reads aloud from Matthew 18: "At that time the disciples came to Jesus asking, 'Who is the greatest in the Kingdom of Heaven?' So Jesus called a child, made him stand in front of them, and said, 'I assure you that unless you change and become like children, you will never enter the Kingdom of Heaven. The greatest in the Kingdom of Heaven is the one who humbles himself and becomes like this child. And whoever welcomes in my name one such child as this, welcomes me."

'Suffer the little children and let them come unto me,' says Rebecca.

'Yes,' he says solemnly, *'and forbid them not, for of such is the kingdom of God.'* He lays the Bible down on the seat then says, 'Hand me the boy.' He reaches across to Rebecca who leans forward and passes over her son. He holds him in his left hand and says to Rebecca, 'Lean to your left Rebecca to keep the boat balanced while I baptise him.' As he slides along the seat, he moves the bowl of water along next to him, and then he slowly dips his right hand into the bowl, swings his left arm holding Samson out over the water and then makes the sign of the cross on his forehead. 'I, Silas Isaiah Crowe, by the powers vested in me as captain of this vessel, baptise you Samson Dalton Crowe in the name of the Father, the Son and the Holy Spirit.'

He pauses then takes a breath as if he is about to say something – what wonders Rebecca, maybe, 'May the spirit of the Lord be with you always,' – what do ministers say at other baptisms before Amen? But he doesn't say any of these words. Instead he says, 'May you rest in peace.' And then in slow motion, he rolls his arm over and lets Samson fall into the sea.

Rebecca sees it all, like a feather slowing wafting to the ground. It is as if she is in a trance, so unbelievable does the action appear and so slow is her own reaction, but then her reflexes and adrenalin kick in.

'Father,' she screams, lunging to the side and leaning over to pluck her baby out of the water, but he is already two, three feet below and she can't reach him. Rebecca is completely undone.

She goes to dive in but her father grabs her, hindering her in her efforts. 'Rebecca, you can't save him. Let him be. Let him go with God.'

'No!' She screams and it is the scream of absolute horror, of sickening dread, of blinding realization that what she has just witnessed is no mere accident, no slight aberration of judgment, but pure malignant intent.

With all her might she fights with her father like she has never fought in her life and through her exertions she nearly capsizes the boat. It is only then that he releases her and she is off over the side but precious seconds have been lost and the grey fog cover means visibility even only a short way down is practically zero. The water is unbelievable. She has never known an excruciating cold like it. The icy liquid clamps around her head like pincers.

She dives down and swings her arms about searching blindly for her son, searching frantically until her own lungs are about to burst with despair, with the incredulity of it all, and with her own bursting need for oxygen. She cannot stay down any longer. Kicking to the surface she breaks air and gulps and thrashes and twirls.

She yells, 'Can you see him, can you see him anywhere? Father, please, help me! Please! You have to help me!'

'He's gone, Rebecca.'

'Nooo,' she screams as she dives under again, down, deeper and deeper into the chilly, icy depths. She can't see a thing but she's hoping she can feel a thing. But eventually, like before, she has to return to the top or succumb. She can't do that. She needs to be alive to be a mother for Samson. Maybe a miracle will have happened and a selkie has rescued him and taken him to shore, she thinks. She focuses on that, she can't bear thinking of the alternative; that her innocent son has sunk to an icy grave. When she surfaces the next time she can barely see a thing either. Her vision is so blurred. Her lips tremble uncontrollably, emitting stuttering sobbing sounds.

Her father yells at her, 'Rebecca, stop this nonsense immediately and get into the boat. Your lips are purple You will barely escape death yourself if you carry on like this.'

'Father,' she wails, 'how can I get back on board when he is down there somewhere, or floating around somewhere? Can't you do something? Can you go back to the stage and bring out your net and drag for him. Maybe he's floating on the surface somewhere out of sight.'

'Rebecca! You are talking nonsense! I will do NO such thing.'

'Father, Father, FATHER,' she screams, her voice jagged. Hot tears trail down her face but she does not feel them. She is numb, shivering uncontrollably in the ice-laden waters of the Atlantic Sea. Already her body is starting to shut down.

'No Rebecca, this is the will of God,' her father yells. 'He spoke to me. That child is the son of the Devil and the only way God could save him was to take him now, before anyone could get to him.'

'Oh God!' sobs Rebecca, 'How could you?'

'I did it because I was told to do it. Just like God commanded Abraham.' After a few moments he reaches out. 'Come on. It is finished.'

All Rebecca's aching heart can think is: but God released Abraham from that command.

She can't bear to look at her father as he rows them back to shore. She wants to claw his eyes out and his heart – if he had one. She closes her own eyes. Tears seep out the side. Her breathing is on the verge of hyperventilation. The icy water and the shock are making her blood gush through her body like a waterfall. She is hot even though she is practically frigid with cold. But her heart, her throat, feel like they are on fire. Such pain she has never known. All of her tears will never douse the flame.

As they come to their stage, she opens her eyes to see her mother and sister waiting anxiously. The fog had muffled her screams but even so they have been away too long and their worried faces turn to relief at their return. Neither notices her wet hair and clothes. Neither notices that she is no longer cradling an infant in her arms until, that is, she jumps up to the stage, by herself, as soon as the boat touches it.

Rebecca sees their pained faces but she has to keep moving or else she will collapse. She will fall down and she will never get up. She staggers past them staring blindly at the path ahead.

'Where's Samson?' asks Morna, in a pinched, panicked voice looking from Rebecca to her husband, who is not looking at her, back to Rebecca. 'Rebecca, where is your son?' she cries.

Without turning Rebecca says, 'Ask your husband.' She is damned if she is going to call him Father.

Rachel took off after her sister. Morna stared after them then she turned to her husband. 'Silas!' she exclaimed. 'What has happened here today?'

Looking up at his wife Silas said, 'Heaven help me, Morna, I pray it was the will of the Lord,' his voice was tight and struggling, 'I didn't want to say anything to you till now, let alone now, I didn't want to believe it myself. But I knew I just had to resolve myself to carry it out, because he told me to.'

'Oh no, Silas! No!' screamed Morna pressing her hands to her ears. Silas stepped out of the boat and walked over to her and firmly pulled her hands away from her head, then held her shaking head between his own two hands.

'Listen to me,' he said.

'I don't want to listen to you,' she snapped, trying to put her hands back over her ears.

'You must. I don't want to tell you this. But you must hear it. You must hear the truth of it. Woman! Stop fighting me for a minute.' His hands tightened around her shaking head. 'The last three nights I have had this dream, this vision, which has chilled me with its foreboding. The same omen each night so that I could not sleep and why you have found me each morning at the table with the lamp by my side and the Bible in front of me praying for guidance.

'Samuel was in this dream and it was like the ends of days, like Armageddon, I swear. The sound was deafening, blackness was tarred across the earth, great flames of fire shot down from the sky, smoke obliterated the landscape and Samuel was with all these other people, I didn't know any of them, lying on the earth, writhing in pain, bodies strewn over each other, struggling to breathe, and one of them was a little boy, about four years old who Samuel was wrestling with, trying to keep by his side, but the child broke free and ran away.

'Then there was this godforsaken blast, like the loudest thunder you have ever heard, and Samuel was struck with lightning and he died along with everyone around him, engulfed in flames.

'And then in the midst of this destruction a little white lamb appeared, looking dazed and confused and it pranced around, barely touching the earth as it was scorching hot in parts and in the distance it saw the little boy who had managed to escape the carnage and it took off after him and the boy could see the lamb coming towards him, so he held out his arms to it, but as the lamb started to run along, it started to grow bigger and then it transformed itself into a pale horse, with a dark rider atop of it and it smote the boy and the boy turned into hot coals and burned to ashes till there was not a sign of him ever being on the earth. After this a startling white archangel appeared and he held a trumpet to his lips and out of the trumpet came wind and rain which blew everything away, washed everything clean and then the earth was green and sweet smelling, the birds were twittering, the trees were rustling. It was like how it was for Noah after the flood. There was peace and stillness and a rainbow even.

'And as much as I've tried to fight it Morna, I feel it in my bones that Samuel is either doomed or evil and this son of his is cursed, or will be cursed. And I swear I heard this voice say to me "Save him, save him while he still has a chance". I thought it was Samuel's voice initially, pleading for the boy, but then I realised it was God's voice, "Suffer the little children and let them come unto me". And that is what I did, Morna. I sent him to be with the Lord, so he can be born into eternal life and not know the horrors of this world.'

'Oh Silas, Silas,' cried Morna. 'What have you done! What have you done?' her hands involuntarily covered her face. Taking them away she stared accusingly. 'You have gone too far this time! You are deranged! Do you hear me? How could you not have talked to me about this?' Her voice vehement.

'It was weighing heavily enough on my mind as it was. I didn't want to burden yours as well.'

'Well, you should have! These are the things I want to be burdened with, before the unthinkable happens,' blasted Morna as she paced backwards and forwards on the stage as her anger battled and raged with her grief, as her mind saw her ragged past and her distressing future, 'Oh God,' she cried, 'How will you, how will we be able to live with this? This will burn a hole in our souls forever. We'll be on a stake till the end of our days.'

'Morna, you've got to banish those thoughts and pull yourself together, for all our sakes. Stand firm in your faith in God. That is all I've got. I've done what I was called to do. I didn't want to. It was the most merciful way to end the child's life. He would have drifted off quickly into a frozen torpor. It was a test of some sort. I don't know why, but it was one of those rare moments in life where I've had to stand up and do what God called for without knowing or understanding the exact reason. Who knows, maybe God has some great plan for

Rebecca, and this is his way of making it happen. It's like he's sending us a message, sending her a message to be done with Samuel and all his ways. And through the birth and now this, she will somehow cleanse herself of him. I don't know. The only thing left now is to pray for healing, for God to show us the way.'

'The way to hell, Silas or the way back from it?' cried Morna. After a few heaving moments she added, 'She'll never forgive you.'

'That will depend entirely on what example you set.' He turned and walked away.

Even before she reached the house Morna could hear wailing. Or was that her own? As she made her way up the stairs to Rebecca's room, she could smell vomit. Both girls were grey-green. Rebecca's damp clothes were in a pile on the floor. She had pulled on layers of wool and was walking round the room in a disorientated daze, sobbing and inhaling uncontrollably. Rachel stood to the side impotent in her helplessness.

'Rebecca.' She walked towards her, 'I'm so sorry, so sorry.' She halted a few steps from her youngest, sensing she did not want to be held. 'If I'd known this was going to happen I would never, ever, have let you get in that boat.' Morna took a step forwards, Rebecca a step back.

Words were failing Morna. She took a deep breath and exhaled, trying to find some measure of comfort. 'There is nothing harder in life than losing a child. I know. I had hoped my children would be spared such pain. One day you will come through this. Trust me. And one day you will find a way to put this behind you. We all have to. I will pray for you, for Samson, for your father and for this family. I urge you to do the same. I beseech you. We can pray together if you like.'

'What?' cried Rebecca in anguish, '"My God, my God, why have you forsaken me?"'

Morna could barely look at her so heavy was her own despair.

'Or perhaps this one: "My strength is gone, gone like water spilt on the ground. All my bones are out of joint; my heart is like melted wax. You have left me for dead in the dust."' She sobbed.

Unable to deny Rebecca's exasperation or her misery, feeling absolutely wretched herself, Morna could only stand there, stunned and wordless, as tears coursed down her face. Finally she said, 'Maybe Psalm 23 might be more appropriate.'

'I'll pray for you,' said Rachel, wiping her face. She dropped suddenly to her knees and leant over the bed, hands clasped, like they did when they were little girls. ' *"The Lord is my shepherd. I shall not want."* ' She swallowed long and hard before forcing her broken voice to go on. ' *"He maketh me to lie down in green pastures: he leadeth me beside the still waters. He restoreth my soul: he leadeth me in the paths of righteousness for his name's sake. Yea, though I walk through the valley of the shadow of death, I will fear no evil: for thou art with me; thy rod and thy staff they comfort me. Thou preparest a table before me in the presence of mine enemies: thou anointest my head with oil; my cup runneth over."* ' Rachel's tears runneth over, her nose was running, her voice was crying. She couldn't continue.

Even Morna couldn't manage the last line about goodness and mercy following her all the days of her life.

Rebecca was back in bed, hunched around her body, still unable to calm her breathing.

Her body shuddered uncontrollably in spasmic waves of shock.

Rachel sat next to the window, glancing occasionally at the form of her sister but mostly looking out, humming hymns softly under her voice. 'It's getting dark,' she said, almost in a whisper.

'What time is it?' croaked Rebecca.

'I don't know, well past lunchtime. Do you want something to eat?'

'No.' Her heartbreak apparent in one plangent syllable.

'Do you want me to leave you alone?'

'You can stay, Rachel, only you.'

The skies grew darker, a violent brew of wind-whipped clouds, a tempest in the making. They could sense the coming storm and then the distant crash of thunder.

'Did you hear that, Rebecca?' asked Rachel. 'The Heavens are welcoming your little boy.'

48

Morna was sitting at the kitchen table staring blankly at the wall trying to figure out the workings of her husband, whom she'd known for thirty years, yet not known, when Rachel joined her. She sat opposite her and they stared at each other, unanswered questions in their puffed eyes.

Eventually, Rachel asked, 'Why?'

'So help me God, Rachel when it comes to your father there are some things I will never understand,' she swallowed, 'this is one of them.'

She told her then what Silas had told her. Rachel sat shaking her head all the while.

'How can it be God's will to kill a baby? Thou shalt not kill, Mother! Doesn't he know he's done wrong?'

'I'm hoping he will come to that understanding.' She sighed deeply. 'What's done is done.'

'We could be next,' said Rachel, vaguely horrified.

Morna shook her head. 'This is only about the child.'

'I would have thought after all the sons he's lost that he would have protected his grandson with a vengeance.' A little while later she said, 'Maybe if he couldn't have any sons he wasn't going to let Rebecca have any either. Oh, poor Rebecca.' Once more Rachel's voice gave way to weeping.

'I don't think that featured at all in his thinking,' replied Morna. 'That's the same as saying, because all the boys die in this family maybe he thought he was doing Rebecca a favour, taking her son before she could spend years loving him then losing him.'

'Maybe he thought that too,' said Rachel, sniffling.

Morna shook her head. 'It is what it is Rachel, and ultimately we have to accept that. What are we going to do, turn him in?' But her tone was, 'we can't turn him in.'

'We should,' said Rachel.

Morna shook her head again. 'Look I'm not excusing your father for what he's done. It's abominable. But, in part I blame myself. I should have sent him away before Rebecca's time. He gets too wound up and worrisome around childbirth – he's worse than me. Births haunt him and I think this one was one too many. It stirred up too many memories. Now he's half-crazed and suffering for it.'

'Well maybe in his suffering he'll think of Rebecca and how much she's suffering.' Rachel shuddered. 'He has gone mad as far as I'm concerned.'

Silas was still down below. Morna half-hoped he would never come up. She felt she was on top of a fence, which, one day she would have to climb down, and on one side were her daughters and on the other, Silas. She thought at least he would return remorseful but, no, he came striding in, full of self-righteousness, which, if she were thinking clearly, should not have come as a surprise.

She opened her mouth to speak her mind, but it was so numb she couldn't put any words together.

'I have more than explained myself,' he said to her unspoken criticism. 'You're forgetting yourself. Your duty first and foremost is to me, your husband.'

That was the first piece that they had to put back together. But Morna worried that her youngest would never find the pieces she needed to put herself back together.

49

Initially Rebecca stayed in her room trying to relive and remember those precious three days with Samson, as if by playing them over and over in her head she would commit them to memory and would never forget them, not even the minutest detail. Then she stayed to avoid Silas but he seemed to be making himself scarce, only seeing her mother and Rachel at mealtimes, if at all. But on the seventh morning after the…she couldn't put any words to it – she could barely speak – in fact she had no desire to talk to anyone – Rebecca found herself sitting down at the breakfast table in the bloody battleground that was her home.

After a long strained, anxious silence Silas said, 'You wanted to live life to the full, Rebecca, well live it. This is what being a woman is all about. Now you know what your mother has been through time and time again, carrying a babe is painful, giving birth is painful, losing one is painful.'

Will this ever stop? 'I know what Mother has been through,' she said, her voice rusted from all the tears she'd cried. 'I always have. I know she has suffered great losses – I will never dispute that – but she has never suffered what I have. She has never suffered the deliberate murder of her own child – and not only that – but at the hands of someone she loved and looked up to!'

'There's many a time the early settlers in this land had to take the lives of their youngest children, so that there would be enough food for the older ones to survive.' Rachel blanched, but not Rebecca. She now knew any terror was possible. 'It's a cruel fact of life, but at times a necessary mercy. It's an act of courage and of love. In time you might come to see this.'

'That was then. This is now!' argued Rebecca. 'The other day it was all about Satan's spawn. Today it's something different. Don't try and use that sad tale of our forebears as a way of justifying what you have done. Our lives aren't that desperate – at least I didn't think they were. And you're forgetting that Samson's not your child, he's your grandchild. You might think you have a God-given right to sit in judgment on me, but you certainly don't have a right to do so with him. And nowhere in the Book of Life do you have the right to sacrifice his life. If such a right exists, then that alone belongs to his father and me.'

'So where is his father then?'

If Rebecca could have, she would have hurled all manner of abuse at Silas for that – if only she knew some. Taking a wretched breath, she fired away. 'When he was born, I thought my own father would do a good job of raising my son until his own father could come back and claim him. How wrong I was to trust you. You took my child from me – a thriving baby boy – he was only three days old,' she faltered and then the wailing started again, but she continued even so. 'All I wanted was to love him and care for him. I didn't know I had to protect him from the monster that was his grandfather!' she yelled.

'I am not a monster!' shouted Silas, crashing his chair as he stormed towards her.

But this time Morna and Rachel did not wait in ignorance and in silence. Rachel was at Rebecca's side, with one hand around her shoulder and the other holding her arm. Morna stood in front with her hands raised. 'No, Silas. That's enough. Leave her alone. You've already broken her enough.' Silas left. The women wept. Just like Jesus.

How many hours, how many nights did Rebecca lie in bed, her body curled around her pain, her intolerable suffering, her baby-bruised insides, her bursting baby-less breasts, while the questions tumbled through her mind. Why did he? How could he? How did she let him? Did she let him? And then all the ifs. If she had never gone out in the boat that day with her father. If her mother had abetted her rather than insisting on telling her father of her pregnancy. If her parents had welcomed Samuel's and her betrothment. If Rachel had not been plagued by rotten misfortune and misguided love. All the ifs, except: If I had not lain with Samuel. In her utter brokenness that if failed to register.

Finally she could take it no longer. All she could think of was her son. Her son. Her son. She wanted to be with him. She wanted to hold him once more. She wanted to go to him. I can't live this life she cried.

In the middle of a still dark May night, she rose, dressed, crept downstairs, grabbed her shawl and her boots and went down below. She untied the Nightingale from the stage, climbed in and rowed out into the black of night. After some distance she slowed, turned the tender around so she was not facing their cove.

She released the oars and moved down into the boat like she had the day Samuel rowed her out to the iceberg. In a minute, she said, I will join you Samson. But first I need to say goodbye to your father. She lay there staring up into the shapeless night, unrushed by time, trying to piece together her parting farewell. When she uttered those final words she wanted them to go sailing across the seas and flying across the hills to him. As she lay there the impenetrable clouds parted, revealing a night superlative. Their ice cave, refracted and magnified. She gazed in bittersweet bewilderment.

'As I lie in our boat, I remember you, Samuel...' And in speaking his name out loud, her resolve broke and too the fresh seal on her tears. She couldn't do it. Then as if to commend her decision, she saw a star being born, so bright, so angelic, soaring across the heavens, so far and yet so close.

And in that moment she knew the only life she wanted, the only life she could live, was a new life with Samuel, one that would outshine and overshadow her old one, one that would free her and free them.

Without hesitation or regret, she rowed back to shore and stole away into the night.

50

Matthew's first words to Samuel were, 'I'm pleased to see your weary face, little brother. Words can not express how relieved I am that you survived.'

'Thank you,' Samuel had said, 'and for my reward I want to know all about your Military Cross that you have been keeping from us.' That was how he wheedled it out of him.

They were sitting around with a few of the gang, enjoying the long hours of twilight on a Sunday, the 12th May 1918, but no one felt like singing, 'Hail Hail the gang's all here'. They were as despondent as the soldiers Samuel had seen last month, the veterans who could remember the sacrifices their fallen comrades had made in taking Passchendaele, only to surrender it six months later. Samuel had seen them struggle with sickness and remorse, their sorrow sometimes painfully borne out by the unmistakable lament of a lone mouth organ.

And while in recent weeks everyone's backs had been up against the wall, they had held on. But attrition aside, many were just plain over it. Doctors too had to fight not to surrender to a hovering malaise. The fellowship of their medical colleagues and the letters from home often were the only things that kept them going.

While Samuel was at the front Lenore's mother had died and she had moved in with the Daltons. She was just days away from having the baby. Matthew was restless. He clearly had no interest in being there and he was not alone. Less than two days later came the news he had been waiting for.

Samuel was outside Matthew's tent in a chair reading when Matthew came towards him calling out his name. He glanced at his brother and he had a sudden sense of homecoming for it was not the brother he'd come to expect of late, but a long lost brother from Samuel's past. Matthew stood before him with the biggest, widest, irrepressible grin all over his face.

Samuel was on his feet. 'She had the baby?'

'She had the baby BOY!' said Matthew reaching into his pocket for the telegram.

JONATHAN FLETCHER DALTON ARRIVED 6.22 AM 13 MAY. 8 LB 8OZS. 21 INCHES. THE VERY IMAGE OF YOU AS A BABY. ALL WELL. LOVE LENORE AND FAMILY.

Samuel ran his fingers over it almost as if the telegram had come directly from his father's own hands and he was touching the same paper that his father had touched just hours before. How comforting it was to get such a joyous message only hours old all the way from home. He looked up at Matthew who had tears in his eyes. He had tears in his eyes. 'We've got some celebrating to do. Jonathan Fletcher Dalton needs his head wet.'

They went to the bars at Boulogne. Matthew returned late, but Samuel stayed on. He wanted to spend a few days by the sea. The ocean always made him feel closer to Rebecca. And he had been missing her a lot of late. He would send her some postcards from the coast and a long letter. Like Matthew he felt an inconsolable ache to be home.

He returned three days later with an unexpected surprise, a Belgian painter, Alfred Bastien, who had been seconded to the Canadian Army to produce works of art specifically related to the Canadian war experience. Samuel chatted with the man at a café at Poperinge. The artist told him he had done little on the medical life of war and would be delighted to look in on the Canadians at Hospital City and do a small private sitting at the same time. All of Matthew's friends chipped in so he could have a sketching in charcoal and varnish to commemorate his becoming a father.

It was a Sunday evening. Samuel and Matthew had been to a pantomime earlier and were ensconced in conversation, enjoying a little bit of brotherly time and a late nightcap. Samuel had temporarily moved into the hut Matthew shared with another three doctors, before he went back to the McGill base.

It was a beautiful still night, the stars putting on their brightest performance as the two of them enjoyed the clean night air in full view of the cosmic splendour.

'I can't believe my son is already a week old,' said Matthew. 'I can't wait to get home. Already I feel I am missing out on so much.'

'I'm sure you do,' said Samuel. 'One year at university seems to race by but over here it drags on, especially the days at the front waiting.'

They sat in comfortable silence for a few minutes. Then one, then the other became aware of a distant drone, like a hovering mosquito, that kept getting louder and louder, closer and closer.

'Matthew, listen, do you hear that?'

'It's hard not to.' They both jumped to their feet, and searched the sky for the source of the loud humming. The next second they heard the crash. A large bomb exploded in a building less than 100 yards away. Screams and cries resounded through the night, exigent and chilling. There was no siren, no warning. They didn't need any. The two of them instantly bolted to help. Then they heard the second one louder and closer than before. Samuel was ahead of Matthew, who cried, 'Hit the ground,' as he flung himself onto his brother forcing him down.

'What in damnation is happening?' yelled Matthew between heavy breaths. 'Don't those sons of bitches know this is a bloody hospital! That it's verbotenland!'

Samuel registered a hit to his leg. And then he heard a strangled 'aagh' from his brother.

'Bloody hell, Matthew! We need to get under cover somewhere.'

'And miss all this fun and excitement?'

'I thought your job was to stay alive at all costs.'

'No, that is your job. My job is to protect you at all costs.'

'Is that what you're doing on top of me?'

'Yes.'

'Well, not at this price, you self-sacrificing fool. You have a wife and child to live for. I don't have any of those things.'

'Come on now, not even Rebecca?'

'Matthew, don't joke at – ' and then he halted as he felt the warmth on his shoulder. He pushed himself up, rolled his brother off him and then he saw him grimace in pain and a trickle of blood spill from his mouth. 'Matthew,' he screamed. 'God! Where are you hit?'

'In the back,' he wheezed, spluttering droplets of blood.

He rolled Matthew forward and leant over to look at his back. It was soaked with blood and lacerated with large holes. He could even see dark silver metal jutting out in places. Samuel's stomach lurched at the sight of it.

'How's it look?' wheezed Matthew.

'Not bad,' choked Samuel.

'You're a rotten liar.'

'Better than being a rotten brother.'

'I would never call you that.'

'Matthew I've got to get you some help, get you on a stretcher and get you into surgery quick smart. I'll be back as soon as I can.'

'Call out for help Samuel, don't leave me.'

'Matthew, I have to get help.'

'Help will come. Don't you leave me!'

'Right, that does it.' Samuel pulled his shirt off and, raising Matthew, wrapped it as tight around his back as possible to staunch some of the bleeding. 'I know that hurts, I'm sorry.' Then standing, he helped Matthew up then he squatted so Matthew could fall onto his back. 'Here we go.' He stood and as he did his calf flared in pain. He ignored it.

'Help!' screamed Samuel in his loudest voice. 'Over here.' He could see kerosene lamps bobbing in the distance. 'Help, someone please. I've got a doctor down. Quickly.'

A nurse appeared at his side. Barely even looking at her Samuel said, 'We need a stretcher and two orderlies, can you manage that? Quickly now, run! Run like you have never run before in your life!'

But before she could take ten steps, they heard the whistle and hum of more bombs.

'Incoming,' wheezed Matthew.

Samuel fell to his knees then lay facedown, his brother still clinging to his back.

After a few deafening, aching, booming minutes, which seemed like interminable hours, there was at last a reprieve.

Samuel rolled Matthew over to look at him. In the bright moonlight, he could see Matthew's face, waning, fading, almost a study in black and white, his life ebbing out of him.

The sight of his brother sucked the breath right out of Samuel. His heart beat so furiously and so loudly he felt for sure it had jumped outside his body and was stomping wildly around the two of them. Think clearly, Samuel! Get it together! Be calm!

Placing his bloodied hand on his brother's face, he looked into his eyes and said, 'Matthew! Still your heart. Keep it calm so it doesn't beat one hundred beats a minute. Think 'resting heart rate', that's what you want. Mine is beating enough for the two of us.'

'I'm doing my best,' said Matthew, clearly struggling with every word with every breath.

'Matthew, you hang in there, you hear. That's an order. I need you to use that brilliant mind of yours and that unshakeable willpower of yours to force your body to stay calm and stay with it.'

'Like when I faced that grizzly.'

'Yes, that's the spirit.'

'Samuel,' groaned Matthew, reaching up and grabbing his brother's hand. 'Do you think my son will grow up to be a doctor?'

'Quite possibly,' said Samuel.

'Will you look after him for me and Lenore?'

'Matthew,' he breathed out in exasperation and terror. 'God! Yes! But let's make a deal. I will teach him how to be a rascal and you will be the one to take him down the path of straight and narrow.'

'But I always was the wild one.'

'Till recently. Yes. Till you married. Yes. But now, big brother, yours is a life of respectability and responsibility. So that means you have a responsibility to your wife and child and to me to stay alive.' Samuel swallowed, 'God, where are those orderlies!' He frantically looked around.

'Samuel,' croaked Matthew and he felt his brother place both his hands on his own still pulling firmly on the bandage at his chest. He could hear the gurgle in his breathing. He wanted to yell, 'NO! NO! NO!' And beat the crap out of his brother for what was happening to him.

'I've had the sweetest life. I filled every hour. I was happy. What a shame we didn't get to Paris, you and I, but it's not so gay right now. Go home to my son, Samuel and love him for me. Tell him,' he spluttered, 'Tell him he made me so very proud.' And with a slow wavering blink he whispered, 'As did you.'

Samuel released his hands and squeezed his brother's shoulders and leant over his brother's face and cried, 'You can't do this, Matthew. You just can't do this. Come back. Come back, you hear me. You are wanted here! Your life is here! With me! With your family!' Samuel felt himself almost unable to breathe. 'Matthew!' he cried more loudly, shaking his brother's shoulders, seeing his brother's face settle in the night, as it slowly relaxed in the moonbeams, casting their silver rays on the last of his shining life, his precious, wonderful, way-too short, beautiful life.

He grabbed Matthew's fingers with his own and squeezed with all his might and cried in anguish and disbelief. He felt the solid band of his wedding ring and was overcome with a new grief. For the woman who did not know she was a widow. For the love lost. For the life lost. For the child who would never know what a wonderful man his father was.

Next morning a reeling Samuel made his way to the communications tent. He needed to send a telegram to his parents before they received an official one from the War Office.

Could he do that? Not, was he allowed, but, was he capable?

He had to get special clearance from Colonel Elder, Commander of McGill Hospital, to jump the queue of military communiqués and media files.

It took some negotiation – and a quaver of his eternal soul.

He sent the telegram to his father's waiting rooms, not wanting his mother to be the first to hear.

DAD. MOM. LENORE.
MATTHEW WAS KILLED SUNDAY NIGHT WHEN
THE GERMANS BOMBED HOSPITAL CITY. I WAS
WITH HIM. HEARTBROKEN. SAMUEL.

Matthew's funeral was held on Tuesday along with the other fallen. He was given a full soldier's burial. Every available staff member from No 1 and No 3, the McGill Hospital, attended and watched as he was laid to rest in a well-tended cemetery near the pinewoods and the sea. He would have liked that, thought Samuel, the pines faintly reminiscent of the great forests of Canada. Samuel buried him with all of Lenore's letters and the other correspondence that had been sent to him over the years. He removed his wedding ring, thinking to give it to his wife, to his son perhaps.

In his saddest, most courageous hour, Samuel said farewell to his brother with some parting words from Whitman.

This is thy hour O Soul, thy free flight into the wordless,
Away from books, away from art, the day erased, the lesson done,
Thee fully forth emerging, silent, gazing, pondering the themes thou lovest best,
Night, sleep, death and the stars.

Exodus

51

When Rebecca did not join them for breakfast Morna was uneasy.

'She's probably out on the headland looking for more icebergs,' mumbled Silas. 'She'll turn up when she gets hungry.'

His dismissiveness did nothing to settle Morna's nerves. 'Come, Rachel.' They checked the barn first. Mica's bridle was there; she hadn't gone riding. Rachel went in the direction of the pines while Morna went below. Nothing seemed amiss until Morna realised that the Nightingale was not moored to the stage. She must have gone for a row. To where? To do what? It was unlike Rebecca to head off by herself without telling one of them. Morna scanned the cove. Near the mouth on the left hand side about 800 yards away she could make out what she thought was the tender. She waited a few minutes but it didn't come any closer. She climbed into their own tender then, unhitched it from the mooring, fitted the oars and started rowing. She had never learnt how to use the motorboat. What was Rebecca doing out there she wondered. Though she had a fair enough idea. Mourning her son.

After about 500 yards she peered over her shoulder squinting in the direction of the boat. She couldn't see Rebecca at all. The boat was drifting. She suspected she was curled up inside. Morna called out but got no reply. She must be sleeping. Another hundred yards and she yelled again. She must be out to it. Finally she came alongside, lifted her oar and grabbed the gunnel of the Nightingale. But there was no Rebecca; there was only her shawl.

In that instant, Morna realised the unimaginable had happened. The knuckles of her hands clutching the gunnel were tensed and white. She lowered her head onto them and wept bitterly.

Later as she stared emptily out the window she berated herself for not being more watchful. Silas was down in the cove, dragging his nets. Morna didn't even have to ask. He strode away immediately once she told him. Had she been the kind she would have cursed him to kingdom come. As it was she felt untold vehemence.

Rachel at first refused to believe her sister had drowned. 'She's too good a swimmer.'

'It wasn't an accident, Rachel.' Her mother's voice was not her own.

'I know what you're implying but I don't see how she could force herself to do that.'

'She was driven by unseen forces. She was weighed down. Dragged down.'

Rachel went through Rebecca's meager wardrobe and dresser and went through them a second time; nothing was missing, nothing was out of place. She had suspicions that Rebecca had fled in the night for either Toronto or even the Western Front. She didn't know how she would manage, but intuitively, she knew whatever Rebecca put her mind to she was capable of doing. Somewhere she felt a false note.

'How come there's no suicide message, a farewell letter of sorts. She wouldn't do this without saying goodbye. I understand how she could leave without saying a word to father, but she wouldn't leave without saying a word to me.'

'Rachel love, Rebecca wasn't thinking of you. She was only thinking of herself and her son and her pain.'

Suddenly Rachel tore upstairs again and started madly looking under Rebecca's bed, in boxes and baskets, rifling through old clothes and books, until she finally found it, under the wardrobe, a small portmanteau wherein Rebecca kept Samuel's letters. It was still there, but inside…were still Samuel's letters. And then she knew with dreaded certainty that there was no false note. Rebecca would never leave without them. She sat on the floor with her back to the bed, her head bowed and cried tears of disbelief. Such a hollow feeling exploded inside her and crept to the blurred unknown boundaries of her soul. Her mother was beside her, kissing her forehead, placing her hand on the bundle. 'I'll take these for now.' Rachel could not remember surrendering them.

Late in the day Silas returned, without a body. But that meant nought. Quietly he said, 'She could have been further out to sea, the tender could have floated in on the tide.'

Morna went to bed without preparing dinner for anyone. She went to Rebecca's bed. At some point Rachel and her father helped themselves to bread, jam and tea. No one slept that night. The next day Morna seemed to occupy a smaller space in their home and from that day on she was never the same again.

The day following Silas went across to Deception and told folk that five days ago he'd gone across Hamilton Sound to collect Rebecca who'd caught a boat to Carmanville. Then two days later she had taken the Nightingale tender to Anchor Brook. By nightfall she hadn't returned. They found the tender adrift near their cove with nothing in the boat but her shawl. They thought initially that she'd beached the boat somewhere and it had drifted away. But after two days of searching they couldn't find her anywhere.

A week later, when they held the funeral service for Rebecca, when mourners came forward to offer their condolences, none of them could string a sentence together.

Rachel's life became all Samuel had predicted and more, for who could ever predict the vicious misery she experienced in those passing weeks.

At home they lived in shrouds of silence. What was there to say? They asked for help from another only when needed. Mostly they were ghosts of monotony. Before long, Rachel realised her rawness was but a shadow of her sister's and any anger she felt towards Rebecca and what she'd done, vanished. But how could she live this harrowed life? How was she going to drag herself up out of this quicksand? Who was going to throw her a lifeline?

Her father returned from Deception with a letter for them all from Samuel. He was in the midst of doing medicals on 5,000 men. She had forgotten about the war, of his being over there, of him, and, worse, that he didn't know. She felt he deserved to know the truth, but knowing what led to Rebecca's death would be an unbearable burden for him. And how could she write about her father drowning his son. She could never commit that to paper.

Dear Samuel,

We are relieved to hear you are away from the front. No doubt you have witnessed things you wished you had been spared. It grieves me immensely to tell you of another. Prepare yourself, Samuel, for I have devastating news.

We have lost our beautiful Rebecca. One day she took the Nightingale out and she never returned. We only found the tender with her shawl in it. We have no answers to our questions nor our prayers. I like to think she caught a ride on a passing iceberg and that by the time it melted she was in easy reach of a tropical island and she managed to swim ashore and there she is living out her days.

Here it is permanently winter, our days and nights dark and chilling. She was the one who brightened our days and now with her gone we are completely lost – separate souls adrift on the sea. I think of you often and the ordeal you went through in 1914 before you came to us, before Rebecca rescued you. And I know that if I am to survive, it will only be through the kindness of one who can rescue me like she did you.

We two who loved her most, how can we carry on?

My love and prayers are with you.

Rachel

52

Rebecca stood before the scented arbour that rose above the maroon and grey front gate aware that her breath was tight in her chest. Her hand hovered over the latch but it did not make contact. With the slightest tremor she lowered her palm, wiped it on her skirt and took a step back as she breathed out her misgivings.

How was it possible that the hardest part of this journey was the last ten steps?

For the last half hour as she walked past grand residence after grand residence in what she discovered to her dismay was the well-to-do suburb of South Hill, part of her hoped that maybe there was another South Hill in Toronto, one less imposing, less immaculate. But here she was standing outside number 15 Claredon Crescent, knowing with certainty, unhinged by a mixture of surprise and hesitation that she was at the right place. This was Samuel's home, rather his parents' home, for Samuel was miles away, oceans away, in Europe, on the Western Front.

Over the four days it had taken her to travel all the way from her island home off the coast of Newfoundland her mind had tossed up many thoughts and she had tossed many back. What steered her way in the end was the fact that four years ago Samuel had come unbidden into their lives for a reason. She did not know if it was fate or destiny, written in the stars, orchestrated by the gods, or the Christian God she had grown up with, but it was definitely for a reason, multiple reasons. For a long time she felt that she had been chosen and in some respects she was absolutely right.

But as her mind tacked back and forth and she dove in and around their history, Rebecca came to see that Samuel didn't really have a choice in the matter at all, and Rebecca felt that, in the end, neither did she. That was why she was here.

Yet, even so, she could not help but feel anxious about her unexpected arrival.

Had Samuel been there to welcome her he would have barely recognised the intrepid young traveller. At Carmanville she remembered the money she had underfoot. That paid for her train ticket and her passage. In Québec, a city full of sights and sounds she had never encountered – automobiles, a tobacconist, a liquor store, bars, cafés, barbers, hairdressing salons – she had paused outside one such establishment at a sign in the shop window that read, 'Long hair wanted. Will pay good money.' Worried that she might run out of funds by the time she got to Toronto, she went inside and timidly inquired. Twenty minutes later she walked out of the salon with a straight bob, cut to the nape of her neck and five dollars in her pocket. Before she had her hair cut she stared for five minutes at herself in the mirror, trying to imprint her own image in her mind, thinking, have I always looked like this? Although she was a stranger to herself, Rebecca thought this drawn woman looking back at her could not possibly be her. She was way too serious, too lean. Rebecca was below her pre-pregnancy weight, so strained was her existence over the past three weeks. She said goodbye to her hair and then she felt even more distant. It felt strange, the air around her neck unusual, a little brisk even on that late spring day.

Throughout her journey there was a constant flutter in her stomach. At one point she told herself. 'It will be okay. How hard can this be? You have given birth to a baby. That was hard.' There she paused. Harder was what came later. She regretted using that example to buoy herself up. She wrapped her arms around her body, subconsciously holding herself together so she wouldn't fall apart.

In Toronto she had to ask for directions four times to get to the Daltons. She deferred on public transport, preferring to save her money. It took her three hours to walk from Union Station up University Avenue, skirting Queens Park and then up Avenue Road until she came across Claredon Avenue, then Claredon Crescent.

The Daltons' home was a stately three storey Queen Anne style Victorian house built in the latter part of the 19th century. She knew from Samuel they had lived there for eighteen years, since Samuel was five. The foundations were in brick, the main body of the house in wood, painted a warm grey with maroon, navy and cream trim. It had four large brick chimneys that rose high above the roof. The house was such a contrast to the one she had grown up in.

With some trepidation she opened the gate and walked up the path to the front door. The garden was abloom in white trilliums, pink tulips, lilac azaleas and trailing roses. Just before she reached the steps a grey squirrel scurried across the path startling her. Tentatively, she knocked on the door and waited. She couldn't hear anyone inside. She knocked again. Still there was no answer. Rebecca turned and was about to sit down on the steps and wait when behind her the door opened. A tall black woman looked at her, eye to eye. Taken aback, it took Rebecca a few seconds to find her tongue.

'Mrs Dalton?' she stammered in her awkwardness.

'Not the last time I looked,' said the woman. 'Whom may I ask is calling?'

'Rebecca Crowe,' she said. 'Samuel's friend Rebecca from Newfoundland.'

'Well I'll be,' said the woman, her blunt formality suddenly giving way to a wide smile. Putting her hand out to shake Rebecca's she said, 'I'm Addie, Adeline. It is a great pleasure to meet you, young lady. You sure are a long way from home. Come in child. You must be ever so weary.'

She followed Addie down a hallway past a large internal staircase of dark oak with a wide carpeted runner and into the large kitchen where there was a large wooden table at its centre. So far everything in this house was large.

'Set yourself down,' said Addie. 'Wait a minute, what am I thinking? You would probably like to use the bathroom first. Follow me.' She led Rebecca back out the kitchen along the hall to the toilet and bathroom and gave her a towel for her hands and face. 'Come back when you're done.'

Rebecca stared at the amenities, grateful she could discover them by herself, without Samuel being there. She would have been utterly embarrassed. She was in a different world. When Addie showed her the bathroom she flicked a switch and on came a light overhead. She'd heard of electricity. She just never understood the concept.

When she returned, Addie had laid out a small spread: fruit cake, biscuits, cheese sandwiches and a cup of hot chocolate – a first for her.

'When will Mrs Dalton be home?' she asked after a short interlude.

'Soon. She's at the hospital visiting her newest grandchild.'

'Did Lenore have her baby?' asked Rebecca.

'She did indeed. I can see you are up with the news.'

'Not quite,' said Rebecca with a small smile.

'She had a boy. Jonathan Fletcher Dalton.'

'A boy,' said Rebecca, her voice breaking on the word, a fault line through her brittleness. And despite her best efforts and her pep talks to herself, the tears came, thundering down her cheeks in warm hot gushes. Rebecca had hoped she had left all her tears in Newfoundland but no, on they came, more weighty tears of loss, of grief and of faint relief at making it to Toronto all by herself.

She sat there with her hands covering her face, crying into her hands, trying in vain not to cry but it was hopeless. Every so often hiccupping, 'I'm sorry.'

'There, there,' said Addie, who had come to sit in the chair beside her. 'You've got nothing to be sorry for.' She placed her arms around Rebecca and pressed her into her shoulder so she could cry there, and take comfort from her motherly embrace.

Finally Rebecca composed herself. 'Goodness knows what you must think of me.'

'I think you are someone who needed to cry.'

'I have cried more in the last month than I think I have cried in my whole life,' said Rebecca shaking her head, her eyes downcast.

'By the look of you, I'm not surprised.' After a pause she said, 'I'm sorry for your heartache, Rebecca, whatever the cause.'

Rebecca tried to give her a small smile in appreciation, but she only managed to make eye contact for a breath, nod her head and look back at her plate. She blew her nose and to change the subject she asked, 'Have you had any news of Samuel lately?'

'Why, yes, only very small news but he is with Matthew right now. Mr and Mrs Dalton sent a telegram to Matthew on

Sunday and got one back today to say that he celebrated the news of Jonathan's birth with Samuel.'

'So he must be away from the front. Thank goodness.'

'Amen,' said Addie. 'And hopefully he ain't going back.'

'How long have you known Samuel?' asked Rebecca.

'Since before he was born.' Rebecca caught the woman's eye. 'I love him like he's my own son.'

'Do you have children of your own?' ventured Rebecca.

'Yes I have, they're all grown up now and all but left home, a bit like you. Come, let's get you settled. How about we put you in Samuel's old room? Would you like that?'

'Yes,' she inhaled.

Samuel's room was on the second floor at the back of the house overlooking an orchard and the vegetable garden. Somewhere there would be a herb garden. Samuel had once told Rebecca his mother could not live without her herb garden. Addie showed her yet another bathroom where she could shower before dinner then left her alone.

Rebecca sat down on the bed and looked slowly around the room. 'Hello Samuel,' she said, 'I'm in your room!' feeling a tinge of excitement, and for the first time since the terrible tragedy, she felt a small wave of reprieve, as if things were going to be all right. She lay down on Samuel's bed and looked at the expanse of sky out the window. She wondered if Samuel lay there looking up at the stars or if he drew the curtains. No, she decided he would leave them open. She rose and walked over to his desk and there above it was her drawing in a rough weathered frame, not unlike the weathered boards of her home. It made her heart gladder to see it there, to know that it had pride of place in his room. 'I will remember you. I will remember this.' She read the words out loud.

Rebecca had a bath, washed her hair and rinsed off under a handheld shower – another first for her – like a waterfall that you could turn on and off at your leisure. She towel dried her hair, combed it out, put on her one and only change of clothing – a new dress and underwear she had bought in Quebec – and went downstairs.

At the bottom of the stairs she heard voices and wondered whether she should go in search of them or find Addie. Succumbing to shyness she decided on the latter. Coming into the kitchen she asked, 'Can I help you with dinner?'

'No, thank you all the same. I just need the pots and pans to do their thing. Come, the Daltons are eager to meeting you.'

With excitement and nerves battling it out in her stomach Rebecca followed Addie back along the hallway into a large sunroom. Inside were two men and a woman. They all rose as she entered. Mrs Dalton came up to her immediately, taking both her hands and looking keenly into her face. 'Are we ever so delighted to meet you? This has been such a happy week for us and your presence here just adds to it, Rebecca.' She kissed her in the European style, on both cheeks like Samuel did when he greeted someone. Rebecca gave way to a smile of relief.

'So this is Rebecca,' said the older man. His voice was well worn, soft and a little scratchy, but warm with it, his eyes deep-set in his defined face. He took her hand in both of his and looked inquisitively into her face with a warm smile and a lightness sparkling in his eyes. 'The young girl who rescued Samuel all those years ago. How we have looked forward to making your acquaintance, young lady,' he said.

'I'm pleased to meet you too, Mr Dalton,' she said.

'Mr Dalton is my son, here,' said Mr Dalton senior, patting Samuel's father on the back. 'Call me Grandpa.'

'Grandpa, then,' she said, with a soft smile.

Samuel's father looked so like Samuel, it startled her. The same height, the same hair, only a little darker with touches of grey. He had Samuel's eyes too, perhaps more tawny, and she felt warmer for their presence. She held onto his hands and couldn't help but stare.

With a gentle smile, he said, 'Do I remind you of someone?'

'Yes,' inhaled Rebecca, breaking into a grin.

'Now you know what Samuel will look like when he's fifty-five.'

'He will look very fine.'

'Ha,' he said, releasing her hands and giving her a hug. 'I always knew I was going to like you, Rebecca. Come, sit, tell us what you think of Toronto.'

'It's big, much bigger than where I come from, much bigger than I expected even. The houses are bigger too. It's different to Québec. That was hilly. Toronto is flatter.'

'Oh it's not totally flat. We have some little hills of our own which we'll show you sometime,' said Grandpa.

'How did you get here?' asked Mr Dalton.

She told them of her journey and how she had spotted whales on the ferry in the Gulf of St Lawrence.

When she had finished Mrs Dalton said, 'We would happily have met you at the station, save you walking here by yourself.'

It wasn't an admonishment or a reprimand; it was a simple statement, another gesture of hospitality, but Rebecca felt the weight of it and the need to respond. Clearing her throat she said, 'I'm sorry for not writing to see if it would suit you for me to come. I hope you don't mind me turning up unexpected.'

'We don't mind at all,' said Mr Dalton.

'That's right,' said Mrs Dalton, 'It would suit us anytime you wanted to come. Don't worry about it. What day did you say you left home?'

Rebecca thought for a moment – the days had been long and eventful. 'Saturday,' she said at last. She was dreading the next question, thinking for sure they were going to ask her about her family but then Mrs Dalton surprised her.

'So when did you last hear from our Samuel and what did he have to say?'

'His last letter was sent in early April,' she replied. 'It started at the ADS and then they had to drop back when the Germans attacked to reclaim Passchendaele.'

'Do you have it with you?'

Rebecca shook her head and was saved from the next question by Addie popping her head in to say dinner was ready. The four of them sat down at one end of the long mahogany dining table. Mr Dalton at one end, Mrs Dalton to his left, Rebecca was placed to his right and Grandpa Dalton next to her. Rebecca had a glass of water in front of her and let Mr Dalton pour her the smallest glass of white wine. 'Let's raise our glasses for a toast,' said Grandpa. 'To Miss Rebecca Crowe, from Newfoundland for visiting us after all these years.'

'Yes,' said Mr Dalton, 'Welcome to our family, welcome to

our home. We hope you feel as much at home here as Samuel was in yours.' He held her eyes.

'Thank you,' said Rebecca clinking her glasses with theirs and taking a small sip. She expected the wine to be sour but that wasn't the case at all. It wasn't sour or sweet, though it did taste a little bit like honey and it was a little sharp. She smiled at them all after she had swallowed and subtly licked her lips.

Putting her glass down she said, 'Samuel told me you drank wine with your dinner. Do you have wine every night?'

'Only on week-ends now and special occasions,' said Mrs Dalton, 'but mind you, don't go telling folk that we do.'

'Of course, no, I wouldn't dream of it,' said Rebecca a little flustered.

Noting her unease, Mr Dalton said, 'Rebecca, please don't misunderstand my wife or us, it's just that Ontario is under a state of prohibition. The sale and consumption of alcohol has been prohibited since 1916 so we need to keep the fact that we have wine and spirits in our house hush, hush.'

'Oh,' said Rebecca, not knowing what else to say.

'Most ridiculous law ever invented,' said Mrs Dalton. 'We nearly moved to Québec when they brought it in.'

'Québec doesn't have prohibition,' said Mr Dalton for her benefit. 'In fact they strongly oppose it.'

'Why did they bring in such a law?'

'Because too many people lack self control and don't know when enough is enough,' said Grandpa, 'and too many bar managers were greedy and would overly entice the working class man to spend all his earnings on beer and spirits rather than on food and clothing for his family. If people were decent we wouldn't need laws. There's too many laws nowadays.'

Rebecca sat there wondering, then asked, 'If it is prohibited in Ontario and you have it in your house does that mean you could get arrested if you were found out?'

'Arrested, possibly. Fined more likely,' said Mr Dalton. 'They might turn a blind eye given our medical profession and the occasional call on us to administer alms at home.'

'And if we got into any problems,' said Grandpa, 'I'd claim it was all mine. Screw them. See how they treat an eighty year old man.'

Rebecca hoped her face was managing to hide her alarm.

'If it is prohibited, where do you get it from?'

'From my brother Michel,' said Mrs Dalton. 'Have you heard of him?'

'Yes,' said Rebecca, adding, 'What is his surname, your maiden name? I thought of that when I was in Québec, but I had no idea.'

'Sibonne,' said Mrs Dalton, 'with an S.'

'Sibonne,' repeated Rebecca, 'that's a pretty name.'

'Tell me,' said Grandpa Dalton, 'do you have restrictions in Newfoundland because of the war? Do you have the war meals guide and meatless Fridays and no fuel Sundays.'

'Not that I know of,' said Rebecca. 'We have meatless months which have nothing to do with the war. March sometimes can be meatless and vegetable-less, if we run out of potatoes and turnips and the like – we call it the long month of March. We should call it the long month of bread because that's all we eat sometimes: bread and tea, bread and tea. Some people call it chaw and glutch. And then in the summer and autumn we can have the opposite, fish coming out of our gills, berries galore, fresh salad and vegetables.'

Rebecca was glad to be talking about wine and meatless Fridays – anything to keep the Daltons distracted. Ever since her arrival she was expecting a question, multiple questions, 'Why have you come here all of a sudden? Unannounced? What's happened?' Which, after all this time, she still didn't know how to answer. But such dreaded questions didn't come. The Daltons were skilled in social graces and perhaps had been tipped off by Addie. To deflect possible questions Rebecca launched into questioning mode herself. She inquired about Mr Dalton's practice and where Grandpa Dalton had worked when he was a doctor and when they finished that topic she asked after Analeise and her children, her husband Randall whom she knew very little about and then how long Lenore would be in hospital.

After dinner they carried their own plates and empty glasses into the kitchen while Mrs Dalton proceeded to wash up, Rebecca dried and Mr Dalton made tea and coffee.

'Has Addie gone home?' asked Rebecca.

'She has dinner with her family every night. You will see her again in the morning. She comes and goes throughout the day depending on what she has on.'

'Does she live far away?' asked Rebecca.

'No, not far at all,' said Mrs Dalton, giving her a look. 'I'll show you tomorrow.'

They returned to the sunroom for tea and coffee. Grandpa had brought out the last letter they'd received from Samuel and gave it to Rebecca. 'You're welcome to read this.'

'Thank you.' She looked at him. 'May I take it to my room to read later.'

'Of course.' He then asked if Samuel knew she was planning to come to Toronto.

'No,' she said, meeting his eye. 'My departure wasn't greatly planned.'

'And what about your sister, Rachel?' asked Mrs Dalton. 'You couldn't convince her to come with you?'

Rebecca felt a surge of panic. This was like the episode with her mother skirting around her pregnancy, almost worst even. She didn't speak. She just looked at Mrs Dalton, sorrowfully, and shook her head.

And then Mrs Dalton asked in her most delicate voice, 'How is your sister? And your parents?'

Rebecca looked at Mrs Dalton, conscious of the blood rushing to her face trying to stop it from crumbling. She couldn't continue to look at the woman for another moment. Lowering her head, she said, almost inaudibly, 'They are no more,' her voice catching on more. 'I cannot begin to talk about it. Please don't ask me,' and she hung her head and cried silent tears.

53

Rebecca didn't read Samuel's letter that night. She lay there utterly distraught about what she'd told the Daltons and what she was going to tell them. What was she going to tell them?

For although she had lied, she had spoken a truth. In fleeing as she had done she had made a decision to turn her back on her family and over the succeeding days she felt increasingly justified. She never wanted to see her father again. That was indisputable. He was dead to her. She had left to come to a place where he couldn't hurt her anymore. To a place where he couldn't control every inch of her life with his sanctimony and his superstitions and his grand, misplaced sense of familial duty. And her mother had supported him in that. She had not stood up for Rebecca when it counted. Later, she had not helped Rebecca leave when she was pregnant and asking for such help. Rebecca always had a foreboding when it came to her father. When she was thirteen staring at an iceberg, he came up behind her and walloped her so hard across the head he knocked her to the ground making her ear bleed. It was so painful. She couldn't hear properly for weeks and was dizzy for days. He was a violent man capable of inhumane beatings and worse. Her mother had failed to protect her and after thirty years with him she should have known better. How could she have married such a man? How could she lie in bed night after night with him? And, most alarmingly, how could she let him get away with what he had done?

And what of Rachel? She was a twenty-two year old woman, not a child. By choosing to stay silent, she had colluded with them. When her father killed her horse Slate, she had sought out Ronnie's help. But this time when the crime was more severe she had done nothing. Shouldn't a daughter disobey a parent when what they had done was morally wrong? Could she not exercise her own judgment? Could she not defend her sister, avenge her sister even, or did she secretly believe the punishment Rebecca received was deserving of her crime?

Because of Rachel's disability and her seniority, Rebecca had always deferred to her and put her first in everything. Everything, that is, except for Samuel. She was not going to bow down there. And if Rachel had not been so caught up in her own feelings for Samuel, if she had not been so blind, maybe she could have seen that it was Rebecca whom Samuel adored and loved, and graciously stepped aside and given her blessing, and Rebecca would not have had to go on deferring to her and shielding the truth from her.

That night as the minutes and hours ticked by, Rebecca asked what could she hope to salvage from all that? And even though her father was in his own extreme and abominable category, how could she have a relationship with her mother and sister, when they all lived under the same roof. In the dead of night she came to her conclusion: she couldn't. She never wanted to hear of, let alone hear from, her father ever again. So it was not possible. They were no more.

How did they die? Sickness? She ruled that out immediately. How could she fend off any questions of a medical nature with two doctors. Did they drown and she wasn't with them. That could be possible. But then why did she arrive on their doorstep with so few possessions and none of Samuel's letters? They were no more. Then it had to be...fire... and she wasn't there. It was at nighttime and they died in their sleep, the house was burnt to the ground. Her clothes, Samuel's letters, everything. And she wasn't there because she had stayed the night with the Evans. In May, why would she be there? She racked her brain. She had ridden Mica over to the Bay and Mica had gone lame on the journey. So she had stayed with Ronnie to let Mica rest and tend to her.

Could she lie like that? She who had never lied until six months ago till her father forced her.

She slept late. When she awoke she heard voices downstairs. She washed her face, hurriedly combed her hair and dressed. She found Mrs Dalton and Grandpa at the kitchen table having breakfast. Addie was mumbling to herself and writing. 'Good morning,' said Rebecca as she entered.

'Good morning, ma chère,' said Mrs Dalton. 'Did you sleep well?'

'Eventually,' she replied, then added, 'The bed was very comfortable. ' Looking around she asked, 'Has Mr Dalton had breakfast already?'

'He'll be seeing his first patient about now,' said Grandpa.

'What about you, Addie?' asked Rebecca.

'I had mine with Jerome and Joel, but I'll have another cup of tea. Would you like some tea?'

'Yes please,' said Rebecca and then, 'Who are Jerome and Joel?'

'Why, Jerome's my good husband, and one day you will have the pleasure of meeting him. Joel's my youngest, and that will be a pleasure too.'

Both Grandpa and Mrs Dalton chuckled at Addie.

'I've heard of a Joel, is he Samuel's friend, Joel?' said Rebecca in surprise.

'That's my boy,' said Addie with a wide smile.

'Where is he?' asked Rebecca

'He's at work. Nearly finished his first year at a big engineering firm down in the city.'

'What does he do there?'

'Engineering. He's helping them build bridges.'

'Joel's the first engineer of colour to graduate from the University of Toronto,' said Grandpa.

'That's my boy,' Addie said again.

'Addie is very proud of him. As we all are.'

'Well, that's wonderful for him. I don't know anything about engineering but I'm sure he can tell me one day.'

'That he will,' said Addie. The next moment she leaned over, put her hand on Rebecca's, and in a lowered voice said, 'It might be hard for you to appreciate this right now, but when you have your own children you just want to give them everything that you didn't have as a child yourself and when you see them go on and live a life that is bigger than you ever imagined, it makes your heart burst with pride and joy. God has blessed me; he has blessed me in so many ways, with a loving husband with four healthy children and with the

Daltons here who helped all of our children get an education. Jerome and I came from nothing except hard work and decent manners and we have been given so much by these good folk.'

Right up to that point Rebecca was doing well, feeling as if that day might be the first in over three weeks when she wouldn't cry. But with Addie's words she came undone.

'Oh Lordy me, forgive me, child, I'm beyond sorry. I didn't mean to upset your pretty face again today.' She squeezed Rebecca's hand.

After she had calmed down, and had two pieces of toast and another cup of tea, Mrs Dalton said to her, 'You have an older sister, right. Not Rachel but another one?'

'Yes,' said Rebecca, hesitantly. 'Esther.' And before she could help herself, she blurted out, 'She died too…in the fire.' What compelled Rebecca to say that? To compound matters further! It was this morbid dread of having to answer the Dalton's unspoken questions, to explain herself. She just wanted to get the story she had concocted out there, over and done with, so she would only have to say it once and never mention it again. But being here in the Dalton's home, for the first time she felt abject shame. Shame at having lain with Samuel as if she were a loose woman, like the ones she'd seen at the wharves in Quebec, shame at the atrocity her father had committed, shame at being related to him, and shame for the way she had left her family with so little consideration for their feelings. What would these good people think of her? So to cover her shame, to cover her actions, she lied and then one lie begat another.

Her face was diffused with colour and the tears rolled down her face not in heartbreak as Grandpa and Mrs Dalton and Addie suspected but in mortification at her own dishonesty, hating her father, hating the injustice of it all, but hating herself the most. She told them about the fire alright. But she told them Esther was visiting as well with all her four children so everyone could meet her youngest and, poof, they were no more too. In a few foul minutes she wiped her whole family off the face of the earth. She ended up in Mrs Dalton's arms but she felt so undeserving she tore herself away and fled back upstairs to Samuel's room.

A few hours later Mrs Dalton knocked on her door.

'Rebecca,' she called. 'May I come in? I've brought you morning tea.'

Rebecca rose and let her in. She felt wretched.

Mrs Dalton put down the tray then gently took her hand. 'Your home is with us now, Rebecca. You will become our daughter. And we never have to speak of this again.'

This time Rebecca did lean her head on Mrs Dalton's shoulder, her eyes closed. 'Thank you,' she whispered.

'I want you to rest up because this afternoon I'm going to take you shopping for some new clothes.'

Rebecca was on the verge of telling her she did not have to do that: she had money but then that might lead to more explaining and the inference that perhaps her leaving Newfoundland had been pre-meditated which it hadn't.

'Would you like to take a walk with me in the garden?'

Rebecca nodded. Outside they came across the carriage house where Addie and Jerome lived.

'So does Addie's husband work for you too?'

'He works for us part time. Before we had the car he used to look after our horses and he has always managed the grounds, in his spare time. But he's always had other jobs as well.'

'Do most people in Toronto have servants?' asked Rebecca.

Turning to look at Rebecca, Mrs Dalton said, 'We call Addie and Jerome our helpers. We help them out and they help us, but in answer to your question, the majority of people no, those who can afford it, yes. Did Samuel never tell you about Addie and Jerome?'

'No,' said Rebecca, wondering why.

'I suspect he had his reasons.'

'I didn't know any of this was back here yesterday when I arrived. All I could see was that big oak tree.'

'I love that tree,' said Mrs Dalton. 'Every home should have one. It marks the seasons and you hit the nail on the head when you said you couldn't see anything back here. It gives both Addie and us some extra privacy. And for Matthew it was his escape route when he snuck out at night to meet his friends. See that branch up there where it forks,' she said pointing to it. 'That's right outside Matthew's old room and he used to swing out there and then slide down. He thought we didn't know what he was up to but we did, we were wise to him.'

After lunch Mrs Dalton took Rebecca on the streetcar to Eaton's department store. It was imposing as well. Rebecca hoped she wasn't obviously goggle-eyed. In ladies fashion, she tried on a number of dresses for herself, but largely to indulge Mrs Dalton who bought Rebecca a navy dress that belted at the waist with a white collar and white trim. She also bought her a powder blue cotton skirt, a matching cotton cardigan along with a soft blue and pink floral top, two pairs of stockings and a pair of low navy lace-up leather shoes to go with her two new outfits. Rebecca told her it was too much. Mrs Dalton said it wasn't nearly enough but they would stop for the day.

Rebecca had only been in Toronto for twenty-four hours but already she felt like it had been the right thing to do. Mrs Dalton was unlike any woman Rebecca had ever met. She seemed to be more woman than mother, more lady than housewife, which in truth she was. Though Rebecca could not name it, she embodied a femininity that was strikingly new to her, not delicate femininity; healthy spirited femininity. Her character was warm and friendly and confident, even playful like Samuel. While Rebecca always thought her mother had a quiet beauty, Mrs Dalton, whom she put around the same age as her mother, had a striking beauty by comparison.

Lottie wore bright tasteful outfits, with necklines that revealed her collarbone, with fabrics that quietly accentuated her figure. She wore her dark curly hair with barely a hint of grey pinned loosely up all over her head. She had olive skin and deep-set chocolate-brown eyes edged in darker eyelashes, and Rebecca noted when she was up close, she painted her lips. Today they were a soft red that only seemed to add to her vibrancy.

If she weren't friendly and easygoing, Rebecca would have felt intimidated and dull next to her. 'Thank you for being so welcoming to me,' said Rebecca as they sat in a café drinking coffee.

'Thank you for coming,' said Mrs Dalton. 'I had been so looking forward to meeting you this summer and then disappointed when that was not going to happen. So despite the sad circumstances that brought you here, Rebecca, I'm happy you're here.'

When they came home from town Rebecca headed to her room. Her spirits had lifted incredibly and she wanted to share everything with Samuel. She decided she should write to him about being in Toronto with his family, but with pen in hand she realised deciding to write to Samuel was one matter, doing it was something else.

Dear Samuel,
Guess where I am? Would you believe…in Toronto…with your family?

What was she going to say, I'm in Toronto. I decided to come by myself and got no objections…

She knew that would arouse his suspicion and fly in the face of everything he knew about her parents and the stipulation that their relationship be kept secret. One thing for certain, she did not have it in her yet to write and tell him everything that had happened. She couldn't even write half of what had happened. In the end she abandoned all efforts, deciding to leave it to another day.

The next morning Lottie took Rebecca to visit Lenore and baby Jonathan. When Rebecca followed Mrs Dalton into Maternity Ward A she entered a large white room with tall narrow windows along each wall between ten wrought iron single beds puffed up with women and pillows. Everything inside the room was white except for the flowers on each patient's bedside cabinet; even the coverings on each child's bassinet were white. They stopped in front of a woman reading a copy of The Evening Star, her face completely screened from view.

'Anything interesting in there?' said Mrs Dalton. 'Because there's plenty interesting out here.'

Lenore lowered her newspaper, a bright smile spread across her face. 'Hello Lottie,' she said and then without pause, 'Hello Rebecca.'

'Hello,' said Rebecca after a small startled delay.

'Hello,' drew out Mrs Dalton. 'Someone has obviously been here before us.'

'Yes, Grandpa popped in again yesterday. I don't think he can stay away. He told me there was a new woman in his life. I told him I'd only been here for five days and he was a tad fickle. What happened to decorum I ask you?'

'Well, he is Matthew's grandfather,' said Mrs Dalton 'Need I say more.' Both women laughed quietly.

Then, looking at Rebecca, Lenore asked, 'How are you settling in to Toronto?'

'Very well, thank you.' She tried to smile brightly 'Congratulations on the birth of your son,' said Rebecca. 'How was your labour? Are you recovering well?'

'I am doing as well as can be expected I think. Thank you.' After a few moments she said, 'You know a thing or two about childbirth then?'

Rebecca stared at her for a long moment, feeling her heart beating faster. Taking a deep breath she said, 'I have, had,' she stammered, her heart haemorrhaging in disgust at herself, she swallowed, 'A sister who had four children. Her youngest was born in March, a little boy she called Reuben.' Her face blushed again and she looked uncomfortably at her feet.

'Oh,' Lenore said slowly, 'of course,' then sincerely, 'I'm ever so sorry.'

Rebecca nodded, not raising her head, her hands squeezed tightly together.

'Would you like to meet Jonathan?' she asked.

Rebecca cleared her throat. 'Sure.'

'Well you could meet him if Lottie would surrender the spot she has claimed there. She fell in love with her newest grandchild the moment she laid eyes on him. He's his father's son. I don't think I got a look in anywhere.' A few moments later she asked, 'Have you heard from Samuel lately?'

'I got a letter about two weeks ago. It was written back in early April. What about you, have you heard from Matthew?'

'Yes a brief telegram on Tuesday. Here,' she reached across to her drawer, 'you can read it.'

LENORE DALTON. TO THE BEST NEW MOM IN THE WORLD. I LOVE YOU. I AM SO PROUD OF

YOU. SAY HELLO TO JONATHAN FOR ME. I CAN'T WAIT TO HOLD THE TWO OF YOU IN MY ARMS. ALL MY LOVE MATTHEW. P.S. SAMUEL CELEBRATED WITH ME AND SENDS HIS CONGRATULATIONS.

Rebecca's eyes overflowed with tears. They funnelled down her cheeks. She kept her face lowered and tried to hide their trail, quickly wiping her face with her left hand as she handed the note back to Lenore with her right. Almost inaudibly she said, 'That's lovely.'

'Yes,' said Lenore, 'Sometimes they say the most perfect thing.' And then quite unexpectedly Lenore reached out for her hand. 'They'll be home soon. I'm counting on it.' She squeezed once in encouragement.

Rebecca nodded and risked a glance and a smile at Lenore. Then she heard Mrs Dalton say, 'Rebecca, come and have a look at this beautiful boy.'

He was lying on his back with his head to the side, a beautiful shaped head with dark hair and dark eyelashes.

'Do you want to hold him?' asked Lenore.

'No, let him sleep,' said Rebecca. 'I'll hold him another day when he's awake,' thinking, sleep on little boy, sleep on today, answer my prayer little angel and don't wake up today.

That night over dinner as they exchanged stories of their day Mr Dalton said, 'Samuel told us many things about you and your sister, how charming the two of you were, but one thing he neglected to tell us was just how unusual and beautiful your accent was.'

'I have an accent?' asked Rebecca in disbelief.

'Yes,' everyone said in unison and laughed at her surprise.

'A soft round lilting brogue,' said Mr Dalton, 'an intermingling of English and Irish and Scottish perhaps but with all the harshness, and pompousness and blurriness left out. And you have this wonderful way of inhaling when you say yes rather than exhaling.'

'I do?' queried Rebecca.

'Yes,' said Grandpa Dalton, 'your voice is like velvet.'

'Is that what you told Lenore?' asked Mrs Dalton arching an eyebrow.

'Never you mind what I told Lenore,' said Grandpa. 'That's between her and me.'

On Sunday morning, Rebecca helped Addie prepare a homecoming lunch for Lenore and Jonathan. Lenore's brother Alistair joined them along with Analeise's family. Alistair was a tall man, taller than Samuel, noted Rebecca, with brown hair that sported hints of auburn in various lights. Without doubt he was handsome, but he didn't unnerve her like Samuel once had. He wore a fawn-coloured three-piece suit, the jacket of which he removed after only a few minutes. Rebecca found him to be most courteous. He asked her about summers in Newfoundland, if she knew anyone in the war and how she was finding Toronto. Rebecca found Randall, Analeise's husband, quiet next to Alistair, but at the same time relaxed and gentle with his children. He was quite striking though, his brown tortoiseshell glasses framing large brown eyes and matching hair.

If Samuel was the image of his father, than Analeise was the image of her mother, an inch or two taller, a few pounds slimmer, her hair more loose and wild about her head. Rebecca liked that about her, it reminded her a little of herself when she had long hair. Over lunch she asked Rebecca if she liked the cinema.

'I've never been. I hardly know anything about it,' she shrugged.

'Everyone who goes to the cinema loves it. Moving pictures. I'll take you sometime. These days I don't get to go nearly as much as I'd like to.' She called out to her mother, 'Perhaps you could look after the children one afternoon while I take Rebecca to a matinee at the Musée.'

Lottie was bouncing Catherine on her knee. 'Take her to see A Dog's Life. Your father and I loved it, or that new one that's just started playing, Amarilly of Clothesline Alley.

'Just name the day, Mother.'

'Alright, hint taken,' said Mrs Dalton, raising a hand in surrender.

54

On Monday morning Rebecca found herself in the kitchen ironing whilst Addie was bustling about, preparing lunch. All of a sudden the relaxed air of the house was broken by a chilling scream from one of the upstairs bedrooms. The two women looked at each other then took off. She heard Addie say, 'God almighty, please let that baby be all right.'

On the second floor, Rebecca followed Addie into Lenore's room, the source of the cries and sobbing. Inside, she saw Mr Dalton holding both Mrs Dalton and Lenore in his arms, his eyes closed, his head resting on Mrs Dalton's. Addie marched over to look at the baby in the bassinet. A few steps behind, Rebecca, softly asked, 'Is the baby okay?'

Addie looked at Rebecca then turned to Mr Dalton with a mixed look of dread and curiosity on her face. Sensing their gaze, Mr Dalton opened his eyes. 'It's Matthew,' he said, 'we've lost Matthew.'

'Sweet Jesus no,' said Addie, slowly shaking her head. 'Don't tell me that.' She collapsed backwards onto the settee and buried her head in her hands.

Rebecca stood there looking at everyone, trying to comprehend what she had heard. She couldn't understand how it could be, but in the dark corners of her mind she felt the sinister whisper. I am a bad omen for these people. I brought death into their home. Things happen in threes! Who will be next? I should never have come here. I best leave, but where? Who else am I going to hand over to the angel of death? The baby's crying brought her out of her mind's death trap. Everyone else was too overwrought with his or her own grief to notice. Slowly she walked over to the small child, bent down, picked him up and holding him to her chest she carried him out of the room.

Downstairs, she changed Jonathan's nappy and put a pot

of water onto boil. In the laundry she found a clean tablecloth, which she wrapped around herself and across her front and back, securing it with a knot, placing Jonathan inside firmly against her front. She thought he was hungry but she couldn't feed him. She hoped he would settle. A little while later she carried a tray with a pot of tea and four cups upstairs to Lenore's room. The family had separated and was half sitting, half lying on chairs and the bed. Mr Dalton came immediately to her aid.

'I thought you might like a cup of tea,' she said. 'Sorry, Mrs Dalton, I don't know how to make coffee yet.' She gave her a quick glance.

'Tea will do fine my dear. Thank you.'

All of them were so far embroiled in shock and disbelief they didn't notice Jonathan strapped to her body.

Rebecca hesitated, not knowing whether to stay or go, not knowing what to say or do. In little more than a whisper she said, 'I'm sorry about Matthew.'

No one replied they just nodded and cried into their cups.

Strangely with Matthew's death, Rebecca was at last able to close the door on her own grief – almost. She got her strength back, her reserves returned and she became the silent angel of salvation around the Daltons' home, helping each family member somehow, someway get through each day.

She cooked small meals for them, made fresh bread, made soups, omelettes, scones, whatever Addie suggested in an absent off-handed way. Addie took Matthew's death almost as hard as Mrs Dalton. She would be in two states; deathly silent or a blithering mess slumped over the kitchen table.

Rebecca went to St Lawrence market all by herself and bought supplies with money Grandpa gave her. She laundered, dusted, cleaned, made countless cups of tea, made beds, watered the garden and in between all that she would feed Jonathan with fresh goat's milk she would buy every second day from the market. The shock of Matthew's death had affected Lenore deeply; she couldn't nurse her son without pouring rivers of tears over his head. She was too upset and couldn't settle and neither could the baby. Because she was breastfeeding, Mr Dalton balked at giving her opiates to calm her down. Rebecca tried to give her chamomile tea but she would barely touch it.

In just a few short days, her milk supply ceased to flow and Jonathan cried louder and desperately in hunger and in pain. Grandpa Dalton stepped in. He took Rebecca shopping and then Rebecca took over bottle-feeding while Mr Dalton started administering brandy and opiates to give Lenore much needed rest. Rebecca took to carrying Jonathan strapped to her chest nearly everywhere she went. Her very presence soothed the boy and his soothed her. She loved the weight of him on her. Some afternoons she'd take him upstairs whispering to him, 'Let's see what your mommy is up to,' thinking she could hand him back to Lenore, but more often than not Lenore would be lying on top of the bed covered with a light cotton throw, staring at the wall, lost to the world. Occasionally Rebecca would untie the wrap and tuck Jonathan in front of her, placing Lenore's hand on the little bundle so she knew he was with her and then she would silently leave the room.

55

It was Ronnie Evans who brought it to their attention, riding over the hill like he'd done the day he told them England was at war with Germany, except this day Silas was away, trapping. He sat down for a cup of tea and Morna felt he looked drawn and older and not by just a few years. Perhaps she was projecting her own altered state.

Without any preamble he began. 'The Germans it would appear have no regard for human life or the Hague or Geneva Conventions – particularly the latter. They no longer recognise the neutrality of medical personnel or hospitals.' With a heavy sigh he continued, 'Last Sunday night they bombed Hospital City where the Canadian Stationary Hospitals are located.'

He already had their attention with his sombre disposition, but Morna's and Rachel's senses were instantly heightened. Rather than regurgitate what was in the newspaper, he laid it out in front of them, his hands shaking. 'Best you read it for yourself.'

They skimmed the front page, looking for what he couldn't tell them.

```
Hospital City, at Etaples, France, as its name
implied was a large community of row upon row of
makeshift Allied hospitals caring for the sick
and wounded. Temporary hospitals made of tents
and wooden galvanized huts. The thought of the
Germans attacking these medical stations so far
from the front was just preposterous, their
position and their purpose well-known to both
sides of the conflict. Last Sunday, May 19, when
nursing sisters were returning to their quarters
after an evening concert, they heard a loud
humming sound from the sky, a large bomb
exploded directly in front of them. Sleeping
quarters of orderlies and the other personnel
were blown to bits. Sick and recovering soldiers
had to dive under their beds for what little
```

```
shelter they offered. That night nearly every
hospital in the vicinity was bombed. All told
sixty-six Canadians were killed or died shortly
thereafter from injuries or burns. Seventy-three
were wounded.
```

Rachel raised her head and looked at Ronnie, 'Was–'
'Keep reading.'

```
The hospital was at full capacity with 2,218
patients being cared for by 142 nurses. Three
Canadian army nurses — Sister Macdonald from
Brantford, Sister Lowe from Binscarth and Sister
Wake of Esquimalt — were killed making them the
first Canadian nurses to die in the war. Two
doctors, both brothers from the Dalton family in
Toronto, rushing to help were caught by an early
explosion, the youngest killed, the other
wounded.
```

Rachel's hands immediately covered her face. 'No, no, not Samuel, not Samuel, not Samuel,' she cried. Morna reached for one of Rachel's hands and held it next to her own heart while she looked out the window.

'I'm sorry, lass,' said Ronnie. 'I know you've already had enough heartache for one lifetime.' He squeezed his hands together, 'But I didn't want you to be waiting and waiting for Samuel to write to you and his lack of response add to your misery.' His sigh was lacerated. 'This news would never have reached us normally. It's only because the Hun attacked those hospitals in the rear and killed Canadian nurses that the newspapers ran that report. No doubt Samuel was with Matthew at the time and because it's tied up with all this mess, we get to read about it.' Rachel was speechless.

'I wonder if he got the letter about Rebecca?' Morna murmured.

Ronnie shrugged. He looked at Rachel and reached over to squeeze her shoulder. 'He was the most splendid young man, my dear. One of a kind, that's for sure. And we are blessed for having known him.'

When Morna told Silas about Samuel's death, he ran his hand down his face. Quietly he said, 'That dream I had was a premonition then. He was destined to die.'

He showed no sorrow which under normal circumstances

would have infuriated Morna but now given everything, just left her cold. 'Like our grandson, right?' Her voice bitter. 'Was Rebecca destined to die too? Did you dream that?'

Silas went down below and dragged the Nightingale out of the water. A day later he doused it in fuel and burnt the last remains of Samuel from their lives.

Dear Mr and Mrs Dalton and family,

We read with dismay the details of the bombing of Hospital City and then with sadness and heartache the disturbing news that both your sons were injured, Samuel fatally.

Your youngest son we remember fondly for so many things: his boundless energy and willingness to dig in and help, his cheerful personality and his thoughtful ways that brought grace and good humour to our home. I will, however, most remember Samuel for the charming man who made both my daughters' hearts sing. Yet, he understood and loved our youngest Rebecca like no other and she returned his affection completely.

His tragic passing seemed to rub salt in our very own raw wounds – so sudden after Rebecca's drowning – the Nightingale tender and Rebecca's shawl all we found adrift in our bay. Rachel wrote to Samuel but we doubt that news ever reached you. It goes against the laws of nature when the Lord calls our children home before us. I know we are not meant to question why but many days I struggle. My only comfort is that Samuel and Rebecca can be in death what they could not be in life – together for eternity.

I do feel a degree of responsibility and regret for what has happened; that by Silas' and my actions last summer we drove Samuel away to the war. Had we said: 'Yes, next summer' to his request to marry Rebecca then I fear he would have stayed put in Canada and this tragedy might have been avoided. For that I am deeply sorry and humbly ask for your forgiveness and understanding.

We will remember your family and Samuel every night in our prayers and trust Matthew has made a speedy recovery.

My deepest sympathy,
Morna Crowe on behalf of the Crowe family,
Second Chance, Newfoundland.

56

The Daltons, Lenore and Rebecca did not find out about the inaccurate news report till some days later and when they did, it barely registered. They had a telegram from Samuel that was indisputable. It had been confirmed by a cable from the war office.

'How could they get such a thing wrong?' Rebecca asked.

But none of the Daltons were too perturbed. Even Lenore was understanding. 'Rebecca,' she said, 'whether it's right or wrong, it's not going to bring Matthew back.'

Grandpa added. 'In war my dear the stakes are a lot higher than a misprint in a newspaper.'

They decided to wait till Samuel returned before holding a service for Matthew. Mr Dalton sent him a telegram:

I HAVE ALREADY LOST ONE SON TO THIS BLOODY WAR. I DON'T WANT TO LOSE ANOTHER. PLEASE COME HOME FOR EVERYONE'S SAKE.

They got a short reply back.

I'LL LEAVE WHEN I CAN.

But after that, nothing. The days dragged on like water dripping slowly and irritatingly from a leaky faucet.

Rebecca was walking barefoot with Jonathan on the petanque green in the Daltons shaded front garden the day the postman delivered her mother's letter. She'd made a habit of going out on the lawn just before the postman came at three o'clock. She was always hopeful for news from Samuel, not that he knew to write to her there, for she had not found a way to write to him since her arrival, but any news from Samuel would be welcome. The Daltons sensed her hopeful longing and were content for her to collect their mail.

She recognised her mother's hand instantly. Her heart raced, her mouth went dry. She quickly folded the letter in half and shoved it down her front, relieved that there were other letters to pass on. That night in her room she read the letter and was awash with more waves of guilt and grief.

She had been doing her utmost to block out all thoughts of her family back in Newfoundland. And the details of her last night were sketchy at best. When she got to Deception in the pre-dawn, she hid onboard one of the boats loaded and bound for Carmanville. As she cooled down after her exertions she realised she had left her shawl behind in her haste. Obviously she had not bothered to secure the tender either. All she could recall was leaping onto the stage and racing up the stone path. Maybe subconsciously – perhaps consciously – she wanted them to think she had drowned, for in thinking that, they wouldn't pursue her by any method. And now she realised that was what had come to pass. That was how she bought her freedom. She had been telling a falsity – that they all were dead – and they were doing the same about her. But in their reality it was the truth.

That night she cried for her mother and her sister and the pain she no doubt had caused them. And she cried for herself, for the tangled mess she was mired in. She longed for Samuel to be with her so she could talk to him and work out a way to right her world again. For how does one undrown oneself? How does one unburn people? How does one make that right?

One month and one day after Matthew was killed, the Germans showed they felt no remorse in killing innocent doctors and injured, out-of-action soldiers. On the night of June 27, 1918, a German U-boat torpedoed the Canadian hospital ship Llandovery Castle anchored off the coast of Belgium killing all 234 people on board including 14 nursing sisters. 'When is this ever going to stop?' Lenore cried out in anguish upon hearing the news. The latest tragedy not only saddened her, it angered her and with the anger came the return of her fighting spirit. 'How dare they?' she said, marching across the second floor landing while she jostled Jonathan in front of her. 'How dare they!' It made her more determined than ever to support the war effort. That night at dinner she announced that she wanted to go back to nursing. She floored everyone.

'What about Jonathan?' asked Mrs Dalton.

'Well I'm hoping everyone can help with Jonathan. I only intend to work part-time, but if I can work part-time and another nurse can work part-time then that will free up one nurse to go to war. We are practically losing nurses faster than we can turn them out.' Lenore looked around the table at the silent faces. 'Can you please help me with this? I can't stay at home all day and think about what I've lost.'

'What about what you've gained? A son,' said Mr Dalton.

'I know I've gained a son, but spending day in and day out with him just reminds me all the time of what he and I don't have any more. Having other people's woes and misfortunes to fill my head will help me forget about my own, so that when I'm with Jonathan and my family I can be more grateful for my own good fortune,' she argued.

Lenore got her way and got out of the house. She also got Rebecca out of the house. After spending days sorting through her mother's effects and her father's effects that her mother had never dealt with, in what was now Alistair's home, Lenore decided Alistair wasn't the cleanest, tidiest man put on earth and he needed help. She asked Rebecca if she'd like the job. Two days a week she would do Alistair's laundry, clean the house, maintain his small garden and cook an evening meal. The arrangement suited everyone.

With the small wage she earned Rebecca tried to offer Mrs Dalton board.

'You're not paying me board,' she said flatly, 'don't be ridiculous. Did Samuel pay your parent's board all the time he stayed with them?'

'He tried to.'

'Fine. So did you. Now give it up.'

'It just doesn't seem right,' said Rebecca.

'I tell you what, Rebecca, you can pay me board if you like and then I can pay you for your household services. It will be roughly the same. Shall we just move the money around the table?' Rebecca could see the battle was lost. 'Save your money. You are in the city now, there are plenty of things you can spend it on and if nothing takes your fancy then save it for your future, save it for a holiday with Samuel somewhere, sometime.'

'If I could I would spend it right now on bringing him home.'

'Wouldn't we all?' said his mother.

'When do you think he might turn up?' asked Rebecca, restless and daunted.

Mrs Dalton, disheartened, merely shook her head.

Addie said, 'Now ain't that the million dollar question.'

57

Some men returned from war with untold emotional trauma, with niggling aches that would plague them for years, old war wounds that no operation would ever fix. Others struggled day in and day out to live a normal life with lungs scarred by horrendous mustard gas. Many, recovering from sheer exhaustion and exposure to the terrors of the trench, took months to surrender their war. Quite a few carried a shell with them till the day they died, others the desire never to leave home again, but not Samuel, no, not Samuel. He came home laden with guilt.

He never wanted to leave France. Even though he believed Matthew's soul had soared westward to Canada and the remnants of his human remains were all that were buried in French soil, Samuel still felt that by leaving he was abandoning his brother. Every cell in his body seemed to tether him to a small radius around Matthew's grave. He would walk on the soil, on the sand, in the sea, but he could not venture far. Such an unfinished feeling enveloped him.

In the end he left because he felt duty bound to Lenore that he couldn't afford to be another one of the fallen. He needed to go back to Toronto to do what he could for her and the baby as he promised Matthew. He also went because of his father's plea.

In paths untrodden Samuel made his way home. But he went dragging his heels. If he could he would have sailed to Toronto via Africa and the Cape of Good Hope across the bottom of the world, the Roaring Forties, around Cape Horn, Terra Del Fuego, the West Indies, the Bahamas, up the Eastern American seaboard, homeward bound, on the ocean, out of contact with everyone for months. In his mind's eye that is what he did because in those wretched days and weeks after Matthew's death, Samuel resigned himself that he could no longer think about Newfoundland, about Rebecca. He didn't want to be sailing past the island and thinking of her because, for the time being, she was lost to him. She had to be, at least for a while. Somewhere in those early weeks he resolved himself to his fate and his future: the future of being a father to Matthew's son, a partner, a husband perhaps to Lenore if she so desired. Desired? Perhaps decided, once all things were considered, for family, for the honour of his brother. It wasn't his heart's calling but in the repercussions of war, how many people got what they desired. He alone had survived and that privilege came at a price. He didn't negotiate the terms. They were presented to him as a fait accompli.

He did not telegraph that he was coming home. He just turned up. He didn't even knock. He walked around the back of the house and came through the rear entrance to the kitchen. The first person he saw was Addie.

'What are you doing here?' she asked in a voice that she would ply on a young Samuel whenever she found him in the kitchen prowling for food.

'I thought I'd save you a walk to the front door.'

She walked over to him, took both his hands in hers and said, 'Let me have a look at you.'

He looked down at her wearily, a faint smile on his lips. Her eyes were deep brown, with depths of knowing, clear and wise but that day they were smarting as she nodded faintly and said, 'It's good to have you home, my boy.' She wrapped her arms around him. They stood together rocking each other for a very long time. Addie hummed softly in her throat, a tune from his childhood as they stemmed their tears. Finally she rubbed his arm up and down. 'My word, it's good to have my hands on you again.' And then she pulled away. 'Are you hungry, you want some food? A drink?'

'Maybe later. Where's Mom?'

'Upstairs with Lenore, in Analeise's old room.'

The door was slightly ajar. Samuel knocked on it lightly. 'Come in,' he heard Lenore say.

His mother's back was to him and Lenore was sitting in a chair, burping the baby. She gasped then his mother turned round and he barely had time to say, 'Hello Lottie,' before she launched herself at him.

'Oh,' she cried, 'you're home. You're home at last. Oh thank God.' She hugged him, long and forcefully, and cried in his arms. And he, unable to help himself, shed tears as he embraced his mother with equal measure.

He looked at Lenore and saw she was crying too. 'I didn't mean to upset you all. You've probably been upset enough.'

'No,' said his mother, pulling away slightly from him, looking into his face. 'I am crying tears of joy that you have been returned to me.' She smiled through her tears. 'And look,' she said, touching his drawn face, 'you are still my beautiful boy even if you are a little battered around the edges.' She pressed her face into his neck and kissed him again.

'Here come and look at another beautiful boy.' She led him to Lenore and gently gathered Jonathan in her arms, 'Meet Jonathan. Jonathan, this is your Uncle Samuel. Isn't he something?'

Samuel could feel more tears trapped inside his heart. He sat down next to Lenore on the small sofa and lay Jonathan on his knees.

'Don't worry, little fellow,' he said, his voice constricted. 'I have had practice at this. There's two ahead of you.' He gently brushed his hand over Jonathan's head and then he said, 'Oh Christ, he is like Matthew.' His voice catching on Matthew and the tears trickled down his face. Lenore placed her arms around him and hugged him from behind, her cheek against his shoulder. Tears trickled down her face as well.

'I'm counting on you, Samuel, to teach him all the things his father would have taught him.'

Samuel nodded. When he could speak he said, 'All of the things?' giving way to a half-laugh.

'Well maybe not every little thing,' she said with a small laugh herself.

Samuel wiped his eyes and blew his nose then said, 'Mom, can you give me a few minutes with Lenore?'

She got up to leave. 'Does your father know you are home?'

'No,' said Samuel with a single shake of the head. 'You two are the first.'

'I'll ring him. He'll be home as soon as he hears. Here, let me take Jonathan.'

After she left, Samuel stayed still with his head resting on the back of the sofa, looking up at the light hanging from the ceiling, his eyes still watering. 'I'm so sorry, Lenore. I'm so sorry I couldn't save Matthew.'

'I know, Samuel.'

He turned to face her. 'Believe me, if I could have died in his place I would have. I spend most of my days wishing I had.'

'Come on, Samuel. He wouldn't want that.'

'I know. But he wouldn't want this either.'

There and then, sitting on the sofa, a sombre Samuel told Lenore all about the last night of Matthew's life. Reaching under his collar he pulled out a cord he had worn round his neck since the day Matthew died. It had Matthew's wedding ring knotted to it.

'Here, this is his. For you, for Jonathan.' He gave it to her and told her he buried Matthew with all her letters, with everyone's letters.

'Thank you,' she whispered almost inaudibly.

And then seeing that she was breaking in two Samuel took her in his arms and hugged her for quite a while. When they separated, he cleared his throat and ran his hand over his hair. 'I've been trying to work out when would be the right time to talk to you about this. And then I think, well maybe it might help with everything else that is going on in your head, give you some options to consider.'

'What are you talking about, Samuel?'

'Just before Matthew died, he asked me to look after Jonathan and you, and I gave him my word. I would do it anyway even if he hadn't asked me.' After a pause he continued, 'You know that my parents will support you and their grandchild for the rest of your lives. But that may not be what you want for yourself or for your son.

'This idea may not appeal to you in the slightest and that is fine by me, the whole decision is yours and yours alone. But Lenore, if you want to raise your son in a normal family environment, with a husband and with other children even, then I would be honoured to be that man for you and the terms of that relationship could be as you wish, for the love of my brother, and for Jonathan. I had the best brother in the whole world, and I would hate for Jonathan to be an only child and in the end I don't think it is something Matthew would want for him either. Whatever you decide I will be there for Jonathan and for you.'

Samuel paused then continued, 'In time you may decide you want to stay single or you may decide that you want to marry again for love. If so, I want to raise my hand as a suitor and ask that you give me, us, the opportunity of getting to know each other not so much in our connection to Matthew, but in what connection we could have with each other.' He stopped and shook his head lightly. 'That was a clumsy proposal, I know. Not romantic in the least. But I just want you to know, I offer you my hand in marriage.'

Lenore reached for his hand and held it in her own while she wiped her eyes and continued to struggle with her breathing. After some minutes, in a wobbly voice, she said, 'Samuel, you do me and my son an incredible honour. Matthew would be unbelievably proud. I cannot give you an answer, but I will promise to think about it.' She squeezed his hand. 'But please tell me, what about Rebecca, don't you love her, don't you want to marry her?'

Samuel looked at her and then down at their clutched hands. 'I don't think that is meant to be. Once upon a time things may have been different, but not now. The less said the better.' His serrated sigh cut through the air.

Mr Dalton's exalted cry broke the silence. From downstairs he yelled, 'Samuel, Samuel, where are you?'

'Here, Dad!' He released Lenore's hand and strode out to the landing and into his father who nearly knocked him off his feet in greeting and then he saw his eighty-year old grandfather hurriedly trying to climb the stairs, his eagerness and excitement apparent in every jerky movement.

'What took you so long? Did you swim home?' Grandpa croaked as three generations of Dalton men folded their hearts and their lives in each other's arms.

58

July in Toronto was hotter than Rebecca had ever experienced in her life. She was walking home from Alistair's wishing she could go swimming. She pictured jumping off the stage and immersing herself in the icy sea. She never thought she would miss her home but on a day like she was having she longed for cool, clean water, for the sighting of icebergs in the distance. Two days earlier they had quietly celebrated her nineteenth birthday. Rebecca had hoped Samuel would have been back but that was not to be. When she blew out her candles and cut the cake she wished for him.

She opened the front gate and walked up the path, up the stairs then left around to the long verandah shaded in the early evening. She was headed straight for the kitchen for a cool glass of Addie's lemonade. She was lost in thought and could vaguely hear Mr Dalton's voice. She looked at the group sitting in the wicker chairs ahead, casually taking them in and then she saw him. She stopped suddenly. Then she drew back as if she had walked into a glass door. His back was to her. His hair was incredibly short, but she would recognise his voice and his straight back and his neck anywhere. Everyone else was aware of her presence bar Samuel. One by one they let the conversation slacken and one by one they looked tentatively in her direction. Her heart was racing. Slowly in the silence Samuel sensed something behind him and turned his head to look over his shoulder.

She watched his face completely drain of colour. She felt the smile on her own face falter. She heard his voice say, 'Rebecca?' It sounded like he did not quite believe his eyes. He stood and turned around to look at her.

'Hello Samuel' she said. She squeezed her hands together. She wanted to jump into his arms but the presence of everyone and Samuel's aloofness stopped her. 'Welcome home,' she said with her best smile. He was not smiling. He was not Samuel. Taking a few steps towards him, she stretched out her arms in a beseeching gesture of welcome.

He took both her hands but rather than pull her into his embrace he held her at a distance. 'What are you doing here?' he said softly, almost in disbelief. She noted the emphasis was on the 'you' rather than the 'are', that was something. At least he didn't sound angry but he was far from elated. His citrine eyes looking into hers were so sad, almost incriminating as if he were saying to her, 'I wish you had not have come here.' She couldn't figure him out, he seemed far from the natural, easy-going Samuel she knew and loved. 'Look at you,' he said, still holding her at a distance and then she understood the thing that upset her most – aside from those first few seconds – he could barely look her in the eye. 'You look so different,' he said.

'I've had my hair cut. Do you like it?'

'Very chic,' he said, brushing it with his right hand and this time he did look at her completely and in his face she saw sorrow and untold regret and inexplicable anguish.

She heard Mrs Dalton say, 'Come and sit down, Rebecca. We are celebrating over here.'

'Can I have a quick shower first? I feel like a walking rag today.'

'Yes of course, dear.'

Rebecca walked away, hot tears searing her cheeks.

Samuel watched her departing back. His face flushed at his own callousness. His mother said, 'How about that for a homecoming surprise?'

'Big surprise.' Samuel turned to his mom and gave her his best attempt at a smile. Raising both his eyebrows he asked, 'When were you planning on telling me?'

'Why tell you and spoil the surprise?'

'What about you, Lenore, were you going to tell me?'

'I was planning on telling you, Samuel, but I didn't have a chance. Your dad arrived home and things moved along from there.' He gave her a disconcerting look.

'Aren't you happy she is here?' asked his father.

'Of course,' said Samuel, smiling for everyone's benefit,

'just unprepared, that's all. Still trying to get my head around it. Wondering how you managed to pull this off?' He smiled again as he looked around at their faces. 'Whose idea was it?'

Lottie cleared her throat. 'Rebecca came here under her own steam, a very brave move on her part. She arrived just after Jonathan was born, before Matthew...,' her voice trailed off. 'She was in a bad way when she got here. Running from the most dreadful disaster.' Lottie lowered her voice. 'All her family were killed in a house fire. Apparently she only managed to escape because she was staying with people in Deception that night. We don't know much beyond that. I suspect you will be the first person she will tell all to when she's ready.'

Samuel felt as if his heart were in a vice. Everyone's eyes were on him as the beasts of burden waged war within him. He had never felt so torn. Before standing he exchanged a troubled look with Lenore. 'I must go pay my respects.'

'She's in your room Samuel. If you want your room back, you'll have to move her into Matthew's or take what's on offer on the top floor,' his mother called after him, but he was already halfway up the stairs.

He could hear her in the shower. He walked into Matthew's room and walked over to the window. He looked out over the solid arms of the ancient oak. Soft voices wafted up from below. But they weren't the voices he wanted to hear. What he wanted to hear most was the voice of his brother Matthew, the voice of reason and understanding, the voice of calm who could help him navigate a path through this impenetrable minefield, whose very presence would invalidate this minefield. He noted with some irony that this time last year he had landed himself in an unpleasant predicament because he had kept his mouth closed too long, whereas this year it was by opening his mouth too soon that he found himself in the most unenviable of situations. What was he going to do now?

If Rebecca were not here could he marry Lenore after a suitable period of time, if she would have him? Possibly.

If Rebecca were here and her family at home all safe and well, could he still do it? Possibly, after he had helped build a new life for Rebecca in Toronto.

Could he still do it with Rebecca here and all her family gone? He sighed deeply. Could he force his heart? Somehow he did not think he could. What about hers? He knew how she felt about him. He had known since last summer, but more than just him, she had made that clear to everyone coming here as she had done.

He heard Rebecca come out of the bathroom and after a few minutes he knocked on her door.

'Come in,' she called.

She was wearing a pale blue skirt and a pretty floral top and had just finished combing out her hair. She looked fresh and alive and summery and the sight of her made his heart plunge. He went to her and took her hand. 'I'm sorry. I wish we could do this homecoming again. My head's all over the place.' He pulled her into his arms and gave her an all-embracing hug.

'It's alright, Samuel,' she said, hugging him back. He could tell she had been crying.

'Mom told me our loss pales in comparison to yours. I'm so sorry, Rebecca.'

'I'm sorry for you too.'

'Want to tell me?'

She shook her head.

He waited till he realised she was not going to be forthcoming. 'No?' he asked, a little surprised by her lack of response.

'No, Samuel.' She stepped away from him. 'After I told your mother she said I never had to speak of it again and I don't want to, Samuel. I can't.' Her voice was strained, her eyes were quivering.

'Okay, I don't want to pressure you.'

She lowered her eyes and nodded. Then she reached for his hand. 'Come here.' He resisted. 'Samuel! What's the matter? I just want to look at you.'

He let her lead him to the bed where he sat down on it facing the window and the late afternoon light, trying to calm his face as Rebecca stared at him and he stared back, all the while he barely breathed. She placed her hand against his cheek. 'So many things to read in your face, Samuel, so different to the first time I saw you.' She paused for many long moments and then she said, 'Do you want to tell me why you

351

were so cold and strange to me down there?'

He blinked at her and found himself foundering in her presence. Here was Rebecca, the woman he loved like no other, the one he had thought about every day for the past twelve months, if he were honest, the past four years, and the one he had tried to banish from his thoughts for the past two months. Her beauty was unbearable, her sadness chilling, the nadir of her whole life he held in his shaking palms, trying not to crush it. He wanted to take her in his arms and make her feel like she was home at last. He wanted to feel home at last. He wanted to rewrite the last three months of his life, of Matthew's life. But in setting the course he had, she had become untouchable to him. He needed to be resolute, for her sake as much as his. He could not encourage her, he could not succour her; he could not relieve her. All he could do was level with her and now was not the time.

Exhaling, he stood up and stepped away from her towards the window. 'My life has become unbelievably complicated these last few months.' Out of habit he ran his hand over his head.

'Tell me.'

He looked at her again, emotionally drained, speechless.

'Touché,' she said.

'Oh, so now you're teaching me French.' He pulled a face at her. Somehow that managed to ease the tension between them. 'Let's talk another day. I need a shower myself and then dinner.'

59

The next morning Samuel rose late. When he came into the kitchen Rebecca was kneading bread. 'I thought I'd find you in the garden, not in the kitchen,' he said by way of greeting. 'You were always the outside girl. Rachel was the inside one.'

'Well, sleepy head, if you were up two hours ago, you would have found me outside, when it was cooler.' She closed her eyes and pretended to collapse.

Smiling momentarily he said, 'Having a hard time getting used to our Toronto temperatures?'

'No, not so bad. I'd happily go swimming.'

'We'll have to take you to Sunnyside or some place. What have you been up to since you arrived?'

After she told him he said, 'You've nearly done it all.'

'I haven't been to Niagara yet.'

He met her eyes briefly then looked away. 'It's not going away anytime soon.'

Samuel busied himself getting breakfast while he tried to work out what he was going to say to Rebecca. And how? And where? He'd had a terrible night. He'd barely slept, but that was routine lately. 'Have you been to the Toronto Islands?'

'No, where are they?'

'An island girl like you hasn't been to the islands. Goodness me, what is the world coming to? We should go today.'

'Yes, let's!'

They made a picnic lunch and caught the electric trolley car then the ferry just a short way across Lake Ontario to Ward Island. They waded along the water's edge; she, carrying her shoes and a bag with towels and their swimmers, he the picnic hamper and his own shoes. After a few moments of silence, Samuel asked, 'How did you get here?'

'I suspect I came here by the same route you took to get

home last year,' she replied offhandedly. 'Thank you for making me take that one hundred dollars. I had need of it.'

He stopped walking and looked at her. She stopped and looked at him then beyond to a park bench. She motioned her head, 'Let's sit for a bit.' He took her hand. They wandered over and sat down. 'I love the trees in Toronto. They are so different to the trees we have in Newfoundland. I hope they never get cut down.'

'They won't get cut down unless they are dead or get struck by lighting or some other disaster.'

Without any preamble Rebecca said, 'It's been a hell of a year, Samuel, I don't know where to begin.' There she paused and looked into his eyes. He had to resist flinching from her gaze. What was that in her eyes? It was as if she was begging or searching for assurance, forgiveness maybe. And on one level he did want to assure her so she would continue with her story. But on another level he couldn't assure her. And forgiveness – who was he to be meting out forgiveness. He could not nod in encouragement. All he could do was force himself not to look away.

'Go on,' he managed at last.

'My father…what can I say…he went from being unreasonable to being irrational. And we all suffered for it. Our only reprieve were the months he spent working in the lumber camp.' She was looking out at the water as she spoke. 'There were things that happened Samuel…I didn't want to burden you with.'

'What sort of things?'

She looked at him, her eyes once more quivering, her lips trembling. With a frown creasing her brow, she shook her head. 'It's all history now. I don't want to speak ill of the dead.'

He squeezed her hand. 'I'm so sorry. I wish I could have been there for you, with you.'

'There were times when I wished that too,' she gave him a sad tinge of a smile as tears teetered on the brink of her eyelids then slowly coursed down her cheeks. 'They are no more, Samuel.' She squeezed his hand this time. 'It has taken some accepting, but that is how it is.' She continued to look straight ahead.

He sat looking at her profile, holding her hand firmly,

sensing for now that was what she needed from him and what he could give her. 'I'm so sorry. I can't begin to imagine what you've been through. Losing Matthew was bad enough. I can't imagine losing my whole family.'

Rebecca seemed to bite her lips as she tempted to calm herself.

'When was this?'

'Late April,' she said almost inaudibly.

They found the changing sheds and shortly after Rebecca appeared in a new clingy dark-green, one-piece swimming costume. It came well above her knees and exposed most of her arms and had a pretty floral cap to go with it.

'That's new,' Samuel said when she came up to him.

'Yes. My homemade costume was quite nineteenth century. Thanks for telling me.' She nudged him slightly.

'What was I going to say? Beside, I didn't care what clothes you wore.'

'That's right. If I recall, you cared more about me not wearing clothes.' She glanced up at him with parted lips and just a hint of a teasing smile. He looked away and stayed away. In the water that day there were no near-naked bodies, no clenching of hands nor arms around the neck, not even the smallest suggestion of a kiss.

After lunch they walked over to the far side of the island. 'Not as much seclusion here as at home,' she said after a while.

'You should see it on the weekends. This is private.' He glanced down at her. Then he reached for her hand. She turned to face him. He looked into her eyes with all the earnest he possessed. 'A lot has happened to me in the last year as well.' He glanced away then steeled his eyes back to hers. 'It has been the most eventful year of my life: moments of incredible beauty and happiness and moments of unspeakable sadness.'

'I know,' she said, squeezing his hand and looking at him with empathetic, adoring eyes, eyes he could barely manage to look at. It took at least one chamber of his heart just to maintain eye contact.

'It's been enormously challenging and made me question everything I believe in.'

She nodded in agreement and smiled encouragingly. But he could not smile back.

He reached for her other hand and held them both in his own. Taking an aching breath he said, 'Please forgive me, Rebecca, but I don't know what is to become of us.'

'What do you mean?'

'I know we made plans last year to be together, but Matthew's death has thrown everything up in the air.'

'What do you mean 'up in the air'?' She released his hands. 'Has Matthew's death made you wary of marriage? Nervous of marriage? I know you're not superstitious Samuel, so what is it?' She looked up at him, waiting for a reply. 'You're not planning to go back to the war are you, afraid something might happen to you and that I end up being a widow?'

'No, that is not in my thinking anymore.'

'What then?'

He looked at her, struggling with what was inside him that needed to be inside her.

'It's not Matthew's death per se, but the fact that Matthew died leaving a child who is now fatherless.'

'I know,' she said softly, reaching for his hand once more trying to comfort him. 'You will be the closest Jonathan has to a father and we will make sure of that. I know Lenore will be happy for us to take him from time to time and I would want to. I feel incredibly close to him and he's not even my own son.'

'Rebecca,' he said, 'remember the first time I visited you in Newfoundland, when I went on the boat for the week with your father?' She nodded. 'I was trying to convince him to let you and Rachel leave and go away to St John's or come here, under my father's auspices, to further your education. As you know he wouldn't hear of it. He kept on at me about duty, familial duty; that your position, your duty, was to your family at home there. I heard what he said, but I didn't agree with him. I didn't believe you needed to be present to be dutiful. I really had no comprehension of duty. But in the military you get a sense of duty. You certainly get a sense of following orders, and now, for the first time in my life, I understand familial duty and that is to my dead brother and his son and his wife.'

'Sorry, Samuel, this heat is obviously going to my head, I don't understand the implications of what you are saying.'

'I'm saying I need to put them first before all others, before myself, before you even. I need to consider their needs and their wants before my own. I need to provide for them.'

'So?' she said. 'You can still provide for them, we can provide for them when we are married.'

'I'm not sure that we can,' he said, looking aside. 'What happens if two or three years down the track Lenore decides the best thing for Jonathan would be for him to have siblings to play with, to be raised in a normal family?'

'She can marry, no one will stop her.'

'Wouldn't it be best that those siblings were as much as possible his own flesh and blood?'

'We could give him young cousins to play with, that would be the next best thing, don't you think?'

'No. My brother meant the world to me. I would have hated to be an only child and I would not wish that for Jonathan.' Samuel didn't like how Rebecca was staring at him, but even so he continued, 'If I were to father other children that Lenore might want then it would be the closest possible family they could have.'

'So what are you proposing? To offer your services?' snapped Rebecca unable to quell her distress. She pulled her hands away from Samuel and took two steps back.

'Please, don't be like that.'

'Well what?' she demanded.

'What I'm trying to say in a very inarticulate, ineloquent way, is that I can no longer fulfil my promise to you. I need for you to release me from my offer of marriage.'

'But you have affianced yourself to me!'

'I know I did, but I can't go through with it anymore. Not now. I need to be single and available in the event that Lenore decides she would like to remarry. I may not be the person she chooses but I don't think it is fair on her or Jonathan for me to preclude myself as an option.'

'What about fair on me?' demanded Rebecca unable to disguise her dismay. He noticed her hands by her sides, her fingers outstretched. She was doing her all to maintain her composure. This was killing him too.

'Samuel, you are going overboard. There is dutiful and dutiful, duty in this instance does not imply marriage.' She paused. 'At least not to Lenore,' she said dryly.

'Rebecca, I am sorry. I really am. If I could make things different I would.'

'I can't believe what you are saying. Just stop and listen to yourself and think for one minute. What happens if you go down this crazy path and you wait three, four, who knows how many years and then Lenore decides she does want to remarry but not you?'

'Then she marries someone else. I will respect that and I will be free to marry someone else.' He looked at her. 'I know this sounds insane to you, utterly absurd, I can appreciate how you may not understand it at all, because I never understood duty up till now.' Touching her shoulder, he said, 'I am truly sorry.'

Ignoring his apology, Rebecca said, 'What then for me in your grand scheme of things?'

'I don't know. It's like I said at the beginning I don't know what's to become of us.' Rebecca would not look at him. She just stared straight ahead, slowly shaking her head. 'What are you thinking?' he asked. 'Please, tell me.'

'I am recalling my father's voice. It is like he is haunting me, taunting me. "If it is good enough for Jacob to wait seven years," he is saying.'

'I don't expect you to wait seven years. I don't expect you to wait at all.'

'Well what am I meant to do with my love for you then?' she burst into tears. He hated himself for making her cry. 'Somewhere over the past twelve months you may have lost your love for me, but I haven't lost my love for you.' She turned and ran away.

'I never said that,' he said, running after her.

'Leave me alone, Samuel,' she yelled back, 'Just leave me alone.'

He let her be and waited for her to return, and waited and waited. Samuel felt he was drowning in the whirlpool of his own soul.

He climbed a tree. It was one of his favourite past times. He thought he might be able to see her from an elevated position, but no. After an hour he decided to head toward the jetty, wondering if she was waiting for him or if indeed she had left by herself. He came across her after about ten minutes, wandering along, slowly making her way back to him.

'Can we go home?' she said, her eyes swollen, her voice rough.

'Yes, of course.' He reached for her hand but she wouldn't give it to him. 'I'm sorry for upsetting you, Rebecca. I don't want to upset you or hurt you.' He went to touch her face but she pulled away.

'Well you have and unless you drop this whole crazy idea then you will continue to upset me and hurt me and what good is sorry if it makes no difference.'

60

She didn't speak to him all the way home. She could barely hold herself together, particularly in light of his perfidy. The last twenty-four hours were close to the worst twenty-four hours she had ever experienced and this year she'd had quite a few.

She had expected Samuel to come home sad, with a need to put his family first, but she thought that her presence would be a comfort to him. While their reunion may not have been passionate, given the circumstances, she thought it would have at least been warm and affectionate. But perhaps what had passed between them last summer was all a dream, like childbirth was a dream, like what followed was a dream. If only.

Yesterday when she sat him down on the bed in her room, his strong oval face catching the late afternoon light, she nearly swooned as his refined form. His hair was about a quarter of an inch long all over his head, revealing a perfect shaped head, a hard head. He had bristles clustering along his angular jaw and his round chin. The absence of hair on his head, the lack of its bright, light straw colouring only seemed to accentuate his features. His cheekbones were pronounced, his beautiful pink lips ringed with stubble. She longed to trail her fingers over them. But his lips were clamped firmly together. There was no smiling. His eyes were glassed over. The dark circles under them had made his tawny eyes look darker, more forest-like, but sad as if he had seen too many tree burnings in one lifetime. It was as if layers had been peeled away and that was what remained. She ached to forgive him for his casual offhand treatment of her. She wanted to instantly take away his pain, kiss his lips, claim them for herself. But the moment was evanescent. Her want was not reciprocated.

At the Daltons she went straight upstairs to have a shower. She wanted the water falling on her head to somehow ease the torturous notions racing through her troubled mind. She thought Samuel had more rectitude than that! Was this God punishing her? Making Samuel come out with all that because she had lied about her family?

Today she had been so close, so close to telling him the truth. But he was so distant! Like yesterday! His eyes guarded, almost defensive and she thought with a sinking feeling, no, this is not going to be all right. If I tell him, it will be irrevocable, and what is the truth going to do now? Will it change anything? Will I feel vindicated? No. What will happen if I say I am the daughter of a madman, a man riddled with malice? Samuel's already acting strange, maybe that will scare him away from me. For weeks she had been doing her best to recover and to think of her family recovering. Sad and negative thoughts only seemed to weigh her down, and that morning when she looked at Samuel he had enough weighing him down. He had just lost a brother. It was not the time to find out he had lost a son as well. Wouldn't it be better for him to think her family had passed on, for him to think of them in the best possible light, than to tell him the unspeakable truth? And so that is what she did. On one hand an uncalled for act of kindness…she had looked long into his eyes and hoped he would understand and absolve her…on the other hand an unpardonable breach, like the original sin that had started it all.

Things were no clearer after her shower. She went in search of Jonathan. He was in his bassinet fast asleep. She did not want to disturb him so she just stood watching his little stomach rise and fall. Watching him, serene and at peace, Rebecca doubted that even if Samuel were serene and at peace could she have brought herself to speak of her son, their son. It was all still too raw. She stayed for many minutes trying to salve her wounds. She was still looking over him when Lenore came in.

Rebecca glanced at her. 'I hope you don't mind me being in your room. I thought if Jonathan were awake I'd take him for a walk in the garden, but he's napping away.'

'No,' said Lenore, 'I don't mind. He likes you Rebecca. I can tell. You have a knack when it comes to settling him.'

'Well at least I'm good at something,' she said with a half-smile.

'Rebecca,' said Lenore taking a step towards her, touching her forearm, 'has Samuel said something to you?'

'Yes,' her voice strained.

'Oh Rebecca, please don't hate me.'

'Why would I hate you? I don't have enough friends as it is, and you've done nothing wrong, have you?'

'No, I don't think I have.'

'So has Samuel talked to you about his plans to be an available husband for you should you so desire?'

'Uh-huh,' said Lenore unable to hide her discomfort.

'What did you say?'

'Well it was quite unexpected as you can imagine. I said I would think about it. But Rebecca, believe me when I tell you, I am not about to marry Samuel. I'm still in love with Matthew! I'm still trying to find a way to come to terms with him not ever coming home. Part of me wishes he was listed as missing, 'presumed dead' even, at least then I could hold out some hope of him coming home when this wretched war is over. I can't fully believe it in my heart yet. My head tells me it is the case but my heart doesn't want to.'

'Was Matthew like Samuel?'

'Yes and no. I don't know Samuel as well as I know Matthew, but I think I could say that Samuel has all the best parts of Matthew, but I would say Samuel has a more serious and more sensitive side. Matthew was rarely serious. He was playful and adventurous.'

'Samuel can be playful and he is adventurous.'

Swallowing, Lenore said, 'I'm sure you know him better than I do.'

'I thought I knew him very well, but I'm not so sure any more. I can't believe he proposed to you. Not that you're not a lovely lady, Lenore, but I thought a person could only be betrothed to one person at a time.'

In dawning realisation, Lenore said, 'Samuel proposed to you?'

'Yes!'

'Of course he did,' she shook her head, as if she were seeing things with instinctive clarity.

'And when were you planning to get married?'

'When he finished his medical studies.'

'And what has he told you today?'

'That he wants to break off our engagement, for me to release him from his promise so he can be free in the event that you decide at some point in the future you might want to remarry and want him to be your husband.' Rebecca steeled her eyes to look at Lenore. 'Do you think that might be a possibility?'

'Oh Rebecca, I would never take Samuel away from you if he was yours.'

'Well Lenore, it's obvious he is not mine. He is his own being to do what he wants with. Are you going to give him an answer, tell him yes, no, maybe?'

'Honestly, I haven't given it a thought since he mentioned it. But now that you have enlightened me I will speak to him, but honestly I don't know if saying 'No' to him right now will make much difference. He believes what he is doing is the right thing.'

'How can it be right to hurt the people who love you?'

'People do that all the time.'

'You're right,' said Rebecca recalling things she had no desire to recall.

'Rebecca, you'll have to give him some time. He's hurting and grieving and trying to right the world at the moment. With what happened to Matthew, the world's all wrong to him now. He means well, but he's lost his bearings.'

'I thought I was his bearing.'

'You probably are, he just can't see clearly at the moment.'

61

Days went by and they barely spoke to each other. Samuel avoided her or avoided the house, choosing to spend time at home when she was at Alistair's. He'd visit Analeise, play with Benjamin and Catherine, take his grandfather to visit old friends, spend time with his father in his practice, spend time chatting with Lenore in her room, holding Jonathan, but after a while it seemed he was not just avoiding Rebecca, he was avoiding them all. He'd go off by himself and take long walks and return around dinnertime, sometimes not even then. He'd come in, say hi to everyone then go up to his room.

A place deep inside of Samuel was broken and everyone's heart was breaking watching him. They would look at him as he walked into a room and walk out again. He would barely speak to anyone; barely make eye contact. Everyone felt his unravelling yet felt powerless to do anything about it.

Rebecca was falling apart watching him become more miserable day by day, feeling that her own destiny was becoming just as hopeless. His sadness touched a raw nerve inside her. She longed to just cradle his beautiful broken self in her arms. One morning, she went out on limb and said, 'Samuel, can I hold you?'

He looked at her and she saw something come down over his eyes. 'I don't need holding. Thanks all the same.' And then he was gone.

The back of his neck was the one part of his body that she saw the most of, usually as he walked away from her. She had fallen in love with his nape all over again. He had taken to wearing collarless shirts since his return. They had the smallest edge exposing his long strong neck, his now glowing suntanned neck. His heart may not have been perfect but his neck was and she wanted nothing more to reach out and caress it, kiss it, smell the scent of him at the base of his scalp, like she used to do when they rode together back in Newfoundland.

August came and went. For Rebecca it was possibly the most painfully awkward month of her entire life. Days of long reverberating silence between her and Samuel. They had barely spoken in three weeks and she was becoming increasingly alarmed and upset. She'd been told once that if you did something for three weeks it would become habit forming for life. Was this how her wonderful planned life with Samuel was to end?

Could she even be with him in comfortable silence any more? She longed for him to just be at ease with her again, like he had always been. She oscillated between wanting to say something and wanting to say nothing at all, wanting to give him the slightest touch, a semblance of a smile, brush past him as she walked out of the room or stroke his hand whenever she handed him Jonathan. Thinking of anything so that her fingers might speak a language of love to him that her heart and her mouth just couldn't seem to manage. But Samuel seemed to be a master at keeping his distance. Always civil, rarely, if ever, encouraging her in the slightest, safest conversation.

Most nights she'd go to bed and lie awake and toss and turn with restlessness and anxiety, and then in the end she'd get up and go downstairs and make herself a hot drink to try and help her sleep. Tonight was another one of those nights. She crept downstairs and made her way to the kitchen. There was a light on, though she couldn't hear anyone, but when she walked towards the door she saw Samuel sitting at the table. He looked up at her.

'Sorry,' she said, 'I didn't mean to disturb you. I couldn't sleep. I thought I would make myself a hot chocolate. Do you want one?'

'No, thanks. I've just had one. There should be coals in there still.' He barely looked at her.

She busied herself stoking the wood oven, pouring milk in a pot, placing it on the hot plate, putting cocoa and a teaspoon of sugar in a cup.

'Couldn't you sleep either?' she asked.

'I don't sleep much these days.' His eyes were downcast. 'Haven't slept much for months. I think I've got used to living on hardly any sleep.'

'That's no good. You need to find something to help you sleep.' She turned away from him and made her hot chocolate, then she rinsed the pot under the tap, scrubbed it out with a brush, rinsed it again and dried it, all the while she felt her heart being squeezed as she was thinking, please say something to me Samuel, please talk to me.

Picking up her hot chocolate, she looked at him and said, 'I'm sorry you can't sleep, Samuel. I hope you get some sleep soon.'

'Yes. Thanks.' The briefest glance of acknowledgement.

She walked out of the kitchen and down the hallway, telling herself to keep it together, but after a few steps she stopped and turned around to look at him. He had a book in front of him that he was looking at, but she didn't think he was reading it. He was just staring at the empty words on the page.

She held her breath and kept looking at him, her heart beating out a sorrowful lament, Oh Samuel, Samuel, you were once my light and you dispelled my darkness. How I wish I could do the same for you. I feel the waves of death are all around you but look here, here is your Evening Star, your Morning Star, trying to show you the way, trying to shine my light in front of you. But you are ensnared in thick fog like we have back in Newfoundland, fog that no sunshine can penetrate. It depresses you, it's like a deathly vapour that has invaded your lungs, your soul, your very being and eventually its dampness will fill your lungs and you won't be able to breathe anymore.

'Rebecca?' she heard him call out to her though he didn't turn his head.

'Yes,' she called back softly, lest she wake anyone up.

'Why do you linger?'

Why do I linger! She walked back into the kitchen and sat down in the chair opposite him. In her softest voice she said, 'You know in your heart Samuel why I linger.' She waited. Deep, dark, oppressive moments. He wasn't looking at her, just at the table in front of her. 'Once you placed your hand across my heart and wondered how I couldn't know the truth inside.'

Samuel glanced up. Unable to deny her, he said, 'That is what I'm trying to do, to listen to my heart.'

Rebecca suppressed her exasperation and tried a different tack. 'Samuel, I can hardly bear what you are going through. It grieves me the way you keep punishing yourself, putting yourself through hell each day and I can't work out what for. You didn't kill your brother. You are in no way responsible for his death. Stop blaming yourself. And now to add to your worries and your misery you have constructed this untenable solution in your mind as to how you can spend the rest of your life making amends for your brother's death, which is just ludicrous. Can't you see that? You are punishing yourself over Matthew's death and persecuting yourself over your plans to marry Lenore, turning yourself away from the one person whom I thought made you immensely happy.'

He raised his eyes to her, 'People who go to war don't come back happy, Rebecca. It is something you need to resign yourself to.'

'I'm not convinced that is the essence of the issue,' she continued. 'Do you remember there was once a time when you said what was most important for you was to love the woman you married? Hmm, remember that?'

'If I recall correctly, during the same conversation I said I could marry a widow.'

'Samuel! Please don't be flippant. We had a commitment. I thought you made me a promise? But more importantly I thought we made each other happy – deliriously happy once upon a time – and that we loved each other.'

'I did, we did. But too many things have changed.' He paused. 'I also made my brother a promise.'

'Yes, but he didn't expect you to marry his wife. Raise his son, look after his wife by all means, but not marry her.'

'Why not? She is a good woman. She will make a fine wife.'

'I know she is a good woman. I thought I was a good woman too. But perhaps I was a naïve woman, an easy woman, a foolish woman.' Rebecca lowered her head. She had said it at last, named her sin; what some days she feared was the reason she was being punished over and over: first

367

Samson, now Samuel. In her purgatory Samuel's bold voice reached her.

'You are a good woman, Rebecca Crowe.' She looked up and this time he did look at her, directly, earnestly. 'You have never been nor will you ever be any of those things.'

'Well then what difference does it make if you won't change your mind? For me? For the person who saved you all those years ago. For the person who has loved you all this time.'

'He saved me too. Not once but twice, the last time it cost him his life.'

'But…' said Rebecca. But what? She didn't know what else she could say to convince him otherwise. She was stumped.

'Welcome to my moral dilemma,' he said, his eyes boring into hers. 'Do you want it?'

Two nights later they came across each other upstairs outside the bathroom.

'After you,' he said.

'No, it's all yours.' She walked away. Then she stopped. 'Samuel,' her voice inflecting slightly.

He stopped. She turned and waited till he turned to her. 'Can you tell me one thing please, because I have been thinking long and hard about what you said the other night, and there's just one thing I don't understand.'

She tried to keep herself composed but she could hear her own voice stretched tight across the nervous lump in her throat, 'As you know I never knew Matthew, I wish I had. But if Matthew is the wonderful person everyone claims him to be then something tells me that he would rather you marry the woman you love than a woman, his widow no less, out of obligation or duty, even if that duty was to him. Tell me that's not the sort of person Matthew was.'

'Matthew was the most fiercely loyal person I ever knew, an example to us all. You have no idea. This conversation is over.'

'This conversation is too close to the bone, is what it is.' She stared at him so pointedly, wanting the force of her stare to pierce some part of his soul.

But what he said when he replied was: 'You have been

raised in the church and I imagine you know your Bible inside out. Isn't there a scripture that says something like, "What God the Father considers to be pure and genuine religion is this: to take care of orphans and widows in their suffering and to keep oneself from being corrupted by the world".'

This time she was the one to walk away.

Samuel may have been doing little to make Rebecca feel at ease but everyone else was. Grandpa, Addie, Mr Dalton, Samuel's mother were all doing their best to boost her spirits.

One day his mother said to her, 'Samuel has always been a person of emotional extremes, Rebecca. From the time he was born. Everything about his emotional temperament has always been larger than life, except for anger. We have never seen him really angry; he just channels that inside himself. I don't even know where that comes out; I think he just gets quieter with it. But joy and happiness have been his hallmarks; we have always loved him for his ability to take great pleasure in the moment. If he was confused and unsure of himself, he would worry for weeks and nothing anyone could say would make any difference. Matthew was the opposite. He never seemed to worry about a thing. He lived his life fearlessly and got on with it. But Samuel was different. When he was remorseful, it was noticeable. When he was a little boy, if Matthew ever went somewhere without him, he'd mope till he came home. And this time, he's not coming home. Samuel's life is spinning out of control, while we just wait and hope and pray that when it stops, it stops once more at happy and joyful.'

'He's mired in guilt over his brother's death' said Grandpa. Just that, thought Rebecca? 'And mark my words this guilt will take longer to pass than the healing of any physical ailment.'

'Can't you talk to him about it?' said Rebecca, 'Tell him how silly it is, how it was an accident, how you don't hold him responsible.'

'You don't think we haven't tried?'

'Yes, of course. Sorry.'

One night in late August Lenore finally levelled with Mrs Dalton about Samuel's double proposal.

Rebecca felt she could never bring it up. Clearly Samuel

had kept their engagement a secret and she, having never spoken a word about it when she arrived, felt like a complete fraud at the mere thought of bringing it up, let alone talking about the latest instalment in the saga that was fast becoming her life.

But as their days seemed to become more and more oppressed, and everyone continued to suffer and wonder at Samuel's mournful behaviour over Matthew's loss and his distant treatment of Rebecca, Lenore had stepped forward and explained what Samuel was unable to explain. Rebecca was on her way back from Alistair's at the time but she came into the kitchen at the very end of it to hear Addie say: 'That boy's got rocks in his head.'

'Are you talking about Samuel?' she asked.

Mrs Dalton just looked at her and said, 'I apologise, Rebecca on behalf of my son and all he has put you through. If it were not for the death of his brother his behaviour would be totally inexcusable.' Putting her hands on Rebecca's shoulders, she said, 'If you still love him then all I can say is, please be patient with him, please forgive him. I have faith he will sort himself.'

'That's all that I'm holding onto,' she said quietly, 'holding firmly onto what I once had.' She excused herself and went upstairs.

That night Mr Dalton tried to talk to Samuel about his quixotic course of action. And although Samuel listened to his father, and nodded to his father, and talked to his father, in the end nothing changed. He still remained undeterred.

Somehow, someway Samuel had managed to come crawling home, his body encased in chitin, so impenetrable was he, so seemingly lacking in compunction.

Rebecca could not help but wonder, is this my Calvary? Once upon a time she thought the tragedy of her horse Slate was her Calvary, but then that had been surpassed by what had happened to Samson. But what about this?

Rebecca sought refuge in the only one whose connection to her was purely innocent, who nurtured her soul, whom she believed truly loved her out of some inexplicable instinct. Rebecca was the first person Jonathan ever smiled for. One day while she was changing his nappy and singing a gentle dreamy lullaby she looked down at his face and his shining happy face was just looking wondrously up at hers. It melted her heart. She bent down and kissed him on the nose and he smiled, he laughed, he giggled even and so she continued to hug him to her chest, carry him around bound to her, trying to think light loving thoughts when she was with him, not the deep dark thoughts that consumed her as she walked from Beaconsfield to South Hill twice a week. Now she knew how the people of Israel felt. She too had not found what she was looking for by going into the Promised Land. Here in exile her heart was breaking. She thought of God and her father, she thought of Samuel and herself as she tried to understand who was responsible for sending such waves of misery and sorrow crashing over her soul.

At the end of August, Rebecca decided she could no longer handle the situation. What she couldn't handle the most was the person she was turning into, a person who seemed to be just holding herself together every day, constantly setting herself up for disappointment and heartbreak by being on the periphery of Samuel's presence. What ate away at Rebecca was the fact that she couldn't understand how a person could just box up such intense feelings, such blinding love for someone and then put it away, out of reach, like in an attic where it would collect dust and spider webs and become forgotten. She knew she had boxed up feelings for her family but she believed she had just cause for that; she had been provoked beyond all measure. But Rebecca just couldn't get her head around how Samuel could deny his feelings for her, how he could get over loving her. He had never said so in actual words but his actions spoke a clear cold message: it is over. Despite her best, well-intentioned efforts, he refused to be dissuaded. The trenches around his love for her were so well barricaded, she was the one injuring herself time and again trying to go over the top, trying to penetrate them from any direction.

Rebecca eventually got to the point where she felt her very presence around Samuel was doing more harm than good. Coming up to him one morning, she said, 'Samuel it is clear to me that you are very uncomfortable around me lately and I'm very sorry for making your life so unpleasant.'

'I'm uncomfortable with a lot of things lately.' His eyes flickered in her general direction.

'Well I don't want you to be uncomfortable in your own home. You should feel at peace here. I've spoken to Alistair and I'm going to board with him. That way if you want to see me you know where to come looking.'

'You don't need to do that. And that's not the best move in your situation, for a single woman to be sharing a house with a single man.'

'There is nothing going on between Alistair and I and besides he is hardly ever home. What else am I to do? I can't go on living here.'

'Listen, you don't need to do anything,' he paused, 'because I am leaving.'

'You are?'

'Yes. Fifth year at McGill starts in a few weeks. I'm moving back to Montreal. I need to finish my medical studies.'

'Oh,' said Rebecca, 'of course.' She tried to hide her disappointment.

But Samuel only told Rebecca a half-truth. He was going to McGill, but only going so he could arrange his deferment. Then he was going to head north, north to nowhere.

'I'm lost here, Dad,' he said one evening to his father. 'And I'm no help to Lenore and Jonathan. If anything I'm dragging you all into my own morass. I should never have come back. It was a mistake.'

'You didn't want to stay on over there,' said his dad. 'You just didn't want to come home and face us. But we don't hold you responsible or blame you for Matthew's death. He could have just as easily been killed whether you were there or not. The fact that you were with him when he died has been of immense comfort to us. That he didn't die alone, that he died in the arms of a person who loved him dearly. There is no better way to die, Samuel.'

His mother came across him a few days later as he was packing. 'You're going away, aren't you? For how long?'

'For a while.'

'You will come back in one piece?'

'Mom,' he said, shaking his head and looking at his feet.

'Samuel, I want you back. I've already lost one son. I don't want to lose another.'

All Samuel could do was stare at her.

'Go,' she said, 'but come back, whole if you can manage it, jubilant even.' She pulled him into her arms and said, 'But I'll take you whatever way you come. You won't always be broken.'

On the day he left, Samuel got up early, around half-past four, had a quick bite to eat and walked out the back door, around the side of the house, through the garden towards the front gate. As he was walking away, he heard Addie call out after him. He stopped and turned around and looked at her as she walked up to him.

'The Samuel Dalton I know and love would always say goodbye before he left to go away for a while. I'm going to forgive you just this once and send you off with my blessing even so. You are living in the shadow of death, Samuel. You need to step out into the light and live your life. I hope you come back to us blazing in glorious sunshine, my boy.' She reached up and kissed him on the cheek. And then he was gone.

62

As devastating at it was, Rachel accepted the news of Samuel's death with fatalism. It was how her mother had written in her letter to the Daltons. Rebecca and Samuel were meant to be together and in death they were. She also saw it as a sign – three strikes and she was out. There was no point her ever holding out for a suitor. That was futile.

She recalled clearly the conversation she had with Samuel on the very last day she ever saw him. Well, where was she going to start? She knew that if he were alive that's what he would be encouraging her to do.

Her mother and father were two people who were now married on paper only. The conversation around their dinner table was sparse at best. Her mother's appetite was sparse at best. She had lost weight. Her clothes hung on her. In a matter of months her hair had turned white. She was no longer middle-aged. What was to become of her mother? And if something happened to her mother, what of her? Could she stay looking after her father?

One morning she woke up with resolve and went to her mother as she was stirring in Rebecca's bed, now her's.

'Mother,' she said, 'what's the state with our accounts at the Merchant? Are we in credit?' In all her life she had never asked such a question.

'I don't know. Normally we are by the end of the season.'

'Well, I'd like to borrow some money, so I can go to St John's and get myself a job. I will pay you both back. One day maybe I can train to be a teacher, but I can't leave you here with Father. You need to come with me, or you need to go to Esther's. We'll both go to Esther's for starters.'

A few days later Rachel told her father of their intentions. She told him in a way that did not seek his permission. Just simply that come September, she and her mother were going to visit Esther and most likely would stay on for a while.

Silas didn't object. He merely said, 'I see.'

And then a week before their planned departure he said, 'Perhaps I'll join you at some point.'

Both women looked at him but made no comment.

The next day Morna said to Rachel, 'I'm still coming with you but I won't stay.'

'Why not? What is there here for you, Mother? At Salvage you have a daughter, a son-in-law and four grandchildren to keep you occupied.'

'I know. That's six other people's lives at risk if your father were ever to come make a home there and snap like he did this year. I'm not ever going to be party to that again.'

'But you'll die here. There's no life. There's no love. There's no joy in this home.'

'I'll die knowing I did what I could for my surviving children.'

'I can't let you do that. Mother, don't you see, you're not well.'

'I know I am not who I once was. I never will be. But one day I will recover enough to go on living. I have done it before. I can do it again.' A speckle of flint in her raspy voice.

63

The fall of 1918 on the battlefields of Europe was known as Canada's 100 days. The Allied troops, spearheaded by the Canadians, succeeded in breaking through German line after German line, forcing the retreat that eventually would end in the Armistice. They marched to glory, Samuel to gloom.

He went to Montreal, spent as little time there as possible, called in to see his Uncle Michel who was away at his office in Québec, which suited Samuel just fine. Onto Québec he travelled, spent two days with his grandparents and after talking to Michel arranged to catch a ride on one of his boats headed to Chicoutimi. Down the St Lawrence Waterway up the Saguenay River into the only navigable fjord in North America he sailed, into the liquid domain of the beluga whale, the minke whale and the notorious Greenland shark.

He passed Tadoussac, the juncture of the two mighty boiling rivers, once the traditional bartering point for Iroquois and Algonquin peoples. Bypassing the Laurentian Mountains, past untamed cliffs and imposing headlands fading in diminishing layers of indigo blue, deep into the Canadian Shield he travelled, trailing up the Rivière Péribonka, into secluded areas that were once the sole hunting and fishing domains of proud native tribes like the Huron. Away from civilisation, away from his life.

With a pack on his back filled with supplies, blankets and warm clothes, knives, a fishing rod, a small wood axe and rifle strapped to his body, he hiked for days, gorging on blueberries and freshwater fish that he caught in streams and lakes at dawn and dusk. He lost count of the lake trout, walleye, smallmouth bass, northern pike and whitefish that he ate. He lost count of the days too. Deliberately. He lived by the signs of the light overhead and the shortening, darkening days. He saw white tailed deer and moose and beaver but he shot none, biding his time for when he would settle down. Ducks fell victim to his fire occasionally, but not the herons or the majestic peregrine falcons that soared overhead.

He went up the Savanne, a tributary that flowed into Lac Onistagane. Occasionally he'd find a birch bark canoe stashed under trees beside a lake and he'd help himself to it, paddling for a few hours before returning and storing it exactly how he'd found it. He was never far from cold clean flowing water, never far from forests that went on and on as far as the eye could see, never far from the landscape that he and Matthew yearned for during those long unbroken days on the Western front.

After days of feeling the chill wind of the arctic announcing the onset of winter he came to rest at an abandoned trapper's hut on a lake on the 52nd parallel. With him he still had over half of his supplies of oats, flour, tea, dried milk and lard. He brought no books to read, no paper to write on, no letters from home, sacrificing all for other items more necessary for his survival. As it was, he had enough weighing him down.

Back in Toronto Rebecca had plenty weighing her down as well. One evening she said to Mrs Dalton, 'Do you ever feel as if you have lost two sons, not one?'

'Sometimes,' she sighed. After some moments she added, 'Then I think of you, Rebecca and all that you've lost. I try and be thankful for what is my lot, thankful for my grandchildren, thankful that you were spared and are with us to gladden our days, thankful that at least Samuel's away from the war and I'm hoping he'll come home healed one day.'

And then Rebecca felt like a complete phoney, realising that Mrs Dalton had lost a son she had loved for twenty-eight years, where as Rebecca had lost one she'd loved for only three days, and not a father, mother, two sisters and nieces and nephews as they were led to believe. She was deeply ashamed.

She wished there was a way she could tell the Daltons that her family was alive – to clear her conscience and to ease their minds. But what could she say?…'I'm sorry I misled you. They are alive, but I couldn't live with them any longer. I had to get away.'

She couldn't offer up that explanation without offering up what came before. She definitely didn't have it in her yet to bring that up. Mostly she wanted to forget it all, though understandably, mostly she wanted to remember her little boy. She had thought she would find a way clear to the truth once Samuel had come home and she had told him. But not only was the truth dashed, so were her dreams.

Right now she didn't know what was to become of her nor what to do. She had days full of guilt and worry. Worried that Samuel might return whole but just as determined to forge a life without her. Worried for her mother and Rachel and what was happening in their lives. Worried that some day, some how, her fabricated falsehoods would be revealed for what they really were – bald faced lies – and she would be forced to leave in utter humiliation.

Inert and contrite she was completely taken by surprise when over dinner one night Mr Dalton suggested she resume her school studies. Telling him she would think about it she went to talk to Addie, concerned that it was an expensive undertaking that she could neither afford nor did she expect the Daltons to pay. Addie said to her, 'Mr Dalton thought that all through before he even suggested it to you, honey. He don't expect you to pay for a cent. He just wants to help you along in your life a bit. You've been given a golden opportunity coming here, Rebecca. Most folk would never offer such a thing to a girl your age. It wouldn't even enter their mind. They'd expect you to be out working for the remains of your days.'

In the end she accepted on the condition that she pay for her own uniforms and textbooks. Grandpa said she couldn't pay for her textbooks because he wanted to buy her the textbooks and so it was settled. In September, Rebecca went back to school. She had to sit an entrance exam before she was accepted, but then she was in, attending classes where she was four years older than every single student around her.

Rebecca felt more intimidated going to her new all girls' school than she had coming to Toronto. With no friends she felt like a complete outsider. Only her strong interest in learning and her ability to concentrate in class got her through the day. That and the fact she knew she would be returning to friendly faces at the end of it. On her second morning she sat at the Dalton's breakfast table struggling with her nerves and swallowing her food, trying not to give vent to the squeamishness in her stomach. She was conscious of Grandpa eyeing her closely. After he salted his omelette he said to her, 'Rebecca, an observation if I may?'

'Yes, Grandpa.' She stopped what she was doing and looked at him.

'You remind me of Samuel when he was about to set off to McGill for his first year after he had been out of the school system for a while.'

'That's probably right.'

'Well in the end he managed and I'm confident you can too.' He paused shaking his napkin. 'Have you ever heard of Ralph Waldo Emerson?'

'No.'

'He was an American. Died about sixty years ago. Came from Boston, entered Harvard College when he was fourteen no less and paid his own way working as a tutor, a messenger, and a waiter at the college. He ended up becoming one of America's best-known essayists and poets. I have a book of his you are welcome to borrow. He once said: *What lies behind you and what lies ahead of you are but small matters compared to what lies within you.'* Grandpa paused while Rebecca considered what he had just said. 'You have everything inside you to get you through today and tomorrow and the one after that, to get you through the year, your whole schooling. I know it and you know it, so don't worry about everyone else, just worry about yourself and know that inside, here,' he said tapping his own chest, 'you have what it takes.'

Before she knew it, her days were as full as they had been back in Newfoundland. Eight subjects kept her occupied during the day. Then there was cleaning and laundering at Alistairs. Every day she would spend two hours at least poring over Jonathan, talking to him, bathing him, taking him for walks, feeding him. Every morning she would rise early and do two hours of homework before joining the Daltons for breakfast and heading off to school. And every day as she came home she would hold her breath, like all of the Daltons held their breath, waiting for news from Samuel. Every day she was disappointed and then in the end she gradually came to expect no news. She no longer asked, 'Any news from Samuel?'

Then one day she arrived home and lying on the kitchen table was a letter. Not from Samuel but for Samuel. From her sister, Rachel. It had been redirected three times. Her trembling fingers lifted it up as she tried to read the postmark. Fortunately it was illegible. Even so she felt the blood drain from her face. Lottie came upon her in her whitened state.

'Rebecca,' she said. 'I'm sorry, I didn't know what to do with it.' She looked at Rebecca, her eyes full of apology. 'Obviously Rachel posted it just before the fire. I didn't know whether to hide it away for Samuel. I didn't want to upset you but this no doubt will mean more to you than it will ever mean to him, being you sister's last words and all.'

Rebecca nodded. She struggled for her voice. 'May I keep it,' she managed to croak.

'Yes of course dear.'

Upstairs Rebecca sat with the unopened letter weighing heavily in her lap. After what seemed like an eternity she stood up, walked into the bathroom, tore the letter into tiny pieces and flushed it down the lavatory along with all the troubled emotions it stirred.

64

On the 11th hour, of the 11th day, of the 11th month, in 1918, World War I came to an end. Germany surrendered. The Treaty of Versailles was signed. They called it the war to end all wars. Peace. At last. But there was no peace for Rebecca. No peace for the Daltons. No news from Samuel, no watershed. And worse, unimaginably, a new war was being raged in practically every home in Toronto, in every home in Canada, up and down the length of North America, and, unbelievably, in nearly every far-flung corner of the globe.

The kiss of purple death had come to claim its victims. Originally thought to have come from the battlefields of Europe, the unforeseen epidemic was spread quickly by war-weary soldiers returning from the front before and after the Armistice. Spanish Flu first appeared in Montreal and Toronto during the last days of September. In six short weeks it claimed over 3,000 victims in Montreal out of a population of 640,000 and a similar number from Toronto's population of 490,000. To halt the disease the Board of Health instituted emergency measures closing all places of public meetings. Much of everyday life came to a stop.

Addie and Rebecca took over looking after Jonathan while Lenore and Mrs Dalton swung in to caring for Toronto's sick and ailing as part of the Sisters of Service volunteer nursing brigade. Mr Dalton saw case after suspected case at his practice and did successive house calls late at night, often to confirm death reports and write death certificates. A vaccine was made freely available, but no results could be promised with certainty. Not taking any chances, Mr Dalton vaccinated the entire family bar Jonathan, including Addie and Jerome. If anyone left the house, they wore a mask. Everyone who came into contact with Jonathan wore a mask. As winter approached it was hard for people to relax and celebrate the end of the war when the slightest cough, the merest fever, the subtlest variation in one's lip colour could be a death sentence.

In his supreme solitude, Samuel was spared the Spanish Flu. He hunkered down in the face of blizzards and snow flurries and fierce winter squalls. Although it was twice as cold as it had been the winter before in Europe, Samuel felt cocooned in a blanket of pure newborn snow. After days of gelid deluges he would emerge to a pristine frozen landscape like he had never known before. Gradually he started to feel cleansed by his austere surroundings. He had little desire to hunt but knew for his own survival he must. A thick covering of ice cemented the fish deep below the lake's surface. He could spend all day chipping away at the ice and then chances were he would fall in and half freeze to death himself. He would leave fishing to the spring.

Bringing the rifle with him had been a difficult decision. When he first held it in his hands, he had trembled with a chilling urge to use it – to rid himself of what was most unwanted – his life. A disturbing temptation like none he had ever experienced. But for the memory of Matthew. He felt completely lacking in valour as it was, saying in one breath he wanted to be there for Lenore and Jonathan and then running out on them. He had let down the people who had mattered most to him, he couldn't face their expectations nor his own sense of failure. He was a distasteful disappointment even to himself.

For a long time he never loaded the rifle. He knew that was reckless. Anytime he could come across a bear or a wild cat. But such was his self-regard or was it self-preservation. For some time he wondered if he would be able to resist the allure of the magic bullet out in the deep black heart of the frozen forests. He recalled conversations he had with his father and his grandfather back in August as he fought to get a grip on a world that had been cast awry. His grandfather had said, 'All the great battles are fought within.' Samuel had remained silent. He couldn't argue with such wisdom. His grandpa had also told him that each and every man who had come home from the war had achieved something remarkable; they had survived.

'Whether you can see it or not, they all carry scars of the devastation, the carnage, the waste they have experienced. You feel alone and helpless, but you are not, Samuel. Find some young men in a similar situation to yourself, who can understand what you have gone through, what you are going through. We can only help so much.'

But what his grandfather didn't seem to grasp, what no one could understand, was that in the lurid aftermath of finality, Samuel felt Matthew's life should have been spared, not his. To Samuel, the unholy judgement that took Matthew but spared him was cosmically askew. In surviving, he felt unworthy. From the earliest age, Samuel had been in awe of his older brother. He was original and smart, funny and fearless. He was the cornerstone of Samuel's boyhood and his adolescence. He was there when their father was absent. And when Samuel followed Matthew to McGill to study medicine he strove diligently to honour his brother's memory. Matthew's life had purpose and direction. Everything he did, he did with great generosity and verve. He eclipsed Samuel in every single way.

His father had told him that in going to the war he – Samuel – had made an equal sacrifice. 'You were just as prepared to die as he was. Don't convince yourself otherwise. Don't harbour this guilt,' were the words he said to him one evening as they sat on the verandah and gave themselves over to twilight.

He remembered that conversation. It went something like this: 'Samuel, I'd rather Matthew wasn't dead either, but I'm grateful at least one of my sons has come home from the war. You are alive and that is what I focus on. We will remember Matthew always. We will mourn him for eternity. But at some point we have to get on with the living, for the sake of the next generation if nothing else.'

But it was the "sake of the next generation", of Matthew's son, that was killing Samuel the most. The hollowness of that future was impossible to bear.

Christmas came and went, New Year too. Back in Toronto Samuel's family and Rebecca marked a very subdued Christmas, trying to find meaning in the continuum of life, trying to celebrate the gift of life, of birth, of the essence of the season. They lavished their attentions on the three young children. All of the presents they bought for Samuel lay under the Christmas tree, still in their fancy wrappings, waiting for his return. For Rebecca that winter was punishingly cold: the separation from her family – bizarrely – the absence of Samuel and the extreme temperature – minus 30, a dry cold that crept into your lungs and froze the hair in your nostrils. But after a few weeks she decided she preferred it to winter in Newfoundland where the damp seeped into your bones and chilled you for months on end thwarting any desire to go outside.

Nineteen-nineteen was upon them. Samuel had no notion of it whatsoever. In mid-January he spent one whole day tracking a buck, across a flat frozen terrain, masked by towering pines. When he killed it he was miles away from his hut, miles from shelter. He didn't have a hope of making it back by nightfall or of lugging it back under the unknowing cover of darkness. He knew before long any carnivore within a twenty-mile radius would smell the blood and come for the kill. He built a large roaring fire, roasted the saddle, ate that and sat up into the night, his rifle loaded this time, resting it across his knees, staring into the fire, into the still night, waiting for unwelcome visitors that didn't show.

A week later he was outside his hut, another fire blazing, satiated by another meal of caribou, a million stars blazing in the crystal dome above. He had steered himself not to look up at eventide. He had looked at it too long out of habit, searching for the Evening Star, his heart and soul leaping across the night sky towards Rebecca. He was schooling himself not to do that. He had not forgotten her. At one point he knew he would need to uncover everything, blow the snowy powder off and examine without any evasion his life and her life. Night by night he was coming to terms with that, day by day he was feeling uplifted by the tiniest degrees, by the beauty, the emptiness, the oblique comfort of his surroundings.

By his own calculations it was late and Venus would have long vanished to be outshone by the brilliance of Hercules,

Perseus and Hydra. He rose from his spot by the fire and strode out across the frozen lake and looked up to the clear night sky. With a blanket over his shoulders he stayed there for half an hour, more, his bearded face uplifted, recalling how he used to study the stars when he was sailing, trying to remember the stars near the Equator, Capricornus for one.

Eventually he turned and walked back.

Ten yards from the fire he saw movement out of the corner of his right eye. He jerked his head and there was an adult wolf snarling at him, baring her teeth, pacing side to side, patting her feet on the snow as if it were a bed of fiery coals and she dare not stay in one place for too long. Behind her were two other wolves, smaller, her cubs, finishing off the buck that he had been bleeding. He thought he had tied it high enough in the tree. Obviously not.

His rifle was where...inside, outside, next to the groundsheet? In that palpitating moment he couldn't remember. He'd heard their howls earlier but paid no heed. Well, he thought, will this be my comeuppance? I have thwarted death long enough, is this how it ends?

He held his ground and the she-wolf held hers. As long as he stayed put, she seemed content to stay put. Samuel thought about placing the fire between him and the beast, moving around the far side, but the last thing he wanted to do was to startle and enrage the wild animal. Beautiful, he noted, amazing eyes, but still wild. Slowly he edged towards the fire, till he could feel its temperate glow on his face.

Her cubs finished and rubbed their noses under their mother's neck. She didn't respond or look at them; she continued to stare straight at Samuel. He stared back unwavering. Then, her young turned tail, disappearing into the night. What then for her? For him? Had she eaten anything before he came upon her or was she biding her time waiting to feast fully...on him? Samuel wondered if he had left the moment to move too late. Would it have been smarter to move away from her and around the fire towards his blanket and the hut while she had the distraction of keeping watch over her cubs? By waiting as he had done, he now had her complete undivided attention.

She sat down on her back legs and continued to watch

Samuel. He thought she wanted the food and that was why she wasn't leaving and her sense of self-preservation kept her from turning her back on Samuel. He could only follow her example, though he didn't care if she wanted a meal. What was she waiting for? For him to make one wrong move and she would launch for his jugular. In his mind he talked to her. I am harmless. You can trust me. Let me go inside and you can eat to your heart's content, without fear or malice. Sometime later, he had no idea how much later; he sensed they had somehow in some way come to an unsignalled détente.

The fire had died down, a small flaming beacon now burned between them. Slowly, deathly slowly, he walked around the fire, keeping his distance from the flames and from her. Neither Samuel nor the she wolf took their eyes off each other. He got to his blanket and then with his foot, he felt around and found his rifle. He allowed himself the smallest sense of relief, but he did not gaze down. He continued to watch the wolf as he slowly lowered himself onto his haunches and reached for the rifle with his left hand. He could feel its cold metal barrel through his thick gloves. He resisted the urge to snatch it up in one limbering motion. Rather, he rested his right hand on it ready to pick it up and fire it in a split second if he had to. Every cell in his being was awakened to his life and her life right there in front of him. Such a beautiful savage creature, with more right than he to be in this untouched world. Did he want to kill it? No, he didn't think so. Did he want to scare it off like his brother Matthew had done with that bear all those years ago? No, not even that. She might mistake his fire for an attack and counter attack. Or, she might run away and he might never again get to see such a wondrous creation so closely.

And then she did something truly amazing. She took three steps towards him and lay down in front of him, completely in front of him, like some mythical ingénue. She rested her head on her front paws and stared assiduously at Samuel, like she was spellbound. He was spellbound. Tentatively he lowered himself onto the groundsheet and he sat and waited and watched as this captivating specimen of nature continued to gaze at him, without movement, without blinking.

He watched until the fire had burned down to embers,

until his feet were nearly numb. Her eyes had a power and a beauty and a sadness that Samuel could not deny and without warning he found himself crying, from a well deep inside, releasing his lode of pain. Tears came unbidden, staining his face, unclenching his soul. It was as if by looking at her for as long as he had done, opening his eyes to her, he had let her in and she saw inside him, saw all things. She saw what he was hiding from himself, from the rest of the world. In their primal communion she spoke to him. She was Matthew, she was Rebecca, she was his very self, her very self. All were immanent in her. Her knowing and her wisdom were absolute.

Like Romulus and Remus, he had been rescued by a she-wolf. And like the ancient gods had ordained, only one brother was to survive: Romulus through a murderous act of jealousy, Samuel through a selfless act of love. As night drew on, the she-wolf raised herself up and threw her head back to the velvet sky and howled for her pups. And in her howling there was healing. She cried in the night and her cries were answered but no wolf came to her. In the morning she was gone.

Three days later Samuel followed. He headed southward taking his direction from the longest branches. With each new day he slowly felt himself unfurling. At some point as is the wont with new growth, he started to bloom, reaching for the sun, reaching for the light, the anticipation of new life pulsing through every cell in his body.

65

Rebecca was lying in bed reading an English text but she was finding it difficult to concentrate. It was late and she was tired but try as she might she just couldn't sleep. In the end she just lay there, becoming increasingly worried over Lenore who two days ago had come home from work at St Michael's Hospital saying she felt utterly exhausted. She had not got out of bed since. They thought the flu epidemic had subsided. And now this: sudden and sinister, striking completely out of the blue.

Mr Dalton had insisted on complete rest. He was emphatic. He warned her under no circumstances was she to place her heart or herself under any stress. They fed her fluids constantly. Mrs and Mrs Dalton cared for her around the clock and they banned all visitors. They were all back to wearing masks. They thought they caught it early, yet they prayed for a miracle. Rebecca struggled with that. She had lost her faith in the power of prayer. Too many of her prayers had gone unanswered.

Rebecca was drifting and then she stirred. She thought she heard a soft knock.

'Come in,' she said, but no one entered. Then the knock again. This time she turned to the window. Is someone knocking on my window she wondered? A third knock, as something bounced off the pane. She stood and went to the window and was met by another knock, a small stone or piece of wood deflecting off the glass. She pushed up the sash window and poked her head out in the cold night air to look down at the white carpet of snow below. Staring up at her was a man bundled in winter clothes. He looked like Samuel.

'Rebecca,' she heard him call to her. It **was** Samuel.

'What are you doing? Are you locked out?'

'I don't think so. I know where the spare key is.' He smiled up at her. 'Come outside.'

'Now?'

'Yes, come and look at the stars with me. Rug up. I'll meet you at the back porch.'

Months of rejection, months of silence, months of absence, now this? Rebecca dared not get her hopes up. She changed out of her nightie and quickly piled on layers of clothing. Downstairs she retrieved her anorak from the cloakroom and her winter boots and walked through to the kitchen. She sat down and pulled her boots on and then unlatched the back door.

Samuel was standing there in front of her, a fur fleece hat on his head, only his chin to his eyebrows exposed. 'Come.' He extended his gloved hand to her.

She took it. 'This better be worth it. Is it the aurora borealis?'

He didn't answer. He led her past the oak tree, past the driveway to where in summer they played petanque. Over his arm he carried two blankets. He wrapped one around Rebecca and helped her to the ground, then wrapped the other around himself. Pulling her into his shoulder they lay on their backs looking up at the stars. Rebecca was silent. She didn't know what she was looking for and she did not know what to expect.

'Can you see that constellation of stars up there?' said Samuel pointing with his gloved hand. 'Can you see three stars dotted together?'

'Yes,' she said, 'I see the three stars in a row.'

'They are Orion's Belt. Sometimes they are called the three kings. If you go out at a slight angle top and bottom from the two outside stars you will see four more bright stars, Can you see that? Look for an hour glass shape.'

'No,' said Rebecca 'No, wait, yes, I can.'

'Good, that figure is Orion and below that and to his left are some smaller stars, they are his hunting dogs – can you see them. And at his knees, either side is the river.'

'Yes, Samuel,' she said, 'now that you point it out I can see it quite clearly.'

'And then over there above him to the right is another constellation, Taurus the bull. Orion is also called The Hunter and he's only visible in the northern hemisphere for a few months each year, from November to April. Taurus is also more prominent in the winter sky.' He paused. 'I have been watching these stars for weeks, looking out for Andromeda as well, the chained maiden, the female warrior holding a sword.'

'Did you find her?'

'Yes, I found her.' He paused again. 'You know who first introduced me to the stars?'

'No.' She paused. 'Grandpa?'

'Possibly, indirectly, but no – Matthew.'

'Matthew,' she echoed.

'Before I started elementary he started tutoring me. I think he had been doing his impatient best waiting till I was old enough. He had a fascination for the stars and you know, in the past few weeks I've come to realise that I think it was because of Matthew that we came to meet; that I steered myself in the hapless direction that I did, towards the position where you found me because of the night navigational lessons he raised me on when I was ever so young and impressionable.

'These stars have been glowing at me for weeks. Where I was Rebecca there were no city lights to obscure one's vision. I was in the wilderness, miles north of Québec city, to the west of Labrador. Some nights the sky was majestic with no one around me but silence and a sprightly old she-wolf and the voices of all those I held dear. And their message was strong and persistent. They shone a light so bright inside me I couldn't hide. It lit up the locked chambers of my heart and thawed the winter that had set in my soul. It breathed new life into my bewildered being so that I could no longer shy away from looking at the Evening Star or searching for it in the pre-dawn chill. And when I felt its calling, when the darkness disappeared from my life and I felt Matthew's eternal blessing, eternal guidance, believe me when I tell you, I could not come home fast enough.'

He turned her face to his, the plumes of their expelled breath intermingling. 'Rebecca, if it were in my power to rewrite the past year I would, from the moment Jonathan was born I would make so many changes but, most of all, I would change everything I said and did to hurt you. And if I could I would make good on everything I wrote to you about when I was overseas: every plan, every promise, every pledge. I am so sorry. Sorry for the pain, the heartache, the tears, the anger, the frustration. You had enough to bear last year. You certainly didn't need any more from me.'

'You were suffering too, Samuel. You were coming to terms with things outside of your control. I had some idea about that.'

'Yes but that was no excuse,' he reached down into her blanket, found her mittened hand, brought it up and kissed it. 'I don't know how you feel about me anymore and I don't know if you will ever trust me enough to love me again. I accept that might take time, but I want you to know I never stopped loving you. Even though it seemed as if I turned away from you it wasn't you I was turning away from. It was my life, what I saw as my impossible, undeserving life. All I can offer you is my deepest, most profound regret and ask that you give this pathetic worthless man a second chance.'

Rebecca could no longer deny her emotions or the unmitigated love she felt for him. 'You are not worthless,' she cried. 'You are worthy!' She lay her hand on his clean-shaven face, 'You, the most handsome of men.' Through her tears she kissed him. He kissed her back with heartbreaking tenderness. They kissed like their first time when they were in the cobalt blue cave of the iceberg. They kissed like they had on the night they gave themselves to each other completely. They kissed as if Samuel had just returned from war to the best homecoming gift he could have possibly hoped for. And through their kisses they emptied and filled themselves of each other and surrendered to the sweetness of unbridled relief.

After some time, Samuel broke off. 'We could really do with a fire.' He helped her up and they walked to the porch and shook out the blankets and lightly stomped their feet. They took their boots and coats off, placed them in the cloakroom under the stairwell. At the bottom of the stairs Samuel softly said, 'Rebecca?'

'Yes?' She turned and reached out her hand. But he didn't take it. Instead he bent down and lifted her into his arms.

'Up the stairs?' she whispered in surprise.

'All the way,' he whispered, 'I've carried elk heavier than you.' He carried her up the stairs to her room, his room, and placed her on top of her rumpled bed.

'Where are you going to sleep?'

Smiling softly he said, 'With you.' Her eyes opened in alarm. He laughed. 'I promise all I will do is sleep beside you.' He bent down and kissed her. 'I want to wake up with you in my arms. It has been too long coming and I'm not going to go another night without you asleep in my arms. Will you lie down with me?"

She peeled down to her thermals. Samuel took off his cap. She noted his hair had grown out. And then he took off his jumper and trousers. She didn't recognise the clothes; he'd bought them in Québec on the way home where he stopped for a night with his grandparents. He was wearing long johns. He removed his skivvy and climbed into the bed with her. It was late, well after two in the morning but Rebecca felt wide awake. She remembered Lenore and thought about telling Samuel but decided to leave it till the morning. Morning would come soon enough. Rebecca lay on her back, her head resting on Samuel's bare shoulder as he lay on his side, one arm under her neck, the other across her front, his face pressed to the side of her head.

'Samuel,' she whispered, 'do you remember your last night in Newfoundland?'

In an instant he moved on top of her, his head suspended above, his lips mere centimetres away from hers and then he lowered his face and kissed her ardently, his lips on fire, opening his mouth, opening hers, his tongue touching hers, sensually stroking each side, inside and around her lips. Rebecca felt the burn, the tingle and the warmth flare up and down her body. She whimpered softly into his mouth in delicious remembrance, her hands roaming over his beautiful naked back. 'Do you want me to just go to sleep beside you?' Samuel whispered.

'No,' said Rebecca, and then in resignation, 'Yes.' She kissed him briefly. 'Are you the prince of darkness come to have your wicked way with me?'

'If I recall you had your wicked way with me also.'

She blushed. Gently shaking her head she said, 'Not now Samuel, not here. Besides, I have to go to sleep. I have to go to school tomorrow.'

'You go to school now?'

'Yes,' she said, 'what else do you think I have been doing with my time?'

'Well you're going to be a married school girl soon,' he said kissing her lips. He lifted his head and flashed his brilliant strong white teeth, the glorious Samuel smile of old.

'Will I still be able to go to school when I'm married?'

'I don't care what you do, Rebecca as long as you are my wife. Can we get married tomorrow?'

'Tomorrow? You're not serious!'

'The sooner the better as far as I'm concerned. I want to spend my days and nights making love to you. I want to be on permanent honeymoon with you.'

'But then I couldn't go to school.'

'No you couldn't,' he whispered, 'but, believe me,' he said as he brushed her lips with his, 'I'd make you forget all about school.'

'Samuel,' she moaned. Minutes later she finally got her breathing under control. 'Maybe we should wait till I finish the school year.'

'Maybe. How many weeks is that? Five or six?'

'Six!' she exclaimed. 'More likely twelve.'

'Three months!' he said almost in horror. 'I can't wait three months! Can you wait three months?'

'With you by my side, I can wait three months.' She stroked his face.

'Well there's no way I can wait three months with you by mine.'

'Sure you can,' she teased.

'Is that a challenge?'

'Maybe?'

'Shall we see who can hold out the longest?'

'That's not what I meant, Samuel.' She affectionately tried to push him away.

'Let's see how we go tomorrow. You are having a school free day, Miss Crowe. Plead sick, proffer any excuse, I don't care. You are not leaving my side for a single minute.' He rolled back on his side, turned Rebecca on hers and pulled her into him like two well-worn spoons, kissed her on the neck and then they slept.

66

Daylight was creeping into the room when Rebecca awoke. She had slept way past her usual wake-up time and didn't stir until she heard Mrs Dalton calling her name.

'Yes,' she called out, 'in here.' She rubbed her eyes and tried to sit up. Samuel's arm was draped across her.

'Samuel,' said Mrs Dalton, 'what are you doing here?'

'I snuck in last night,' his voice sleepy. He raised himself up onto his elbows.

'That much is obvious,' said Lottie, welcoming her son home with a tender smile and reaching down to hug him. 'Dare I say it, but I'm pleased Samuel is the reason you are still in bed. I don't think I could cope if you were off colour too.'

'How's Lenore?' asked Rebecca.

'Not good,' said Mrs Dalton, 'She's asking after you.'

'What's the matter?' said Samuel sitting up.

'She's not well Samuel, not well.' Mrs Dalton grimly shook her head. 'The dreaded influenza. We are crossing our fingers and praying for a miracle.'

'Influenza?' said Samuel quizzically.

'Where have you been?' asked his mother incredulously. 'To the North Pole? You don't know people have been dropping dead with this insidious illness!

'I have been a long way from everything and everybody.'

'Have you? Well I look forward to hearing all about it.'

They heard Mr Dalton calling out for his wife.

Samuel and Rebecca both jumped out of bed and followed her to Lenore's room, Samuel pulling on his skivvy on the way through.

Mr Dalton was sitting beside Lenore's bed, his hand resting on her forehead. He turned to them as they came through the door. "Samuel,' he said in surprise, standing up to embrace his son. 'When did you get here?'

'In the middle of the night. What's up? Can I do anything?'

'I wish there was,' said Mr Dalton, his face sombre. 'You two should have masks on.'

Rebecca raced out of the room and returned a minute later. They fixed their masks and crept up to the bed.

'Lenore,' Samuel spoke softly, 'can you hear me Lenore? It's me, Samuel. I've come home at last. I've come out of my hibernation and it's time for you to do the same.'

Lenore opened her eyes and stared at Samuel and then she looked at Rebecca. 'Is he for real?' she asked.

'Yes,' said Rebecca, touching Samuel's shoulder and squeezing Lenore's forearm. 'He's come back. The Samuel we know and love has come home.' Her eyes smiled above the white mask.

'That's good,' said Lenore dryly. 'About time. Where's Lottie?' Rebecca noticed blood on her lips.

'I'm here Lenore,' she said coming up to Mr Dalton's side.

'And Jonathan?'

'With Addie.'

'Good,' she nodded. 'Keep him there till this is past. Keep him safe.' Mr Dalton brought a glass of water to her lips, and Lenore took a few swallows. There were smears of blood trailing down the side of the glass into the remaining water. Lenore tried to take a deep breath but that clearly pained her. 'I need to say something to you all and I don't want this to go unsaid,' her voice was hoarse. In alarm Rebecca looked at Mr Dalton. He stared back at her. His eyes were unreadable. 'I don't know if I will pull through this or not. It has taken me low,' whispered Lenore.

'You'll pull through,' said Rebecca trying to fill the room with her optimism.

'I want to', she said, her breath serrated. 'But in the event that things go from bad to worse I want to talk to you about Jonathan.' Looking towards Samuel and Rebecca she said, 'I don't know how things are between the two of you now and I don't want you to explain. I doubt I have the energy to listen even. All I want to say is this: I love you both. Rebecca, if I could choose one person to be the mother of my son, it would be you.' Looking at Lottie, she said, 'Not that you wouldn't be a wonderful mother to my son Lottie, but you are already a wonderful grandmother to him and I would hate to burden you with another child, but Rebecca has youth on her side and she loves my son just as much as any of us and he loves her. I know it; with every waking living breath he loves her.

'Samuel, I know Matthew would want you to be the father of his son in his absence. I second that. But I'm not going to make you promise me anything as a dying wish. I just want to tell you that I bless you both and that I trust either one or both of you to raise Jonathan. But please don't forget Alistair, he's short on family too. That's what I want you to know if the worst should happen. And if the best should happen and I do pull through, Samuel, I want to see you marry for love. It's what Matthew would want too.'

'Thank you,' he said. 'I will.' His arm went around Rebecca.

'Good,' Lenore grimaced as she swallowed. 'That's how it should be.'

Samuel stood up and moved towards Lenore placing his hand on her shoulder. 'Get well. We have lots to catch up on.'

Rebecca caught him level a look at his father before they left the room.

'I'll be downstairs in a few minutes,' Mr Dalton said as they departed.

Outside, no one said a word. Mrs Dalton, Samuel and Rebecca just looked at each other, not wanting to voice their gravest fears.

'I'm going to shower,' said Samuel, turning and walking away.

Ten minutes later he joined his parents and Rebecca in the kitchen.

'Where's Grandpa?' he asked uneasily.

His mother raised her eyes. 'We packed him off to Analeise's.'

'How long has Lenore been ill?'

His father hesitated then said, 'Three days.'

'Three days!' exclaimed Samuel. The two stared at each other until Samuel asked, 'Have you been home with her all this time?'

His father shook his head. 'Only yesterday.' He continued to look intently at his son.

Taking a deep breath, Samuel said, 'I'll sit with her today if you like.'

His father shook his head again. 'No. Maybe tomorrow you can. Just get used to being home today.' Glancing in Rebecca's direction he said, 'I take it you're not going to school today.'

'No' she said. 'Sorry. I hope I haven't disappointed you.'

'Not at all,' said Mr Dalton. 'Go for a walk with Samuel. Get some fresh air into your lungs. Just avoid people where you can.'

Mrs Dalton interjected, 'Maybe, Leonard you should let Samuel give you a few hours break. You must be exhausted and in your position you can't afford to get sick.'

'Yes, Dad,' said Samuel. 'Mom's right. I've had more than enough downtime lately. I don't mind relieving you.'

'Listen up, people,' said Mr Dalton. 'I want to sit with Lenore today and as head of this house I occasionally like to get my own way. Is that understood?'

After breakfast Samuel and Rebecca visited Addie who had her hands full trying to dry nappies on racks raised high to the ceiling and keeping young Jonathan occupied. Addie asked about Lenore. Samuel gave her a brief summation. But his unwillingness to talk about Lenore's condition conspired in their favour. He was left with little choice but to talk about himself and his exploits over the past six months.

After lunch, just as they were about to leave Mr Dalton called out for Lottie. She was in the midst of doing the dishes. 'Here, let me finish,' said Rebecca. Mrs Dalton wiped her hands and hurried upstairs. Five minutes later Mr Dalton called for Samuel.

'Coming,' he yelled.

But when he got to the bottom of the stairs his father leant over the railing and said, 'I was thinking if you feel up to it, call in and see Grandpa when you're out. He's been worried about you. He would want to see you.'

'Yes, of course,' said Samuel. 'We probably won't be back till dinner then.'

'No rush.'

They returned around seven o'clock as darkness was descending, entering as always through the back door. The light was on in the kitchen and there was a metal pot on the stove and a tea towel covering a fresh loaf of bread on the table. Samuel lifted the cloth. 'I hope Mum doesn't mind. I'm famished. Do you want a slice?'

'Please,' Rebecca said as she placed the butter dish on the table. The house was eerily still. 'It's quiet isn't it?'

'Any place would be quiet after Analeise's.'

'Uncle Samuel, Uncle Samuel, Uncle Samuel,' teased Rebecca. 'Good practise Samuel. One day it might be Daddy, Daddy, Daddy.'

'I hope we get some peace and quiet to ourselves first,' said Samuel. He looked directly at her. 'Tell me again how many children you want.'

Rebecca froze. She felt her heart beating loudly in her ears. She tried to clear her throat. 'Four,' she almost croaked. 'How many children would you like?'

'If you're up for four, then I'm up for four.'

'Would you have agreed if I said eight?'

'Heavens no, that's way too many. And besides I know you don't want eight.'

Samuel stepped towards Rebecca and pulled her into his arms. 'All the time I was away, did you ever give up hope that I would come back to you?'

'*Dum spiro, spero.*'

'Ah,' said Samuel, 'Venus is speaking her native tongue. '"While I breathe, I hope".'

'Yes,' said Rebecca, hoarsely.

'I can't tell you what a relief it is to find you here and willing to chance your life with me. I thought after my heartless treatment last year, family or no family, you probably would have gone back to Newfoundland and I would have had to go back and find you.'

'There is no going back,' said Rebecca leaning into Samuel's chest. 'I'm here because I believe in you. I believe in you above all things.'

'Do you believe this mixed up man has it in him to be a good father?' asked Samuel.

'You will make a fantastic father,' she said, sensing sadness and remorse bubbling close to the surface. 'Look at the role model you've had.' She paused. 'We will make beautiful children together,' her voice catching.

'Is that so?' Samuel grinned at Rebecca who was doing her best to smile. They gazed into each other's eyes and then softly, Samuel said, 'I'm sensing you want to be the mother of my children?'

Rebecca felt herself tremble. Looking up into Samuel's face, she felt her life was at an impassable crossroad. Was this the moment? she wondered. But no sooner had she thought that did she feel her gut twist in panic and recoil. Her heart screamed: I already am Samuel. I was! But the words sank inside her aching chest. She just stared up at Samuel shaking her head as salty tears splashed over the rims of her eyelids, and trailed down her face.

'Oh Rebecca,' said Samuel, hugging her tightly for many minutes while she surrendered herself to tears of abandon and loss. Eventually she calmed herself and Samuel lifted her face and kissed her eyelids. 'If ever there was a yes that was it.' He squeezed her tight. 'I promise to marry you. I promise to give you children, to help you raise a family so our lives can be filled with laughter and love, not sorrow and heartache.' Bending his head to kiss her, he said, 'And this time I promise to keep my word.'

Some time later they parted. Covering up the bread, Samuel said, 'I wonder how our patient is.'

Walking out of the kitchen, they went down the hallway where they heard Mr Dalton say, 'Samuel, we are in here.' They followed his voice into the front room where both Mr and Mrs Dalton were nursing small tumblers of amber liquid. Brandy.

'How's Lenore?' asked Rebecca.

Mr and Mrs Dalton exchanged a look. 'I'm afraid she's gone,' he said.

'Gone?' said Rebecca in disbelief, 'to hospital?' her every fibre fighting to dispel the dreaded finality of his words.

'No Rebecca,' said Samuel, pulling Rebecca into his arms. 'She's gone to be with Matthew.'

Ten months after Matthew's death, the Daltons

remembered their eldest unforgettable son along with his beautiful, incomparable wife. In the dismal days following Samuel's return they never found it in themselves to hold a service for Matthew and so they honoured both Matthew and Lenore as they laid the two of them to rest, two shining tombstones side by side. As they were in life, so they would be in death.

Lamentations

67

On the first Saturday after school broke up in June 1919, Samuel and Rebecca were married. It was a small wedding attended by Samuel's immediate family, his Uncle Michel and Aunty Marguerite who brought with them Samuel's grandparents. Samuel did not invite his cousins, conscious that Rebecca had no family to invite. Addie, Jerome and their grown up children were all there, as were Samuel and Matthew's good friend, Anthony Clarkson and Lenore's brother Alistair.

Rebecca was adamant that she did not want a church wedding – much to everyone's surprise. 'Enough things happen to you and you find it hard to believe there is a God anymore,' she said by way of explanation. 'Don't you find it hard to believe in God after what happened to your family?'

'Don't you want God to bless your union?' asked Lottie.

'God took away from me what meant most to me,' said Rebecca.

'Now that's not entirely true,' said Samuel, drawing her into his arms.

How could she deny him that?

'I know!' he said. 'The ocean brought us together. Why don't we get married by a captain on a boat?'

She blanched and faltered and for the first time in her life snapped at Samuel. 'There is absolutely no way I'm getting married on a boat.'

'Okay,' he said, raising his hands in peace, 'it was only an idea. I thought you might like the idea.'

'Well, I don't,' she said, trying to get a hold of herself.

In the end they were married in the Dalton's garden on the petanque green where they had lain in the snow when Samuel returned home whole. The trees rustled lightly in their new summer growth. Grandpa Dalton escorted her to the small party waiting for them under the shade. Weeks earlier, Analeise had asked her who was giving her away. 'No one will be giving me away,' she had said.

Grandpa had misheard her inflection and thinking she was saddened by her lack of family had stepped forward and said, 'Rebecca, I would be honoured to give you away.'

Rebecca looked at him then turned to Samuel standing behind her. Samuel put his hands on Rebecca's shoulders and said, 'Grandpa, I think what Rebecca is trying to say is that she is hers to give away. She's not anyone's to give away.'

'Ah,' said Grandpa.

But then Rebecca had said, 'You can escort me to my wedding, Grandpa if you like.' And that seemed to please everyone.

No one including Rebecca could have been more surprised at the dress she wore to her own wedding. It was a La Belle Époque gown in gold and black lace over old gold satin. With relish she ignored the saying, "Married in yellow, ashamed of your fellow." Because she wasn't getting married in yellow, she was getting married in gold! It was elfin-like and regal with flashes of rich platinum, the most elegant example of French fashion from the past thirty years. The rich young women on the Titanic would have eyed her dress with envy. The skirt had a slender swag front and the back fell into a train from a pleated semi-circular fantail. Her arms were bare except for the smallest draping of old gold guipure over the shoulders. The same lace ran around her décolletage and in a vee at the front and back of the dress at hip level. Her hair was loosely rolled and pinned up. She was simply dazzling.

Rebecca was conscious of everyone watching her but as she approached the wedding guests she had eyes only for one person and he had eyes only for her. When Samuel took her hand and pulled her towards him he was speechless for many seconds. Finally he said, 'I am the luckiest man alive and you,' he squeezed her hand, 'you have never looked more beautiful.'

'You said that once before,' she said smiling up at him.

'So I did,' he paused. 'I meant it then and I mean it now.'

A Church of England minister performed the wedding with minimal religious fanfare. 'We are here today to bear witness to the marriage vows of Samuel and Rebecca and to hear their declarations. Where there is love there is sanctity. And where there is marriage there is sacredness. Today Samuel and Rebecca stand before us ready to be joined in this most holy of unions.' Turning to Rebecca he said, 'Are you, Rebecca Olsen Crowe, lawfully free to marry Samuel Rousseau Dalton?'

'Yes,' beamed Rebecca.

'And you, Samuel Rousseau Dalton, are you lawfully free to marry Rebecca Olsen Crowe?'

'Totally free,' said Samuel, looking into Rebecca's upturned face.

Analeise read a blessing bestowed upon Grandpa Dalton on his wedding day, a Gaelic classic: You are the star of each night.

Then to everyone's surprise, the girl who didn't want any religious overtones to her wedding, dedicated a Psalm to Samuel.

'O God, you are my God, and I long for you. My whole being desires you; like a dry, worn out, and waterless land, my soul is thirsty for you. Let me see you in the sanctuary; let me see how mighty and glorious you are. Your constant love is better than life itself and so I will praise you. I will give you thanks as long as I live; I will raise my hands to you in prayer. My soul will feast and be satisfied, and I will sing glad songs of praise to you.'

Samuel responded. 'I love you to distraction and hereafter am prepared to love you continually throughout the years as much as he who can love you most. I invite you to share my future, to be my equal, to walk by my side into an unknown life, full of remote possibilities and redeeming love.'

After they had exchanged wedding vows, Rebecca whispered, "I feel I took you to be my husband years ago, when we first kissed under the iceberg.'

'I know.' He squeezed her hand. They turned around to face the minister.

'Do you have the ring?' he asked.

'Yes,' said Samuel.

'Repeat after me,' said the minister.

'It's fine,' said Samuel turning to the minister. 'I know what I want to say.' He took Rebecca's hand. 'I give you this ring as a symbol of my undying love. This ring is whole and complete and never-ending as is my love for you. And each time you see this ring on your finger, each time it catches the light, or you feel it around your skin, remember today, remember our love for each other, our commitment to each other, remember our suffering and our strength and what we went through to arrive at this day and remember how happy we make each other and how we complete each other.'

'I will,' said Rebecca as Samuel lifted her hand and kissed the ring on her finger. Samuel glanced at the minister.

Is there more?' the minister asked.

'Yes.' Samuel reached into his pocket and pulled out another ring. This time he reached for Rebecca's right hand placed the ring in her palm and folded her fingers over it. 'Rebecca, couples in the Roman Empire were the first to place betrothal or 'truth' rings on the fourth finger of the left hand believing that a vein in that finger, the 'vena amoris', runs directly to the heart.'

Her breath caught in her throat. She was completely mesmerised by him. His whole heart was in his eyes.

'I give you this ring to place on my finger as a symbol of my love and my loyalty and my honesty. That you should know I will always be truthful unto you. From my heart to your heart,' he said, as he touched his heart and touched hers and squeezed their hands together.

Rebecca placed the ring on Samuel's fourth finger, lifted it to her lips and kissed it. Their eyes never leaving each other's. After a few moments Samuel turned to the minister.

In a loud voice he announced, 'Samuel and Rebecca, I now pronounce you husband and wife. Young man, you may kiss your bride.'

Samuel took Rebecca in his arms and gave her a long, rapturous heartfelt kiss to the cheers of teary onlookers.

In the three months leading up to their wedding they had maintained a hard-earned vow of celibacy. Rebecca's decision was driven by her fear of finding herself pregnant again and Samuel disappearing through forces outside of their control. She fully believed in Samuel and his commitment to her but her faith in the rest of the world had been sorely tested. The reason she gave Samuel was that she didn't want to spend her days at school re-playing all their nightly encounters in her head. She wouldn't make it through the school year.

'I see,' said Samuel, 'so you would rather spend your days thinking of the encounters ahead.'

'Yes,' she said trying to avoid his eyes. 'I think that would be easier.'

'Bollocks!' said Samuel. 'Either way you are going to be distracted. At least my way it is going to be more worthwhile.'

Rebecca gave Samuel a flustered look.

Taking her hands, he said, 'Relax, when have I ever forced myself on you?'

She looked at him. Her eyes giving him the honest answer.

'That's right, never. I just kneel at your altar accepting any offerings you give me.'

Feeling overwhelming tenderness, she placed her hand on his cheek and said. 'When we are married I will give you offerings galore.' She went up on her toes to kiss him.

With his mouth at her lips he murmured, 'I'm pleased to hear that, because when we are married, I will not be reticent in demanding my dues, of that you can be certain.'

Rebecca trembled. Her stomach flared.

So there was no sweet love making before their wedding but there was plenty of ardent Saturday afternoons spent on a picnic blanket, plenty of feverish hands running over clothed bodies and in the early mornings, plenty of hugs and kisses to the back of the neck, only and always to the back of the neck. They had made a vow that they would not go into each other's rooms at night, but before long an unspoken morning ritual surfaced. Whoever woke first would sneak into the other person's bed so the other could wake in the arms of the one they loved. After the third morning, Samuel instituted a no kissing on the lip order. He said it was too much too bear and that he wouldn't be responsible for his actions beyond that if they started.

On their wedding night they farewelled their guests at ten and made their way to their suite. 'What a long day,' said Rebecca, walking into the room. She fell backwards on the bed and swung her legs up in the air. 'I'm pooped.'

Laughing, Samuel said, 'You're not allowed to be pooped yet.'

They lay on the bed and laughed together. Rolling towards her Samuel said, 'Have you seen the size of our bathtub?' He kissed her. 'It's like a mini Lake Ontario. Let's have a bath.' He got up and went to run the water.

When he came back he had removed his jacket, vest and tie, his shoes and socks. Rebecca was admiring her wedding ring. 'I feel bad,' she sighed. 'I haven't bought you a wedding present.'

'Don't feel bad. Don't you know? The bride is the wedding present.'

Her cheeks blushing, Rebecca said, 'I'll have to think of what I can give you for a wedding present.'

'While you think about that, I have one wish for tonight.' He led her to the bathroom.

'What's that?'

'No speaking, absolutely no questions under any circumstances.'

Through lowered eyelashes she said, 'I think you have two wishes, Samuel.'

'Au contraire, my beautiful wife, one is my wish and the other is my due.'

He kissed his forefinger and pressed it firmly against her mouth. She looked into his eyes as she kissed his finger. Then Samuel trailed his fingertips down Rebecca's neck across her clavicle to the curved neckline of her dress all the way across her décolleté. His eyes followed his fingers then they returned to Rebecca's. He walked round behind her and unfastened the long line of hooks at her back. Slowly he peeled the dress forward down to her elbows and ever so gently he pulled one arm out and then the other. Her dress fell to the floor. Rebecca stepped out of it. Samuel tossed it over the towel rack behind him.

She stood before him in a black corset, black gold garter belt, black satin panties and soft silk stockings. Samuel appraised her. To her credit, Rebecca stood firm, her breath shallow. He stepped forward and Rebecca reached up to place her arms round his neck to draw him down but he took her hands and squeezed them, lowering them to her side. Slowly, sensuously, he traced his finger around the top of her corset. He did it a second time, this time he ran his finger inside and gently played with her nipples. They tensed and tightened under his delicate touch. Rebecca moaned.

He ran his hands down the side of her body and then he traipsed his fingers deftly across the tops of her thighs. Rebecca was desperate for Samuel to kiss her, but he was drawing this out as if dawn was a long time coming. Samuel crouched and ran his tongue around the top of her stocking, stopping where the catch was and releasing it, then onto the next catch, one leg and then the other. He rolled her stockings down and lifted one foot and removed a shoe and a stocking and then another. He unclipped her garter belt and let it fall to the floor. He took two steps backwards surveying her like a masterpiece. His eyes mirrored her own. The anticipation was almost an end in itself.

He came up to her and this time she did not reach for his face. She lowered her hands, undid his belt, pulled it through the loops, placed it over his neck and pulled him to her to kiss him. They kissed until they were breathless and heaving and somewhere in there Rebecca's fingers found Samuel's buttons and undid his shirt, tugging it out of his trousers. More kisses, sweet, rainfall kisses. Samuel's lips wandered along the curve of her neck to her earlobe, to her nape. Breathless, sensual kisses, completely unrestrained.

Rebecca couldn't help herself; she moaned deeply, moans of pleasure and arousal. With her hands behind him she pulled Samuel towards her. She could feel him pressed up against her. After some moments he crouched and trailed his lips to the center of all her nerve endings. She was burning with unrestrained heat and dampness. He kissed her. He soused her. She placed her hands on his head and almost swooned at the delicious sensation of his lips on her through the warm wet fabric of her underwear. Her body was flooding with feelings and memories that had sustained her for nearly two years. She was desperate to cry out 'Please! Samuel!' but all she could manage was to bite her lips and press her tumescent self deeper into his mouth.

He broke off and looked up at Rebecca and she looked down at him, her eyes pleading. He stood and she watched as he undid his trousers and shorts and stepped out of them. He wanted her. God he wanted her. She wanted all of him on her, inside of her, over her. He crouched down again and this time he removed her panties, she felt him blow on her, she felt him give her the lightest kiss while her flesh pulsed in desperate need and then, then, he placed his warm wet lips on her and in mere seconds she came, collapsing over him, gasping for air, for Samuel.

Before she knew it she was in the air and he was inside her walking towards the bathroom wall pressing her against the cool green tiles and pressing himself deeper and deeper into her, blindingly kissing Rebecca's neck, her face, her mouth, seeking out her eyes. His eyes full of heightened determination, surely hers were full of Samuel and his power over her. He flexed. She tensed. She was groaning and gasping and he was breathing hard and fast and furiously and then he made her forget about her breathing as she surrendered to the pull and the fire inside her, inside him. He took her to the edge and with her strangled 'aagh' he cried out 'yes' and they both came, flooding in endorphins and tingling helplessness, burying themselves in each other's necks.

Many minutes later, when Samuel had finally managed to get hold of his breathing, when he had finally managed to remove her corset, he carried Rebecca to the bath.

They made love again, he on top then she on top, tumbling like water babies, like water gods, concupiscent lovers that they were. She loved it. He loved it. In the still of the night Samuel opened a bottle of French champagne iced for hours and they drank out of one glass, trickling champagne into each other's mouth with each resuscitative kiss. They drank from each other's umbilicus, from their breastbones, from the hollow at the base of their throats, one immemorial night of effervescent love. No speaking, their clamant fingers, their craving mouths paying homage to each other's body.

And as dawn approached sending currents of amber across the sky, Samuel flung back all the curtains, laid his wife on the small mahogany dining table and made love to her once more, watching her from a belvedere height as the sun reflected off golden panes of glass and bathed her in gilded light and her body refracted rose hues that gave her skin a royal flush and her hair dazzled in wild Nordic fury and her face projected the heady sight and feel of him. In breathless ecstasy and wonder Samuel thought that somewhere, some god, was indeed shining their perpetual light on them.

68

They spent the first week of their holiday at Niagara Falls, staying in a charming little inn within walking distance of the mighty river. They walked for miles along the pathways, had secluded picnics under canopied trees amidst fields of fragrant summer flowers. They went to the Canadian Falls – the beautiful Horseshoe Falls – and marvelled at its sheer velocity. They returned to see it at dawn and at dusk. They visited the Museum where they learnt all about the daredevils who tried to survive a jump over the falls or walk on a tightrope over the falls, or – Rebecca's favourite – the forty-six year old woman who went over in a barrel with her cat.

They went to the Cave of the Winds behind Bridal Veil Falls, sometimes called Aeolus's Cave after the Greek God of Winds. 'Can you hear him calling for you?' whispered Samuel in her ear. 'He's saying Venus, Venus, where are you? But you can't hear him, Rebecca. You'll never be able to hear him for you have been made deaf to his overtures, deaf to anyone else's overtures bar mine.' They had romantic candlelight dinners and it took them back to the night they celebrated their engagement with Ronnie and Margaret Evans. They would be happy to know they were married at last.

They made love many times, sometimes noisily and sometimes in silence. In the absence of words, their eyes more than anything else spoke the wanton language of lust, of desire, of deep-seated love.

After a week they caught the train back to Toronto and then without stopping another train onto Lake Muskoka where they had rented a small lodge on the lake for three weeks. One week by themselves, one week with the whole family – Grandpa, Lottie and Leonard and Jonathan, Analeise and Randal and their two children – and then a last week by themselves. Samuel and Rebecca did not want to go a whole month without seeing Jonathan. They wanted to swim with him in the lake and show him all the summer butterflies and the squirrels and the elk.

And at some point on their honeymoon Rebecca hoped she could find it within her to tell Samuel the truth about everything. When he was in the shower she would practise different opening lines.

'Samuel, remember that day we went to Ward Island, remember when…'

'Samuel, remember when you came back from the northern wilderness and we were outside looking at the stars and you asked me to forgive you… well…remember I said I knew something of what you were going through.' Did Samuel know anything about guilt brought on by lies?

'Samuel, remember the first time we went hunting and you said to me my father was one of a kind…'

None of them sounded right. Every time she thought of the telling she was gripped by fear – almost like she had that day on Ward Island. They were together and happy now, if she told him would it spoil their idyll, their wedded bliss? No, she wouldn't mar their honeymoon with this. Maybe some other time with Jonathan in her arms she would manage.

On Saturday all the family arrived in two cars. 'Hello honeymooners,' said Grandpa coming up and giving Rebecca a hug, even trying to lift her off the ground. 'It's time to stop horsing around. It's time for family time.'

'Family time is fine,' said Rebecca putting her arm around his shoulder.

Leonard on overhearing her comment, said, 'That's good, because we have some family news to share.' In the days following Lenore's death, Mr Dalton and Alistair had instigated the procedures for Jonathan's adoption. Alistair had taken affidavits and statements from Samuel, Rebecca, Leonard and Lottie as to Lenore's wishes for her son and filed all the necessary paperwork with the Charges of the State Registry and while Samuel and Rebecca were enjoying the first week of their honeymoon, the official adoption papers for Jonathan had come through, 'I know in the circumstances it's an odd thing to celebrate, but what it does is secure Jonathan's future and for that we should be grateful,' Leonard said.

'And,' said Analeise, 'it means Jonathan now has a mommy and a daddy to call his own.' She winked at her brother. 'Welcome to the club, Samuel.'

Samuel smiled at Analeise though to Rebecca he looked a little perturbed. She reached for his hand. 'You'll grow into it.' She smiled up at him.

'I dare say it's something he'll have to get used to before long,' said Grandpa.

'Yes,' said Lottie, 'we thought as a practice run, you can have him all to yourselves for a few nights this week, what do you say?'

Rebecca raised her eyebrows at Samuel. She was happy to take Jonathan but she wanted Samuel to be happy to take Jonathan as well.

'He sleeps through the night,' Lottie reminded them.

Samuel wrapped his arm around Rebecca, pulling her in close to kiss her on the temple. 'We'll gladly take him in the middle of the week,' he said, loud enough for everyone to hear.

After their honeymoon Samuel took Rebecca to Montreal for the McGill dedication service in memory of the nine medical students who gave their lives to the Great War. Samuel was going to pay his respects to his friend James Maplethorpe and have a long overdue lunch with James' parents.

In Montreal, he showed Rebecca McGill University and Mont Royal. He took her to the Royal Victorian Hospital and showed her where he had spent many hours during his third year as an intern and where he would soon return. They came across the tablet erected in honour of John McCrae. They read his inimitable poem:

In Flanders Fields the poppies blow
Between the crosses row on row,
That mark our place; and in the sky
The larks, still bravely singing, fly
Scarce heard amid the guns below.

Samuel remembered the poppies blooming, he remembered his surprise at their blooming in the midst of that barren wasteland but mostly he remembered sitting around braziers with his brother and Jack McCrae and how incredibly special those times were and how they would never come again. He hung his head and cried and when he tried to shake off his tears he said, 'At least he can keep Matthew company.'

When Rebecca heard who John McCrae was, what he had meant to Matthew, how Jonathan came to be so named, she kissed Samuel's wet cheeks. 'Such a perfect name. You must tell him this story when he is older.'

They stayed with Uncle Michel; in fact Samuel was going to board with his Uncle and Aunt when he moved back to Montreal to finish his medical degree. Samuel showed her where he played ice hockey, where he used to row, Parc Lafontaine, Notre Dame Cathedral and when Rebecca was inside gazing at the ceiling, her face alight with wonder and joy, she squeezed Samuel's hand and said. 'Now this is a church I could have got married in.' It reminded them both of their iceberg.

In August they returned to Toronto. For one week they looked after Jonathan all by themselves while Addie and Jerome holidayed with family and Lottie and Leonard went to Québec to visit her parents and Grandpa visited a friend in Orillia. They spent their days in each other's sublime presence. It was as if their honeymoon lasted for ten weeks. After a year of such intense sorrow, the abundant happiness of the newly weds seemed to be the antidote the Dalton family needed to completely re-enter their old lives.

In September Rebecca went back to school while Samuel started preparing for his return to McGill. In those final few weeks together he wanted to walk Rebecca to school in the morning and be there when she came out in the afternoon. She insisted on walking the last three blocks by herself because she did not want every schoolgirl talking about her behind her back. Lowering his voice he asked, 'What do teenage girls talk about these days?'

'I'm not saying.'

'You're denying me!'

'I am. I deny myself even. It's drivel, Samuel. That's why I have hardly any friends at school.'

'Does that bother you?'

'Very few things bother me Samuel, now that I have you in my life, now that I am your wife.'

Samuel spent his days trying to determine what his medical specialty would be. Through his own ordeal and observations while at the front, what interested him most was the subject of mental health. The condition of men suffering mental anguish moved him more than anything he'd come across in the medical profession. It seemed to be the biggest challenge and hold the most unknowns. On the lake, not far north of Toronto, was the town of Cobourg where the Cobourg Military Hospital was located. It was also the psychiatric hospital for the Canadian Army Medical Corps. Prior to going to Montreal, he paid the hospital a two-day visit and, based on what he saw, decided to apply for an intern position.

Good news and bad news awaited him in Montreal. The bad news was that a medical degree had been extended to a six-year rather than a five-year one. Had he gone back to medicine in 1918, he would have graduated under the five-year scheme. Now he had to do an extra year to gain his qualifications. He wasn't pleased about that and he imagined Rebecca wouldn't be either. The good news was that he could do a three-month internship at Cobourg in his fifth year and a three-month internship in his sixth year. That would put him closer to Toronto and mean he and Rebecca could see each other more frequently.

Spring 1920, the days were lengthening, but it still felt like the heart of winter, the ground draped in snow, the thermometer struggling to register above zero during the day, but some brave trees were valiantly blooming with little green shoots, welcoming the change of season. It was a Wednesday afternoon, the next day was the tenth of March, Samuel's birthday, and on Friday after school Rebecca was catching the train to Montreal to be with him. She came rushing out of school eager to race home and do all her study and essays as she didn't want to have to take a single textbook with her to Montreal. The weekend was for Samuel.

Two blocks out of school, she looked up and saw him standing in the middle of the cleared footpath, his hands in his pockets looking straight at her, smiling straight at her with all his teeth, his out of this world smile. She took off and within seconds she launched herself into his arms, schoolgirls or no schoolgirls behind her. She kissed him on the lips, deeply, passionately. He kissed her back, his tongue parting her lips, reaching out for hers. She could feel his fingers pressing into her back, through her coat and as he kissed her he swung her around in an arc, her feet circling above the white expanse, her hair flowing in the blurry surround. When he at last he lowered her, she breathlessly said, 'What are you doing here?'

'I couldn't wait for my birthday present.'

They nearly ran all the way home. Samuel led her around the side of the house and with his fingers up against his mouth signalled, 'Ssh'. He whispered, 'Come, climb the tree with me, like Matthew and I used to do when we were young.' They took off their shoes and put them in her school bag. He flung it over his shoulder, climbed up to the first branch and pulled her up then she followed him up the tree towards Matthew's old bedroom and he showed her how to swing across and put her foot on the sill and grab the window frame. She swung her foot out onto the sill and reached out for him, climbed through the window and within seconds she was unbuttoning her coat as he was bolting the door, clothes were piling up on the floor as Samuel was getting an early taste of his birthday present.

Later, when they went downstairs Addie looked up at them and said, 'Huh. I didn't hear you two come in.'

'That was the whole idea,' remarked Samuel.

And when Addie laughed, she didn't so much as laugh as chortle, in wicked remembrance, in lusty imaginative overtones, such was her mirth.

Rebecca wagged school on Thursday and Friday to be with Samuel who had to leave on Saturday afternoon. She wanted to spend every waking hour and every sleeping hour with him and to have family time with Jonathan. They rugged him up and took him for long walks, the packed snow creaking under their heals. Samuel would carry him on his shoulders and Jonathan would pat Samuel's head and laugh uncontrollably and wriggle his legs urging Samuel to run. Rebecca would look up and smile and he would laugh even harder, so delighted was he in Samuel's presence, so delighted were all three of them.

69

It was the week that dragged her back to her unrelenting past: the twenty-third of April, the twenty-sixth. Rebecca was grateful Samuel was away. Last year he had been home and she had dared not bring it up, so relieved that he was back and normal again but so saddened by Lenore's passing, as was everyone. Death still hovered over them. Even so, they sensed her downheartedness.

Samuel had asked, 'Was it a year ago?' She had nodded mutely, letting herself be comforted by his embrace.

On the first anniversary of her son's birth she had walked into the school gates and out the other side and walked and walked and walked till she came to a small park dotted with freesias and warm sunshine. There she sat and gave herself over to thinking completely about their son. She tried to think solely of Samson and blot out any image of her father. But his presence invaded her mind sending her into a downward spiral, till he was no longer a trespasser but the central figure in her senseless wretched week.

She thought of her mother and sister, Rachel, one year gone, and part of her ached for them, but she couldn't seem to separate them from the whole vile episode and she knew with certainty that not enough time had passed. She was far from being ready to write to any of them.

This year she tried to make a pact with herself that she would only mark Samson's birthday had he lived. She would try and imagine him as a two year old and what he might be like, what mannerisms he might have. He would be walking and she imagined clasping his hand and stopping to explore everything that caught his eye.

She thought of Catherine, Analeise's daughter, who was one year and one day older than Samson, and of Jonathan, only three weeks younger, and imagined the three of them sleeping together in a bed to keep each other warm, like she and Rachel had done when they were small.

She did slightly better the second year.

70

By summer 1920 Rachel had secured herself a position with the Newfoundland Postal Telegraph Service in St John's, sending telegrams and connecting calls. She was one of a pool of twelve women who worked shift work seven days a week.

She and her mother had stayed on with Esther to the spring of 1919. Their father did not join them for Christmas, choosing to go to the lumber camps early like a lonely dejected bachelor. During the summer of 1918 in the midst of the Crowe's heartache, Nellie Simpson had married Jonah Knowles. None of them had gone to the wedding but Silas had asked the newly married couple to housesit and tend the animals. They had been living with Jonah's parents and gladly accepted.

Months later, in March 1919, when they left Salvage, Morna went north, Rachel south. They agreed to meet up at Esther's again one day, Rachel telling her mother she never wanted to return to Deception. Through a relative of one of Esther's neighbours, Rachel found a room in a boarding house at Bowring Park, St John's, and cleaning duties to pay her way. She lived a lean, lonesome year but she managed, powering through her senior years in one year. She wrote regularly to her mother and Esther. Slowly she made friends with women she worked with, but mostly in her spare time she'd go to the St John's central library, read newspapers and borrow books. There she felt she was amongst kindred souls. Strangers who wanted company yet could hide their shyness and secrets in the library's silent hallways.

But outside one day she did talk to a young man as she held the door open for him in the midst of a fierce squall. He walked with a cane and had one trouser leg knotted at the knee. Rachel's eyes must have overflowed with sympathy but he curtly repelled her compassion. 'Don't feel sorry for me.'

'Fine' she replied, nearly undone by his rudeness, 'I'll feel sorry for those who didn't make it. I know a few.'

He looked at her then, his pale grey eyes sad and smarting, not just from the wind she thought. 'Feel sorry for their loved one's. They need it most,' he mumbled, uncomfortably looking aside.

'But then we come full circle back to you,' she murmured.

He brought his eyes back to hers and she thought they reminded her of their cove on an overcast day, so achingly familiar.

'Who are you?' he whispered almost in anguish.

'I am Rachel.'

His name was Andrew. He had survived Beaumont Hamel and upon his return and rehabilitation had trained to be a teacher. He had a prosthetic but he didn't like to wear it. They married a year later.

71

In September 1920, Samuel moved to Cobourg for his final three-month block at the hospital then he worked a three-month block at Kingston followed by a three-month assignment at the Ontario Hospital, commonly known as 999. He found the latter, despite many people's best intentions and numerous reforms to be a soul destroying place, the complete antithesis to Cobourg. Over 1200 psychiatric patients had passed through Cobourg and there wasn't a single suicide, homicide or serious accident amongst any of them. 999 on the other hand felt like a rat-infested prison, a public health hazard, an absolute pit of despair and worse, he felt powerless to effect any major changes. At the end of his final year of medicine, Samuel felt disillusioned with the major psychiatric treatment of patients in Canada and felt the best he could do for anyone was to do his utmost to keep them out of any such institution. But where did that leave him? He graduated but felt he was back to being sixteen, trying to work out his future.

To celebrate his graduation and to mark the occasion of their second wedding anniversary he took Rebecca to Québec to show her his favourite town in Canada, the way he wanted her to see it, to immerse her fully in the French Canadian culture, to visit his grandparents, to give two-year old Jonathan some time with his great grandparents and to steal Rebecca away for a night at the romantic Chateau Frontenac. He had been to the city many times but had never stayed there and always promised himself that one day he would. Now was the perfect time.

Matthew had once told him that when he found the woman he loved he must take her to one of their Premier Rooms. And so they did. They spent an evening with his grandparents and a morning, getting Jonathan comfortable with Grandmère and Grandpère who just charmed the pants off him (or was it the other way round?) and then they left for the hotel.

They were shown to their room and Rebecca did what she always did when she entered a bedroom that was hers or about to become hers, she walked in, fell back on the bed and swung her feet up in the air. Samuel loved this little quirk about her. He had told her on their honeymoon that he hoped she would still be doing it when she was ninety. I hope I can still do it when I am ninety she had replied. Today she did it and when her feet were in the air, she gasped loudly.

Samuel eyed her with concern. 'What have you done?'

'Nothing,' she said slowly placing her feet on the floor. She pointed her finger to the ceiling with a look of stunned incomprehension. 'There is a mirror on the ceiling.'

Samuel glanced up. His mouth started to tremble then he burst out laughing and fell onto the bed rolling his head from side to side.

'Samuel!' said Rebecca. 'What's so funny? How is it funny?'

Samuel continued to laugh struggling to gain his breath. He laughed so much he cried. Wiping his eyes, he sat up and said, 'I'm sorry, Rebecca. You just had to know my brother. This is Matthew to a T.'

'How?'

'Do you know what we are doing here?'

'It's our anniversary?'

'Yes, but that's not it.'

'It's a fabulous hotel?'

'Yes. But, no. Try again,'

'I don't know, Samuel. I give up.'

Taking a deep breath he tried to calm himself. 'Matthew once said to me that you never really make love to a woman till you make love to her under a mirror. I, of course, pooh-poohed the idea. And he said to me, "Suit yourself Samuel. It will be your loss."

'He also told me another time, in a completely separate conversation, when he knew you and I were secretly engaged that to show you how much you meant to me I should take you to the Chateau Frontenac and book a Premier Room, which as you have seen, is what I have done. So now that we are here in this room, under that enormous mirror, weird as it might be he's laughing along with us. He's saying I got you Samuel and the joke is on me.'

'A bit of a wasted joke though – he doesn't get to appreciate it.'

'But we do,' said Samuel, becoming serious. 'You don't have that odd aversion to mirrors still, do you?'

'No,' said Rebecca, a little indignant.

'Good, I'm pleased.' He reached for her blouse and starting to undo the buttons. 'Let's not waste any time.'

'No champagne first?' she asked.

'There will be plenty of time for champagne. Trust me. We need to make the most of daylight. Mirrors always cast a much better reflection in natural light.'

She glanced upwards. 'It feels a little weird, don't you think? Like someone is watching us.'

'Trust me,' said Samuel, as he ran his finger down her open front. 'The only one watching you will be me.'

That night after dinner they christened the bath like they had on the night of their wedding and afterwards as they were lying in the bath with a glass of champagne in their hands, Rebecca's head resting up against Samuel's shoulder, he said, 'I tell you what, we may not have made a baby these last two years, but we made you a perfect posterior.' Today I saw it in a whole new light and I think there are muscles there that I never noticed before.'

Rebecca turned to look at him. 'Are you disappointed in our inability to have a baby?'

'I am a little bit perplexed, amazed even, that after all the love we have made there is no baby on the way, but I'm not disappointed. We are still young and there is much of our life still ahead of us.' He kissed her across her brow and whispered, 'Look back on our life. I was hungry, and you fed me. I was thirsty and you gave me drink, I was a stranger and you welcomed me into your home.' He stroked her face. 'And every day you feed me, water me and welcome me home in every sense of the word and if that is my lot in life then that is enough for me. I have you and I have Jonathan and with that alone I consider myself richly blessed.'

'Samuel,' she said, her voice thick with emotion, 'I can't

explain how I know, but I just do. I know in my heart we will have a baby of our own one day. I don't know why it's taking so long but I know it is possible. We can do this. We just have to keep trying.'

'I will always keep trying,' he said as he lowered his mouth to claim hers.

72

Their time that summer had been enlightening in two ways. One, Rebecca had not fallen pregnant despite their ceaseless lovemaking. Samuel was beginning to think there was a problem. Was this meant to be a sign, a direction for him to focus his career?

And two, when Samuel looked back on his life he realised his happiest times, Rebecca aside, were when he was learning from someone who really inspired him. From his grandfather and father when he was young, from his classics teacher at school, from his brother Matthew when he was older, from his Uncle Michel and, when he travelled, when every day was new and unexpected. He knew that for him to have a career in medicine of any description he would need to work with someone who truly inspired him, someone whom being around and working with would make every day seem an exciting adventure. Once he had come to this understanding, one man came to mind.

John Gerald Fitzgerald had made great strides in the area of public health. He prepared the first anti-rabies vaccine in Canada, the first free antitoxin for diphtheria; he formed the University of Toronto Antitoxin Laboratories uniting an academic institution with the commercial production of biomedical products – a move unprecedented anywhere in the world – aiming to provide preventive medicines freely to all Canadians, regardless of class or income.

During the war when the labs were renamed the Connaught Laboratories, they pumped out vast quantities of vaccines, dramatically reducing the numbers of soldiers dying of disease in the trenches.

While Samuel never thought his future lay in pathology, he admired Gerry Fitzgerald for the egalitarian visionary that he was. He saw in him a man who could lead and inspire others and possibly be a mentor for him as John McCrae had been to Matthew.

In August 1921 Samuel went to meet Mr Fitzgerald, a man only thirteen years his senior with boundless energy and monumental ideas. To his great surprise Samuel discovered they both had favoured a career in mental health towards the end of their medical studies and both had become disillusioned with the practice. Gerry abandoned neurology and psychiatry in favour of public health and preventative medicine.

Samuel took to the man and the man took to Samuel. He encouraged Samuel to focus his studies on public health education and policy. Their meeting was meant to go for only one hour. Three hours later, Samuel was still there and his mind was full of possibilities. He left and went home to talk to his father, his grandfather and his wife. The next afternoon Gerry called to say he had a research grant for Samuel to undertake a Masters in Public Health Policy at Harvard or Johns Hopkins in Baltimore. They chose Boston. In the end they were away for two years.

After one year and much persuasion by Samuel, they took themselves off to specialists to see if they could uncover the mystery of their non-existent baby. Everything seemed to be working normally as far as Samuel was concerned. The specialist whom Rebecca saw hemmed and hawed and apologised in advance for what might appear to be an improper and delicate question before asking, 'Is it possible Mrs Dalton that way back in your youth, before you met Mr Dalton that you perhaps had intercourse with someone else? It's just that sometimes unknown to themselves women can contract diseases that render them infertile.'

Rebecca looked him squarely in the eye. 'I can assure you that I have only ever had sexual relations with my husband and if you want, you can call him in here to attest to my virginity. Could he make me infertile?' She wondered if he could tell that she had given birth to a child. 'I can't understand it,' she continued, 'the women folk in my family have always been fertile. This is as you can understand an anomaly to us.'

They stared long at each other till the silence boomed in the room, till Rebecca could no longer maintain eye contact, until her heart leapt in her throat and she could barely hold out, let alone breathe. An anguished 'No!' escaped her mouth as she covered her face with her hands, tears pooling into them, her face burning up, ashamed and horrified, knowing that if she wanted answers, if she wanted a baby, she had to tell a complete stranger what she had never told Samuel.

Alarmed by her outburst, the specialist said, 'Mrs Dalton, shall I fetch your husband?'

'No,' she said, shaking her head and lifting her face. 'Please, no!' Swearing the doctor to secrecy, Rebecca told him that whilst her husband was away at war, she had given birth to a boy which she had kept from him for fear of worrying him unnecessarily, planning to write to him after the birth, but the baby had died in his sleep when he was just a few days old. And she never told Samuel because: 'Too much death back then, too painful, too many bad memories,' she gasped, her arms wrapped around her body, hugging herself as she rocked back and forth. 'I'm sorry,' she stuttered.

Dr Simms sat across from her, his hands clutching his pen, listening intently.

'Did you know?' Rebecca sniffed.

'No,' he replied with a single shake of his head. 'You are one of those fortunate women whose body is unmarked. There is no physical evidence of you ever having a child and I doubt any of my colleagues could tell either. I just had this sense you weren't telling me everything.'

He looked at her with compassion then exhaled deeply. 'It is as you say an anomaly. Particularly as you two have produced a child together. Everything seems to be in order. You say your menstruation is completely regular. There are no blockages that I can ascertain. I imagine it's just a matter of timing and, naturally, having regular, I would go as far as to say daily relations with your husband.'

Rebecca left the room no wiser, no freer, by her admission. Perhaps if she had got an answer, an explanation from the specialist she reasoned with herself, then she could have gone home that night and told Samuel, told him everything…but she had nothing, no promise, no consolation. All she had was her appalling secret and lies. How was she ever going to face that?

They returned to Toronto in the summer of 1923 for Samuel to join the Faculty of Medicine at the University of Toronto. Gerry Fitzgerald had become the University's Professor of Hygiene and was overhauling undergraduate medical education and introducing mandatory field courses in public health. Samuel would develop and deliver part of the new syllabus. Toronto was abuzz with medical developments. Four Canadians had recently discovered insulin, the treatment for diabetes, and received the Nobel Prize. Connaught Laboratories' output of insulin and other preventive medicines put it on par with the Pasteur and Lister Institutes in Paris and London. At the same time Gerry had attracted a $1.25 million donation from the New York-based Rockefeller Foundation for the establishment of a School of Hygiene – only the third in North America.

Samuel, Rebecca and Jonathan returned to Toronto as this exciting news was breaking, but much to their surprise it was eclipsed by another major windfall. Lenore's brother Alistair had recently married the widowed daughter of one of his clients. Irene, his bride, had lost her first husband in the war when their daughter Penelope, now six, was two years old. All the Dalton family attended the wedding; the Daltons being Alistair's adoptive family after Lenore had passed away.

In a surprising act of generosity, Alistair sold the house that had once belonged to his parents, gave twenty percent of the proceeds to Samuel and Rebecca, and put another twenty per cent in a trust for Jonathan to mature when he was twenty-five. With this funding Samuel and Rebecca were able to purchase a modest home, their first, in Summerhill. No baby, but they had family around them again – Jonathan loved his cousins – and in September 1923 he started school. Two weeks later, Rebecca started Art College. She decided she would end up at 999 herself if she were at home alone for hours during the day.

73

Paris, the city of love, the city of light and gaiety, of crème buildings with black slated tiled roofs and petite iron balconies. The Louvre, the Seine, the Eiffel Tower, Sacré Coeur, the Moulin Rouge. Café au lait, croissants, chocolat, soup du jour, wine, music and dancing. Monet, Gauguin and Rodin. It was everything Samuel had ever told her and much more.

They went to Paris to celebrate their sixth wedding anniversary, to celebrate their love, to make a baby. After all, how could you not make a baby in the city of love?

Leonard and Lottie had visited two years earlier on an extended holiday to England, France, Italy and Greece. Before she left, Lottie had dug up a small bag of dirt from under the oak tree which Leonard had carried in their luggage all the way from Toronto to England to Calais to Poperinge and onto Etaples to Matthew's grave, where Lottie emptied it, so Matthew could be at peace under Canadian soil. Then they sat and had a picnic remembering their son on the day that, had he still been alive, he would have turned thirty-three.

Lottie had returned with a whole notebook full of places to visit, pensions and charming little hotels to stay in, places to have breakfast and lunch and dinner. At Samuel's request and without Rebecca's knowledge she had organised their entire tour as a surprise for Samuel and Rebecca's sixth wedding anniversary. Jonathan had stayed home with his grandparents. Every day Rebecca and Samuel would send him a postcard. She imagined him having afternoon tea at his grandparent's home in South Hill reading his daily postcard.

When she had finished school Rebecca wanted to lavish her time on Jonathan, on her husband, to fully devote herself to the elusive art of making a baby. She rested, she indulged her family, she played and she loved. They loved to distraction. Making a baby became a reckless, breathless, deliriously exciting challenge to them both and to their surprise took their love to a whole new level. They enjoyed their bodies so often and so frequently that the urge, the desire to have sex completely overshadowed the purpose of why they were having sex. They had long languorous sex, they had quick sex, they had bath sex, they had risky sex at other people's houses, they had picnic sex, they had car sex, canoe sex, they had early morning half-asleep sex, they had see how long we can go without having sex sex, they had before lunch sex while Jonathan played outside, they had we all need a little rest after lunch sex. They had quiet sex, noisy sex, sticky summer sex and warm-never-ending winter sex under all the covers, breathless midnight moonlight sex, any which way sex. But despite their intimate understandings of each other's bodies, the immense pleasure they derived from it, the clenching climaxes, the out of control orgasms – no baby, not even the slightest suggestion of a baby was forthcoming. Thirteen times a year without fail Rebecca would continue to bleed in time with the full moon, her body flowing to the mysteries of its own tide. All the while she kept on assuring Samuel, I know we can make a baby. We can. We will.

So now Paris. L'amour. Warm summer, late afternoons, completely naked, daylight love. Two beautiful, long graceful bodies, at their physical peak feasting on each other, one body half lying, prostrate, collapsed on the other. Nerve endings tingling. Taste buds alive. Gasping, exhilarating love. Giddy, champagne-infused love. Their bodies entwined, their fingers entwined high above their heads, face to face, mouth to mouth, passing tongues and passions between them, their throats dry and thirsty for water, for wine, for each other, whispering in French, the language of love, only in French.

The year was 1925. Rebecca celebrated her twenty-sixth birthday in Paris. Samuel had turned thirty a few months before. His hair was thick and long and straight on top, short at the back and the sides. Hers was thick and long, halfway down her back again. No fashionable pageboy bob for her, no wavy permanent flapper set. They had the look of casual freedom about them and when they looked into a mirror, when they looked into each other's eyes, at each other's bodies, both liked what they saw. Still young and beautiful and in love in Paris. Lovers in Paris. They turned heads everywhere they went. A living, walking, breathing monument to the city of love. Even the locals wanted some of what they were having. They would never forget Paris.

But even so Paris did not bless their boundless love with a longed-for baby.

Rebecca was becoming increasingly exasperated with her inability, their inability, to produce a baby. She couldn't understand what was wrong with her body? What was wrong with Samuel's? She asked him one day was he exposed to any poisonous gas while he was in the war, thinking that might have something to do with it. No, he said. He asked her if she wanted to go and see another specialist. And what do you think that will achieve she asked? She felt fettered by her secret but at the same time she couldn't even begin to imagine how she could tell Samuel now after all this time.

Part of her felt like writing old Mrs Hooper, the octogenarian midwife back in Deception, to see if there was something she was meant to be doing, taking, something peculiar to getting pregnant a second time. Her obsession with a baby started to smother everything. She couldn't understand how they could not have made a baby in Paris. She had pinned all her hopes on Paris as if that was her last chance and for the first time in their married life, she started to lose interest, in lovemaking. She saw herself as barren and decrepit, unable to make a baby for her husband after all the love he had given her. Making love became a disappointment to her, a sharp reminder of what they had tried for, for so long, yet didn't have. What was the point? She felt like cursing her parents, her father mainly. But then she remembered that phrase she had learnt in Latin: *De mortuis nil nisi bonum*. Say nothing but good about the dead. But her parents weren't dead. Or were they?

Fall came and she became vapid and withdrawn, not just to Samuel, not just to Jonathan, even to herself.

In all this time the person she was grateful for was Lottie. She understood their frustrations and heartache and disappointment and to her everlasting credit, Lottie nor any of the family, ever said, 'When are you going to give Jonathan a baby brother or a sister?' She never said, 'When are you going to give me another grandchild?' She held her tongue and did her best to boost Rebecca's spirits until one day she found Rebecca crying when she came to visit and that was when she took Rebecca in her arms and said, 'Rebecca, I wish I could wave a magic wand and make it all happen for you. I wish I were a genie in a magic bottle and could grant you three wishes. I pray for the two of you every day and I will keep on praying.'

That Christmas a large wooden box with Samuel's name and address painted on the top in stencilled letters was delivered to their door. Two men had to carry it, it was that heavy. She told them to leave it on the porch in the sub-zero temperatures for Samuel to deal with when he came home. She had no idea what it was. 'What is it?' asked Jonathan, when he came home from school. He knocked on the wood. 'It's not a coffin is it?'

'No, it's not a coffin.'

'Do you know what it is?' said Jonathan to his father when he came home.

'I have some idea,' said Samuel. Looking at Rebecca he said, 'So does your Mommy if she thought hard about it, if she thought about her trip to Paris.'

Rebecca looked at him and took her mind back, then, it came to her. She shuddered and not just because of the cold and the snowflakes lightly falling to the ground. 'Did you go ahead and place the order?' she asked.

'Yes,' he said.

'What is it, Daddy?'

'It's a statue, two statues of your Mommy and me.'

'Miniature statues?'

'No, life size, but only of our torsos. From our hips to our necks.'

'So how can you tell that it's you?'

'Well once you get to know someone's body, your own body you can tell these things. But more than that it's art. A celebration of a person's special talent and the beauty in life.'

'Can I see? Are you going to open it?'

'Ah, Samuel, do you think this is a good idea?'

'Rebecca, how do you want our son to grow up? Afraid of the human body or in love with it?'

She reluctantly conceded. Samuel left to find some tools.

While he was away, Rebecca said, 'Jonathan, I want you to know that these statues won't have any clothes on them. It will be just of the body, from here to here,' she demonstrated, 'like Daddy said, but they won't be the colour of the body, or normal skin. They will be burnished, black, charcoal looking. Understand? Two people, an adult male and an adult female body.'

'Yes, Mommy,' He stared at the lid of the box, waiting for it to open like a magical trap door.

Samuel prised the box open and lifted the top. Inside was a swaddling of red and green velvet. 'Can you give me a hand with this box please, Rebecca?'

Jonathan held the door open while they carried the box inside and deposited it on the floor in the hallway. Samuel bent and lifted the red velvet bundle out of the box and Jonathan helped him unroll it. When he stood it on its base it was like they were looking at a little bit of ancient Greece in their living room. 'Could be Zeus or Apollo,' said Rebecca looking at it.

'Is that you, Daddy?' asked Jonathan.

'Yes,' he said, 'do you think it looks like me?'

'I don't know. Take off your shirt!'

Samuel rested the statue on its base and pulled off his jumper, his shirt and his long-sleeved undershirt. He knelt next to his statue. Jonathan took a few steps back and eyed them both, as did Rebecca. Samuel looked up at Rebecca. 'Very impressive,' she said with a weak smile.

Jonathan came up and rubbed his little hands across Samuel's shoulders, and then across the statue's shoulders.

'Ah,' he gasped, 'the statue's very cold! But he continued to rub his hands across the statue's chest and his father's chest once more. 'Very good.' He pronounced. 'Let's see the other one.'

They pulled the green bundle out of the box and unraveled it. Samuel placed it next to his statue. Jonathan stared in awe at the statue's breasts. Samuel couldn't help but smile. He looked up at Rebecca and was about to say, 'What do you think?' when she burst into tears and ran upstairs.

Jonathan turned to see her departing back. 'Doesn't she like hers, Daddy?'

She was upstairs lying on their bed crying when she heard

Samuel whisper, 'Rebecca.' He kicked off his shoes and crawled across and put his arms around her. 'I didn't mean to upset you.' He kissed her on her neck.

'I know.' She squeezed his hand. 'But tell me, what do you see when you look at the statue of me?'

'I see a beautiful woman, a shadow, a black negative of the real one in front of me right now. What do you see?'

'I see a pathetic excuse for a woman. A childless woman. A woman with breasts that ache to nurse a child.' She was if anything unconvinced.

'I see a woman who is incredibly sensual, the very epitome of womanhood and inherent in that is a woman who one day will bear children and nurse them at her breasts. I see a woman in the prime of her life offering herself to a man at the peak of his wanting to celebrate their love for each, wanting to celebrate their bodies, wanting to create something beautiful out of their union. I still see it. It's all ahead of us still.'

'Yes, Samuel,' she said, the certainty in her voice eggshell thin.

'We've got to keep loving each other Rebecca if we want to have a baby. We can't give up. There won't be any baby without sex, without love, unless you believe in Immaculate Conception, unless you believe the angel Gabriel is going to pay you a visit.'

'Huh,' she said almost in disgust. If the truth were known some days she did wonder about Immaculate Conception. If indeed that was how Samson had been conceived and that would explain why that baby had come unbidden into the world. In her darkest hours she wondered if Samuel had actually fathered Samson or whether he had been a holy child or worse as her father swore, implanted by Hades.

'Rebecca, remember our wedding day, remember what I said when I placed the ring on your finger.' He reached for her hand and found her ringed finger. 'To look at this ring as a testament to what you can survive, what we can survive together and the riches and rewards ahead of you, ahead of us. We are just going through one of those trying times that couples go through in their marriage, but all is not lost, when you think about it we are infinitely better off than we were before we married. The pain of losing all our loved ones has

436

diminished and we have Jonathan. Please don't forget Jonathan,' he begged. 'He loves us as much as any child could love their parents. He is a little angel and for him alone we should offer our thanks. But mostly Rebecca, please don't forget us. That is the best part of our lives. Us. We didn't make a baby in Paris, but we made those two busts downstairs and I thought they might remind you of the best thing about Paris. Us. That we have each other. That we are together.

'I know your heart is breaking because we haven't had a baby yet. I yearn for a child of our own too. But my heart is breaking more over what is happening to us. Open your eyes to us. You have given us up, as if we are part of the problem rather than part of the solution. Jonathan and I are here, right now in your life, wanting you to love us, wanting you to be totally present to the moments you spend with us. That is what I yearn for most. That's what I want most, to love you again like we loved in Paris, to have you love me again like you did in Paris, like we have done all our married lives before Paris. Where is the Rebecca who I know, who I love? Did we lose her in Paris? I will never love Paris again if we did.'

She inhaled deeply then sobbed in release. With an effort she turned to face Samuel and placed her hand on his face. 'I'm sorry. I'm sorry,' she cried. 'I'm sorry I've been so absent. I'm sorry I've been so withdrawn. I'm sorry I have let this wanting to have a baby get the better of me.' Neither of them stanched her tears.

'You're forgiven,' said Samuel pressing his lips to her forehead.

'I haven't forgotten us. I swear I could never forget us.' She kissed him on the lips, wiping her tears on his cheeks.

'Well I'm pleased to hear that.'

'I remember the good times we had in Paris, Samuel. I loved Paris.'

'Me too. We had days and afternoons and nights of good times and didn't we have fun making those casts?' Samuel had covered Rebecca's body in clay and she had covered his. It had been one erotically charged day.

'Yes,' she said, surrendering a little sigh. 'But we weren't thinking too far ahead. At the time I didn't ever think we would go ahead with the full models. Where are we going to put those things?'

'On the front porch for all the neighbours to admire.'

'Maybe we just leave them in the box.'

'We are not leaving them in the box. Don't you think they are beautiful?'

'Yes,' she cried.

'Good, well they are coming out. They are going on display.'

He kissed her and she kissed him back both tasting her salty tears. They kissed deeply and slowly, a healing kiss, the beginning of make-up love.

'Do you feel like going on display now?'

She caught his eye. 'We'll have to be quick.'

'Oh I can be quick, not that I always like to be quick, but needs must.' He had already pulled her shirt off and her skivvy and had his hands on her brassiere – the days of the corset were long gone – when they heard a little voice say, 'Mommy, are we going to have dinner soon? I'm starving.'

They turned to look at Jonathan, the stealth walker, standing in their doorway.

'Yes, honey.' She smiled at him.

'What are you doing on top of Daddy?' he asked.

'Oh…just playing.'

'Can I play too?'

'Sure honey, come up here and we'll all have a roll around the bed together.'

74

When Morna arrived back home in May 1919, she pulled on her apron and got on with the life she chose. Silas and her were civil to each other and even considerate. Both did their duties in terms of their partnership and providing for the other. Upstairs they slept in separate rooms. They talked about happenings in the bay, about developments in the newspaper, about updates from their daughters. Sometimes they chuckled at something. They rarely laughed. They certainly didn't guffaw.

Every two or three years they managed a trip to Salvage in the spring to visit their daughters and grandchildren. They never mentioned Rebecca or Samuel or Samson.

With the passing of the years Silas kept to himself more and more. Morna enjoyed the company of Ronnie and Meg, Mabel Hendersen and others in the bay. She'd ride Mica over and back, using a stump to help her get on and off. She thought of Samuel and Rebecca every time she caught the mare.

She asked herself, how does one regain respect and trust? What would her husband have to do for her to feel differently towards him? What would she have to do to reinstate her respect for him? For even though she carried on, she worked hard to find things that she could respect him for, because, sometimes, what she couldn't respect him for was too overwhelming.

For years she held out for an apology. A simple sorry for what happened to Rebecca – an admission that he felt responsible for driving their daughter to take her own life. But nothing ever passed his lips.

If Rebecca had not drowned herself, perhaps Morna would have forgiven him for what he did to Samson. Strangely her daughter had not been as strong as Morna thought, though perhaps she was stronger, strong enough to say: enough.

One night in 1925, not long after they had just marked the first birthday of Esther's seventh child and Rachel's second, Silas picked up his Bible and flicked through the thin yellow pages. The book fell open at Matthew 18, the 'Suffer the little children to come unto me' passage that he read the day he baptised Samson. It was the first time he had looked at that since that irreversible day. There immediately below the section he'd read in the tender was the verse:

'If anyone should cause one of these little ones to lose his faith in me, it would be better for that person to have a large millstone tied around his neck and be drowned in the deep sea. How terrible for the world that there are things that make people lose their faith. Such things will always happen but how terrible for the one who causes them.'

Slowly awareness trickled through and to his utmost horror, Silas realised that he was that person. And the little one referred to in the Scripture was not Samson but Rebecca. What had he done?

'My God! My God!' he yelled, his hands squeezing his head as he rocked back and forth, his face misshapen, as if the muscles were pushing and pulling it in all directions, almost as if he were having an apoplexy.

Morna had never seen him in such a state. She came towards him, but stood a little distance away unsure as to how to help.

'I've damned her to hell for all eternity.'

'Damned who?'

'Rebecca!' he said in utter anguish.

'I turned her away from God and then she chose death. How can she ever be saved? My God, forgive me! Forgive me!' he bellowed. 'Save her. I'm sorry! I'm sorry!'

'What exactly are you sorry for?' asked Morna, bewildered.

'I'm sorry that by my actions I have denied her eternal life.'

'You don't know that for sure.' Though in that moment Morna had her doubts. She remembered Rebecca's hollow upset words the day Samson was drowned. At long last the anger and the hurt Morna had held in check for such long years broke loose and she hurled the words forth in fury and bitterness.

'Well, thank you for denying me the joy of having my daughter by my side in eternal life! It wasn't enough to deny me the joy of her presence in this life! What have you got to say about that? Are you sorry for that? What will you say to our daughter when you're resting in peace with her son in heaven while she's burning down below in the pit fire of hell? Are you sorry for that? What will you say to Samson – separated from his mother as well for all eternity? You better think about that, Silas, work out how you are going to make amends because every day you live is one day closer to the grave and you're going to be a long time dead.'

The next morning when Morna arose Silas was down in the kitchen with the lamp burning, poring over the Bible like how he had done all those years ago before he baptised and banished Samson. Here we go again she thought, and she was instantly on guard. He had a notepad next to him and would jot down lines from time to time. He sat at the table all day engrossed in what – she wasn't sure – how to undo the impossible.

He went down below the following morning and when he came up for lunch he said, 'I have never been good at apologies. They have never come easy to me. I don't know why that is but it is. I can't sit here now in front of you and apologise. So I am writing down, the words I can never seem to say.' He handed her a sealed envelope addressed to Ronnie Evans and asked if she would mind taking it across that afternoon.

Ronnie,

You have always been a good neighbour and a good friend, a man we can always count on. I ask your help now because I know you will give it. My life is drawing to a close. And I don't want Morna to suffer alongside me, so I will do what needs to be done. I hope by my actions I cause her but little pain, for she has had enough pain for one life. Please help her to leave here and go to

Salvage to be with Esther and family. They will ease her days. She deserves to be happy.

Thank you and goodbye,
Silas

Ronnie would not let Morna return to the house. He took Jonah with him instead. They borrowed a motorboat and in less than half an hour were in the Crowe's cove. He feared he would be too late and he was, but to his relief, nature had intervened. They found Silas lying on the stage, lifeless. Nearby was a large splintered hole. Below in the shallow water they saw a large boulder. Ronnie marveled at how one man could have carried it so far.

When Morna returned to her home she found two letters on the kitchen table.

My dear Morna,

You have been a good wife and a good mother. I have tried my best in many things but now I see in some things I have been a tool of the devil. That is not an excuse because I know God gives us free will.

Many times these passing years I have taken comfort in the verse, "It is better to suffer for doing good, if this should be God's will, than for doing evil." But now I know with dread that I have not done God's will. I have done the opposite.

As you said the other night, in a little while I will depart this earth and, God willing, enter into Heaven and a new earth. I think you will find on earth at least the punishment will fit the crime. When I face judgment I will do my all to bargain for Rebecca's life, trade places with her if that is what it boils down to. For my sins are far greater than hers.

You and I have lost our share of children along the way. But to lose Rebecca like we did was the hardest. I know her loss grieves you still to this day. And I know we lost her because of me.

I am not fit to be her father. I am not fit to be your husband. I am sorry. Take care, my Morna. Say goodbye to Esther and Rachel.

I hope one day we meet again in peace.
Silas

Next to her letter was an unsealed one, addressed to Rebecca, clearly meant for Morna to read and, after she had read it, she realised for her daughters as well.

75

Samuel had been invited to talk at a Public Health Forum in St John's, Newfoundland, organised by a group of local doctors eager to adopt initiatives being implemented in Ontario. Of all the Maritime Provinces, of all the major metropolitan regions in Canada, St John's had the poorest child mortality record. There would be presentations and workshops on a range of medical, nutritional, educational and social issues concerning the health of minors.

Over dinner one evening he said to Rebecca, 'I know the thought of Newfoundland is painful, but maybe enough time has passed. Maybe you can go back, to the southern part at least and create some new and happy memories of Newfoundland. I understand if you don't want to come, but I am going to this conference and I thought you and Jonathan might like to accompany me. Don't say no straight away, think about it.'

Understandably she was decidedly non-committal. Jonathan on the other hand jumped at the idea of the trip, literally jumped at it.

'Do you like the idea of an overseas holiday?'

'Yes,' he said clapping his hands.

'Would you like to go on a big ferry?'

'Yes!' he said springing up on his toes.

'Would you like to go see the country where your Mommy comes from?'

'Yes,' his head nodding a hundred to the minute.

'He's not going to see where I come from.' Rebecca was not keen at all.

'I'm not talking Second Chance, Rebecca. I'm talking St John's. Have you ever been to St John's?'

'No.'

'Then why don't you want to go?'

'What for, Samuel? What's there to see and do there?'

'Well I know it's not Paris, but I think we could still enjoy ourselves and have fun. I hope I haven't spoilt you for the simple things in life. I have only been there briefly in 1914 and I would be happy to see it again.'

'Well if you've been there then, why don't we go to Nova Scotia or Prince Edward Island? Now there's a place I wouldn't mind visiting.'

'Well maybe we can go there another time, but I'm going to St John's as that is where this conference is and I was hoping my wife and son would like to join me.'

She acceded at last.

'Thank you. Maybe we can go to St Vincent's Bay if the whales are there. And if we have time I would love to go to Gros Morne National Park. I hear that is meant to be beautiful.'

'Yes, I've heard the same.'

As they walked around St John's, Samuel, not Rebecca, gave Jonathan a history lesson on Newfoundland. 'This is where the North American day dawns first, the easternmost edge of the continent. And this town, St John's, is the oldest English-founded city and Water Street, the oldest street in North America.'

Jonathan was only half listening. 'How do you say the name of this place again Mommy?'

'NewfoundLAND like underSTAND. The emphasis is on the last syllable.'

'NewfoundLAND, NewfoundLAND,' Jonathan practised under his breath.

They walked out along the northern side of the peninsula till they came to the Narrows that form the entrance to the waterway and could admire the magnificent sheltered inlet that was St John's Harbour. They explored Signal Hill National Historic Park, the Queen's Battery, Cabot Tower, and the site where Marconi received the first trans-Atlantic radio message in 1901.

They all agreed St John's was charming. They loved the way the city rose from the harbour front, with narrow streets and terraces of colourfully painted clapboard terrace houses.

Along Water Street they walked, along Duckworth and Gower, gazing at three storey houses adorned in ocean shades of deep blue and green with contrasting window trim.

'Different to Deception and Seldom Come By?' asked Samuel.

'Yes,' said Rebecca. 'Brighter. Different to any place I've been.' But the wind was the same and the light. In the late afternoon, it was warm and haunting and beautiful. She couldn't work out if it was making her nostalgic or whether it was in itself melancholic. It was oddly comforting and at the same time oddly unsettling. It seemed to reinforce those strangling feelings of isolation she had in her youth. She shuddered as she tried to shake her sense of unease. She almost felt like she was going to get sucked into a lost world and Samuel and Jonathan would not be able to find her. She gripped both their hands tightly.

'What do people do here, Mommy?'

'Fish mainly, sail the oceans.'

'See all those boats down on the waterfront,' said Samuel waving with his hand, 'St John's is a sailor's town.'

'What do they fish for?'

'Cod mainly. They go to the Grand Banks and spend weeks on end fishing for cod. The inshore fishermen fish for cod too and flounder, and herring, lumpfish, lobster and capelin. They jig for squid as well.'

'What's jig for squid?'

'It's a method of catching the squid. If we see someone doing it, I'll point it out to you.'

'And they catch salmon too, Rebecca, some of the world's best salmon.'

'Yes,' she said, remembering. 'And in spring, the men head north to hunt harp and hood seals. They give birth to their young on ice floes. Some people like to eat seal flippers.'

'Do you, Mommy?'

'No, Jonathan, I don't like the thought of seals pups being killed. They are too innocent and helpless. We should let them live their lives for a while. But a lot of people don't have much choice in the matter. Food isn't always as easy to come by here as it is in Toronto.

'When I was growing up a seal saved our family's life once.

It was the end of March and we had not had a good summer the year before so by the end of winter we were without food. Early one morning my father decided to head off to the merchant to see if we could get an advance on our account for some food. Before he left he had this urge to go down to our stage and there on a floe just a few metres from the shore was a large seal. He crept back home for his rifle and we lived off that seal for nearly three weeks. It filled our bellies when there was nothing else to.'

'When was that?' asked Samuel.

Rebecca looked at him. 'In early 1917,' she said, almost inaudibly.

'You never told me! Why didn't you write? We could have sent you some supplies.'

'You can guess why Samuel.' There was no mistaking her meaning. Samuel just shook his head.

Tugging her hand, Jonathan asked, 'Couldn't you catch any fish?'

'No Jonathan, they had gone away. It sounds strange when the sea is full of fish but there are times when people spend weeks catching hardly any food. And it's not just a matter of catching what they need for themselves; they need to catch more fish to exchange for flour for their bread and other meat to supplement their diets and for clothes to wear.'

'So they need to catch the fish 'cos it's like money to them.'

'Yes,' said Rebecca, as she gazed out to sea.

Jonathan tugged her hand, again. 'Mommy, what are you thinking?'

'Just remembering a way of life. Why don't we read the newspaper tomorrow while Daddy's at his conference and we can learn more about what people do here?'

76

On the first day of his conference Samuel strolled the twenty minutes from their hotel in Queen Street to the recently opened Memorial University College in Parade Street. Being new, the campus lacked stately trees and established gardens and, it would appear, outdoor shelter of any description. With university in recess the conference was being held in the main lecture hall. Inside the central front stairs there was a long corridor that ran the length of the entire building, bench seats up against both walls. As he was one of the opening presenters, Samuel followed a directional sign, looking for the entrance to the hall, oblivious to the people waiting on the seats. A female voice called out, 'Samuel. Samuel Dalton.'

He turned and a woman he'd just passed stood and stepped forward. He smiled, thinking perhaps she was on the conference secretariat there to assist him, but a second later his smile faltered. The blood drained from his face. He felt his heart pound and his stomach lurch.

'Rachel?'

'Samuel!' she cried, as she came up to him and placed her hand on his arm. 'Samuel, I thought you died in the war. For years I thought that till just the other day when I read about you and I thought how could there be two Doctor Samuel Daltons from Toronto.'

'That was a misprint. It was Matthew who was killed.'

Rachel slowly shook her head. Her eyes scanned his face while his scanned hers.

'I thought **you** were dead,' Samuel said, 'That you died in a fire.'

He was incredulous. Rebecca, the woman he had loved for more than a decade, his wife of seven years, had deceived him. He couldn't believe it. But more than that, the question that thundered down was: why? Why would she tell such a lie?

What had happened to her to make her do such a thing?

'Me, no,' said Rachel, shaking her head in confusion. 'Why would you ever think that?'

Samuel stood there utterly stupefied. His wife's sister wasn't dead, but she hadn't contacted Rebecca in how many years? And why hadn't she? Wouldn't Rachel know where Rebecca was? Or had she contacted Rebecca and had Rebecca kept that from him as well? Shaking his confounded head, he let out a ragged sigh. 'Because Rebecca–'

'Rebecca!' Rachel stifled a strangled gasp and grabbed Samuel's arm as she stumbled forward. He steadied her with his free hand. 'Oh, I knew it! I knew it in my gut, I knew it!' She inhaled sharply, 'When did you last see her?'

For the briefest instant he hesitated. 'Half an hour ago.' Samuel hoped in telling the truth he was doing the right thing. Where was his ice-maiden of a wife when he needed answers?

'She's here! In St John's?'

Samuel nodded. 'With our son, Jonathan.'

'Where is she?' Her earnest eyes pleaded.

'At the Bluestone Inn.' He glanced at his watch. At that very minute he wanted to be there himself but he didn't have time. He would have to spend all day in suspense, unless he opened his mouth right then and started asking Rachel questions. But did he really want to do that? No, he wanted to give Rebecca the chance to explain herself first. Did he want her to have the pressure of them both bearing down on her? He sighed again. 'I'm sorry I can't take you there. I'm on in fifteen minutes I'm afraid.'

Rachel nodded. She looks as if she were in daze, then she raised her eyes to Samuel, they filled with tears, her lips trembled. 'Do you think she would want to see me?'

'Oh Rachel,' he groaned, pulling her into his arms and pressing his cheek to her head, 'Don't even give her the choice.'

77

Samuel called out as he let himself in. 'Hello, I'm home.'

Running up to him, Jonathan said with a laugh, 'This is not our home, Daddy.'

'Isn't it?' said Samuel, picking up his son and giving him a hug and a kiss on the cheek. 'I know it's not, but it is in one sense. My home is wherever you and Mommy are. It doesn't matter that much about the location. It's about the people.'

'You sometimes call Nana Dalton's place home.'

'I do, don't I? That's because it was my home for many years and it will always be a home for me. And for you,' giving him a squeeze. 'Just like our home will always be your home, even when you are a grown man and living elsewhere with children of your own. What did you get up to today, bud? Did you go to the park?' asked Samuel lowering the boy.

'Yes, this afternoon. I played with Simon and Mary. Simon's four and Mary, well she's only two, and they live over Pippy Park way and we can go and play with them tomorrow as well.'

'That's good.'

'Mom said they are my cousins. And the lady Rachel is my Aunty. Is that true?'

Samuel exhaled. 'Yes.' He gently squeezed Jonathan's shoulder. In a tight voice, he asked, 'Where is your mother?'

'She's lying down. She said she had a headache.'

'I bet she has.'

'That's why I'm here playing pairs like she asked me to. Do you want to play with me?'

'Yes. Once I see how Mommy is. Be a good boy like you always are.' Samuel swept Jonathan's fringe across his head.

Samuel quietly opened the door to the bedroom and walked towards the bed. It was dark inside the room except for the dull light of the lamp on the dresser giving an ancient and mellow gloom to the room. Rebecca was lying on the bed with her back to him. 'Rebecca,' he said softly as he came up to her. 'Rebecca,' he said again.

She rolled over and said, 'Huh' in a voice that came from a raw and broken place. Her nose was red like her eyes.

Reaching out he touched her shoulder with his left hand and said, 'Are you alright?'

'No,' she cried in a broken whimper.

'Move over.' He nudged her on the hip so he could sit on the bed beside her. 'Was it good to see Rachel again?'

'Yes,' she cried in the same choked whimper.

'What –'. He broke off. What was he going to ask her? Only she could decide the telling.

'Samuel,' she cried, pushing herself back up on the pillow. 'I –,' she faltered. She tried again. 'I…' The word hardly sounding like I, in a voice that bore little resemblance to her own. 'I'm so sorry,' she breathed out at last and inhaled a small sob as she placed the back of her arm across her forehead, a damp white handkerchief crumpled in her hand. 'I'm so sorry.' She squeezed her eyes closed to trap the tears. She failed. Her face was awash with wetness and misery.

'Sshh, come on, it's okay.' He brought her into his embrace. 'It will be okay. Let's just get this over with.'

She clung onto him fiercely while she cried, and cried and cried and tried to settle herself, all the while Samuel gently rocked her and tried to soothe her with his gentle, swaying shh. After a while, with her head resting on his shoulder, he heard her say in a hollow voice, 'I don't know where to begin, Samuel, I just don't know where. I know there are things I should have told you. Told you a long time ago, but after a while, I just wanted to remember them the way they were. The way they were that first summer you came. And that's how I wanted you to remember them. But I also have these other memories and once I tell you they will be inside you too and it will be between us and there will never be a way of undoing that and I'm frightened that might cloud what you think of them and destroy the good memories you have.'

'And so you don't want to tell me?'

A strangled 'no' escaped her mouth. She shuddered. 'But I

know I have to.' Sniffing, she said, 'Now that I have seen Rachel again. Oh, I have missed her. I have ached for her. I have ached for her like I have ached for a child of my own.'

Samuel pressed his lips to her head and whispered, 'So tell me, Rebecca.'

'I am so ashamed.' The tears cascaded down her cheeks, dampening his shoulder. 'I have let anger and bitterness come between me and the people I love. I have let arrogance and stubbornness become a part of me. You name it, I own it. And I cannot even look at you, so ashamed am I at what I have kept hidden from you all these years.'

'Rebecca, look at me.' He pulled her away from him. 'Look at me.'

Slowly she raised her sad shaking eyes to him.

'There is nothing you can say or do that will make me think anything less of you. I have known you now for nearly half of your life. You have always been and always will be a good woman, Rebecca Crowe. Rebecca Dalton.' He placed his hand over her heart. 'I know it. You know it and I am eternally blessed that you are my good woman. So let us have this out. Maybe with the passing of time, there are some things we can salvage.'

With her head lowered, Rebecca blew her nose. Quietly she said, 'I need a drink please, Samuel.'

'Water or something harder?'

'Both,' she croaked, almost inaudibly.

When he returned she was sitting up on the bed, her hair undone, loose around her shoulders, in her hand, a piece of paper

'Here you go.' He placed both glasses onto the side table. She gulped a few mouthfuls of sherry and like bitter medicine washed it down with the water.

'What do you have there?' he asked.

'A letter from my father.'

'Is your father still alive?'

'No,' she cried, shaking her head slightly, her lips trembling. 'He died last year, apparently.'

'I see,' said Samuel.

'I'll let you read it later.'

He waited. There was a long silence. Then Rebecca took a

deep breath and said with a shaking voice, 'There's a story I want to tell you'. Wetting her lips she wavered but managed to maintain eye contact with Samuel. 'For most people, this is a biblical prophecy, but for me it is a story from the past.' Samuel looked at her face intently, his hands on her thighs, having no idea what to expect. Inhaling she continued:

'One day a great and mysterious sight appeared in the sky: a young woman, whose dress was the sun and who had the moon under her feet and a crown of twelve stars on her head. She was soon to give birth, and the pains and suffering of childbirth made her cry out.'

Her voice broke, but she carried on:

'Then another mysterious sight appeared in the sky. There was a huge red dragon with seven heads and ten horns and a crown on each of his heads. With his tail he dragged a third of the stars out of the sky and threw them down to the earth. He stood in front of the woman, in order to eat her child as soon as it was born. She gave birth to a son, who was to rule over all the nations. But the child was snatched away and taken to God and his throne. The woman fled to the desert to a place God had prepared for her, where she was taken care of.'

She finished. Her chilling blue eyes gazed deeply into Samuel's.

Samuel did not blink. He did not breathe. After an immeasurable length of time he inhaled and asked, 'Did you have a child? Did something happen to your child?' Rebecca looked at him through a wet blurred haze, unable to answer him, unable to enlighten him. Her head rolled slowly from side to side in her lament as she sucked in her lips holding whatever was inside, inside. After a spell, he asked a different question. 'Was it Rachel then?'

'No, Samuel,' she cried as her head teetered, wavering mournfully of its own volition. 'I had a child. **We** had a child. You and I. A little boy. His name was Samson. He lived for three days.'

There was prolonged silence…an eternal moment…then a throaty whisper. 'Oh Rebecca,' and overcome with emotion he hugged her hard, the letter pressed between them, as he rocked her back and forth muttering, 'I'm so sorry. I'm so sorry. I wish you could have told me. How could you not have told me! To carry this around all these years by yourself?' What happened?'

She responded with a strangled moan.

'Come on, don't stop now. Out with it, you're doing so well. Come on, my brave Venus.' Samuel rubbed her back and did his all to coax her.

When at last she regained a semblance of composure Rebecca looked at Samuel and shook her head in finality. 'That, I cannot speak about. I have lived it once and that was too much. I won't live it again through the telling, but here, read the letter and you will know what came to pass.'

Dear Rebecca,

I write to you as if you are still living fore there are things I need to say to you. I pray that you are above and can see the words on the page and know what is in my heart. With the fullness of time I see how I wronged you and how I wronged God. What was I thinking that I could interpret dreams? I am no prophet of God. I let evil be my guide wreaking my revenge on Samuel and you by taking your innocent son.

As you know the Bible says, "if you forgive others the wrongs they have done you, your Father in Heaven will also forgive you. But if you do not forgive others, then your Father will not forgive the wrongs you have done." So Rebecca, I tell you in all that I hold sacred that I forgive you. I forgive Samuel too, for the shame and the heartache and the nightmare we found ourselves in. I forgive you most for ending your life and tearing our family apart for it was I who drove you to that. And I see now that I am at fault.

The day you lost a son, was the day Morna and I lost a daughter, perhaps even more dear to us, for we had the loving of her for 18 years. You were the son I never had. All of us have been punished by your actions and mine. But now I see it is me that must carry the burden of both for my crime is far greater. Morna has been denied a daughter and Rachel and Esther a sister they loved dearly, as well as a grandson and nephew. I pray that Samson in Heaven will look down on me and forgive me for plunging him into such an early, icy grave, for robbing him of his mother.

My greatest wrong and my greatest fear is that I turned you from God and you have ended up in damnation for all eternity. If that is the case I will do my all to take your place. I have prayed many times over to be forgiven for taking not one but two lives and for turning you from the Lord. I trust in him, yet still my heart is not at peace. For how could it be when I have done this to you – this, the greatest of sins – and I fear for where you are.

My greatest prayer is that you are in heaven with Samuel and Samson. I pray that when next we see each other, you will have found it within you to forgive me, so we can comfort each other in mercy.

Your sorry father,
Silas Crowe

Samuel put down the letter. With a lump in his throat he could not dislodge he reached for Rebecca. 'Come here, you.' He hugged her. He squeezed her. He rubbed her back and caressed her arms as they cried together, drowning in tears of sorrow, tears of heartbreak, tears of love. When they eventually broke apart, Samuel wiped his eyes, gently did the same to Rebecca then kissed her eyelids. When she opened her eyes Samuel said, 'Did you see him drown the boy?' his voice breaking on 'boy'.

Rebecca nodded.

'Where did this happen?'

'About ten minutes row from our stage.'

'What were you doing on the boat to begin with?'

'We had gone out to baptise Samson.' Samuel stared at her, waiting. 'When he finished baptising him, he just rolled his arm over and let him fall into the water.' Rebecca started crying again. Samuel grasped her hands and squeezed them. 'I dived in after him, but I couldn't find him. I'm so sorry.'

'Rebecca, look at me! You have **nothing** to be sorry for. Believe me. Where were your mother and Rachel while this was happening?'

'They were waiting for us onshore. It was fogged in. They never saw a thing.'

She told him then about the night she planned to drown herself, how just before the point of no return she could not go through with it, how she fled in the night, how and why she came up with the fire story, the two letters she'd intercepted.

All the time Rebecca spoke, Samuel's eyes did not break from Rebecca's. From time to time he brushed her face with the back of his fingers. When she finished he exhaled deeply. 'To think that you went through all of this and made your own way to Toronto by yourself and I didn't welcome you with open arms, I am so ashamed.'

'Your family welcomed me with open arms and that meant everything to me at the time. I went there, knowing you weren't going to be there. When you returned you had enough heartache of your own.'

Samuel's heart ached for his wife. He searched her eyes. 'How did you survive?'

Rebecca sighed. 'I had faith and hope and love for you.' She paused. 'Being in your presence and being able to look on your face was the best I could hope for some days. That is true. And your family comforted me. They were an extension of you. I had Jonathan and if I could have I would have carried him around with me on my chest all day, as a sort of armour against the world and a balm against the pain in my heart.'

Samuel kissed her tenderly on the lips. Holding her hands in his, amazement in his voice, he said, 'I can't believe we made a baby you and I?'

'Yes,' she inhaled.

'Well that means we can make one again.'

'I've been trying to tell you this for quite a few years.' Her lips curled into a sad smile.

He smiled in return, lightly shaking his head. 'You had proof though. No wonder your faith has been so strong.'

'Have you given up faith? You who once told me never to give up hope.'

'No, Rebecca I have not given up. I will never give up,' his voice full of conviction. 'Even if I have to make love to you till my dying days, I'll manage.'

'Oh life is so hard.' She released her hands and pushed him back on the bed.

He looked up at her leaning over him. 'What was he like, my son? Can you tell me?'

Her eyes quivered.

'You don't have to tell me right now, in your own time, when you're ready. Just don't leave it eight years,' he said with an optimistic smile. Suddenly Samuel sat up. 'Speaking of sons, we've forgotten about Jonathan!'

They both leapt off the bed and raced into the next room. Jonathan was curled up on the lounge fast asleep. 'Oh the poor little mite, he hasn't even had his dinner,' said Rebecca. 'Shall we put him to bed?'

'No,' said, Samuel, reaching for a throw to lie across the boy. 'Let's put ourselves to bed first.'

That night, honesty was laid bare in their bed. After years of concealing such deception, of suppressing something so unbelievably cataclysmic, so painful, Rebecca felt reborn with her admission. Samuel finally saw her for what she was, understood the abomination she had run away from, understood her personal struggle with her denied feelings towards her family, her lies and betrayal. And through it all, he did not condemn her nor her family. His whole heart, his kind eyes, his caring hands and lips were full of compassion and wonder at the woman he had fallen in love with many years ago. They made such intimate, achingly tender love. She felt more open and flowing almost as if she and Samuel were in a dream, floating above the bed. They lay in each other's arms, wrapped in nuances of their loss and suffering, entwined in the healing caress of whispers and sacred kisses.

In the afterglow of midnight, as they lay spooned together, Samuel softly said, 'Tell me about Rachel. And your mother.' While she talked he ran his hand tenderly up and down her arm. 'And now she's married?' he asked 'I didn't have time to talk to her this morning.'

'Yes, she is Mrs Townsend. Her husband's name is Andrew. He is a schoolteacher. He was in the war and apparently he knew Toby.'

'Really? When are you seeing them again?'

'Tomorrow. She wants us to come by tomorrow afternoon and for you to come for dinner after your conference.'

'What did your father die from? Do they know?'

'They think his heart gave out on him in the end,' said Rebecca, reaching for Samuel's hand and squeezing it.

'A broken heart.' His words like a spell in the still night.

78

At five Rebecca arose, a habit from her childhood, leaving Samuel to precious sleep amidst rumpled sheets. She made herself a cup of tea, drew the curtain and leant against the sideboard, nursing her drink as she stared out the window down at the street below to a bench seat opposite the hotel where yesterday her sister and two children had sat waiting patiently for her to appear.

She didn't notice them when she walked outside the hotel, nor did she notice them following her to the park. It was only when she heard a boy's voice ask, 'Can I ride the other swing?' that she looked at the family.

The woman was well groomed with dark hair, short and waved, pinned down with a small hat. There was nothing familiar or out of the ordinary about her attire but her face was so like Rachel's that Rebecca took two steps forwards, unsure if she was imagining her.

And that was when the lady cried out, 'Look out, Rebecca,' warning her that she was about to be hit by her energetic son on his swing.

She jerked and then gasped, and with her hand outstretched, stumbled forward, almost crushing Rachel in her embrace as if she had spent the last eight years looking for Rachel and finally found her. 'Rachel!' she cried.

'Rebecca!' her sister cried.

They stood, heads pressed together, eyes running, mostly in silence, their tears saying everything.

Like an excited maiden remembering every glance, every word, every moment of a romantic encounter, alone in the stillness of early morn, Rebecca replayed this scene over and over in her head and the apologies and explanations that came after. And she knew, like she knew Rachel was her own flesh and blood, that everything was instantly and long forgiven.

Samuel rang the doorbell. Moments later Jonathan opened the door.

'Dad,' he said, 'come meet Simon and Mary.'

Before Samuel could say, 'In a minute,' Jonathan had dragged him into the front room where his cousins were playing. Mary had brown curly hair and was watching her brother pull a wooden train and its carriages around the room. Simon's hair was lighter and straighter as if he spent more time in the sun without a hat on. He was completely absorbed with the job of train driver.

'Hey you two,' said Jonathan, 'this is my dad.' No one turned to look at Jonathan. 'Simon,' said Jonathan, his voice a little louder. The boy stopped and looked at Jonathan who said again, 'This is my dad. He's your uncle.'

The little boy looked at Samuel as if he met a new uncle every day. 'Hello,' he said and then waited for Samuel to dismiss him so he could get back to his game.

Mary's expression was one of guarded interest. Samuel smiled. 'Hello, you must be Mary.' She nodded in reply.

Rachel and Rebecca were in the kitchen sitting around the table drinking tea when he came to the doorway. Samuel didn't say a word. He just looked at Rachel and then she stopped talking and looked up and saw him. Her eyes watered. 'Thanks for making the headlines with your health conference, Samuel.' She said, her voice rough.

His throat was so constricted he couldn't even manage to say hello back as he walked towards her. She stood up and walked into his open arms and cried wet salty tears on his shoulder. He looked at Rebecca and could see her crying and smiling. He beckoned for her to join them and she came and he hugged her as well, a sister on each shoulder, their heads bowed, the three of them lamenting over their years apart.

They decided they would drive north to see Rebecca's mother who now lived with Esther, and Jonathan could get to meet more cousins. Over breakfast at their hotel he piped up, 'Mommy, how come you told me you lost your family when they have been here all along?'

Rebecca put down her tea and looked at her son and then

almost despairingly at Samuel. One Saturday a few years earlier, after a sleep over with his cousins, Benjamin and Catherine, Jonathan had come home demanding to know why he had only one set of grandparents when his cousins had two sets: Analeise's parents – Nana and Grandad Dalton – and Uncle Randall's parents. Why didn't he have two sets of grandparents?

That was the day they told him all about his adoption and his real parents, Matthew and Lenore. He took the news exceptionally well, if anything it seemed like he felt even more special knowing that unlike other children he actually had had two sets of parents. They explained that Lenore's parents – his Uncle Alistair's parents as well – had died before he was born, hence why he only had one set of grandparents. That satisfied him until his face became excited. 'What about your parents Mommy, where are your parents?'

With a quiver in her voice she told him. 'Honey, I lost them too. We had some sad times back then but hopefully all of the sad times are behind us now.' How she hated lying to her son. What to tell him now?

'I'm sorry, that must seem a strange thing for me to have said but at the time they were lost to me. We had a big misunderstanding in our family. I thought my father didn't love me any more and I didn't know if I loved him, if I could continue to love him.'

'How come?'

'You see we hurt each other, not physically but here inside our hearts,' she touched her chest with the palm of her hand. 'It wasn't as if we deliberately meant to hurt each other, it was more by our actions, we weren't thinking of the consequences. And we needed time apart to understand and to heal. Hurt inside takes a long time to heal, to get over sometimes.'

'Do you, did you, still love your father?'

'Yes,' said Rebecca, her voice breaking.

Samuel put his arm around Rebecca and reached for Jonathan's hand. 'The ties you have with your family, no matter how tormented they may be at times, Jonathan, are like no other ties. They are irrefutable. They cannot be refused. And sometimes when you try to refuse them or deny them, often the person you end up hurting the most is yourself.'

'You have to still love the sinner, Jonathan,' said Rebecca, 'just not the sin, and sometimes it can take a lot of hard work to get to that point.'

When they arrived at Salvage they decided to park the hired car about a quarter of a mile away from Esther's place and let Rachel go ahead and prepare her mother and Esther. They would be shocked. Rebecca hoped they wouldn't be angry. Samuel and Rebecca stood outside the car, leaning on it, anxiously waiting for Rachel to appear and give them a wave to come on down. The three children were content to be out in the fresh air, gazing at the ocean, playing hide and seek around the car, around the adults. Samuel and Rebecca steered their eyes towards the house, the signal from Rachel seeming to be a long time coming.

But then they saw Rebecca's mother come racing out the door and they heard her calling out Rebecca's name and with her skirts in her hand, she ran towards them fast and determined but by this time Rebecca was already twenty yards closer to her calling out, 'Mother! Mother!', as they ran towards the other and threw themselves into each other's arms. The years of anguish no longer tearing them apart. They were together again, succumbing to tears of relief and, as her father had hoped, tears of mercy.

Her mother cried more tears – bitter tears – when she learnt how Samuel and Rebecca had not been able to have any more children. She looked at Jonathan deep in conversation with Reuben, Esther's fourth child and said, 'I hope at least he is some comfort to you both.'

'He is the best,' said Samuel. 'We couldn't love our own child more. And every so often my brother, Matthew, visits through Jonathan, the most precious flashes of such rare communion. Jonathan has no idea what's going on but there are moments I just can't breathe, his presence seems so real.'

'Yes,' said Rebecca, squeezing Samuel's hand and giving her mother a smile. 'He is adorable. He has been like that ever since he was a little baby.'

The next minute, adorable Jonathan touched Morna's hand. 'Excuse me,' he said. They stopped talking and looked at him. 'Now that I've met you, will you be my grandmother?'

His hopeful eyes searched her face. 'Most of my friends have two sets of grandparents but I only have one.'

'I would love to have another grandchild.' She reached out and pulled Jonathan to her, 'But you must promise me you won't wait eight years before you come and visit me again. I like to see my grandchildren more often than that.' She kissed him on the head. 'You know one of my friends has forty-six grandchildren and with you now I have ten. And she has seven great grandchildren would you believe?'

'I have great grandparents,' said Jonathan. 'I have Grandpa Dalton and I have Grandpère and Grandmère Sibonne.'

'Well aren't you blessed?'

'Did your husband die?' asked Jonathan matter-of-factly.

'Yes.'

'Do you think he would have wanted to be my grandfather?'

'I'm sure he would have.'

'Do you have a photograph of him?'

'No dear, I don't.'

'What about a drawing or a painting?'

'I don't have that either.'

'That's too bad.'

'Yes my boy, it is, isn't it?' agreed Morna staring off into the distance. As an afterthought she said, 'Maybe your mother can draw him for you one day.'

They stayed two weeks with Morna and Esther. Rachel's family stayed for two weeks as well, bunking down with an elderly widow just along the way. It was noisy and boisterous and bubbling with laughter and fun and all sorts of tales: old wives tales, fish tales, superstitious tales; the salt of Newfoundland. The days were full of baking and seafood fry-ups. Jonathan learnt all about splitting cod and jigging for squid and keeping an eye on the weather as banks of fog rolled towards the shore and rolled away and clouds scurried overhead.

Every day was play day, every day held the promise of a new adventure. Jonathan had four cousins older than him, one, Reuben by only seven weeks and five younger than him. He didn't feel left out at all. Newfoundland was the best holiday he had ever had. Rebecca went for long walks and talks with her mother and with Rachel. Esther wanted to know from Rebecca all about Samson and what happened that day on the boat. For the first time since he was born she was able to talk about Samson and strangely that made him seem more real and she was able to talk about him without getting upset. Sometimes all four women would sit round and drink tea and ban everyone from the house, but not for long, everyone was constantly coming and going and neighbours dropping in to say hi. It was as if they lived each day in a kaleidoscope catching the fractured light, the circadian rhythms of daily life at a Newfoundland outport, storing memories of what had become a surprisingly joyous holiday in Newfoundland, a wonderful welcome to a home away from home.

79

Rebecca felt mortified at the thought of coming clean with the Daltons after all the years they had spent together. 'Samuel,' she said, 'they trusted me and took me in without question from the first day and it looks like I never trusted them, and I lied to them.'

'Well in the grand scheme of things I don't think they are going to think of you as untrustworthy or as a liar.'

'You're just saying that because you are my husband and you love me.'

'Yes on both accounts but I'm not just saying that. They are your family now and they love you too.'

'But how would you feel if you had been kept in the dark all these years?' He gave her a look. Rebecca groaned. 'Forget I even said that!'

Samuel pulled her into his arms. 'Look, I will be with you all the way and I guarantee you one thing: it will not be the hardest thing you have ever done.'

Her eyes met his and held onto them. 'You're right.'

'So, what is the hardest thing you've ever done?'

Rebecca's eyes scanned Samuel's as her mind flashed past some of its rarely visited warrens, then she lowered her gaze to his mouth and said, 'Oh, I think,' then she paused and a small smile played on her lips, 'making love to you every night.' She twisted and tried to turn and race away from him, but she wasn't going anywhere.

'If that's the case,' he said to her in his huskiest of voices, 'anything else must be child's play.'

With an exuberant eight year old, more exuberant than he had ever been after the unexpected delights of their holiday, Samuel and Rebecca decided they needed to take matters into their own hands.

'Jonathan, don't go telling everyone about your cousins, straight away. This is important,' said Samuel.

'Why not? What's the big secret?'

'This is Mommy's family and she wants to tell the adults first about getting together with them and once she has done that you can tell everyone about your cousins and about what you got up to, about the clambake and the fish you caught and how much you ate and where you slept and how you couldn't stop talking at night when you were meant to be sleeping.'

'I did sleep.'

'Eventually.'

They sat in the wicker chairs on the Dalton's verandah before lunch on Saturday, the first Saturday of fall, though summer hung relentlessly in the air. Jonathan was playing with Benjamin on the petanque court, but playing chase or something. Catherine was playing with Daniel, her younger brother, under the oak tree, under her mother's watchful eye, while all the adults were assembled in the hushed shade drinking Analeise's homemade ginger beer. When Rebecca phoned to set up lunch, she had asked if Addie and Jerome could join them as well.

In a double chair with Samuel beside her holding her hand Rebecca looked around at everyone, looked at their expectant faces, their faces full of love and hope and she suddenly realised, too late in fact, that they could only be thinking one thing and what she was going to tell them was far from that thing. She felt crushed.

'Oh,' she said, 'I think I know what you are all thinking and I'm sorry to say I'm not pregnant.' She shook her head and looked at them in apology as her mind lingered on the word pregnant and then she blinked and tried to remember when she last bled. She couldn't remember much beyond the turmoil and excitement of the last month. Turning to Samuel, she softly said, 'When was the last full moon Samuel?'

He looked at her, suddenly intensely alert. 'Over two weeks ago, the last week at Esther's. Remember we went out in the boat just the two of us and watched the full moon come up?'

Rebecca held her breath. Samuel held his. Her heart was racing as she tried in vain not to entertain the possibility as this little voice inside her said, 'You always bleed on the full moon.'

Samuel, his face incredulous, his voice incredulous, softly echoed her thoughts, 'You always bleed on the full moon.'

'You are pregnant!' exclaimed Lottie. 'You've just realised it, haven't you ma chère?'

Rebecca looked into Samuel's face, her eyes searching his for the answer, for the truth and his were full of unexpressed, no longer suppressed hope. Her eyes filled with tears and Samuel smiled at her, smiled his out-of-this world Samuel smile. He pulled her close, possessively, fiercely, and said loud enough for everyone to hear, 'Yes, it is possible.'

Her fallow years were over.

The Promised Land

80

After Rebecca told her Toronto family everything that had happened, all her transgressions and begged their forgiveness, no one spoke, but there was a barely a dry eye in the circle around them. Lottie's hand was across her mouth. She had dark trails running down her cheeks. Addie kept on wiping her face with a handkerchief. Eventually, she mumbled. 'I wouldn't be in a hurry to tell a tale like that to anyone either.'

But nine years and twelve days after the birth of her first child, when a little girl named Abigail Hera entered the world on the fifth of May 1927, just eight days before Jonathan's ninth birthday, everyone knew just how momentous the occasion and how precious the child. Jonathan took one look at her and said, 'It's going to take a long time before she's big enough to play with me.' But that didn't bother Abby, for she simply adored her Nana Dalton and her Nana adored her.

In October 1929 when Rebecca was heavily pregnant with her third child the world as everyone knew it came plummeting down with the massive stock market crash turning a recession into a full depression. Henry was born in the cold heart of winter. He came into the world following a straightforward delivery, lived for a day then mysteriously died during the night. They were stunned and shocked. They berated themselves over whether they had missed any signs. He had seemed normal and healthy and then his life just petered out. It was the bleakest winter they had experienced since 1918.

In the summer of 1930 they went away to a rustic cottage on the shores of Lake Temagami to put some distance between them and their heartache. That holiday healed them. Rebecca's intuition was right. It brought laughter and happiness and joy back into their family so they could get on with the living and the loving. They made another baby that holiday. When he was born nine months later they named him Morton Apollo, Morton after Grandpa Dalton. If Jonathan was the spitting image of Matthew then Morton was Samuel's son in every way: the same colouring, the same thoughtful gaze, steady, reliable, and respectful.

By 1933 twenty-seven percent of the Canadian labour force was out of work, one fifth of the population was dependent on government assistance and Rebecca was pregnant with her fifth child. The baby was due at the end of August and for the first time in her life Rebecca was heavily pregnant through the heat of a Toronto summer. Evangeline Demeter was named Evangeline after a Frenchwoman who had helped Samuel during the war, and Demeter after the Greek goddess of corn as Rebecca had craved corn during her pregnancy. Evangeline was their quiet baby, born at the absolute bottom of the depression but born with a special grace that everyone found enchanting. Initially they thought she might be called Evie or Angeline, but Morton got stuck on Gene and Gene she became. Gene was quietly inquisitive, imaginative and somewhat introverted and of all their children the least predictable. She had honey blonde hair and large eyes even more intensely green-blue than her mothers.

When Gene was a baby Rebecca took to cradling her to her front like she had done all those years ago with Jonathan. For some reason her protective instincts with this child were incredibly heightened. For weeks she wondered if her behaviour was a subconscious sign that this child would be her last, yet on a conscious level she hadn't given that any thought whatsoever. Then in the middle of a deep dark winter's night it came to her in a shudder.

She had been lying in bed, sleepless, trying to think of the names of Henry VIII's wives. The saying she had learnt at school kept playing over and over in her head: Divorced, beheaded, died, divorced, beheaded, survived. All of a sudden her mind went: Drowned, survived, died and then she stopped in alarm – not because her fourth child – Morton – had repeated the pattern and drowned but because she had seen a completely different pattern, a completely different set of threes. Lost one – Samson – kept one – Abigail – lost one – Henry – kept one – Morton. Was she going to lose this one as well? She didn't sleep anymore that night. For several weeks she took to watching Gene even more closely, watching with bated breath every time Abby wanted to hold her baby sister. Morton thank goodness was too young for any holding. Somewhere in the middle of her wariness Rebecca resolved to have at least one other child. They stopped at Joel Adonis Dalton.

Joel was faster and louder than the lot and Lottie thought he reminded her of how wild Matthew had been as a young boy, game for everything, gregarious in nature. He latched onto Jonathan, which was another reason why he reminded them of Matthew.

Six months after their youngest son was born their eldest left home. When Jonathan finished school he struggled and erred over what to do with his future. Samuel told him to take his time, not to rush, how he had been the same way. Jonathan was interested in medicine but he was also keen to become a pilot. Eventually he decided and when in September 1935 Jonathan left Toronto, said goodbye to his family and his grandparents, and moved to Montreal he became the fourth generation of Dalton medicine men.

81

Four summers later in 1939, with the world teetering on the brink of another war, Rebecca planned a holiday for her family and Rachel's on Prince Edward Island. She had booked two bungalows next door to each other on the Gulf side near Cavendish for three weeks in July. Morna would be joining them as well.

Then, at the beginning of June, Rachel called with disappointing news: Andrew's mother had been diagnosed with advanced leukaemia. She only had a few months to live and he wanted them all to stay home to be with her in her dying days. Rebecca was upset but she understood. She felt worse for her sister.

Unable to deny how much she was looking forward to seeing her mother and sister again, how much she was longing for her children to spend some time with their grandmother – her mother – with their aunties and uncles and cousins on her side, Rebecca cancelled not one but both houses and announced to Samuel that she wanted them all to go back to Newfoundland for a holiday. If their Newfoundland relatives couldn't come to Canada, then the Canadian relatives would go to Newfoundland. The promise of Prince Edward Island paled in comparison.

Her mother would be turning seventy-one in the fall and Rebecca realised with a pang how little she had seen of her in the last twenty years, how little she had seen of Esther and Rachel. She thought of Andrew's mother and then with dread her own…thinking how long…how long do you have left? Swallowing, she sent up a silent prayer, 'A long time still, please.'

They would spend one week in St John's with Rachel, two weeks in Salvage with Esther and Morna and another week in St John's on their way home. Jonathan was staying put in

Montreal, working part-time as a lab assistant, part time for his Great Uncle Michel, prepping part-time for his next year and quietly courting full time a second year medical student, a young lady born and bred in Montreal. When he told Samuel and Rebecca he wouldn't be able to join them; that he had lots going on in Montreal over the summer, Samuel and Rebecca had looked at each other. Rebecca raised her eyebrows, a small smiled played on her lips. Samuel just came straight out with it, 'Does lots have a name?'

'Candace,' Jonathan replied, dryly.

Ah, Candace, Rebecca's heart whispered. 'Has Candace ever been to Newfoundland?' she asked. 'Perhaps she would like to join us on holiday? Tell her parents, she will be safe with us.'

'Like we were safe,' whispered Samuel. Rebecca continued to smile at Jonathan but behind her back she slapped her husband.

Rebecca thought grandchildren were a way off for her and Samuel, though some days she would wonder what dimension Samson would have added to their lives had he lived. Maybe he would have been like Samuel, fathering a love child. Had he lived he would be a man now in every sense of the word.

Some days she thought of Samson as Jonathan's equal, but other days she thought something entirely different. Matthew was gone from their lives forever. Samuel, thankfully, had been restored. Samson, Samuel's son, her son, had been denied them but Jonathan, Matthew's and Lenore's son, had been their salvation, hers in particular. It was almost as if he had been given to them to restore their faith. And because he came into the world when he did, he embodied not just everyone's hopes and dreams, but also their memories. It was as if he were Matthew and Samson incarnate. He was their very own trinity. Rebecca wondered if Jonathan ever sensed that. She had never told him about Samson. She had never wanted to burden him or alarm him, but one day, she vowed, when he was a little older, she would tell him, so he would know on another level, just how special he was to the two of them.

Telling Samuel about Samson had been a watershed moment in her life and once it was done, she was no longer filled with dread and despair but she had moments, many before that fateful day – throughout her barren years – and many after when she wished that Samuel could have known his first born for just one day and held him in his arms and run his hands over his silky hair, like he had with Henry. To know that he was real. He was real for her, hauntingly real. Yet some days, she wondered how real he was for Samuel. In many ways Samson felt like her son, not their son and she wished it could have been otherwise.

Perhaps that was why on her second day at Esther's sitting across the table from her mother and sister, each of them bouncing one of Esther's grandchildren on their knees, she hadn't balked when her mother said, 'I'm thinking I would like to go visit the old place one more time and I'm wondering if you would like to come with me. I haven't been back for fourteen years. Thought I never would once I'd left, but lately I'm of a different opinion. There's folks there I'd like to see again and I feel this calling to pay my respects to your father.'

Rebecca heard that and felt the weight of it on heart. The weight of knowing she had never gone and paid her respects to her father. Never replied to that heartfelt letter he had written her all those years ago. Could she go back? She remembered once saying to Samuel, 'Very few things bother me now with you by my side'. It was twenty-one years since she had left. Twenty-one years since she fled her father. Twenty-one years since she had given birth to Samson. How did she feel about going back? And being there, how would she feel about her father? About Samson? She had long forgiven her father, but she had not forgotten. A mother never forgets. What about her other children? Did she want to take them? She told her mother she'd think about it and think about it she did, all afternoon, all evening and at night during pillow talk with Samuel.

'What do you think, Samuel? Do you think it is a good idea to go there?'

'I would love to see that place again. I know it doesn't have the best memories for you, but for me it holds wonderful memories.' Rebecca could sense every romantic nostalgic bone in Samuel's body was in favour of the idea.

'It has some good memories for me too,' Rebecca admitted quietly.

'Let's take the whole family,' urged Samuel, 'show them where you grew up, where we met, so they know the most unlikely things can happen in the most unlikely places.'

She knew he was thinking beauty and love, happiness and adventure, but when he said that she thought of something else entirely. That was the problem. That was her pendulum. 'If I go, I don't think I'd want to take the children, only you.'

'Why not?'

The rational part of her couldn't give a real reason, only the irrational…because I already lost one child there. I don't want to lose any more, no matter how outlandish and far-fetched that possibility might be. Remember bad things happen in threes Samuel? For years she had thought the three were Samson, Matthew and Lenore…but after Henry her fear got the better of her some days and she would shiver involuntarily.

What she said was, 'I don't think I can do what I need to do with our kids around us. I don't think we can do what we need to do. This is not about them. This is about us and Samson, your son,' she said pointedly then added, 'our son.'

'You don't think having them along will make it easier, remind you of what blessings you have?'

'I want those blessings to return to. I want my children to feel safe and loved. I don't know how I will be back there and I don't want them upset by a distraught mother.'

But as she lay there in the dark, wide awake, her head nestled on Samuel's arm, staring at the ceiling, staring into her past, or was it her future, Rebecca made peace with the idea. Not for her mother and not for her father, but for herself, to go back, to remember her father and with Samuel to remember and acknowledge their lost son.

The next morning at breakfast before Rebecca said a word to her mother or Esther, Morna said, 'I meant to say yesterday that Ronnie and Margaret Evans are still alive.'

Rebecca caught Samuel's eyes. They held each other's gaze. So many memories flooded through her mind. She imagined Samuel was having a similar rush of images and emotions. Still looking at her, he said, 'How old are they these days?'

'They must be well in their eighties. He at least.'

They headed off the next day. Their four children stayed behind with Esther.

82

On the boat to Seldom Come By Samuel and Rebecca sat out on the open deck, at one with the elements. The wind whipped her hair around her face but she didn't care. Samuel put his arm around her shoulder, leaned into her and softly said, 'I wonder if we'll see any icebergs?'

'We can only hope.' With a smile she turned to look into Samuel's face, recalling the thrill of that magical day, now a quarter of a century ago. 'I remember,' she whispered.

'I remember too.' He kissed her on the forehead as he pulled her in tighter. They pressed their faces together. Eventually she rolled her face away into Samuel's neck and then opening her eyes turned to gaze at the horizon.

They had packed lightly and had not telegraphed ahead to let anyone know they were coming. Ronnie and Margaret were smaller versions of their old selves; lined and spotted from years of wind and sun and hardship. Their voices croaky, their faces creased but this time from happiness. How their eyes glistened when they recognised Samuel and Rebecca. How they hugged them and insisted on them staying with them.

Rebecca had brought a photograph of their family for Ronnie and Meg. When she knew Jonathan wouldn't be coming with them to Newfoundland she had organised a family portrait for her mother and sisters. Esther said she could take hers...she would share Morna's.

They talked long into the night. The men drank sherry long into the night. At one point Ronnie squeezed Samuel's shoulder and said, 'It's so good to have you back, Samuel. So good! How does it feel to be back?'

Samuel looked at Ronnie not knowing where to begin. 'I am reminded of Henry Wadsworth's, "My Lost Youth"'.

'Often I think of the beautiful town that is seated by the sea,' said Ronnie.

"Yes,' said Samuel, 'especially the part about a mist before the eye.'

Rebecca decided she could not put off going to visit her father's grave. She told Samuel she was going to do it the very next day, by herself, get it over with and then perhaps later the two of them could visit it together. She left not long after breakfast. Her mother told her where to find it. 'It's at the top, far away from the other crosses, overlooking Deception, almost on the ridge as if he were halfway home.'

No wonder her mother's memory was so accurate. She had been there before breakfast and already weeded the plot and left some wild buttercups that she must have picked along the way. His grave was right next to her own. How eerie it was to see her name on a speckled cross. She shuddered. Thank God she hadn't brought the children.

Rebecca had a small posy of pansies that Margaret had given her from her own garden. They would wilt quickly, thought Rebecca, but at least they would add a small sprinkle of colour. She crouched down on her knees and looked at the worn wooden cross in front of her. The paint was all cracked and peeling, in fact there was more wood than paint. They must sand it and repaint it before they left. Her fingers traced over the letters Silas Isaiah Crowe, 1860 – 1925

She read the words in her mind but out loud she said, 'Hello Father'…and then she cried, cried with relief that she could once again call him Father, that in some way, by doing so, she was back in the fold. He wasn't Silas to her anymore but her father, the man who gave her life and, on balance, a rich and remarkable life. More enlightening, more revealing, more fulfilling than she could have ever imagined when she was a young girl growing up on Second Chance. And though Samuel had made a large part of that possible, she could not deny that she had chartered that life because of who she was – Rebecca Olsen Crowe – and who she was, was intrinsically linked to who her parents were, where she came from and what lessons she had learnt growing up even if some of those experiences had been egregious, the lessons were still well-learnt.

But strangely not one of those lessons had prepared her for this: sitting by her father's grave. Where did she begin?

'Hello Father,' she said again. 'It's me, Rebecca. I've come back to Second Chance at last, after twenty-one years. Some days it does not seem like twenty-one years, that's for sure. I got your letter. Thank you. It's at home in my Bible. I got your apology too. Thank you. I got your forgiveness as well.' She looked down at her hands resting in her lap, her lined palms facing upwards, struggling with herself. She inhaled deeply, trying to stop her throat from tightening as she added, 'What I got the most though is that you loved me, even though you never said so during those embattled years we had together. And that you continued to love me after everything. And that, I think, meant more to me than anything.' Wiping the tears from her face, she smiled lightly at that admission. She had never even told Samuel that.

'I can sit here now and practically cite that letter back to you…I forgive you even though I think I will never fully understand but I believe if you could relive those days now, you would do things differently and that makes my heart gladder. I have married Samuel and I hope that makes your heart gladder. We have been blessed with five beautiful children, three boys and two girls and they are all angels. Jonathan, Abigail, Morton, Evangeline and Joel. I had another son as well called Henry who died in his sleep after one day. Samuel is a wonderful father. He and the children are my morning, noon and night. They utterly fulfil me. I understand now that come what may, whatever they do I will always love them and how that was the case with you.' She paused and looked down at her hands folded in her lap.

After a little while she said, 'Like Dante I have drunk from the River Lethe and the River Eunoë. My soul remembers good deeds.' She took a deep breath and looked up and around her to the rocky outcrops, to the grey glimmering sea and the soaring gulls. Finally her eyes came back to rest on the cross. 'I wish right now that you could be by my side to see what is in my eyes and to know what is in my heart. Know this…we would be crying tears of sadness and of joy.'

She bent forward and kissed her father's name.

That afternoon they borrowed a boat and Samuel rowed Morna and Rebecca around to their cove. No family had lived there since Morna walked off the property. The stage was falling down. They beached the dinghy and slowly ambled up the overgrown path to their house.

The outside was showing signs of neglect and abandonment. There were cobwebs and lichen around most windows and eaves. The wood was bleached a pale grey, cracked in many places. The back door was padlocked, the lock somewhat rusty but the key that Morna had left with Ronnie worked like a charm. Inside the house was mostly as Samuel and Rebecca remembered. To Rebecca's surprise the furniture had been left behind. Morna said she really had no need for it. Shipping it to Salvage would have been an unnecessary expense. They walked around the rooms, mostly in silence, lost in their memories, until they got to Rebecca's bedroom. She walked in and stood at a spot not far from her bed and said, 'Samson was born here.' Samuel looked at her solemnly, nodded and walked over and folded her in his arms. After a while he left the women alone and went outside.

The sun was low in the sky as Samuel dipped the oars slowly into the water and began rowing out of their bay. They had asked Morna if she wanted to come but she had declined. She said she'd make her own way back walking across the barrens. They could see her at the top of the path beyond the argent trail they made through the greying waters. No desolate swell of the sea this evening. No dank and heavy fogbank. No icy growlers or frozen shards. At Rebecca's feet was a wreath of summer flowers Samuel had made earlier, fashioning it out of a disused lobster pot. Together all three of them had picked the pale yellow sea-roses that dotted the cliff tops and woven the vivid green stems through the wicker strands. Samuel had added a few bulrushes.

They didn't speak but their eyes buoyed each other up, speaking volumes in the silence. After a while Rebecca softly said, 'This will do fine, Samuel.'

He lifted the oars and pulled them through the oarlock. He reached out for Rebecca's hand and together the two of them stared at the sea in front of them for many long minutes.

Finally Samuel spoke. 'Hail Samson. This is your father, Samuel. I'm here with your mother, Rebecca.' He paused.

'This visit is long overdue and we're sorry for that. We're also sorry, deeply sorry, for what happened to you, that we weren't able to protect and save you in your hour of need.' Samuel inhaled. 'I want you to know that shortly after I found out what happened to you I grieved for you immensely. I was like some women after childbirth. And I was angry, angry like I had never been before in my life – and never been since for that matter – knowing that I could have had you as my son and watched you grow up, but that was denied me. Eventually I had to learn to let the anger and grief go, follow the example of your mother.'

Samuel paused and looked up from the water to Rebecca before he continued. 'We want you to know, Samson, that you are stamped on our hearts for all eternity. You are our first born, the embodiment of our sweet love of youth. And for that we love you. Being here right now, we think of you and want you to know you bring our spirits back. You remind us of our love for each other for twenty-five years and all that we have been through.' Samuel locked eyes with Rebecca. 'You have five siblings who would have adored you and looked up to you. They may have annoyed you too at times, but even so, I'm sure you would have loved them equally in return.

'We will always remember you with pride and with love, with sadness, and with longing for what might have been. Come visit us in our dreams, colour our nights and during our days, while we breathe, while we live, while we love, we will treasure you, Samson. You will always be a part of our family.' He squeezed Rebecca's hand.

'I remember you, Samson,' said Rebecca, her voice strong and clear and loving. 'I remember what a beautiful baby you were. I remember how incredibly happy you made me and every day since the day you were born I think of you with love and wherever you are, my love goes out to you. Please forgive me for what happened to you. I know it was inexcusable but please forgive me even so and know that when I look at our other children I see you.'

Slowly, carefully, Rebecca and Samuel leant to the side – there was no balancing the boat from opposite ends that evening – there was no foreboding. Gently, they placed the wreath on the water with utmost care, with utmost tenderness.

Samuel reached for Rebecca's hand and squeezed it tight but their eyes did not leave the floating circle of flowers. They watched the wreath bobbing on the water, riding the lightest ripple, solemn and at peace. Then in the shifting light, in the shifting waters, without warning, without a wave, a seal appeared. It nudged the wreath with its nose, tapped it with a flipper, disappeared for a moment or two and just when they thought it had gone for good it returned to claim the ring of remembrance for itself.

Four days later they were back in Salvage, being deluged by their children.

'We had the best time while you are away!'

'Yes. Aunty Esther and I made crabapple jam and I can make scones now all by myself.'

'Jimmy taught me how to jig for squid, Mom. Mom! Are you listening to me?'

'Yes, honey, did you?'

'Gene and I made a fort, Mommy. Do you want to see it? Dad, do you want to see it?'

'Soon,' said their father.

'We love it here, Mom. Can we come back and holiday next year?' Gene tugged her arm.

'Yes!' echoed Morton. 'This is the best place. You were so lucky to grow up here. Can we go out in the boat again tomorrow?'

'Yes,' cried the other children.

'Well I didn't exactly grow up here, Morton, but I hear you.' Rebecca looked at Esther, apologetically. 'Have they been like this since we left?'

'No, thank goodness. We wouldn't have coped if they had. It's like four of Jonathan all at once.' They laughed remembering how excited Jonathan had been on his first visit.

The next morning Rebecca and Esther were preparing breakfast ready for the second sitting – Esther's husband David and her eldest boys Reuben and Thomas had already eaten at four-thirty before heading out on their boat – when Samuel came rushing in from outside.

'Guess what?' He was puffing slightly from his excited dash.

Rebecca turned to look at him. He was smiling his out of this world Samuel smile. His eyes were dancing.

'What?' she said, grinning back at him. Even after all this time she still found that smile so infectious. Even with a few lines around his mouth and eyes.

'Guess!' said Samuel.

'The men are back already?' Rebecca glanced at her sister.

'It would be amazing if they were,' said Esther.

'No,' said Samuel. 'Think of a different sort of present from Poseidon.' Samuel's eyes were twinkling.

'Whales,' cried Rebecca.

'No,' said Samuel, running his fingers through his hair and shaking his head at her. 'Come on,' his voice full of weary pretence.

'No!' she replied; her no sounding like an excited 'really!'

'Yes!'

They tore outside. Samuel grasped Rebecca's hand as he led her up the hill behind Esther's house and over the ridge to the headland beyond. Rebecca felt herself flooding with anticipation and excitement. It couldn't be. Well it could be, even though they were a lot further south and it was late in the summer. It wasn't unheard of. What an unexpected delight! Way off in the distance to the north she saw it. White towering peaks piercing the skyline.

'Hah,' she cried, 'how about that!' She squeezed Samuel's hand and looked at his ecstatic face. There was something magical about an iceberg, something otherworldly about sharing an iceberg with Samuel, a miracle of sorts. She lifted her face to Samuel and kissed him, between grins and with parted lips she kissed him. 'Oh Samuel,' she murmured, 'Wait till the children see this. We'll have to show them.'

'Will that be before or after we go out there by ourselves? Before or after we make love in a boat blessed by an iceberg like I wanted to do all those years ago.'

'So you really did want to back then!'

'Of course!'

'Let's go right now!' she enthused. 'We'll take the children after breakfast.'

Twenty minutes later they were powering out of the bay in a small runabout, the Salut, borrowed from a neighbour along the way. The iceberg looked marginally closer – about eight to ten miles away, as with most icebergs travelling about half a mile an hour. Would it come closer to shore or would it veer away? She was glad they weren't rowing.

Samuel pressed the throttle down a bit further. Rebecca's hair streamed behind her in the wind, the salt spray teased her tongue and face. Such an exhilarating morning, like horse riding along a beach, like Sable Island almost, like the very best of her youth.

Windswept and exuberant she turned and gazed in rapture at Samuel. She felt alive, utterly alive, replete in her happiness. In that moment she was herself, a beautiful forty-year old woman with a child's heart. She remembered her childhood, her desperation and loneliness. Today she did not feel lonely anymore, nor desperate, nor wanting.

Above the drone of the motor she called out to Samuel. 'I think I love Newfoundland!' her voice catching, unable to hide the surprise or emotion of her realisation. 'I know some of the worst experiences of my life happened here, but so did some of the best, with you, with Rachel, my mother, Esther.'

'Have you just figured that out?' Samuel was grinning at her.

'Maybe.' She pressed her lips together. 'Maybe I can say it now.'

They motored for the better part of an hour. Imagine rowing, she thought! But when she saw it up close she thought, wow! I would have rowed out to see that. With a whoop, she stood up, carefully balancing herself in the boat, her eyes shining at the glamorous form, lustrous in golden light.

She turned around. There was Samuel standing beside her. They laughed like teenagers, they hugged like old friends, but when they kissed they kissed like delirious young lovers.

With his mouth next to her ear, he whispered, 'Have I told you how much I love the smell of salt water in your hair?'

'I don't think you have this year,' she said, smiling up at him.

He looked at her, longingly, and then they turned to look once more at the alabaster expanse in front of them. It was a magnificent iceberg. It had a curved archway, a natural Arc de

Triomphe. Either side of the arch were two pristine pinnacles, one with a waterfall trailing down its side that kept on flowing and flowing as if it had an infinite source of pure aqua.

They sat back down and Samuel eased the motor barely out of idle. Slowly, they circled the massive floating massif. It took ten minutes to do a complete orbit. From a certain angle she could see its cirque, the pool of melt water feeding the fall. When she was young she used to dream about being able to climb up there and swim in one of those. She knew it would be unbearably cold and the idea totally preposterous, yet it was incredibly tantalising. Even today she felt drawn to the possibility, the idea of diving overboard, swimming to the iceberg and climbing up the walls to sit on top. It would be like sitting on top of the world up there.

Samuel circled once more till he reached the far side of the crystal arch then he cut the motor. 'Now,' he whispered. Together they drifted down to the bottom of the boat, to the wellspring of their youth and lay there gazing at the pearly arch, the pearly gates, here on earth as it is in Heaven. Samuel turned his head and kissed Rebecca on the lips, kissed her like a young man kissing a young woman at the very start of their relationship. She kissed him back and she was fifteen all over again, tingling with exhilaration, tingling with Samuel. She could feel and taste everything he felt for her. Still. What consuming comfort, to know someone so well, to love someone so deeply, to delight in someone so much. This day she would cherish forever.

THE END

Australian-born Sherryl Caulfield is a marketer, writer and traveller. After twenty years working for some of the world's leading technology brands and a stint with Outward Bound, she longed to write about the human experience and the redemptive qualities of nature. In 2006, haunted by an encounter with a woman she met in Canada, Sherryl started what has now become known as The Iceberg Trilogy.

You can find more information about Sherryl and her books at www.sherrylcaulfield.com.

This includes:

- Discussion Topics for book clubs on Seldom Come By

- Frequently Asked Questions on Seldom Come By

- Music links for the soundtrack of Seldom Come By

On her website you can also sign up for her newsletter to be kept up to date with major book releases.

If you want to get in touch with Sherryl you can do so by:

Sending her an email to: info@sherrylcaulfield.com

Or by visiting her Facebook page: SherrylCaulfieldAuthor where she often runs giveaways, posts images from her books, provides project updates and chats to her readers.

Book 2 of The Iceberg Trilogy, Come What May, will be released in 2014. Book 3, Come Full Circle, will be released in 2015.

Acknowledgements

Naturally, a lot of research goes into writing a historical novel and while I consulted many sources, I wanted to single out the two that I valued the most: More Than Fifty Percent. Woman's Life in a Newfoundland Outport, 1900 – 1950 by Hilda Chaulk Murray and the Canadian Medical Association Journal, which has every issue dating back to 1911 available online. Not only did these resources provide factual and cultural details, they also provided a portal to the language and characters of the time. To the best of my abilities I have portrayed the war events as they happened with only minor liberties taken to serve the purposes of my story.

You can read more on historical aspects in the Frequently Asked Questions on my website: www.sherrylcaulfield.com

The inspiration to write The Iceberg trilogy came about following a holiday I had to Canada one northern summer. Since then, many people over many years have helped me shape Seldom Come By into its final form. To all of them I am incredibly grateful.

To my first two readers: my partner, Mark, and your surprised comment, 'Actually, I'm quite enjoying it'; and my sister Anita, for your tears in all the right places; thank you both for your years of support and assistance.

To my wonderful reviewers from across the globe – Jessie Carter, Ruth Schaffer, Teresa Marinovich, Cathi Roberts, Jill Roberts, Carolyn Wood, Sandie Squires, Jeannette Kirby, Jane Brisbane, Julie Fison, Gabrielle Reinhardt, Leah Sparkes (my Newfoundland guide), Svetlana Stankovic, and Su Sprott – thank you for being part of this journey. To manuscript assessor, Stephen Stratford and literary agent, Pippa Masson, thank you for your interest and guidance. Finally to Jan Caulfield, Kylie Depper, Malcolm Meldrum, Margarita Dalmeida, Angela Mangnall, and Jeanne Pryde – thank you for being in my cheer squad and encouraging my dream to see this book published.